Rex

The Walkers of Coyote Ridge, 6

DEAD HEAT RANCH
Boots Optional
Betting on Grace
Overnight Love

DEVIL'S BEND
Chasing Dreams
Vanishing Dreams

MISPLACED HALOS
Protected in Darkness
Salvation in Darkness
Bound in Darkness

OFFICE INTRIGUE
Office Intrigue
Intrigued Out of the Office
Their Rebellious Submissive
Their Famous Dominant
Their Ruthless Sadist
Their Naughty Student
Their Fairy Princess

PIER 70
Reckless
Fearless
Speechless
Harmless
Clueless

SNIPER 1 SECURITY
Wait for Morning
Never Say Never
Tomorrow's Too Late

SOUTHERN BOY MAFIA/DEVIL'S PLAYGROUND
Beautifully Brutal
Without Regret
Beautifully Loyal
Without Restraint

STANDALONE NOVELS

Unhinged Trilogy
A Million Tiny Pieces
Inked on Paper
Bad Reputation
Bad Business

NAUGHTY HOLIDAY EDITIONS

2015
2016

Rex

THE WALKERS OF COYOTE RIDGE, 6

NICOLE EDWARDS

Published by Nicole Edwards Limited
PO Box 1086, Pflugerville, Texas 78691

Rex
The Walkers of Coyote Ridge, 6
Nicole Edwards

This is a work of fiction. Names, characters, businesses, places, events and incidents either are the products of the author's imagination or used in a fictitious manner. Any resemblance to actual persons, living or dead, business establishments, events, or locals is entirely coincidental.

COVER DETAILS:
Image: © Wander Aguiar | WanderBookClub.com
Model: Preston Thompson
Image: © Vitaly Korovin (picture frame - 14901223) | 123rf.com
Image: © picsfive (background - 14359053) | 123rf.com
Back Image: © Lindsay Helms (36305261), © picsfive (tape) | 123rf.com
Design: © Nicole Edwards Limited

INTERIOR DETAILS:
Formatting: Nicole Edwards Limited
Editing: Blue Otter Editing | BlueOtterEditing.com

ISBN:
Ebook 9781644180020 | Paperback 9781644180037

SUBJECTS:
BISAC: FICTION / Romance / Gay
BISAC: FICTION / Romance / General

Prologue

September 15, 2004

"I'M SERIOUS, RAFE. I'M GONNA do it," Rex Sharpe declared. "I'm gonna turn this place into a bed-and-breakfast. A big one. Fancy, too. People are gonna come from all over just to hang out here." He smirked. "And they won't wanna leave."

In less than a month, Rex would be seventeen, and he already knew *exactly* what he wanted to do with the rest of his life. It all revolved around this place, the old, eight-thousand-plus-square-foot farmhouse that sat right in the middle of town surrounded by the land his family had owned for generations. The same eight-thousand-plus-square-foot farmhouse that was practically falling down around them because their old man was a drunk and an asshole.

But if Rex had anything at all, it was hope. So much he floated on it these days, his dreams so close he could practically taste them.

"Whatever," his kid brother said with a dismissive sigh. "You can't do that. Dad ain't gonna let you. He said he's gonna sell it."

"The hell he is," Rex snarled. On the day Rex turned eighteen, it would all belong to him and his brother. That would be the day Rex could throw the old man off their property and do right by their heritage.

"I heard him tellin' Jolene he's gonna make a bundle," Rafe insisted, his gaze locked on the floor as he flipped the broken sole of his boot open and closed.

Rex wasn't going to argue with Rafe. Billy Don Sharpe was out of his mind if he thought he would do anything of the kind. No way would Rex allow that crazy old fucker to sell what rightfully belonged to him and Rafe. The old man didn't have any rights to it since Billy Don's own father had ensured it wouldn't end up in his hands. Chester Sharpe had shown Rex the will, which stated the land and everything on it belonged to Rex and Rafe should something happen to him.

That meant Billy Don just got to stay there for one more year. If Rex had a say in the matter, the mean old bastard wouldn't even get that.

"It's gonna happen, Rafe. I promise." Rex peeked out of the old shack they'd started using as a hideout from their father. At one time it had been a tool shed, but his old man had long ago hocked all the tools to buy beer. "He ain't gonna stop me. One more year, Rafe. That's all we gotta wait."

"You ain't seventeen yet," Rafe corrected, sounding like the twelve-year-old he was.

"I will be in twenty-three days."

"That feels like forever, Rex," Rafe grumbled. "For-ev-er."

Still very much a kid, Rafe thought a week was forever, but Rex understood what he meant. Sometimes a week did feel like a lifetime around here. But a year … They could hold out for that long. They had to.

"It'll be here before you know it," he assured Rafe. "Just have to be patient."

The wind rattled the old boards of the shed as they sat silently for a minute.

"Well, I wanna help," Rafe finally said, his brown eyes widening. "Will ya let me help, Rex? Maybe I can handle the horses. You can do all the rest."

Rex chuckled as he sat back down on the dusty wood floor and glanced at his brother. "We're gonna have people to help us. Lots of people. They'll work here. In the house and in the barn. We'll pay 'em good, treat 'em nice so they stick around."

Unlike their daddy, who ran off everybody. Including all of Mama's family. Rex and Rafe had loved the rare chances they got to spend with their aunts and uncles, but Billy Don had seen to it that Mama wasn't allowed to associate with them anymore. Hell, even the teachers at Rex's school didn't want to deal with Billy Don.

"Like that place Mama took us to?" Rafe asked, his eyes wide with wonder, his voice quieter than usual. "That big ol' cowboy place with the swimmin' pool and the hay rides?"

"It was a lodge," Rex told him.

"It looked like a log cabin to me. Will it look like that? Can we make it look like that, Rex?"

Rex considered it for a moment, grinned. "Sure. Just like that. We'll rebuild the house, make it nice. Lots of rooms for people to stay. Put in a pool and a hot tub. We'll get a barn, some horses."

"And chickens? I wanna get some chickens."

"Fine. We'll get chickens, too."

Rafe stared at him for a moment as though considering something. When he spoke, his eyebrows lifted slowly. "Only one problem, Rex."

Rex narrowed his gaze, waited for Rafe to clarify.

"You don't know how to build a house."

Rex chuckled. "I'll learn. When I graduate, I'll find someone to teach me. Then I'll be able to do all the work by myself."

"Me, too. You said I could help."

"You will." Rex would make sure his kid brother got to help.

Rafe's gaze dropped to the floor, his shoulders hunching forward as he continued to pick at the toe of his boot. "I wish Mama was here. I miss her, Rex."

That familiar pain jolted through his chest. Rex missed her, too. Just thinking about Mama made his heart hurt, the ache still too fresh.

"I wish he was in jail," Rafe hissed. "That's where he belongs."

Rex could only nod in agreement.

According to the police reports, Mama had died from a head injury when she'd fallen down the stairs. According to Billy Don, Adele had been drinking. Rex knew better. On both counts. Adele had a glass of wine on occasion, but even that had been rare. And Rex knew she hadn't fallen down the stairs. Billy Don had more than likely hit her. Hard. Like he always did.

Unfortunately, Rex hadn't been there when it happened, and the sheriff wouldn't listen when Rex tried to tell him to look into it further. He acted like Rex didn't know anything. Didn't help that Sheriff Carl Monroe was one of Billy Don's oldest friends. If only Jeff Endsley, the deputy, had been there. Then perhaps someone might've done something.

They'd laid Mama to rest just nine months ago, one week after Christmas and only two months after their grandfather had passed away from a heart attack. Rex figured Billy Don had something to do with that, too, but he couldn't prove it. Billy Don had hated Grandpa. They were always arguing. Billy Don was the one yelling, cursing, saying horrible things about Mama right to Grandpa's face. Grandpa had defended Adele every chance he could, but as it turned out, not even Grandpa could put Billy Don in his place.

And now Rex and Rafe were on their own, stuck with Billy Don until Rex turned eighteen. The only two people Billy Don hadn't chased off were now six feet under.

Rex's ears perked up when he heard the back screen door slam. Rafe instinctively scooted farther against the wall, tucking his knees in close to his chest, making himself small.

"Rex! Where ya at, you little fucker?" Billy Don let out a sharp whistle. "Get yer ass in the house. Dinner ain't gonna cook itself."

Rex frowned. He'd been hoping the old man had passed out. Between the whiskey, the beer, and whatever he shot into his arm, it happened more often than not. Evidently, they wouldn't get that lucky tonight.

"You stay here for ten minutes, then come up to the porch." Rex squeezed Rafe's shoulder gently. "Make sure there ain't no yellin' before you come inside."

Rafe shook his head. "I wanna go with you."

"Lemme see how his mood is first," he warned his brother. "If he's swingin' fists, I don't want you in the house."

Billy Don was always itching for a fight, always beating on someone or something. It was the very reason they didn't have a dog anymore. When Rex had witnessed Billy Don kick the dog hard enough to send him sprawling across the room, Rex had lost it. He'd ended up with a black eye and a split lip when he lit into Billy Don, but Rex had somehow managed to deflect Billy Don's rage. They'd only had Rascal for two weeks when Rex had begged Grandpa to take him, to give him to someone who wouldn't hurt him. Grandpa had done it, even though Rafe had cried. Sure, Rex had felt bad for his brother, but not bad enough to change the outcome.

Most of the time, when Mama was alive, she'd been the one who dealt with the backhanded blows, the punches, and the nasty words. No matter how many times Rex tried to intervene, to stop the old man from hitting her, it only made things worse. At that point, Billy Don would hit her harder. Right up until that asshole killed her.

Now that Mama was gone, Rex was trying to keep the old man's focus on him. Being that Rafe was four years younger, it pained Rex to see his kid brother getting hit. If he could stop it, even if it meant taking the blows himself, then by God, he would.

"Don't let him hit you, Rex," Rafe whispered.

Rex pushed to his feet. "It'll be fine." He put his hand on the door and peeked out to ensure his old man wasn't still out there. "Ten minutes. If you hear yellin' inside, don't come in. Just come back here. I'll let you know when it's all right."

Rafe's eyes were wide, but he nodded his head, his mess of dark hair flopping over his forehead. Rex knew the kid wouldn't listen. He was hardheaded, a trait that seemed to run in their family.

Once he confirmed the coast was clear, Rex slipped out of the rickety shack and raced toward the back porch that was in worse condition than the tool shed. As usual, Rex's gaze scanned the huge farmhouse as he neared it. One day this place would belong to him and Rafe and they'd turn it into something nice, something worthy of their grandfather's legacy, a place everyone wanted to come. And Billy Don wouldn't be allowed anywhere near it.

Rex opened the screen door and stepped inside. Before his eyes could adjust to the dim interior, he was knocked forward, his father's big hand smacking him upside the head, making him stumble.

"Where you been, boy? I hollered ten minutes ago."

Rex's fists clenched at his sides, but he bit back the anger. It was getting harder and harder not to hit the old bastard. But he knew if he did, they'd likely cart his ass to jail and no one would be there to protect Rafe.

"I told you to get yer queer ass in here," Billy Don hissed.

Rex blanched just like he did every time his father said that. He wasn't sure if Billy Don actually knew that Rex found himself attracted to guys rather than girls or if he just got off on being crass. It turned his stomach all the same.

"I'm here," Rex said, putting distance between him and the drunk old man. Billy Don smelled like he hadn't showered in a week.

"Where's that snot-nosed brother of yours?"

Rex shrugged.

The old man turned to look out the screen door.

Knowing his father would go looking for Rafe simply because he wanted someone else to knock around, Rex figured he had to distract him.

"What'd'ya want for dinner?" Rex asked, heading to the sink to wash his hands. "I'm not sure what we've got. You ain't been to the store in a while."

"We got spaghetti, don't we?"

"Yeah." Besides the makings for PB and J, it was the only thing they ever had in the house.

"Then make it," his father ordered, turning around to face him. He had a beer in one hand, a cigarette in the other. "Jo's comin' over. You make sure there's enough for her."

Rex inwardly cringed at the mention of his father's girlfriend. He absolutely hated Jolene Snyder. Not only because she'd been coming around ever since their mama died, but also because she creeped him out. Always trying to get close, sitting beside him, putting her hand on his leg. When he tried to get away, she would whine to his old man until Rex was forced to sit there and endure it.

"You have a problem with that, boy?"

"No, sir." He kept his eyes down so his old man wouldn't see the hatred he felt for him.

"Good. 'Cause tonight, I'm gonna let Jo talk to you 'bout a few things." He sneered at Rex. "Said she's got a plan."

Rex frowned. He'd rather let his father beat on him than have to talk to Jolene.

Thankfully, the old man disappeared into the living room. Rex started the water to boil on the stove, then motioned Rafe into the house when his brother appeared in the doorway.

"Jolene's comin' over," Rex whispered. "You're gonna have to stay outta sight tonight."

All the color drained from Rafe's face. Rex got the feeling Jolene had managed to corner his brother at least once, but possibly more. He didn't want to think about what that vile woman had done to Rafe, either. While Rex did his best to stand between Rafe and the adults Billy Don brought around, he couldn't always be there.

"I don't wanna stay here," Rafe insisted, his voice a rough, high-pitched whisper. "I don't wanna see Jolene. Don't make me, Rex. Please don't make me."

"I know." Rex pulled the spaghetti box out of the pantry, went to work getting the pasta started. "I don't, either, but we ain't got no choice. We ain't got nowhere else to go."

"What about Mama's brothers or sisters? Did you call them yet?"

"Haven't had a chance," he said, although it wasn't exactly the truth. While he wished they could do something about Billy Don, Rex wasn't that naive. The last time he'd seen any of his family had been at their mother's funeral. Aunt Lorrie had told them to call if they ever needed anything, but Rex wasn't sure she knew what she would be getting herself into if he did.

So he was putting it off.

"Bring me another beer, boy!"

Rex shot a glare in the direction of his father's voice. He hated that old man. Hated everything about him, but most importantly, he hated that their father didn't give a shit about his own kids.

Not wanting Billy Don to come into the kitchen again, Rex hurried to grab a beer out of the fridge. He popped the top, delivered it to his father, then returned to the kitchen to find Rafe sitting on the floor, his knees up to his chest, back against the wall, gently rocking himself.

"I ain't gonna let them hurt you," Rex whispered, making noise with the pans to cover up the sound. "I swear it, Rafe."

His brother's dark brown eyes lifted, and Rex could see the fear and something that looked a lot like shame. "I hate her, Rex. Hate her so much."

"Me, too," Rex assured him. "But don't you worry 'bout nothin'. I got it all under control."

While the noodles boiled in the water, Rex made peanut butter and jelly sandwiches. It took five minutes for Rafe to scarf down one, along with a full glass of milk. Rex made quick work of two while he nuked a bowl of spaghetti sauce in the microwave.

"Go on up to your room," Rex whispered to Rafe when he was done. "Read a book or somethin' till I can finish up down here."

"Promise not to leave?" Rafe asked, his eyes pleading. "You're not gonna go see Bristol, are ya?"

"I swear it. I ain't goin' nowhere tonight." Rex mussed Rafe's hair, nudged him toward the back stairs. "Now, go."

Once Rafe was out of sight, Rex made his father a plate, delivered it to him before returning to the kitchen to clean up the mess he'd made.

He was a few minutes shy of being finished when the shrill whine of Jolene's car signaled her arrival.

Rex peered out the small window above the sink as the little silver Toyota bumped down the driveway, coming to a stop right outside the door. His teeth clamped together, anger filling him at the sight of Jolene driving their mama's car. When Mama died, Billy Don had given the car to Jolene as a present rather than let Rex have it like he should have. Rex had already learned how to drive, even had his license thanks to his grandpa.

Of course, Billy Don said Jolene deserved the car for all she did around their place. Rex knew it was more of a payment for sex than anything else. He still didn't know why Jolene was hanging around Billy Don considering the twenty-seven-year age difference, but hey, it wasn't his place to care, either.

On the other hand, he did know why his old man kept *her* around. As soon as Billy Don had put the car keys in her hand, Jolene had dropped to her knees right there on the back porch, unzipped Billy Don's jeans… The instant Rex had realized what was going on, he'd raced upstairs wishing he could bleach his brain to forget what he'd seen.

Hurrying to dry the last of the dishes, Rex prayed she would finish her cigarette outside, giving him ample time to disappear upstairs. He tossed silverware into the drawer, slammed it shut, and was just about to turn when he heard the screen door squeak on its hinges. He grabbed the rag to wipe down the counters, got busy.

"Hey, handsome," Jolene said in that raspy tone he was sure wasn't natural. "Sure smells good in here. Whatcha makin'?"

Rex's shoulders tensed but he didn't turn around and he didn't speak.

"Did you save me some supper?"

Without a word, Rex motioned toward the plastic containers he'd set on the counter by the stove.

"Aww, ain't you sweet," she said, her voice far too close for comfort. "I knew you were thinkin' 'bout me."

As he wiped the counter with one hand, Rex hurried to put the last plate in the cabinet, tossed the dish rag in the sink, and turned to go.

"Where're you goin' in such a hurry, Rexi boy?" Jolene asked, plastering herself against him.

He fucking hated that nickname she'd given him. Almost as much as he hated the way she smelled. Like tobacco, cheap perfume, and sweat. A disturbing combination that made his stomach twist in a knot.

Rex eased around her, doing his best not to make eye contact. From the moment Billy Don had introduced him to Jolene, he'd felt there was something seriously off about her. Mentally.

She could've been pretty if it weren't for her frizzy, bleached-blond hair, her black-lined, bloodshot eyes, and her fire-engine-red lipstick that clashed with her yellow teeth. Never mind the fact the woman didn't know what real clothes were. She was always wearing short-shorts and a tank top, showing off far too much skin, including all the track marks that ran down her arms. No doubt she was an addict and it didn't do much for her appearance. For a woman who was only twenty-one, she sure looked a hell of a lot older than that.

"My father's been waitin' for you," Rex told her as he kept to the perimeter of the room, heading for the stairs.

Jolene grinned, one hand sliding over her breast. "I'm worth the wait. Where's Rafe?"

"He's not feelin' well."

"Oh, that poor baby." She flicked her cigarette ashes toward the bowl on the table. "I'll have to come up and check on him in a bit."

"He's fine," Rex told her. "I'm takin' care of him."

Jolene suddenly blocked his path out of the kitchen and Rex forced his gaze to hers. At sixteen, he was already six three, a good foot taller than Jolene. She didn't seem bothered by the fact that he towered over her. In fact, he was almost positive she liked that he did. Whenever he looked at her, she always batted her eyes and licked her lips. It grossed him out every single time.

"Always takin' care of everyone else, Rexi boy," she crooned, then flipped her hair over her shoulder. "You're all grown up. A man already." She smiled, flashed dingy teeth. "But don't you worry. That's why I'm here. You need someone to take care of *you*."

Rex's stomach threatened to revolt.

When she reached for him, he jerked back, his elbow hitting the wall. "I'm fine takin' care of myself."

Her smile lost its sweetness and matched the meanness he saw in her eyes. "I know you are, handsome. I know you are. But sometimes you don't get to make the rules. Your daddy says I'm in charge when I'm here, so you might wanna be nicer to me." Her gaze raked over him. "You wouldn't want me to put you over my knee, would you?"

Jolene's cackling laugh sent chills down his spine. She seemed far too interested in doing just that.

"No, ma'am," he said, his tone serious.

"That's too bad," she pouted. "Might be kinda fun."

Rex continued toward the stairs, not turning his back on her. He didn't trust the woman any more than he trusted his father.

Her eyes followed him, but thankfully she didn't say anything else. As soon as his foot hit the first step, Rex turned and bolted, his boots slapping against the wood. Loud enough his father hollered to tell him to keep it down.

Once he was safely upstairs, Rex made a beeline for Rafe's room. He found his brother sitting on the bed reading a book. "Come on. You're stayin' in my room tonight. Bring your book."

Rafe didn't argue. Not that Rex had expected him to.

"Can I sleep in the closet, Rex?"

"Yeah, sure. Grab a pillow and blanket."

Maybe if they were lucky, Jolene would get high and pass out right along with their old man. Otherwise, it was going to be a long night.

Unfortunately, that was the night that changed the rest of their lives.

One

Fourteen years later
Saturday, January 5, 2019

"I GET THE FUNNY FEELIN' WE'RE NOT gonna meet the deadline, Duke," Rex Sharpe told his dog as they stood in the living room and surveyed the space before them. "I mean, six months *might* be doable if I had a crew."

But he didn't.

He peered over at Duke, his three-year-old, floppy-eared retriever mix. "Perhaps you'd be willin' to pitch in?"

Duke didn't even have the decency to acknowledge him.

"Seriously?" Rex chuckled. "Maybe swingin' a hammer's not in your wheelhouse, but perhaps we could find somethin'."

Duke cast a half-interested look his way.

"What? As much as I want to, I can't do it all by myself."

And if he tried, Rex was going to have to modify the timeline. Again. Never mind the fact that he had overhauled the entire plan at least a dozen times, usually pushing it out a year, then another and another, hoping, with significant optimism, one day he'd find the motivation and get his ass in gear.

At some point, *optimism* was going to take on an entirely new meaning.

And then a year ago it had hit him. He'd woken up one morning raring to go, ready to work. He'd done well for a while, putting in twelve-hour days to focus on the attic. Once that was done, in an effort to keep the momentum, Rex had given up the small apartment he'd been renting to move into the house. But as usual, he had found a few dozen excuses not to get started on the old farmhouse he was turning into a bed-and-breakfast. Most of those mitigating circumstances had been ridiculous, but hey, what could he say?

"I'm an optimistic procrastinator, Duke. That's all there is to it."

Duke let out that familiar doggy sigh. The one that said he'd heard it all before.

"What? There is such a thing," Rex insisted, peering around the empty room. "And fine, maybe it's a decade or so overdue, but still. A man can only do so much, right? I cleared it out. That's a start."

Duke didn't seem to agree with him, but Rex knew he wouldn't. His dog was nothing if not skeptical.

Despite the timeline being roughly thirteen years overdue, and the plan pretty much nonexistent at this point, Rex wasn't ready to throw in the towel. He had faith that this place would come together. Eventually. Maybe not in the next six months like he wanted, but he was trying.

In fact, he finally had something to show for it. For the past eleven months, give or take a week or three, Rex had worked nonstop. And thanks to his dedication, he'd managed to remodel the third floor completely, turning what used to be a dark, musty attic into a functional living space for a future manager. Two bedrooms, one bath, a small eat-in kitchen, nice-sized den, lots of windows to let in light, even a couple of balconies. It was exactly how he'd planned it, and all that hard work had added an additional one thousand square feet of living space.

Not that he'd needed more. The eight-thousand-plus-square-foot farmhouse that sat dead center in the middle of downtown Coyote Ridge was big enough already. While the house resided on a decent five acres, Rex also owned the two thousand acres of farmland behind it that had once been considered part of the adjacent town. At some point, it had been annexed into their county, officially making it part of Coyote Ridge.

Needless to say, he had more space than he would ever need.

For himself, anyway. However, it was perfect for the dream he'd had since he was a boy. A dream that involved turning the dilapidated old house into something functional, utilizing every inch of space for what would be a phenomenal getaway.

Sooner or later.

And converting the attic into living space, as well as moving in, was just the beginning. The rest, starting with this—

"Son of a bitch!" Rex dropped the hammer, grabbed his hand, and growled through the pain.

Two hundred seventeen. No. Make that eighteen. Yep. That was the number of times he'd hit his damn thumb with that damn hammer since he started the ridiculous task of rebuilding the place.

Fucking hammer.

He took a deep breath and stared at the wall. Or rather what *would* be a wall. Technically, right now it was only a few two-by-fours being put in place to hold up the floor above, so it didn't quite qualify.

Yet.

Considering Rex would have to rebuild and remodel thousands of square feet, you'd think one little wall wouldn't give him so many problems.

Fucking wall.

He inhaled deeply, exhaled slowly. In. Out.

With the first phase—the third-floor conversion—completed, it was time for Rex to focus on the house. Tearing it down to the studs hadn't been easy. Day in and day out, his ass had been ripping out and hauling more debris than he cared to think about, and truth be told, there were times Rex wanted to say to hell with it all. It would be easy to sell, move somewhere else, and forget the only dream he'd ever had.

"Easy's for pussies," he mumbled to himself.

He wasn't going to give up now. No fucking way. He'd worked too damn hard for that.

"Do you think I should've sold it, Duke? Left this small town and started over somewhere else?"

Duke gave a light snort but didn't lift his head up off the floor.

"If I'd done that, who would've picked you up at the pound, huh, buddy? Answer me that."

There for a while, Rex had come damn close to selling off the family property, leaving the small town he and his younger brother, Rafe, had grown up in, and finding somewhere else to put down roots. A place they wouldn't be the outcasts, the misfits, the kids whispered to have done the vilest of things. The rumors were endless.

While Rex and Rafe had been cleared of all crimes, people still weren't quite sure they believed what had happened that fateful night fourteen years ago. Some even claimed it was premeditated. Rex would admit, he'd entertained the idea of his father dying a time or two, but never the way it went down. While he had hated the old man, Rex wasn't that evil. And he knew Rafe wasn't, either.

There were only a handful of people who knew the sordid details of what had happened that night. Rex would've preferred to keep it a secret, but telling the tale had meant keeping Rafe out of jail. So, after some encouragement from his aunts and uncles on his mother's side, Rex had relayed the information. Then he'd had to do it again, filling in the holes for the sheriff. Of course, Sheriff Monroe—having been the lowlife that he was—had been more than happy to air their dirty laundry with anyone who asked.

Unfortunately, you couldn't have secrets in a small town. And still, some had felt it necessary to pass judgment over the years. Not so much anymore. While the town had constantly questioned what was going to come of the vacant house that sat on Main Street, somewhere along the way, they'd gotten used to it.

Of course, there were still rumors. Some ridiculous, others insulting. And those damn rumors were the reason selling had seemed the logical thing to do. If, of course, Rex was the type to run from his problems.

Which he wasn't.

Not by a long shot.

So, he'd stood his ground, dug in his boots. This had been his father's childhood home, and his grandfather's, and his great grandfather's, and so on and so forth. While he had no desire to let Billy Don's legacy live on, there was no reason to let one bad seed ruin the entire orchard. Before Billy Don, the Sharpes had built a well-respected reputation in town. They were upstanding citizens, hard workers, always willing to lend a hand when necessary. And with that same hard work and loyalty his ancestors had shown, Rex had proven he was part of the good bunch despite who his father was.

Unfortunately, procrastination was a trait he'd inherited right along with trustworthiness and dependability. So, no, his pet project wasn't coming along quite the way he'd initially envisioned. Then again, he'd been a naive teenager when he originally thought it would be a piece of cake to transform this old run-down farmhouse into a bed-and-breakfast that would draw people from all over.

Fucking dreamer.

There was no denying that life had taken a series of twists and turns that had gotten him off track for a while. But he was right where he'd always dreamed he would be. Sure, the path to get here had been riddled with bumps and bruises and boatloads of disappointment, but his intentions were still the same. He would turn what was nothing more than a house haunted with bad memories into something worth staying in.

And he would do it alone if he had to.

Of course, that would take far longer than he wanted, but a man could only lure his friends to pitch in so many times. As it was, his family were his closest friends. Cousins, mostly. CJ, Jaxson. They'd been there for him through it all. While they rarely balked when he asked for their help, Rex knew it wasn't fair to them. Payment in the form of a six-pack only went so far.

If only Rafe would come home.

Rex sighed. "Not gonna happen," he reminded himself.

Truth was, Rex figured he would never see Rafe again. It was a fear that had the power to steal the air from his lungs. He missed his brother. Had since the asshole walked out of his life a decade ago.

Seemed no matter how often Rex asked his brother to come home, he was either met with silence or resistance. Clearly the man had no desire to move back to Coyote Ridge. Too many bad memories, perhaps? Or maybe Rafe simply blamed Rex for what had happened. That was his worst fear. He'd spent years wondering if that was the real reason Rafe had left.

Either way, Rex had to move forward. He had to prove he had what it took to do right by his family. And maybe Rafe would come back one day to see all that he'd done.

So here he was with the constant reminder looming before him. Desperate and eager to expel the demons from his childhood home and start new memories for himself, his brother, and anyone who wanted to venture to this small patch of Texas real estate Rex called home.

Getting this place up to par hadn't been easy up to this point, and he expected no less in the days to come. Transforming the farmhouse into a bed-and-breakfast was, in theory, a brilliant idea. Or it had been.

Back before he had actually started working on the damn thing.

Back before he had truly understood *just* how much work it needed.

And fuck all, it needed some serious work.

New hardwood throughout would mean new trim. New trim would mean new paint. New paint would mean new fixtures. Not to mention the new AC units, new doors, and windows, all of which had to be replaced for energy efficiency.

Those were just the bones.

That didn't include all the work that would go into each of the seven bedrooms—five upstairs, two down. And of course, remodeling the kitchen, dining room, living room, game room, the four existing bathrooms, plus the four Rex intended to add. The only thing he could check off were the approvals from the Coyote Ridge historical committee, the inspector's go-ahead on the structural soundness, and the completion of the third floor.

And to think, he was only a year into it.

Some thought Rex was crazy for wanting to stay in Coyote Ridge, to live in the house with the ghost of his dead father. And sure, there were bad memories, but there were a lot of good ones, too. Ones Rex wasn't ready to forget. Like the evenings when he and Rafe would sit with Mama and watch television. The days when Grandpa would take them out to the barn, let them muck out the stalls, then take them back inside for ice cream after a job well done.

Which meant Rex needed to get his ass in gear because excuses were no longer part of his vocabulary. He had to get the place open so he could start bringing in some money.

His thoughts drifted back to Rafe as he scratched the top of Duke's head. "Where do you think he's at, boy? Still in Corpus? Or maybe down in Houston?"

Truth was, Rex didn't know where Rafe was because Rafe wanted it that way.

"I suspect he'll come back when he's ready." At least that was what Rex continued to tell himself.

Year after year, he waited patiently for his brother to come back. Rafe had left Coyote Ridge the day he turned eighteen. Hightailed right it out of Dodge without so much as a note. It had taken Rex nearly a year to track him down after that, but he finally had. He would never forget the day Rafe told him that he didn't want anything to do with him. Even the thought made his chest ache.

These days, Rex did his best to keep in touch, texting Rafe at least once a week. Most of those went unanswered, but every so often, Rafe would respond, letting Rex know he was fine.

"I miss the asshole," Rex grumbled as he pulled his ball cap off his head and ran his fingers through his hair. "Definitely miss him."

Hoping that one day he'd come home was what motivated Rex to pick up that damn hammer again.

JACK CUNNINGHAM PULLED INTO HIS APARTMENT COMPLEX, a sigh slipping out before he even bypassed the security gates.

"I need a vacation," he decided.

The feeling grew stronger as Jack weaved between the buildings. He maneuvered into his empty space just as he was overcome with the urge to flee, to run far and fast to somewhere else. *Anywhere* else.

"A *long* vacation," Jack added as the idea burrowed deeper into his brain and threatened to take root once and for all. "Someplace quiet." His gaze scanned the balconies. "Where there aren't any people. A cabin in the woods. No. Too creepy. Maybe just a hotel. Somewhere no one knows my name."

A small smile tipped his lips.

"Yes. That's exactly what I need. Better yet, make it a beach on a tropical island."

For the record, there was no one in the car and he wasn't on the phone, yet Jack couldn't seem to stop talking aloud. He did it all the time. Thankfully, there was rarely anyone around to listen to his ridiculous ramblings. Not that it made the small quirk any easier to swallow.

Jack shut off the engine and stared up at his apartment building.

"Not gonna get a vacation, am I?" He sighed, dropped his head back on the headrest.

Nope. Not in the cards because, as the saying went, he had made his bed; now he had to lie in it.

For the record, he hated his fucking bed.

He also hated his fucking apartment.

As a result, he hated his fucking life.

Now that Jack was parked in his designated spot in front of his apartment building, the repressed groan he always fought so hard to keep in escaped. It was a rough, gravel-filled sound chock full of…

"Self-loathing and disappointment. That's what I've succumbed to."

Another sigh followed a quick roll of his eyes. This was the absolute worst fucking part of his day. The coming home part. In fact, he would prefer to eat glass. Or fall down a flight of stairs. Or get a root canal. Without anesthetic.

Sad but true. Jack would take any of those ten times over, rather than walk up those damn stairs and face what was on the other side of that door.

As usual, a million *if onlys* began running through his head.

If only he wasn't so impulsive.

If only he could be more patient.

If only he could just say no.

If only he could treat his relationships the way he did his work. It seemed all rational thought was relegated to his craft, leaving nothing for the most important decisions in his life.

Such as, you know… "Asking a woman to *marry me*." He laughed without mirth. "That's an important decision, right? Probably one of the most important in a man's life. Yet I don't seem to put much thought in it at all."

To add insult to injury, Jack had fucked up not once but three times. *Three.*

Not at the same time, of course. He wasn't an asshole. But he was twenty-nine years old, and he'd been engaged three times to three different women.

"Third time's a charm, right?" Jack huffed a breath.

No. No, it certainly was not. It was a fucking nightmare.

Thankfully, he hadn't yet made it to the altar during any of the aforementioned bouts of lunacy, so there was that. As for his latest *what was I thinking escapade* … well, there was still time to fix it because the wedding countdown was now at T minus forty-one days. Fiancée number three had whipped up some fancy shindig that was to take place on the most clichéd day of the year. Valentine's Day.

And right now, she was up there in his third-floor apartment probably waiting for him to come in and make a final decision on what sort of fabric doily would be under the place setting. Truth was, he didn't give a damn.

Hence the reason coming home was the absolute worst fucking part of his day.

"Suck it up." Jack gripped the steering wheel and inhaled deeply. "You have to go inside."

At eight o'clock, the parking lot was dark, the early-January sun having dipped beneath the horizon. The days were short and the nights endlessly long. Probably had more to do with the company he kept than the stupid Daylight Savings.

He peered over at the cars on either side of him. His BMW M6 wasn't all that out of place amongst the other luxury vehicles. After all, it wasn't an inexpensive area to live in. Most of the tenants were single businesspeople with high-pressure jobs and not enough time in the day. The entire complex was secure.

Granted, Jack would've preferred to keep his car in the single-car garage he paid for monthly, but *no*. Fiancée number three had opted to park her Mustang in there.

"A fucking *Mustang*." Jack rolled his eyes.

He had tried telling her he'd dropped six figures on his ride, but Jack was pretty sure she thought he was made of money, so it didn't really matter. It was a compromise, she liked to say.

"Actually"—Jack snorted—"it's my gentlemanly duty to not force her to get into a cold car in the middle of a Texas winter." He ground his back molars together. "Someone should tell her central Texas doesn't really have winter."

Not that it would matter. She would simply tell him he needed to embrace the give and take of a relationship.

Right.

Tina Townsend did not know the meaning of give and take. As far as their duo went…

"I give, she takes. And takes and takes and…" Another groan escaped. "Maybe I should take up meditation." He shook his head, clearing out the thought. "Actually, what I should do is grow a pair and stop being a pussy about it."

Except, not only was he impulsive, he was also damn good at avoiding confrontation. Which meant Jack tended to drag out these bad decisions until there was no way to avoid World War III.

"This is the life I've built for myself."

Sort of.

Jack opened the door, stuck one foot out. "Okay. Let's do this."

Before he was fully out, he jerked his leg back in and slammed the door.

"Maybe just a few more minutes." He stared up at the newly renovated apartment building that he'd called home for the past three years. In the beginning, he had actually liked the place. Upscale area, friendly neighbors, walking distance to damn near everything. And being in the heart of downtown Austin, it was in one of the most sought-after locations.

These days it no longer felt like home to him.

"Because of Tina, no doubt." Another groan followed.

He could see the lights on in his apartment, and the same apprehension he felt every time he came home consumed him, overwhelmed him. That nauseous churning in his stomach that told him he'd made a huge fucking mistake was back with a vengeance and it seemed to be getting worse lately.

That or he had an ulcer.

Jack dropped his forehead onto the steering wheel and sighed.

"You have to go inside. You can't sit out here all night no matter how much you want to."

Or could he?

After all, it was ball-shriveling cold right now. Perhaps sleeping in his cramped car could become his thing. Sort of like talking to himself. He could embrace it. And when Tina finally got the hint and moved out, *then* he could go back to his apartment.

She was never leaving. He could feel it. Never, ever, ever.

"Fuck. I need a drink."

Jack glanced in his rearview mirror.

Yeah. A drink. That was what he would do. He would grab a beer, chill for a bit. Maybe get a hotel in town. Then, tomorrow, when he'd had some time to process all the shit going on, perhaps he could come home, deal with Tina.

And figure out if he could still go through with the wedding.

After all, with every passing minute, the noose was getting that much tighter.

"Not the answer," he admonished. "Running is *never* the answer."

Except it was so damn easy.

Although he'd told Tina he would be gone the entire weekend, he figured it wasn't helping their relationship for him to put so much distance between them. Of course, he was no closer to figuring out what he wanted. Every time he thought about the wedding, his stomach twisted in knots, his heart threatened to beat right out of his chest, and bile rose in his throat. He needed to have a talk with Tina. As much as he hated to do it, he had to push the wedding off. For now. Perhaps they needed another year to settle in.

Jack took one more deep breath, decided it was time to go inside.

If he were a smart man, Jack would put an end to the problem tonight by shoring up his nerve and addressing it directly. The problem being five foot five inches of whiny fiancée who was likely on the other side of the front door waiting for Jack to walk in so she could rip him a new one.

Tina was good at that.

"*Too* good. But that's going to change," he promised himself. "I'll sit Tina down and we'll talk it out. Figure out where we go from here."

Yes. That was the best plan he'd had in forever. No more running, no more excuses. He would address the issue and they could move forward.

Even with good intentions, Jack knew tonight would be like any other. If, of course, Tina hadn't gone out for the evening, he would sit down to a silently tense meal with the woman he shared a bed with. They'd share a few details of their day, then Jack would clean the kitchen before retreating to his office—a.k.a. the breakfast bar—and work on some of his drawings while he waited for Tina to give up on watching whatever ridiculous reality TV drama she was obsessed with and go to bed.

Only when he was sure she was asleep would he join her.

On weekends like this when Jack spent endless hours on an upcoming deadline, Tina was usually fit to be tied. It didn't help that Jack had sprung this weekend trip on her at the last minute. Technically, he hadn't needed that much time, but these days he tended to come up with any excuse not to go home.

So, in an effort to put some space between himself and Tina, Jack had intended to hole up in a Dallas hotel room and knock out the final character design for the project he was trying to focus on. Unfortunately, he and Shawn, the author Jack was contracted with, hadn't been able to agree, and Jack knew it wouldn't matter how long they went over it. So his plan had gone to shit before it fully formed. Not in the mood to argue, Jack had decided to call it a night and head home.

The lesser of two evils? No. Not by a long shot. But this *was* his apartment.

"Should've gone to the bar, had a couple of drinks, thought this through." Yep. That was where he should be right now. Copious amounts of alcohol usually helped to ease his frustration. For a little while, anyway.

But no. He'd come up with the ludicrous notion that he needed to make amends with Tina since their last conversation had been a fucking fight. The kind that always ended with her calling him a selfish asshole. Not that Tina would care that he was home early. She would bitch and moan, then apologize and pretend it never happened. She was good at that, too.

Unlike Tina, Jack wasn't able to forget because the woman was ruthless in pointing out every one of his flaws, of which he apparently had many.

"Suck it up or do something about it."

Yeah, yeah, yeah.

With one last resigned sigh, Jack opened his car door, forced his weary body out, then shifted the seat forward. After dragging his art case out of the back seat, he released another deep breath, shut the door, then headed toward the stairs. Every step felt like he was trudging through quicksand carrying two hundred pounds on his shoulders.

Jack had texted Tina half an hour ago to let her know he was on his way home. He'd even asked if he could pick something up for dinner, but she hadn't answered.

"Not unusual," he mumbled under his breath. "She's busy. *Always* fucking busy."

Luckily, Tina made a living doing spin classes down at the gym—where they'd met—along with a side gig bartending at a popular club in town. The latter paid for her partying habit and the former kept her from going insane because, according to Tina, she was not designed to sit still. Tina was not the kind of girl who could stay at home and simply relax. She had to be moving around all the damn time.

Another trait Jack had picked up on *after* they'd started living together.

If Tina wasn't claiming to be writing her breakout novel—of which she had written two whole chapters in the year since she started—then she was watching television or spending hours people watching down at Starbucks or whatever corner coffee shop was popular at the moment while she chatted endlessly with one of her dozens of friends. And if she wasn't working on Friday or Saturday night, she went out with her friends, painting the town until the wee hours of the morning.

"What's wrong with spending a night in? Watching a movie? Sharing popcorn?" He snorted. He saw nothing wrong with that.

Tina called him old, but whatever.

In an effort to support the woman he had asked to marry him, Jack agreed they could go out together one night a week. For the nights he preferred to stay in, Jack encouraged her to go out with her friends. He did his best to be supportive, urging her to be the social butterfly she claimed to be, because what else was he going to do?

"Supportive," he griped as he reached the third-floor landing. "That's certainly not a flaw." He lowered his voice to a mumble. "Did Tina ever mention that? Of course she didn't."

God, he hoped tonight was one of the nights she went out with her friends because…

"*Fuck.*"

He was home. And this time, there was no turning back.

Two

REX TOOK ANOTHER BREAK, SIPPING WATER AND glaring at the wall. For whatever reason, the damn thing was working against him, it seemed. It was one of the first projects he had to complete in order for everything to come together. So, what was the deal?

He was having one of those moments when, as he worked tirelessly to get the demolition completed, Rex wondered what the hell he'd been thinking.

"Duke, I think I might've been better off working for that jack-off at Timber Construction."

Since Duke was snoring on the dog bed in the corner, he didn't have anything to contribute, either.

"Why was it I never came up with excuses when I was working for someone else?" The only thing he'd ever wanted was to be his own boss; however, now that he was, he couldn't seem to stay focused.

Truth was, after they'd carted him and Rafe off that fateful night fourteen years ago, Rex had expected the county to take the house because there was no one left to take care of it, no one who even seemed to want the damn thing. No one but Rex, that was.

Only a few days after the incident, Rex and Rafe had been placed in their uncle's custody, the house abandoned. Owen Jameson was the youngest of his mother's siblings, but even with five kids of his own, Uncle Owen had been willing to take Rex and his brother in. In fact, all of his mother's brothers and sisters had fought to take them in. Since his parents' will hadn't specified, Rex's aunts and uncles had talked it over amongst themselves and come up with the answer.

So, without a say in the matter, Rex and Rafe had gone to live with Uncle Owen and Aunt Deborah. It hadn't been easy for any of them, certainly not with that many people under one roof, but Rex was grateful all the same. At least he hadn't been separated from Rafe, even though his kid brother was never the same after that night. With his dream still his main focus, Rex had put his nose to the grindstone, ignored the rumors and constant whispers, and managed to finish high school. As far as he'd been concerned, it was the first step to getting on with the rest of his life.

Rex had been contemplating what his next steps would be when, on his eighteenth birthday, he received a letter letting him know the house was free and clear, in his name, and the property taxes current. He still didn't know who was responsible, because no one came forward to admit it, but one day he hoped to be able to thank them.

Not wanting to leave Rafe behind, Rex had stayed at the house. Since two of his cousins—Donovan and Stone—had already moved out, that left plenty of room for the rest of them. And it allowed Rex to focus his efforts on his plans for the future.

Neglect had left the old farmhouse in worse shape than he had expected, so he spent some of his spare time cleaning it up, maintaining the yard closest to the house. It didn't take long for him to realize it was going to take a sizable chunk of change to overhaul the place. And in order to do that, he had needed money, which meant he had needed a steady paycheck. Working at the Gas 'n Go hadn't paid nearly enough.

After seeing a sign for a job opening at a local construction site, Rex had marched up to the trailer that was the office and applied for a job. Timber Construction had hired him on the spot, ultimately setting the dominoes of the rest of his life in motion. After all, Rex had needed to learn how to *build* a house in order to *rebuild* one. From that day forward, Rex settled in, breaking his back working for someone else while he pinched and squandered the money necessary to build his dream. The money never went as far as he'd hoped, and for a bit, Rex had feared he would lose it all because the taxes on the property loomed every year.

His first opportunity to dump the place and never look back came the year Rafe was set to graduate high school.

A big-named real estate investment firm showed up one day to talk to Rex about selling off his family's land so they could build some fancy master-planned community. He wouldn't lie, he had entertained it for a while. While ignoring it had seemed the logical answer, Rex hadn't been able to. For a twenty-two-year-old, that kind of money was quite intriguing, damn near irresistible. So, rather than make a decision like that on his own, Rex had sat down with Uncle Owen, talked it over with him, and finally come to a decision. In the end, Rex turned them down because he hadn't been willing to part with the dream. The fancy lawyer with the fancy car hadn't been happy with his decision, but Rex hadn't cared. He'd only had a little remorse because he knew he would never see that sort of money in his lifetime.

Of course, not much later, another offer had come in, this one allowing him the ability to keep the house and bank a little profit.

Some suit-wearing lawyer had called Rex, informing him that his client was interested in leasing the land to run cattle. Although Rex had never considered doing anything of the sort, the money had been too hard to pass up, especially since they'd been willing to pay five years of the lease up front. Thanks to that deal, he'd finally had enough money to see the dream of his start to grow legs. Since then, the money continued to come in every year like clockwork, even now, and the cattle still grazed far out in the distance. Rex had allocated every penny toward the renovation fund for the old farmhouse and, until recently, hadn't touched it.

To this day, he hadn't uncovered the name of the person leasing the land, only the name of the company, which had resulted in a dead end.

Taking a deep breath, Rex grabbed the water bottle he'd set on the massive oak table that filled the dining area. He'd built it himself. The table. All eight feet and the bench and chairs that ran down the length. Yep, it was the first piece of many that he hoped to fill the rooms with. At some point, Rex imagined there'd be guests planted around that table, shoveling food in their pie hole while they talked nonstop about nothing important. Now, he wasn't sure that day would ever come.

"Definitely not if you don't get your ass in gear." Rex took a swig of lukewarm water and glanced around, wondering where Duke had trotted off to.

Rex was now at the point where there was no turning back. He either had to move forward or abandon the project entirely. The problem was, he wasn't a quitter and he was bound and determined to prove that to himself, his brother, and the people of this town. Ever since he'd started tearing things down, the questions had come, everyone wanting to know what he was doing, what he intended to do. So far, he'd managed to dodge their curiosity, but he knew that wouldn't last forever.

There was just so much shit to do and he'd been crazy to think he could do it all himself. The third-floor renovation had proven that. Even if he worked day and night for the next three years, Rex knew he wouldn't get it done alone. Which meant he had to reach out, had to seek assistance from those who'd offered to help. Real assistance. The kind that came with a payment for services rendered.

For all intents and purposes, the house was ready for work to begin. He had the architectural design in place, the plans approved already, the second floor completely cleared out. Rex had even acquired all the permits necessary to begin work. He kept telling himself that once he knew what to call the place, he could get underway. But that was just another excuse in a long line of them.

Fucking name.

Rex could build damn near anything with his own two hands, but it seemed coming up with a name that would describe exactly what it was he was hoping to accomplish was an impossible task. He was creative to a degree, but obviously not in that regard.

Personally, Rex was fine with Bed-and-Breakfast. Not original, but so what?

Of course, even he knew that wouldn't work. Rex wanted something that suited the place. Something to draw people from all over, to encourage couples to spend a weekend snuggled indoors, to share a meal with strangers, and hopefully one day to embark on the outdoor activities he would be focusing on if and when he ever got the house completed.

One step at a time, Sharpe.

Not that anyone was going to show up, but he was holding out hope. After all, Rex didn't have much of a choice at this point. While he had inherited the dilapidated house, the run-down barn, what was left of the old tool shed, and the remaining five hundred acres that didn't have cattle running on it, he would be sinking a hell of a lot of time, as well as most of his savings, into fixing it up. It had to be successful.

Perhaps that was why he was holding himself back. What if it wasn't successful? What if no one wanted to stay there? More importantly, what if Rafe never came home to see it?

The negativity wasn't helping. Positivity was key.

"Yes," he said on a rough growl. "Fucking positivity."

That was what would push him through the tough times, through the days when he could hardly walk because he'd been on his knees for hours on end installing the wood floors. It was certainly what got him through the nights when the terror filled him, woke him from the nightmares, and had him wandering through the big house to ensure there were no threats.

Fucking nightmares.

Some people dwelled on the negative. Not him. He'd been through hell and lived to tell the tale, so he figured it was time to focus on the positive. He was thirty-one years old, so still young. He had his health, money in the bank, good friends, a decent social life. And perhaps he wasn't the typical B and B owner, but most people hadn't expected his cousin Travis to own one of the most popular fetish resorts in the nation. Right here in Coyote Ridge.

If all went well, Rex would be just as successful as Travis, but in his own way. And if the stars aligned just perfectly, Rex wouldn't be the one dealing with the guests. That was what he would be hiring others to do while he continued working on building the place up.

Maybe once the house was finished, he'd have some time for extracurricular activities again also. Some time for dating, something he hadn't done in … forever. Hell, he'd given up on the idea of getting married, settling down with a man who would live out this dream with him. A man Rex could love, one who would love him back.

That was no longer his priority. As far as he was concerned, happily ever after didn't exist for him.

In fact, Rex had become rather well-acquainted with his hand, which was another reason he was eager to immerse himself in work because he had to get the B and B open. At least when that happened, the potential for a lover was an option.

Rex took a deep breath and glared at the wall.

In order for that to happen, he had to stop making excuses.

Fucking bed-and-breakfast.

Rex reached for the hammer at the same time his cell phone rang. Welcoming the distraction, he snatched it from the table and smiled.

"What's up, CJ?" he greeted his cousin.

"Jaxson and I were gonna hit up Moonshiners for a bit. You up for it?"

He was always up for having a beer. "When?"

"'Bout thirty minutes or so?"

"I'll meet you there."

The call disconnected and Rex once again stared at the wall. It could wait for morning. Tonight, he could relax, have a couple of cold ones, talk to his cousins, blow off a little steam. That way, he'd be raring to go tomorrow.

And while he went and showered off the dust and grime, Rex pretended this wasn't just another excuse in his long list of them.

JACK WAS STILL PACING OUTSIDE HIS APARTMENT ten minutes after he'd made the climb to the third floor. He was pretty sure this was a new record for him.

Despite the fact he was shivering, he was standing there debating on whether he should go in or simply get in his car and drive far, far away. Tina could have the damn place for all he cared. Jack would gladly sign over the lease if it meant she wouldn't bitch and yell at him for something stupid. The thought of arguing with that woman was not enticing him to go inside. In fact, since he'd arrived, he'd considered camping out there at least a dozen times just to avoid her.

Only Jack knew he had to go in because otherwise he was simply a chickenshit.

"Don't be a chickenshit," he muttered.

Jack twisted the door handle and pushed.

It didn't budge.

"Huh. Maybe that's a sign?"

Generally, when the door was locked, it meant Tina wasn't home. The woman had been raised in the country and never locked the damn door when she was home. It had been hell convincing her it was a necessity in the city. Crime in Austin likely involved bodily harm, not merely a raccoon rummaging through the trash.

Perhaps tonight was his lucky night.

Jack dug his key out of his pocket, then shoved it into the lock. When he stepped inside, he was greeted with the scent of cinnamon coming from the candle burning on the counter. Although he wouldn't be robbed blind since Tina was now locking the door when she left, one day he *was* going to come home and find the apartment burned to the ground. Getting her to put out the damn candles when she left was not going over well.

Jack's eyes slid to the coffee table as he closed the door. He frowned at the two wineglasses and the empty bottle of Pinot Noir sitting there. He could hear music coming from upstairs, which Jack assumed meant Tina had been running behind and he was damn lucky she did have the forethought to lock the door.

Setting his art case and his keys down on the barstool and shrugging out of his jacket, Jack peered around the apartment, trying to figure out what was different. Everything looked the same, from the Christmas tree still sitting in the corner, white lights twinkling, making all the blue ornaments Tina had insisted on getting sparkle. Apparently, Tina was waiting for him to take it down. Briefly, Jack wondered how long he could get away with keeping it up.

He let out a long, slow breath, noticing Tina's cell phone sitting on the arm of the sofa.

"Now, *that* is odd."

Tina never did anything without taking her phone with her. Even to the bathroom. The woman spent more time on social media than should be allowed for anyone over the age of twenty-five and likely had posted at least a hundred bathtub selfies in the year and a half he'd known her.

Jack picked up the phone and the lock screen came on. The background image was of Tina and two of her best friends. Speaking of best friends… There was a text from Max, which had come in roughly twenty minutes before the one text from Jack asking about dinner.

As a rule, Jack didn't make a point to be nosy, but since it was right there in front of him, he keyed in her password, then read Max's message.

Max: I'm on my way over. Wear something slutty.
Tina: Slutty is what I do best.

He rolled his eyes and set the phone down. Tina's friend Maxine was always trying to get Tina to go out to the clubs. Most of the time it didn't take much persuasion because, like Maxine, Tina preferred to go out.

"Mmm…"

Jack's eyes shot toward the master bedroom loft on the second floor. He slowly set the phone down as he continued to stare in the direction the noise had come from. Was that the music?

"Unnhh…"

Uh. Okay. *That* hadn't come from the music.

Moving toward the stairs, Jack came up short when the noise sounded again. Definitely coming from their bedroom. He glanced up as though he could possibly see through the ceiling.

Maybe Tina was home. Perhaps she was sick? Drunk?

"Unnhh…"

Jack didn't move, straining to hear more.

"Mmm … unnhh."

If she was sick, then he should leave her alone. If she was hurling, he certainly didn't need to be there. She was testy about that sort of thing, anyway. The one time he'd tried to hold her hair after a night of too much vodka and cranberry, Tina had told him to take a hike.

"Mmm…"

But what if she *was* sick and he *didn't* do anything? She'd be equally pissed. He couldn't win no matter what he did.

"You're an idiot," he mumbled as he took the stairs two at a time, trepidation filling him the closer he got to the top.

"Tina?" he called out as he approached the second floor.

"Unnhh … mmm… Oh, God, Max … that feels so—"

Jack jerked to a halt, his eyes wide as he stopped with one foot still on the step, the other firmly on the second floor. "What. The. Ever-loving. *Fuck!*" His breath lodged in his throat as he stood motionless, surveying the scene before him.

Tina.

Bed.

Naked.

Candles.

For fuck's sake.

All the images came together, coalescing into Jack's worst fucking nightmare.

There on the bed they shared was Tina. His *fiancée*, Tina. She was fucking naked. On her hands and knees. With some strange guy—definitely not Maxine—behind her with his dick in her—

"Holy shit, Tina! *Seriously?* The dude's fucking your ass."

Jesus Christ.

"Jack! You're home!" Tina yelled, dropping to her belly and wiggling out of the man's hold. "You're supposed to be in Dallas until tomorrow."

"Oh, well. That makes it okay then," he snapped, glaring at the scene before him.

Yep, he was home, and Tina was being fucked in the ass—something she'd refused to *ever* let him do—by another man in *their* bed.

He wiped his eyes, hoping like fuck he wasn't seeing what he was most definitely seeing. When Jack opened them again...yep. There she was. Definitely getting fucked in the ass by a dude in their bed.

"Nope. Nuh-uh." Jack shook his head to clear the image now permanently imprinted on his brain. "I don't care. It doesn't matter."

I was planning to break it off anyway.

As a matter of fact, this provided Jack with the perfect opportunity to do just that, right?

This is a good thing.

All fucking excuses because this was *not* a good thing and Jack *did* fucking care. Not about Tina being fucked by another guy, per se. Not about Tina at all, even. But he did care that she was doing it in the very bed they slept in every fucking night. *His* bed. She could've had the decency to go to a fucking motel.

Jack closed his eyes and shook his head again. When his vision cleared, the same image appeared before him. Only this time, the guy's condom-clad dick was dislodged from Tina's ass and Tina was scrambling off the side of the bed.

"It's not what it looks like, Jack!" Tina yelled.

It's not or never, Cunningham. Send her on her way.

When their eyes met, Jack pointed toward the door. "Get out."

Tina frowned. "You get out."

"It's my apartment," he countered hotly.

"My name's on the lease, too."

He felt as though he was in an alternate universe. They were having this argument like she hadn't been getting plowed in the ass by a stranger and the naked asshole wasn't still sitting in Jack's bed.

"Fine. If you won't go, I will." He spun around and headed toward the bathroom. There was so much rage churning in his stomach, Jack feared he would vomit if he opened his mouth.

Fucking shit.

Jack had spent the last six months talking himself *out* of kicking Tina to the curb because that was his MO. He couldn't maintain a relationship no matter how fucking hard he tried. He walked away every damn time, coming up with one excuse after another as to why the new chick in his life wasn't the right one. Two prior failed engagements had forced him to put more effort into being with Tina.

"What did that get me?" he muttered.

Ding, ding, ding. *Three* failed engagements.

Because Tina had been…

He made the mistake of turning back.

"Really, Jack," Tina pleaded as she grabbed a silk robe from the floor. "It's not what it looks like. I was—"

Jack turned away again, unable to look at her lying face. The woman clearly thought he was stupid on top of all his other issues. He took a deep breath, exhaled slowly. The red haze faded from his vision and he felt slightly more in control.

"Let me explain, Jack," she begged. "It's not—"

He spun around, raising his hand to halt her from speaking. "*Not* what it looks like?" Jack clenched his teeth, trying to hold in the anger that rapidly returned. "And what happened, Tina? The guy tripped and fell? His dick *accidentally* got lodged … In. Your. Ass?"

Tina's tits bounced as she sauntered toward him and *finally* closed the robe to conceal her nakedness. Jack's eyes darted over to the naked man now reclining against the headboard. "Max, I presume? Well, I'm Jack. That's … yeah … that's my bed you've made yourself comfortable on. I'd shake your hand, but… Okay, fuck this."

The guy's eyes widened, darting between Jack and Tina.

Jack glanced over at his fiancée. No, make that *ex*-fiancée.

"Why?" He clenched his teeth so hard Jack thought for sure a vein would explode in his head.

Tina's blue eyes were wide with confusion. "Why what?"

She was seriously going to play dumb right now?

"How long have you been fucking this guy, Tina?"

She shrugged, her gaze dropping to the floor. "Not long."

Ah, hell. The urge to vomit intensified.

Jack swallowed back the bile and inhaled slowly, jerking his attention away from the naked man and making his way to the master bedroom closet. Jack pulled a suitcase from the top shelf and began yanking clothes from hangers, dumping them inside. There was already a bag in his car, but it only had what he'd needed for the weekend. He needed enough for at least a week.

He did the same with the drawers in the dresser, shoving as much shit into the suitcase as he could while Tina hovered behind him, moving when he did.

"Jack, please. Let me explain."

"Not necessary. I've got eyes." He damn sure didn't need a play-by-play.

"You can't leave, Jack. Please. We can work this out."

Jack jerked his attention to Tina's face. "Have there been others, Tina? Other guys in my fucking bed?"

She shrugged.

He couldn't get words past the lump in his throat. Sure, they'd been having problems, but did they warrant her fucking other guys? *In his bed?*

Pushing past her, Jack dragged the suitcase behind him, grabbing toiletries from the counter and drawers. Whatever he forgot, he would simply buy.

"Please, Jack. I want to explain."

"Trust me, I don't need details. I'll be outta your hair in two minutes tops."

When Jack stepped out of the bathroom, Max was still there, still naked in Jack's fucking bed. He looked as though he didn't have a care in the world. As though it didn't bother him to be fucking Jack's fiancée.

Still, the smile that split Max's face took Jack completely by surprise.

"I'm open to some three-way action if you are." Max glanced over to Tina, then back to him. "Tina said you were into this sort of thing. Said maybe you'd like me to have a go at you. Some man-on-man action."

Jack's eyes widened, completely unable to hide his horror. "A … go…" He swallowed the dust now coating his throat. "A *go* at me? Seriously?"

Tina had told this asshole about his drunken ramblings?

Max's gaze shot over to Tina once more, then back to him. He appeared unfazed by Jack's complete and utter shame. "If not, we could just show our girl the time of her life." He shot Jack a crooked grin. "Double-team her if you know what I mean."

Our girl? Was he fucking insane?

"Yeah, no. Definitely no. But you're more than welcome to have her. Just be warned, she's high maintenance." Jack motioned toward Max's dick. "That thing probably won't hold her interest for long."

"Jack, please."

He glared at Tina. "I want you out," he hissed. "Out of my apartment by the time I get back."

With that, Jack dragged the suitcase down the stairs, situated his art case under his other arm, then snatched up his car keys, his jacket, and his phone.

He didn't look back.

Not even when Tina yelled, "This is all your fault, Jack. You're a selfish asshole. If you'd given a shit about me, I wouldn't have to find it elsewhere."

Three

"HOW'S THAT HOUSE COMIN' ALONG?" CJ PROMPTED when Rex joined him at a table near the doors roughly forty-five minutes after he'd gotten the call.

Rex sighed. "Almost done demolishing the interior."

"'Bout damn time, don't you think?" Jaxson teased.

"I don't see your ass comin' over to help," Rex countered with a grin.

He took a sip of his beer, glanced around the room. Moonshiners—what everyone considered to be the local watering hole—was packed, which wasn't unusual for a Saturday night. He recognized every single person in the room. Being such a small town, there weren't a lot of outsiders who ventured this way. While Moonshiners was a great spot to shoot the shit, down a beer or two, it wasn't the night out a lot of people were looking for. A couple of pool tables and a jukebox were about all it had to offer.

Jaxson made a show of pulling out his cell phone. "I don't see any messages invitin' me over, either."

Rex flipped him off. "You don't *need* an invitation."

"Maybe I do. Some guys just wanna feel wanted."

Jaxson's smartass comment had them all laughing just as the door opened. Rex peered up to see Braydon Walker stepping through the door, his twin, Brendon, right behind him, followed closely by Travis, Gage, Kaleb, Zane, and Sawyer. Looked like all the brothers had opted for a night out. All except for Ethan, anyway.

"Well, hell. Trouble's in the house," CJ announced, loud enough for the bar to hear.

A chorus of greetings sounded from one side of the room to the other, welcoming the newcomers.

Rex shifted so they could move a few more chairs up to the table.

That was how it usually went when he came over to Moonshiners. What started out as a couple guys meeting up for a beer turned into a family get-together.

"Grab a couple more," Braydon said. "Kaden and Keegan are on their way."

"No hot date for them tonight?" Jaxson asked as he scooted his chair over, pulling his beer closer to him.

CJ laughed. "They're hot for the daycare owner. Not sure they've had a date in a while."

Rex bit his lip, kept his comment to himself. Bristol Newton—a.k.a the daycare owner—happened to be his best friend, had been since they were kids.

CJ's gaze shot over to Rex. "Sorry, man."

Rex chuckled. "For what? Bristol's quite capable of handlin' herself." She might've been his best friend, but she damn sure didn't need Rex defending her honor. Of course, he would if it came down to it, but he knew his cousin meant no harm.

On the other hand, the thought of her dating Kaden and Keegan Walker ... well, to be fair, if that was what she wanted, then so be it. They were good guys and the woman was quite capable of making decisions for herself.

"She still not givin' them the time of day?" Brendon asked.

"Not for lack of tryin'," CJ said. "I saw Keegan hittin' on her at the grocery store."

"You mean he knows where the grocery store is?" Sawyer asked with a smirk.

Rex laughed. While he wasn't close to all of his family members, he did have a fondness for them. There was no denying that Rex had spent more time with Jaxson and CJ than he ever had with the Walker brothers. Being that Billy Don had kept Rex and Rafe away from that side of their family, they hadn't had a lot to do with any of them growing up. Probably didn't help that all except Zane were older than Rex, some significantly. And yet, from the day his father died, Rex's mother's side of the family had welcomed them into the fold.

"Speak of the devil," Jaxson said as the door opened and Kaden walked in, Keegan not two steps behind him.

"Hey, Mack!" Braydon shouted. "Can we get a round over here?"

"Sure thing," the bartender called back.

"Is it me, or is there more silver in his beard?" Brendon noted, watching Mack work.

"Definitely more silver," Braydon agreed with a grin. "Makes him look distinguished."

Rex didn't know Michael "Mack" Schwartz all that well, but only because he didn't make a habit to get up in other people's business. However, he knew Mack had had a hard time recently. He'd heard stories that Mack's kid had come back to town a few years ago and disapproved of his father's sexual orientation. Or something along those lines.

"So…" CJ began, his eyes serious as he focused on Rex. "I heard a rumor that someone saw you skinny-dippin' in your pool the other day. True?"

Rex leaned back, his hand on his beer. "You got proof of that?"

CJ grinned. "Naw. But one of these days, it'll be the hot topic in the *Coyote Ridge Gazette*."

Rex laughed. "I seriously doubt there's that much interest in my naked ass. And to set the record straight, I wasn't in my pool."

"No?" CJ didn't sound convinced.

"No. I was in the hot tub, thank you very much.

That had the table erupting in laughter.

"How's Zoey?" Kaden asked Kaleb, evidently sensing some of the tension.

Kaleb's smile widened, his eyes lighting up. "She's good."

"She at home with all those kids?" Keegan teased.

Kaleb took a long pull on his beer and grinned. "Oh, no. Beau and Ethan are watchin' the boys."

"How's that workin' for ya?" CJ questioned. "Your woman carryin' their baby and all?"

"Ba*bies*," Kaleb clarified, his smile widening. "As in more than one."

"What?" CJ's eyes darted around the table as though getting confirmation.

"You haven't heard?" Keegan asked. "Zoey's havin' twins. Ethan and Beau are gonna have two babies."

Bailey Weber, one of the two waitresses Mack used part-time, appeared, passing around beers. "Isn't it awesome?" she asked. "Twins. They must be so excited."

"Thanks, darlin'," CJ said as he took his beer.

"They're over the moon," Kaleb confirmed. "I think they both nearly passed out when they learned the news."

"Well, can you blame 'em?" CJ tilted his beer to his mouth. "Two? At one time?"

"Why're you all panicked?" Travis interjected with a laugh. "You don't even know what it's like for one."

CJ grinned. "True."

"How far along is she?" Jaxson asked.

"Eight weeks."

"Wow." CJ whistled. "Time flies, huh?"

"That it does." Kaleb tipped his beer back to his lips, glanced over at Travis as though passing the conversational baton.

"So, tell me more about this idea of yours, Sharpe," Travis said, addressing Rex.

Rex frowned, slightly shocked that everyone's attention had turned his way. "Idea?"

"The bed-and-breakfast?" Travis glanced over at Keegan, then back to Rex.

Rex shot a glare in Keegan's direction. He should've known the man couldn't keep his damn mouth shut. Considering Keegan was the only one at the table he'd talked to recently about the B and B, it appeared he was behind this little get-together.

"What?" Keegan asked with a smirk. "It's not like I'm known for my ability to keep a secret."

"No shit," Rex muttered.

"Sad but true," Kaden acknowledged after a long pull on his beer. "He gossips like an old lady."

Keegan only grinned wider. "To be fair," he stated, "I see nothin' wrong with what you're wantin' to do. In fact, I hope the whole town'll get behind you. The sooner, the better."

Rex's gaze swung back to Travis, who was apparently still waiting for his response. Accepting that he wasn't going to get out of it, Rex shrugged, his eyes bouncing between all the faces at the table. "Just thinkin' about turnin' the house into somethin' useful."

"Keegan mentioned you're lookin' to fast-track the project?" Gage inquired.

"To fast-track, I would've had to start a decade ago," Rex admitted, slightly uncomfortable with all eyes on him.

"But it's always been your plan," CJ noted. "Since you were a teenager. I remember when we were in high school, there you were, ramblin' on and on about how it was gonna be somethin'."

"Has it?" Kaden asked Rex. "Always been your plan?"

Rex shrugged, his eyes focused on the beer bottle in his hand. He hadn't considered being interrogated by his cousins when he'd agreed to this outing. "Since I was a kid, yeah. Not sure it's in the budget, though. But I've been savin' up through the years. Leased some of the land for cattle. That income has helped."

"You livin' there?" Travis asked.

Rex nodded, took a long pull on his beer. "Moved back in a few months ago when I finished the third floor. Turned it into an apartment for a manager to live in once it's open. Moved into it when I started to demolish parts of the second floor. Figure if I'm gonna get serious, might as well be all in."

"How long do you expect it to take?" Gage inquired.

"Haven't put too much effort into it yet. But I've started a project plan recently."

"You know our wife does renovations on historical homes?" Gage mentioned, motioning toward Travis, the other part of the *our* in that statement.

"I've heard." Rex took a sip of his beer, wishing like hell someone would change the subject again.

"Keegan was tellin' me about it this mornin'," Kaden noted. "Said you were lookin' for investors."

Rex shot Keegan a side glare. "I didn't *exactly* say that."

Keegan laughed. "Didn't have to." He motioned toward the men at the table. "But I heard it anyway."

"If you're seriously lookin' for investors," Travis said, keeping them on topic, "I'm interested."

"Why's that?" Rex couldn't hide the skepticism in his voice. He'd never had a whole lot of interaction with Travis through the years. Mostly because the man was a solid decade older than he was and always on a different path. Admittedly, Rex was genuinely curious as to why Travis would be offering to invest in something he knew little to nothing about. What was the catch?

"Well, for one, I can see it in your eyes. This isn't just a half-ass thought you had recently. This is somethin' you've wanted for a long damn time. Two, you're talkin' about revitalizing Coyote Ridge. This is my family's home and I care about it. A bed-and-breakfast would be a draw that would get people into town. Even if they're just city folks lookin' for a quick getaway. We're far enough outta Austin to lure people in. A B and B would be a great addition."

Travis paused, took a pull on his beer.

"And don't forget the main reason," Gage encouraged with a chuckle.

"And three," Travis added with a wide smile, "because our wife would salivate at the opportunity to help you out."

That seemed to stir up a few laughs at the table.

"I'd do most of the work myself," Rex stated, a slight edge to his tone. He had no intention of passing over the job to someone else to handle.

"The labor, sure. But do you have the design down?" Gage questioned, tipping his bottle in Rex's direction. "Assuming you intend to change the layout and still keep the historical character."

"No, I don't have the design done. Not completely," Rex admitted. "I've got ideas, yeah. The layout, for example. I know how I want it to look, where I want the rooms, the bathrooms, the kitchen."

"What about blueprints?" Travis asked.

"Actually, yes. Well, no. I have them, but they're not finalized just yet. I recently made a few minor changes. Like I said, I don't have everything nailed down. I've got a friend who's helpin' me out in that area."

"But you'd like to keep the historical charm? The character?" Gage questioned.

"I would on a few things, sure. Like the staircase and the wraparound porch. I'd like to keep them intact, but the entire house needs an overhaul."

"Those are the things our wife can assist with," Travis stated. "And I promise, she's not the sort who'll want to overtake the project. But she does have good ideas."

Rex nodded, realized everyone else was listening to the conversation intently. Not wanting to leave them all hanging, he took a swig of his beer and nodded. "I'd be interested in talkin' to her."

"Like I said, you know what you want," Travis noted. "If our wife's on board, we'd like to be a part of it."

Rex stared at Travis, still wondering what the catch was. He'd learned a long time ago that nothing came for free.

"Talk to Kylie," Kaden suggested. "Stop by their house." He motioned toward Travis and Gage. "You can get a good idea of what she's capable of. She renovated theirs and it's rather impressive."

The table grew quiet for a moment, the topic clearly closed.

Rex glanced at Travis once more, nodded. He would definitely like to discuss it further, see what options he did have. After all, he knew he couldn't do it all himself, no matter how much he wanted to.

"That pool of yours heated?" Jaxson asked, leaning back in his chair.

The tension in the air disintegrated and Rex managed to take a deep breath. He turned his attention to Jaxson. "It is. Runs off the underground gas tank I had installed. Wouldn't say it's exactly *warm*, though."

"Hmm." Jaxson drained what was left of his beer. "Maybe I *will* come by and help out again."

Rex grinned. "Bring the beer next time."

"You want me to work *and* bring the beer?"

"Price of admission."

Jaxson grunted. "Hard bargain, Sharpe," he muttered. "Hard fuckin' bargain."

Rex chuckled, relaxing for the first time in what felt like forever. Even as the place steadily filled to overflowing, the noise level rising to a dull roar, he was glad he'd decided to come out tonight.

"Here you go," Bailey said when she delivered another round. "I'll be back in ten minutes. Nurse those suckers, would ya?"

"Yes, ma'am," Jaxson told her with a wink.

"She's a cute one," Keegan said when she was out of earshot.

Rex's gaze slid to Keegan, his brow furrowed.

"Thought you had your sights on that little daycare owner," Jaxson noted, sounding as confused as Rex felt.

Kaden was looking at his twin, as though he was surprised by his brother's assessment of Bailey as well.

"She's far too sweet for the likes of them," Brendon said, breaking some of the tension.

"Is it true you've shared all the women you've been with?" CJ asked, shifting the focus even more.

"It's true," Keegan said, tilting his beer bottle to his lips. He must've realized it was empty because he set it back on the table, grabbed the one Bailey had just delivered.

"She told you to nurse it, Walker." Jaxson chuckled.

"Yeah, yeah, yeah. I'll start nursin' after I've had a few."

Rex let the conversation drone on around him while he took stock of the room. For whatever reason, he was itching for some action tonight. And not the bar brawl sort, either.

Unfortunately, finding an available guy who'd be up for the same wasn't all that easy in a town the size of Coyote Ridge. Which was a damn shame. Sometimes he wished he could blow off a little steam, but Rex wasn't the sort to venture out of town to the clubs. And to be fair, he wasn't looking for a hookup, either, although he wouldn't necessarily turn one down.

So, while his cousins chatted, Rex sent up a silent prayer that maybe tonight some sexy stranger would just walk through those doors and be willing for a couple rounds. His dick twitched just thinking about it. Been a hell of a long time.

Rex downed his second beer and surveyed the room once more.

Hell, it didn't hurt to wish, right?

"A ROOM FOR THE NIGHT'S ALL I need," Jack mumbled to himself as he toted his suitcase toward the elevator.

The man who'd checked him in had said they only had one room available for one night. As his luck would have it, they had one king bed. Not that it mattered. Jack would've agreed to a pull-out couch just to have a place to sleep. He hadn't expected there would be no vacancies when he started out on his trek tonight, but that seemed to be the case. He was only forty-five minutes outside of Austin, and from what he could tell, there wasn't a whole lot going on out here in the sticks, but clearly, he was missing something.

One night was good, though. Tomorrow, if he couldn't get Tina to leave, he would look for a place that had a longer-term option. A week, perhaps. Give Tina time to pack her shit and go. And once she was gone, Jack could go home and get back to life as he'd known it before the third fiancée came along.

Jack stepped into the room and let the door close behind him. The first thing he noticed was the slightly musty smell. He glanced around, surveyed the sink, the bathtub, the toilet, then went over and pulled the blankets back on the bed. Looked clean to him. It would do.

After depositing his suitcase on the luggage rack, Jack used the restroom, then flopped onto the bed before clicking on the television. He fluffed the pillows behind his head, tried to get comfortable as he skimmed through several channels. It didn't take five minutes before he realized he could not sit still for another minute. His blood was humming in his veins and the thought of sitting in that room for the rest of the night had his head spinning.

Launching himself up off the bed, he grabbed his keys from the dresser, along with his wallet and his leather coat. He debated on leaving the jacket. Not like it would do much good. It was one Tina had gotten him. Fashion over practicality, that was her motto. It was ball-shriveling cold out tonight and the weatherman was predicting another cold front in the forecast. At this point, a leather coat was about as practical as an umbrella in the desert.

"Wouldn't mind some snow, though," Jack said as he walked through the empty lobby. As he started toward the doors to the parking lot, he paused and peered over at the man who'd checked him in. "There any bars around here?"

The guy nodded politely. "A couple, but they're not places I'd frequent." He smiled. "However, if you head down 79 a little ways, you'll hit Coyote Ridge. I'd recommend Moonshiners. Nothing fancy, but they've got a good atmosphere and a decent top shelf."

"Thanks." Jack hurried to his car as the wind nipped at his ears. "Seriously need to invest in a warmer coat."

As he pulled out of the parking lot, he was focused solely on finding this Moonshiners, grabbing a drink, and forgetting that this day had ever happened. In fact, he wanted to forget the past year and a half had happened.

"Gonna need more than one drink."

Twenty minutes later, Jack was pulling into the parking lot of Moonshiners. He weaved through the rows of trucks and finally found one empty spot alongside a huge four-wheel-drive monster. The good news ... all four tires were still on asphalt. Bad news ... his car stuck out like a sore thumb.

A few minutes later, he was stepping inside. The drone of conversation overpowered the jukebox banging out some old country song. There was a sea of hats. Cowboy bar. Of all the joints…

Jack didn't look around, didn't make eye contact with anyone as he headed for the bar. There was one available stool on the end farthest from the door, next to a heavyset cowboy with a barrel chest and a black hat perched on his head.

"This seat taken?" he asked simply to be polite.

The guy didn't respond, just shook his head, indicating it was available.

Jack perched on the wooden stool and waited until the bartender made his way back down.

"Jack and Coke, please."

The bartender's eyes scanned his face momentarily before he nodded. Jack wasn't sure what that meant, but he hoped it was approval. As it was, he knew he was the one thing that didn't fit in this puzzle. All the rednecks made him feel like the city boy he was.

"Ain't from 'round here, are ya, boy?" the big cowboy on the end asked. If his slurred words were any indication, he'd been warming that barstool for a while.

Jack glanced over. "No."

"Didn't figure." The guy touched Jack's leather jacket. "Prolly cost more than most hats in this joint."

Evidently, the guy thought he was funny. Too bad he was the only one laughing.

Feeling slightly uncomfortable having a stranger touch him, Jack casually looked around, hoping to find an empty table. Perhaps one in a dark corner where he could nurse his drink and sulk. His gaze bounced from one table to another, all of them full. His attention lingered when his gaze snagged one particular cowboy in the crowd.

When someone cleared their throat, Jack cut his eyes back to the bar to see the silver-haired bartender watching him intently.

"Sorry." Jack passed over his credit card. "Tab, please."

He received another nod before the frowning man disappeared again.

"Prolly afford to buy a round for the whole place, huh, boy?"

Again, he ignored the guy. Or tried to anyway. The man seemed awfully chatty all of a sudden, rapid-firing questions.

"You here visitin' somebody?"

"You got family round these parts?"

"How much did that coat cost you, anyhow?"

"Your momma buy it for you?"

"Christmas gift, huh?"

Jack didn't answer any of the questions, but that didn't seem to stop the guy. He didn't appear to care for an answer.

"How old are you, boy?"

"Where'd you get the coat?" This time the guy touched the coat, running his hand down Jack's arm.

Okay, so Jack was really getting irritated, but he knew better than to cause a scene. He was just about to get up and wander toward the pool tables in the back when a formidable figure inserted himself right between Jack and the touchy-feely guy.

"Hey, Mack. When you get a chance, can I get a Coke?"

"Sure thing."

"Thanks."

Jack tried not to inhale because the man damn near on top of him smelled good. Not that he usually noticed the way men smelled but whatever.

His thoughts drifted back to Tina and Max, to the way the stranger had offered to "have a go" at him. The thought put him off, but not because a man had made the offer.

And fine, so Jack had admitted—during a drunken stupor, mind you—that he'd fantasized a time or two about men. So, what? Didn't make him gay. Simply made him curious. After all, he'd been engaged to three women. A gay man wouldn't have done that.

"A smart man, either," he mumbled under his breath.

Not that there was anything wrong with being gay or straight or whatever. Jack didn't care one way or another how people chose to live their lives.

The bartender reappeared with Jack's credit card and the Coke for the other guy, passing them both over.

"Thanks, Mack," the good-smelling cowboy said, his shoulder bumping Jack's as he reached for it.

Jack made the mistake of looking up only to realize the man standing beside him was none other than the cowboy he'd locked eyes with earlier. They were so close Jack could see the dark stubble on the guy's jaw, the gold striations in his dark brown eyes. He was an attractive man. Tall, muscular. Finely chiseled features, straight nose, prominent jawline, and a devastating smirk.

Shit.

Shaking off the thought, Jack turned his attention back to his drink and pretended he hadn't just had some weird sensation flash through his entire body. Heat coursed through his veins, and lust fizzed deep inside him. He wouldn't say that had *never* happened before. On a rare occasion, Jack had found himself attracted to a guy. Physically. Nothing he would ever indulge in, of course.

But wouldn't that be the icing on the cake? He could get back at Tina by hopping into bed with a man. That was what she wanted, right? Her reason for inviting Max over?

Wait.

Was he seriously thinking about fucking this guy? Or better yet, having this guy fuck him?

No. No, he was not.

He downed his drink in a hurry, breathing easier when the guy finally slipped out of his spot, taking his intoxicating scent with him. Jack forced himself not to watch as he crossed the room and ended up sitting at the table he'd started out at.

Yeah. Jack could fantasize all fucking night long. Not like that guy would go back to his hotel room with him anyway. Of all the guys in this place, Jack stood out like a sore thumb.

He signaled the bartender again.

Definitely time for another.

Better yet… "Make it a double."

Four

REX HADN'T NECESSARILY WANTED A COKE, BUT his curiosity had gotten the best of him. The instant the city boy walked in the door, he'd been ... well, for lack of a better word, curious. And when their eyes had met, curiosity had graduated to intrigue.

So, with the excuse he had to use the restroom, Rex had left the table. After taking care of business, he'd sauntered up to the bar, then purposely inserted himself next to the city boy to get a closer look, check for a ring. The guy was good-looking in a cultured, preppy kind of way. Dark hair, smooth-shaven, pretty eyes. Not too skinny, not too big. Beneath all those fancy clothes, there was probably a body honed with lean muscle.

And there hadn't been a ring.

"You get his number?"

Rex's attention darted over to CJ. "What?"

"The pretty boy at the bar. You get his number?"

Rex flipped CJ off.

"What? Ain't no harm in takin' some stranger back to your place, shaggin' him for the night."

"As long as you use protection," Zane added with a smirk.

Great. Now everyone was going to chime in.

Of course, it didn't help his cause when his eyes strayed back to the stranger at the bar. When the city boy's gaze locked with his, Rex didn't move. Was that interest he saw? There was no way to gauge whether the guy was gay or not. Rex figured not, but he wasn't above hoping. As their eyes remained locked, Rex willed the guy to show even a modicum of interest. Because hell. Rex wasn't above a one-night stand at this point.

Perhaps if the guy stuck around for longer than a minute...

Two hours later, as it closed in on midnight, the bar was emptying out. Most folks had headed on home to bed. Travis and Gage had slipped out first, followed by Sawyer and Zane. Kaleb had hung around for one more beer but then tipped his hat and headed out. Brendon and Braydon had disappeared an hour ago, claiming they wanted to go home and curl up with their wives.

Rex didn't blame them. The only reason he was still there was because the city boy seemed damned determined to drown his sorrows in whiskey. Not that Rex could do a whole lot to help him out, but he couldn't seem to stop watching the train wreck.

"Well, boys, I think I'm gonna head on out," Jaxson said as he stood.

"You good to drive?" Rex asked, watching as Jaxson swayed on his feet.

"I'll take the lightweight home," CJ offered, holding up the water he'd been nursing for the past hour.

"Think we're gonna head out, too," Kaden added.

Rex nodded. "I won't be far behind you."

As soon as the table cleared, Rex decided to relocate to the bar, check in with Mack. He'd pay his tab and head on home. Feeling a little daring, Rex saddled up to the bar close to the city boy once again. He made eye contact, ensured the guy could see his interest.

Granted, he wasn't getting a gay vibe from him. But there was definitely a hint of curiosity in the guy's pretty gray eyes.

Rex smirked, then turned his attention to Mack. "We settled?"

Mack wiped the bar in front of him. "All good."

A man of few words.

Mack met his gaze, then gave a subtle nod in the direction of the stranger. Rex couldn't decipher what the look meant, but he stayed in place. Figured what the hell.

"I need to settle my tab," the dark-haired stranger said, his words slurring thanks to the whiskey.

"You drive here?" Mack asked as he did whatever it was he did to settle a tab.

"Yeah. Car."

"Prolly shouldn't be drivin'," Bill Hatchett noted from his spot at the far corner of the bar. "Been downin' those drinks like they're water."

The stranger glared over at Bill. "I'm fine to drive. Hotel's not too far."

Rex knew the nearest hotel was a good twenty minutes down the road. No way did this guy need to be driving.

"Don't be an idiot, boy," Bill stated, his eyes going hard. "Kill yourself if you want to, but don't take no unsuspectin' stranger along with you."

That seemed to take the city boy by surprise. He watched Bill for a moment, then reached for his receipt and scribbled his name when Mack passed it over.

After the city boy downed what was left in his glass, Rex waited until he got to his feet.

"Thinkin' maybe you should call an Uber," Rex suggested, moving beside him toward the door.

The city boy came up short, his eyes locked on Rex's face. "Why do you care?"

Rex grinned. "Don't. Just don't want to hear about that pretty face imprinted on your windshield come mornin'."

The guy seemed to consider that for a moment, then started for the door again. Rex met Mack's gaze, then nodded. He would see to it the guy didn't get behind the wheel.

"Which hotel you stayin' at?" Rex asked as he followed him out into the parking lot. The temperature had dropped quite a bit, the wind having picked up.

"How do you know I'm stayin' at a hotel?" His tone held a wealth of accusation. "You following me or something?"

Rex chuckled. "You just said it."

"No I didn't," he argued.

Rex figured there was no point in arguing, so he simply kept pace with the city boy. Rex let him get all the way to his car before he inserted himself between him and the fancy Bimmer.

"Move outta the way," the guy slurred.

"Can't let you drive, buddy."

The glare he earned in return was quite sexy. "I'm not your buddy."

Rex couldn't help it, he smiled. They stood like that for a moment, squared off in the parking lot. He figured the city boy was gearing up for a fight. Decided he'd have to give him one if he attempted to drive. There were a lot of things Rex could tolerate, but ignorance wasn't one of them.

"And you aren't my keeper," the city boy added.

"Well…" Rex tucked his hands in his pockets, glanced around. "I guess I could always call the sheriff."

"Now why would you go and do that?"

Rex shrugged. "Wouldn't want to see you wrapped around a tree."

"Are you hittin' on me?" the guy blurted after several seconds of awkward silence.

Rex grinned. Couldn't help it. "You want me to?"

A shrug was the only answer he got.

Interesting. He could work with that. Rex stepped in close, stared the guy down. He had the urge to find out what the guy's lips would feel like beneath his.

"Where're you from?" he asked, keeping his voice low.

"Austin."

"So you *are* a city boy?"

"So what if I am? You don't like city boys?"

Rex chuckled, moved in closer. "Didn't say that."

When those slumberous gray eyes dropped to Rex's mouth, he recognized that hint of interest he'd been searching for. Too bad the guy was drunk. Otherwise, Rex would've been content to talk him out of his clothes, even if for just a few hours.

But tonight was not going to be his lucky night. Rather than hit on the city boy, Rex held out his hand. "Give me your keys."

"Hell no. I'm not letting you steal my car."

Rex laughed, motioned to the truck behind him. "Trust me, I don't want your fancy Bimmer, city boy. Not my style."

He wasn't sure what the guy was thinking, but a second later, the keys were in Rex's hand.

"You got a key card for your hotel?"

"Not inviting you to my room," the man mumbled.

Rex laughed. "Not askin'."

"Then why do you want to know?"

"Thought maybe I could get a hint as to where you're stayin' that way."

"Oh." The guy dug into his pocket, pulled out a hotel key card.

"Get in." Rex motioned toward the passenger side door.

There was no argument as the guy climbed into the car. Rex was suddenly grateful he'd been around tonight. What the hell would've happened to this guy if he'd let just anyone drive him back to his hotel? Or worse, gotten behind the wheel and attempted the drive himself? City boy looked smarter than that.

Shaking off the thought, Rex sighed, then walked around and got into the car. He felt like he was sitting on the ground as low as it was. He had to shift the seat back several inches to accommodate his six feet five inches.

"How'll you get back?"

Rex glanced over as he backed the car out of the space. "I'll grab an Uber."

The man sighed.

"What's your name?" Rex asked, curious.

"Does it matter?"

"Not really, no."

"I'm not gay."

Rex chuckled. "Good to know."

"Why?"

"Why what?"

The sexy stranger turned his head, stared at Rex. "Why's that good?"

"'Cause if you ain't gay, I ain't interested."

"Would you be?"

Rex shot a look at the man. "Would I be what?"

"Interested. You know, if I was gay?"

"Perhaps."

"Really?" The city boy didn't sound convinced.

"Really."

They drove in silence for a few minutes, but Rex could tell he hadn't passed out yet.

"Could we get some coffee?" the city boy finally asked as Rex neared the hotel.

Without answering, Rex turned and headed toward the McDonald's just a few blocks from the hotel. He maneuvered the drive-thru, ordered one cup of black coffee, then paid.

"I'll pay you back," the guy said.

"No need."

"I'm still not sleeping with you," the guy said.

Rex chuckled.

Because what else was he going to do?

NEVER IN HIS LIFE HAD JACK GOTTEN in a car with a stranger.

Never in his life had Jack allowed a stranger to drive his car.

Yet for whatever reason, he wasn't scared of this guy.

Perhaps the liquor was making him stupid.

He was feeling something, but it certainly wasn't fear. More like lust. A deep-seated ache that had taken up residence as soon as the cowboy had approached the bar earlier. Through the night, it had only grown stronger as they'd traded heated glances across the crowded room. Despite the alcohol, Jack had seen the guy's interest, and admittedly, he'd entertained the notion, until the only thing he could think about was what it would feel like to have this guy fuck him into oblivion.

Yeah. So what if that made him gay?

Well, it didn't necessarily make him gay, right? Curious, sure. Bi-curious, he believed it was called. Of course, he still liked women. Not much at the moment, but surely one day he'd find one he could settle down with. Until then, maybe he should try men on for a change.

No, wait. He shouldn't. That was—

"What room're you in?" the sexy cowboy asked, interrupting Jack's thoughts.

"You're not coming up to my room," Jack stated adamantly when they pulled into the parking lot.

"Okay."

Jack managed to climb out of the car when the cowboy did. He even managed to remain steady on his feet. Mostly. The coffee had gone a long way toward clearing his head. Hadn't done anything to diminish that damn lust sending shockwaves right to his dick, though.

"Where're you going?" Jack asked when the guy started walking toward the hotel entrance.

"Figured I'd hang out inside while I wait for an Uber. Prefer not to freeze my nuts off. That okay with you, city boy?"

Jack frowned, then stumbled a couple of steps. The next thing he knew, the cowboy had his hand on his arm and was holding him upright. They were toe-to-toe, damn near nose to nose. Jack held his ground, didn't back down, staring right into those phenomenal liquid brown eyes. He tried to read the guy's mind, figure out what his next step might be.

Did he want to fuck? Or was he merely feeling sorry for the drunk city boy?

God, he wanted this guy to kiss him. This complete stranger. For some damn reason, Jack just wanted to lose himself for a little while. Feel his strong hands on his skin, those full lips on his. It made no sense whatsoever, but he couldn't deny it.

What the hell was wrong with him?

Jack jerked back, then held out his hand. "Can I have my car keys?"

The cowboy dropped them into his palm.

"And my key card?"

The cowboy smirked, that damn sexy tilt of his lips that had Jack's attention darting straight to his mouth. "Already gave it back to you."

Jack glared at him, tried to remember when he'd done that. Couldn't.

Fuck it.

He needed sleep.

Without another word, Jack marched toward the building. He damn near plowed into the doors when they didn't open fast enough.

"Have a good night, city boy," the cowboy said when Jack headed toward the elevator.

Jack stood there, staring at the button, trying to figure out what he was supposed to do next. Had he punched it already? If he had, then he'd look stupid doing it again. He dared a glance over, noticed the cowboy was still watching him. He jerked his attention back to the button. Surely he'd hit it. Maybe the light was out. That was all it was. Elevators in these places were crappy. And slow.

He sipped his coffee, waited.

Jack had no idea how long he stood there waiting, but it wasn't until the cowboy came over, hit the button that Jack realized he hadn't hit it after all. "Damn it," he mumbled under his breath.

A second later, the elevator doors opened, and Jack headed inside. He turned and noticed the cowboy was still watching him. He was transfixed by the man, mesmerized. He just wanted to know what those lips would feel like on his. All those hard planes and angles under his palms...

Shit.

"Just need sleep," he muttered. Jack glanced down at the panel of buttons. What floor was he on again? Three, right? Or was it two?

Shit.

"Problem?" the cowboy asked when Jack looked up at him again.

"I can't remember my room number."

This time the cowboy seemed a little annoyed rather than amused. That only pissed Jack off. He didn't need a damn babysitter. He would find his room eventually.

Figuring he could simply scan his card on every door until one lit up, Jack hit the button for the third floor. A second later, the doors closed, sealing him inside and ruining all chances of getting that damn cowboy to fuck him.

Shit.

"You do *not* want to fuck him," Jack mumbled when the doors finally opened. "Or vice versa." He stumbled into the hallway, noticed the chairs just waiting for him to relax a bit.

He would take a break for a minute. His head was clearer, but still he wasn't exactly coherent. That last drink had likely been a mistake. Come morning, when he remembered how many he'd actually had, Jack would probably be hugging the toilet and promising never to down another drop.

Again, time seemed to stand still while he sat there staring at the silver doors in front of him. It wasn't until they opened that he looked up and saw the cowboy standing there, grinning back at him.

"Problem?" the cowboy asked again.

"Just taking a break."

The cowboy nodded, then motioned for him to get up. "Why don't you take a break on the second floor?"

"Why would I do that?"

"Because that's where your room is."

"Oh." Jack didn't ask how he knew that. His legs lifted him from the chair, and he marched into the elevator. "I knew that."

"I'm sure you did."

The doors closed when the cowboy hit the button for the second floor. A minute later, they opened again. This time Jack walked out as though he knew exactly where he was going. When he went to turn right down the hallway, the cowboy called out to him, telling him the other way.

"I knew that, too."

"Yep. I figured."

When the cowboy stopped in front of a door, Jack took the key card and swiped it over the door lock.

Nothing happened.

Jack did it again. And again.

Finally, a big, warm hand reached out and took the card from his cold fingers. The next thing he knew, Jack was being guided inside. The coffee cup was removed from his hands and then his leather jacket was being pulled from his shoulders.

"I'm not going to sleep with you," Jack muttered.

"Actually, *I'm* not gonna sleep with *you*," the cowboy countered as he nudged Jack toward the bed. "Sleep it off, city boy. And don't get in too much trouble."

"Wait!" Jack called out when the cowboy turned toward the door. "Why won't you sleep with me? You like men, right?"

This time there was a glimmer of heat in those dark eyes. "I do."

"Then what's wrong with me?"

That smirk returned and Jack felt his knees weaken.

"For one, you're drunk. And two, you told me you wouldn't sleep with me."

Well, shit. That made too much damn sense. "But you want to? Sleep with me?"

The cowboy chuckled. "I'd considered it. Back when you showed up at the bar."

"But not now?"

"You're drunk, city boy. And no matter how hot you are, I'm not into takin' advantage of a drunk guy. Not my style."

For the first time that night, Jack regretted taking a single drink.

Five

REX COULDN'T EXPLAIN WHY HE WAS STANDING in this guy's hotel room. Or why he felt the ridiculous urge to stay, to see what could possibly happen if he didn't slip out into the cold night all alone.

It was stupid.

The guy was drunk.

But still, there was something about him. A vulnerability, perhaps.

Whatever it was, Rex didn't want to leave him alone. He got the feeling the whiskey had been the medicine to dull whatever was ailing him. Not that Rex was looking to fix the city boy. He'd taken on more than his fair share of fixer-uppers, thank you very much. The farmhouse was more than enough for him.

However, that didn't explain why Rex didn't turn and walk out the door. Instead, he took a step closer, then another, until he was once again toe-to-toe with the sexy city boy.

The dim yellow glow from the lamp on the nightstand was all he had to see by, but it was more than enough to know this guy was willing if Rex would just take the reins.

Good thing for the city boy, Rex wasn't the type who took advantage of drunk guys at the bar.

Forcing himself to turn away, he crossed the three feet to the bathroom, grabbed one of the glasses, and filled it with water. He retrieved the packet of aspirin he'd picked up in the small shop downstairs. When he returned, the city boy was still standing. Rex passed over the water and the pills.

"Take it."

The guy stared down at the pills as though they were a snake about to strike.

"Aspirin," Rex told him. "To ward off some of the hangover you're entitled to tomorrow."

The city boy frowned but tossed back the pills, downed them with the water.

When Rex stepped forward to take the glass, the city boy did the same. They were once again toe-to-toe.

"I need to go," Rex said, keeping his tone firm. "And you need to sleep."

Neither of them moved. Hell, Rex wasn't even sure the guy was breathing. But he was damn sure waiting for something.

One kiss.

What could it hurt?

Leaning in closer, Rex allowed his lips to hover. He could smell the whiskey on the city boy's breath. That and coffee. But there was something else, too. An intoxicating scent that had his dick hardening.

Yes. One kiss.

Rex eliminated the remaining space between them, allowed his lips to graze the city boy's. Not wanting to risk dropping the glass, he reached out, set it on the nightstand before returning to feel those soft lips one more time. He was ready to pull back when hard hands fisted in his T-shirt, jerking him closer, sealing their mouths together. He hadn't expected that. The city boy seemed far more reserved, but Rex certainly wasn't disappointed. He didn't have a problem with a man who knew what he wanted.

The soft moan was almost enough to break him, but Rex held his ground, allowed the city boy to kiss him. Rex had tremendous self-control, which was a damn good thing considering all he wanted to do to this man. Hell, his brain was already three steps ahead, stripping them both, rolling on the condom, and sliding into the blessed warmth of his body. It didn't matter that Rex didn't know the man's name. Almost didn't matter that the guy was drunk.

Almost being the key word.

But he wouldn't allow it to go that far. He couldn't.

For one, he *didn't* know the guy's name. And though he was more than willing to indulge for one night, ultimately, it wasn't what Rex was after.

Granted, it was very, very tempting.

Finally, he forced himself to pull back, stared into the city boy's glazed eyes for a moment.

"Sleep," he ordered.

"Stay."

Rex knew he shouldn't. It was a mistake. He needed to head home, forget he'd ever laid eyes on the man who was so easily enticing him to do things he knew they would both regret come morning.

"I need—"

"Stay," the city boy pleaded again, still holding Rex's shirt.

Reluctantly, Rex nodded. He figured the guy would pass out within minutes and he could slip out then, be home before two a.m., get plenty of sleep. No harm, no foul.

Rex pulled the blankets back on the bed, then urged the city boy into it. He moved around to the other side, propped two pillows against the headboard, then reclined on top of the blankets. He didn't bother taking off his boots. After all, what was the point? He wasn't going to stay.

For the longest time, Rex fought exhaustion, staring at the television, waiting to hear the city boy snore so he could slip out. Before he knew it, his eyes were drifting shut, his breaths slowing, and sleep overtaking him. The nightmare of that night so long ago rushed upon him.

Rex woke to the sound of metal clanking against metal.

It took a moment for his brain to come online. He didn't remember falling asleep, but apparently, he had.

His eyes opened slowly, and he recognized his darkened bedroom, the popcorn ceiling overhead, the tattered wallpaper peeling back. The moon was bright, streaming in through the torn curtains, casting shadows from the old oak tree just outside his window.

The floor squeaked and he turned his head to see his father standing at the foot of the bed. The light from the hallway spilled into the room, silhouetting Billy Don in a pale-yellow glow.

A hard hand curled around Rex's ankle.

"What are you doin'?" Rex tried to pull his leg away, but the grip only tightened. Instinct had him jerking harder, but his father's hand squeezed roughly, causing Rex to yelp in pain. "Why are you in here?"

His old man didn't say a word, didn't even look at him.

"Now don't you worry 'bout nothin', Rexi boy. We're just gonna have a little chat."

Rex's attention shot to the side of the bed, to the woman whose words slurred from far too much alcohol and God only knew what else. Jolene was standing there, her hand on his arm as something clicked, tightening around his wrist. He tried to jerk away, but he couldn't. She had handcuffed his wrist to the bed frame.

He yanked his other arm, but it didn't move far, the clanking sound of metal against metal piercing the air. Panic slammed into his chest at the same time he saw the handcuff ringing his other wrist, tethering him to the metal bars beneath him. He tried to move both arms, jerking roughly against the restraints.

Oh, fuck! He was trapped.

Jolene leaned in, ran her hand down his cheek. She smelled like pot and that nasty perfume she favored. The combination was nauseating.

"We just came to talk," she said softly, a creepy smile on her face.

Rex tried to twist out of reach but couldn't.

"Would that be all right with you?"

"No," he said adamantly. "Let me go."

She giggled. "That wouldn't be any fun."

Rex frowned, his gaze darting to the alarm clock on the night stand. Two a.m.

His attention shot to where his father was securing his ankle to the metal rungs at the end of his bed. "What do you want to talk about?"

"Wanted to settle a few things," his old man grumbled.

"Don't worry, honey," Jolene said softly. "It's just a game we're gonna play."

Panic turned to fear, causing Rex to jerk against the restraints. He tried to kick his legs, but one of them wouldn't move. His father gripped the other before Rex could make contact.

"Be still," his father hissed. "Or I'll go get your brother. Make him watch this."

Rex stopped moving. Being restrained to the bed, he had absolutely no way of protecting his brother and they both knew it. They also knew that the fastest way to get him to comply was to threaten Rafe.

Billy Don used a thick zip tie to secure Rex's other leg to the thin metal footboard on his bed. When Billy Don released his grip, Rex kicked out, making the frame shake. He shot an angry glare at his father.

"Let me go," Rex growled, keeping his voice as low as he could. Rafe was asleep in Rex's closet, the safest place he could think to stash his brother while Jolene was in the house.

"Now, now. You wouldn't wanna wake your brother, would ya?" Jolene sat on the edge of the mattress by Rex's hip. "I mean, there really is no reason he should see this. Unless, of course, you want him to."

To see what? What the hell were they going to do to him?

"We can get him if you'd like," Jolene offered, her eyes wild. She was definitely high or drunk or both. "The more the merrier, I say."

"No." Rex shook his head. "Leave Rafe alone." He forced himself to remain as still as possible, but it wasn't easy.

"Then be a good boy," Jolene said, her tone saccharine sweet.

"Why are you doin' this?" Rex asked, his voice sharp as his eyes shot from Jolene to his father, then back again.

Jolene's excited gaze met his. "Because your daddy's worried about you, Rexi boy. Said you been talkin' nonsense."

Rex frowned, confused. When he looked over at his father, he realized the old man had taken a step back, crossed his big, beefy arms over his chest. He seemed content to stand there. Watching.

Rex divided his attention between the two of them but spoke to Jolene. "What are you talkin' about?"

Jolene's hand grazed Rex's bicep and he pulled back to get away from her. The handcuffs stopped him.

"Do you like girls, Rex?"

He frowned, repeated his last question. "What are you talkin' about?"

"Girls. You know. Women." She smiled and it made his insides shudder, fear mingling with the adrenaline already flooding his bloodstream.

"Pussy, boy," Billy Don growled. "Do you like pussy?"

Rex tensed, pure terror causing every nerve ending to spark, his fight-or-flight instinct raring forward.

"Your daddy says you think you're a queer," Jolene explained. "Said you don't care for pussy. That you'd rather suck a dick."

Oh, shit. Oh, shit.

"That's what you said, ain't it?" his father snarled. "That's what you told that fat girl you call a friend. That you're a queer fucker. Wantin' boys and shit."

Rex tried to piece it all together. Tried to figure out what the hell was going on. Why his father and Jolene were in his bedroom. Why they were talking about this at all. The only person Rex had talked to about guys was Bristol Newton. She lived two blocks over and they'd been friends forever. One afternoon, they'd been talking about a guy Bristol liked and Rex had blurted out that he thought he was cute. He hadn't meant to, but surprisingly, Bristol hadn't been disgusted by what he said, and they'd ended up talking about it. But only once. And since then, neither of them had mentioned it.

Had Bristol told on him? Had she said something to his old man?

No. She wouldn't do that. Bristol was his best friend. Plus she hated Billy Don as much as Rex did. The man always called her fat and lazy although she was neither.

"Told Jo ain't no boy of mine gonna be a queer," his father snapped.

Jolene giggled, but it sounded slightly hysterical. "I told him you weren't queer. You're just a confused teenage boy. I've seen the way you look at me." She leaned forward, cupping her breasts near his face. "You'd like to see these, wouldn't you?"

Ah, Christ. Rex was going to throw up.

"Yeah, you would," she said with a snort. "I can see it in your eyes. Can't know what you want till you've had a woman's touch, right? I bet you'll like it just fine."

Rex jerked at the restraints. "I ain't gay," he insisted. "I ain't never said that. Now let me go."

"We're just here to make sure, handsome," Jolene crooned. "Once we do, we'll let you go. But don't you worry, Rexi boy, I'll make this feel good."

Bile rose in Rex's throat, the bitter taste threatening to choke him as Jolene set her hand on his stomach. Rex was still wearing his jeans and his T-shirt. He'd been sleeping fully clothed since his mama died. He hadn't trusted his old man not to burn down the house with his cigarettes and he'd wanted to be prepared to get him and Rafe out if necessary.

Rex jerked away from her touch.

The slap from his father was hard and instant, making his ears ring. He hadn't even seen the man move, didn't realize he was now standing over him.

"Be still, boy!" the old man bellowed. "Jo's gonna fix you and that's that."

Rex jerked awake to the sound of the heater kicking on. The room was hot, the air dry. He knew where he was, why he was there, so there was no disorientation even as the dream faded, the sweat on his skin cooling. Rex took a few moments to slow his labored breaths. He turned his head, caught sight of the stranger from the bar sleeping beside him.

Terror threatened to choke him. What would've happened if he hadn't woken up? Would he have hurt the city boy? Rex didn't sleep in the same bed with anyone for that very reason.

He stared at the sleeping man, his eyes caressing the city boy's face. For some fucked-up reason, the sight of him calmed Rex. It took a couple of minutes, but finally his labored breaths slowed.

Why hadn't he left again? This was stupid. What the hell was he waiting for? The straight guy to drop trou and ask him to fuck him? Rex had no doubt the guy was straight. Maybe a tad curious, but it wasn't in Rex's nature to entertain those who only *thought* they wanted a man for a night. He had no business even thinking about it.

Yet here he was.

Yeah, it was time to go.

Rex scrubbed his hand over his face, squeezed his eyes shut, and willed his ass to get out of the bed. It was the smart thing to do.

Hell, it was the *only* thing to do.

Slowly sitting up, Rex tried to keep as quiet as he could. The bed springs squeaked, and he paused, waiting to see if those curious eyes would open. When they didn't, he stood, made it a few feet before he heard the stranger shift and roll.

Rex made the mistake of turning, looking at him. Those pretty gray eyes were open, watching him intently. He considered telling him he was leaving, but his mouth wouldn't move, and his feet weren't doing much better in that department.

"Thanks for bringing me back here," the man said, his voice rough with sleep. "I appreciate it."

Rex nodded. It was the opening he needed to bolt without a word, but still he didn't take it. After a few seconds, he started to turn but ended up moving toward the bed instead. Rex had no idea what the fuck he was doing, but he couldn't help himself. He leaned over, pressed his lips to the stranger's.

"Maybe … once you figure out what it is you want and all…" Damn, but Rex wanted the city boy to know what he wanted. It didn't seem fair. Rex knew he was looking for a distraction from that fucking nightmare, but still. He could think of a dozen more reasons he wanted this city boy.

And a dozen or two as to why this was a bad idea.

Realizing he needed to go, Rex started to stand but paused when the city boy reached for him.

"I know what I want," the city boy whispered back.

"And that would be?"

"You."

Rex searched his eyes for signs of confusion or uncertainty, saw nothing but pure need reflected at him. Gone were the glassy eyes of the intoxicated; in their place, a man who ached the same way Rex did.

He peered over at the clock. Only two fifteen. He could spare a few minutes, couldn't he?

Curling his hand behind the man's neck, he pulled him up, sealed their mouths together. He kept it tentative, but when the city boy moaned softly, something Rex was clearly powerless against, he moved in closer. One knee on the mattress, one hand propping himself up, he let the kiss ignite. The man was impossible to resist, despite knowing better. Still, Rex let go, allowed the heat to consume them both until he was practically on top of him.

Long minutes passed as they made out. It took everything in him to pull back, but Rex finally managed.

"Please…" the city boy pleaded. "Don't stop."

It was then Rex knew he was in deep shit. If he didn't walk away now, he knew what was going to happen.

Unfortunately, he was powerless to stop it.

Or that was the excuse he told himself.

JACK WASN'T SURE WHAT HE WAS DOING, but he knew he didn't want the cowboy to leave.

Not yet.

He couldn't blame it on the whiskey, either, because he'd slept a lot of it off, his head as clear as it had been when he stepped into his apartment yesterday to find Tina in bed with another man.

Okay, perhaps not quite that clear, but he felt in control of himself.

And though he could tell himself that he was simply trying to punish Tina for what she'd done to him, Jack knew better. He wanted to explore this while he still had the opportunity.

It was the kiss that had done it. That one kiss last night had been the only thing he could think about, dream about. Jack had never kissed a man before and it had been … life-changing. Yeah, he said it. Never before had he ever felt something that potent.

So, when he'd woken up to find the cowboy still there, Jack took it as a sign.

Truth was, he'd been making excuses for most of his life. Trying to convince himself he wanted something he didn't. Perhaps that was the reason for three failed engagements. It was highly likely he'd been looking in the wrong damn place to find what he needed.

Because this cowboy...

Jack wanted him. With a passion he'd never experienced before.

It didn't matter that he didn't know the guy's name. Hell, perhaps that made it easier. One night—better yet, just a few hours...

"You know what you're doin'?" the cowboy asked, pulling back and staring down at him.

Jack liked the sexy drawl, the way those bottomless brown eyes seemed to implore him, searching deeper than anyone else ever had. It made Jack want to let go, to give in to this compulsive action. He'd never been the type for one-night stands. In fact, he'd never had one before.

Jack held on, refusing to let go, enjoying the weight of him. "Don't have a clue," he admitted on a whisper. "Doesn't mean I don't want it."

The cowboy stared into his eyes, seemed to gauge whether he was telling the truth or not. In that moment, Jack wasn't sure one night would be enough, but he wasn't willing to let this moment pass him by.

Pulling the cowboy's mouth back to his, Jack kissed him, allowing the warmth to seep into his soul, soothing the ache that had been there for as long as he could remember. Nothing had ever quenched it. This man, this kiss... Being here with him was everything he'd ever fantasized it would be. Only better. More intense. The heat flashed in his veins, his cock rock hard, desperate for release.

He sensed the cowboy's hesitation, knew he was allowing Jack to lead. Jack could've told him he wanted whatever he was willing to give him. But he didn't say it aloud. Instead, he ground his cock against the rock-hard thigh between his legs. Jack groaned, his lust rocketing to a fever pitch.

How in the fuck had he lived nearly thirty years without feeling this sort of incredible intensity? Sure, he'd been with a few women, but those experiences had paled in comparison to this cowboy's simple touch. Jack wasn't sure what that meant, nor did he want to think about it for too long. Not yet, anyway.

Right now, he wanted to let this play out, to experience every single second he had with this man.

Needing more, Jack reached for the buckle on the cowboy's belt, unhooked it. He fumbled with the button and zipper but didn't pause until he had the steely length of his cock in his hands.

"Heaven help me," he whispered.

"What was that?" the cowboy asked.

"Nothing." He had to stop talking to himself. At least for now.

But holy Christ. He'd never felt anything like the flash fire that consumed him. The smooth warmth of his shaft gliding against his palm. It was foreign, but it felt perfect. Better than.

"Fuck." The cowboy drove his cock into Jack's fist. He pulled back, stared down at Jack. "You sure about this, city boy? If not, you need to tell me now."

"More than sure," Jack confirmed, his breath rasping in his chest, the need overwhelming him.

"I should be stronger than this," the cowboy mumbled, his eyes darkening. "But I want you too fucking much."

Those words were the match that lit the kindling into an inferno. Clothes seemed to melt off, boots and shoes hit the floor, shirts were tossed away, jeans peeled down. And finally … *finally*, they were skin to skin.

Lord have mercy, it felt so fucking good. Jack hadn't felt anything like it in all his life. Every cell in his body came alive. The warmth, the power in the muscles flexing beneath the cowboy's skin. The way his tongue plunged into Jack's mouth, exploring without giving a quarter. Energy pulsed in the air as the kiss grew volatile. Hands roamed, teeth nipped. Jack felt alive for the first time in his life and he wanted this man.

"Fuck me," Jack growled, ignoring the plea that accompanied the words. "I need you to fuck me."

The cowboy pulled back again, stared down once more.

"Now," Jack demanded.

The next thing he knew, Jack was on his stomach, facedown on the bed, the cowboy over him, his full weight pushing him into the mattress. Yes. This was what he needed. The strength, the energy, it sent him higher, his cock throbbing incessantly.

Jack reached back, grabbed the cowboy's thigh, held on tightly, urging him not to wait. He needed to feel him. He could taste his own desperation, the overwhelming need.

The sound of foil had Jack pausing. He hadn't thought about the logistics. "Protection," he mumbled. It shouldn't have been an afterthought, but it was.

"I've got us both covered," the cowboy whispered, easing over him once more. "Don't panic on me, city boy. I won't hurt you."

"Lube."

"I've got you taken care of," he mumbled, kissing Jack's neck as his thick shaft slid between Jack's ass cheeks.

It disappeared a moment later, and a finger pressed against his asshole. Jack moaned softly when the cowboy pushed it inside him.

"Hurt?"

"No." Not a lie, either.

"You wanna feel my cock?"

"Yes." He moaned when another finger was added. "Fuck yes."

The cowboy stretched Jack's ass, fingering him until he was moaning and writhing, damn near begging for more. There was pain, but the pleasure warred, making his cock ache, his balls tightening as he raced toward a climax he wasn't expecting.

When the cowboy's fingers slipped out, Jack pulled himself back from the edge. The near-release receded, allowing him to breathe. And when the cowboy's cock replaced his fingers, Jack tensed.

"Relax for me, city boy," he crooned against Jack's ear, his breath warm. "Feel me."

The cowboy's lips trailed over his neck and Jack found himself moaning, enjoying the rasp of his stubble against his skin. It took effort, but Jack managed to relax, to focus on the way the cowboy moved over him, touched him. Didn't dull the pain at all, but he welcomed it. Hell, he needed it.

"Ah, yeah. Just like that." The cowboy nipped his ear. "Take all of me."

Jack's head was spinning, but it wasn't from the lingering effects of the alcohol. It was from the intensity, and yes, probably a little from the pain. But he didn't want it to stop. Never wanted it to stop.

"Fuck, you're tight. So fucking tight." The cowboy growled low and deep, the rumble vibrating against Jack's back.

Jack's body went cold, then hot as the pain morphed into pleasure. Heat consumed him, made his bones go liquid. The rasp of the cowboy's leg hair against his thighs, the warmth of those hands as they held Jack's hips. Sure, he'd fantasized a few times in his life, but never had he expected this.

Within minutes, Jack was bucking against him, once again begging for more.

The cowboy linked their fingers together, pinning Jack's hands to the mattress, and it felt so good. Letting himself go, giving in. For whatever reason, he trusted this man. He'd never been the sort to trust easily, but he knew the cowboy wouldn't hurt him. The man had taken care of him all night. Water, aspirin. Condom.

Jack grunted and groaned as the cowboy pounded him from behind, driving in deep, retreating, slamming in again. It was heaven. Pure fucking bliss that ratcheted higher and higher until he was on the verge of coming, his cock untouched.

"Damn," the cowboy breathed. "So fucking good. City boy … holy fuck."

When the sexy cowboy slammed into Jack once more, the world tilted on its axis, sensations flooding his system. He was so close. Too close. "Oh, shit… I'm gonna… Oh, fuck, I'm gonna come," Jack warned. He couldn't hold on any longer. "Oh, fuck, yes. Just … like … that."

"Come for me, city boy," the cowboy urged. "Fucking come for me."

That did it. The harsh command had Jack's cock pulsing, a roar rumbling up from his chest. He came in a maddening rush, sparks igniting behind his eyelids, sensations shooting through every nerve ending until he was crying out, the release more powerful than anything he'd ever felt before. Several more hard punches of his hips and the cowboy followed him right over the edge.

They lay in a heap on the bed, Jack crushed into the mattress, praying the cowboy didn't move. He wasn't ready for this to be over, although he knew it was. He could sense it. The cowboy would be out the door and there was nothing he could do about it.

While he didn't regret a single second of what had just happened, he did regret that he hadn't even bothered to get the guy's name.

Six

Later that same morning

REX TOOK A STEP BACK TO STARE at the pile of wood he'd heaped in the corner. Another wall down, who knew how many more to go. If he followed his plans, he would be finished with demolition and move on to reconstruction in the very near future.

Optimism had him thinking tomorrow. Realism had him accepting he'd need a few more days. Maybe a week.

He had spent the past hour clearing out the last of the debris from all the main-floor rooms, choosing to focus there for now. Rather than get ahead of himself and start now, Rex had opted to focus on the last few walls that needed to be cleared out, trying to psych himself up for the visit from his potential investors.

He had potential investors. Some excited ones, if the eight o'clock wakeup call from Kylie was anything to go by.

Her cheerful voice had been a surprise, her request even more so, but Rex had agreed to open the house to the masses. Evidently Travis had gotten his wife riled up about the potential project, and Rex hadn't been able to turn down her request to see the house in its current state. Even though he would've preferred to catch a few more hours' sleep.

It gave him something to do, anyway. Something other than think about the city boy and the heat of his body as Rex had fucked him ruthlessly in the wee hours of the morning. For some damn reason, he couldn't stop thinking about those few stolen minutes they'd spent together.

However, he knew it wouldn't do to get lost in the memories. Last night's encounter would soon fade from his mind, slip away like smoke. They always did.

"Duke, the good news is, we're underway."

The dog didn't even acknowledge Rex, but he had expected no less.

Deciding he needed a breather, Rex picked up the travel mug he'd filled with coffee. It was the second for the day and he suspected there would be a lot more in his future. He was so damn tired. Although he'd been facedown in his own bed by four, it had taken a little while to fall asleep. Not only because his mind was plagued by the city boy but also because that tended to happen when he had one of his nightmares.

Those were less frequent these days, but from time to time, they would creep up on him, terrorize him in the night. Rex thought he'd be past it at this point in his life, but that wasn't the case. And in instances when he felt vulnerable, they became even more frequent.

Last night, he'd been vulnerable, no doubt about it. Rex did not sleep with men. As in the actual act of sleep. Fucking, sure. That wasn't the issue. But falling asleep with a man in the same bed, or hell, even in the same room… no, that didn't happen.

"Shake it off," he said, willing himself to focus on something else.

It took everything in him to stay focused on the task at hand and not drift back to memories of last night. Since the minute he'd walked out of that hotel room, Rex had secretly wished he'd gotten the city boy's name and number. But he wasn't one for regrets, so he forged ahead, focusing on what was important. And right now, getting this place back to its former glory was the only thing he had time for anyway.

The sound of footsteps on the front porch had Rex turning toward the door. A second later, there was a knock, followed by Duke's reluctant bark.

Rex glanced at his watch, realized his visitors were right on time.

"Well, hell." He set the coffee mug down and headed toward the door, wiping the dust from his shirt as he did. He took a deep breath, adjusted his ball cap, then turned the knob and greeted…

Bristol.

"Hey," he said cheerfully, peering around her to see she was the only one there.

"Expectin' company?" she asked, her pretty face aglow.

"I … uh … actually…"

Bristol chuckled. "Don't worry. I heard they're on the way. Thought I'd sneak over first, make sure you were ready for this."

Rex stepped back out of the way, allowed her to come inside. "I take it you heard?"

"I think everyone's heard," she told him, her gaze scanning the room. "The Walkers are descending, and by the end of today, I suspect you'll be one step closer to getting this dream of yours realized."

That was what he was hoping for.

She pivoted around to face him, her light blue eyes glittering. "But that's not why I'm here."

Of course it wasn't. "Want some coffee?"

Bristol giggled. "No, thank you. However, I would like to hear more about the city boy you were seen leavin' the bar with last night."

Rex rolled his eyes, headed for the kitchen to grab his mug. "Nothin' to tell."

"Liar."

He wasn't sure how she did it, but Bristol had always been able to see right through him. Ever since they were kids.

When he realized she was waiting for him to say something, Rex huffed. "Seriously, B. Nothin' to tell. He was drunk. I drove him back to his hotel. Caught an Uber back to town."

Bristol's fists perched on her slim hips. "Who do you take me for, Sharpe? I think you're leavin' out a few hours. Rumor has it, your truck was parked at Moonshiners well after closing."

How people knew this was beyond him. Did they stare out their windows and watch? Or were there cameras planted that he didn't know about?

A knock sounded on the front door, saving him from having to explain himself. He plastered on a grin, motioned toward the door. "Saved by the bell."

Bristol huffed but followed him to the foyer, stood back while he welcomed the distraction.

"Hope you're up for entertainin'," Zane said when Rex opened the door. "Pretty sure half the town's here for this."

Rex peered around his cousin, saw a handful of people climbing out of vehicles, a few wandering around the front, staring up at the house. He recognized Kylie, Gage, and Travis immediately. Braydon and Jessie were getting out of their truck, talking to V, just as Brendon and Cheyenne were pulling in the driveway. Curtis and Lorrie were standing with Owen and Deborah, admiring the porch that was a hazard in and of itself. Rose and Linda—two more of his aunts—were peering down at what used to be an old flower garden, while a few of his cousins— Spencer, Reilly, Ainsleigh, and Elliott—stood back and chatted amongst themselves. Sawyer and Kennedy were waiting for Jared and Hope to approach, while Kaden and Keegan pulled their truck in at an angle, blocking the way for anyone else.

Yep, it was a full house.

"Watch your step," Gage shouted, reaching for Kylie when her foot landed on a board that instantly snapped beneath it.

Travis reached for her other arm, keeping her from falling into the hole.

"Thanks," she said breathlessly. "I wasn't expecting that."

"Yeah," Rex stated, stepping out onto the porch. "Sorry about that. It all needs to be replaced," he added as Travis and Gage helped her toward the open front door.

Replacing the boards on the wraparound porch was on his list of things to do to the exterior. Right along with replacing the warped and faded siding, the crooked, if not missing, shutters, as well as the roof. He figured after he had the potholes filled on the circular drive and he added some additional parking, he'd have no choice but to put in new sod, new flower beds, maybe even plant a couple of trees.

Plenty to do, that was for sure.

As they moved inside, Rex waited to help Curtis steer Lorrie around the worst of the rotted section. He stayed back, guided the rest of his family toward the door.

"The side entrance isn't as bad," he told them, earning a smile from his aunts.

"We know what we're in for," Lorrie told him. "But you think that'll keep us away?"

No, he didn't think it would.

Rex followed them inside but left the door open in case there were any additional stragglers.

"Wow," Kylie exhaled on a sigh, her bright eyes darting to him when he stepped into the foyer. "This is ... *exactly* how I thought it would be."

"Old and dilapidated?" Rex teased, moving around the group.

She chuckled. "No. Glamorous." She looked up at the high ceilings, over to the staircase. "I've spent years wondering what the inside of this place looked like. Since it's been vacant for so long, I honestly considered breaking in just to get a peek at it."

Travis and Gage both frowned over at her.

"But I didn't," she said quickly. "And I wouldn't. But I was definitely tempted." Her eyes continued to scan the space. "God, Rex. It's breathtaking."

Rex scanned the area, tried to see it from her perspective. It had likely been rather spectacular back in its day, back before Billy Don had gotten his hands on it. From the rare pictures he had from his grandfather's younger years, there were some aspects Rex was hoping to ensure remained.

"Oh, it's majestic," Kylie said, stepping into the parlor as Travis and Gage flanked her on both sides.

"A few other adjectives came to my mind," Zane stated with a grin.

"Mine, too," Rex agreed.

He watched as Kylie stared at the empty space, mouth agape, eyes wide, as though she couldn't quite believe what she was seeing.

Honestly, it wasn't much to look at anymore. Now that the renovations were underway, there was a lot that had to be done before they even started on the finish work that would make this place shine. With the old knob-and-tube electrical running throughout, Rex had to focus on getting that up to code first. Never mind the rusted-out plumbing.

"God, Rex"—Kylie's voice was barely a whisper—"this is going to be amazing when you're finished."

He figured she was one of the only people who could see it the way he did. The way it would look once he was finished. From the open foyer with the winding staircase to the second-floor landing that overlooked the wide-open space. He could already picture the rustic chandelier dangling overhead, the gleaming hardwood that would cover every inch of floor. Rex hadn't done anything with the fireplaces scattered throughout the house, mostly because there was no central heat and air just yet, but he even envisioned them in the design.

"Thinking about investing?" Keegan asked Bristol as she walked in and joined them.

"Oh, no," she said quickly. "Far too rich for my blood, but I've always loved this place. Wanted to help Rex show it off."

Keegan shot a smile at Rex. Ever since he'd had the Dumpster first delivered a year ago, he'd had plenty of Coyote Ridge residents asking for a tour. Considering the state, he'd refused, but he knew one day they'd manage to slip inside. At that point, he figured he wouldn't care. In fact, he'd be proud to show it off when it was finished.

"It does have potential," Kaden noted.

"You see potential?" Zane chuckled. "I see work."

"Sure," Kylie added, "it's a lot of work, but it'll definitely be a place people will want to get away to. Whether they're from out of town or not."

Rex hoped that was the case.

"Feel free to look around," he told everyone as they moved about the downstairs. "Just watch your step." Rex turned back to Kylie. "So, upstairs or downstairs first?"

She shrugged, continued to peer around. "I want to see it all, then I want to see it again, so it doesn't matter to me."

"Lead the way, boss man." Gage motioned toward Rex.

"I'm thinkin' we shoulda brought hard hats," Zane stated as the smaller group formed a line going up the stairs.

That actually wasn't a bad idea, Rex thought. Maybe he'd get some, have them on hand for future visitors.

"I heard there were two staircases here," Kylie stated when they'd joined Rex on the second floor.

"There are," Bristol declared, her smile wide as she shot a glance at Rex. "The house was originally built back in the 1800s. Had some upgrades through the years, but the staircases are intact. The other one's down that hallway. Leads down to the kitchen."

"Upgrades?" Zane squinted, ever the smartass. "To what? The air?"

"Funny guy," Bristol admonished. "It doesn't look like it now, but I promise, Rex is gonna have this place shining when he's finished."

Sometimes Rex thought Bristol had more faith in him than he had in himself.

"How many square feet is it?" Travis asked when he approached the second floor.

"The original house is eighty-eight hundred. With the attic conversion, just under ten thousand," Rex answered.

"Wow. That makes this a mansion. In technical terms, of course." Kylie turned to peer around the open room. "How many bedrooms?"

"Not as many as you'd think," Rex admitted. "Originally there were four, all with their own sitting room. Master downstairs, three on this floor. Three bathrooms overall. They used a lot of the space for recreational rooms."

"How many bedrooms do you plan to put in?" Kylie turned to face him.

"I figured seven was a good number," he told her, ignoring all the eyes currently pinned on him. "Each with its own bathroom, then a couple of extras just because."

"Why seven?" Gage inquired.

To be honest, Rex wasn't sure. Seemed like a fair number.

"You've got plenty of room," Kylie noted. "If it were me, I'd aim for eight. Maybe nine."

"She's thinkin' of the income potential," Travis added.

Kylie smirked up at him. "True. But there's plenty of room. And that allows plenty of space for community areas. A game room, sitting area, maybe even a library."

"A library?" Bristol clapped her hands. "That would be amazing."

"That staircase?" Kaden motioned toward the back of the house. "Where's it lead?"

Rex motioned above him. "The apartment for the manager."

"That's complete?" Kylie inquired.

"It is."

"This is quite the undertaking," Kaden mumbled as he moved toward the back windows. "But I'd say it'll be worth it for that view."

The group shifted that way, everyone peering out the windows. Rex waited, giving them time to take it all in. He found himself hoping they'd be willing to help out. He could see the excitement on Kylie's face, heard the way Bristol sighed, her eyes meeting his from time to time. They'd been friends since they were kids and she knew all about his dream. To have her here silently cheering him on meant everything.

Half an hour later, after they'd walked through every room, toured the third floor, everyone ended up back on the main level.

"So, what did you think?" Kylie asked Travis and Gage.

"I think it's gonna take some work," Travis admitted, his tone even, but there was definitely a hint of interest in it.

"I agree," she said wistfully, as though that was the best part.

"Personally," Bristol noted, smiling brightly, "I think it's amazing."

Rex laughed. "I'm not sure I'd go that far. Not yet."

"But it is," his cousin Ainsleigh countered.

"Exactly," Aunt Lorrie chimed in.

"The potential is definitely there," Aunt Rose agreed.

His cousin Reilly put her hand on his arm. "I can practically see it, Rex. This grand mansion gracing Main Street, drawing in tourists from all over, people booking rooms simply to have a chance to stay here, to see what it's all about. It's what you've wanted your entire life, Rex. I'm glad to be a part of it."

Just hearing their praise made Rex believe it possible.

"I agree one hundred percent," Kylie said as she turned to face him. "You've got an amazing opportunity here. I'd love to be part of it, too." Her eyes softened. "That is, if you'll let me."

Rex's heart was in his throat. He'd wanted this for so damn long. And honestly, he hadn't expected to have so many people rooting him on.

"Come on, Sharpe," Zane teased. "Don't leave the girl hangin'."

Rex laughed, unable to stop smiling as he stared down at Kylie. "I'd like that."

Kylie clapped her hands and so did Bristol, as though the place would be open for business tomorrow.

Women.

"What do y'all say we head over to the diner, wrangle us up a couple of tables, and try to bang out some plans?" Travis offered, his gaze locked on Rex.

With a nod, Rex decided this was it. They were moving forward.

Finally.

SITTING IN THE SMALL DINER, JACK TRIED to pretend he fit in with all the cowboys chowing down on eggs and grits while tossing back coffee, fueling up for the rest of their day. Despite the fact he was getting quite a few sidelong glances, Jack liked the place with its rustic decor and smiling waitresses. The moment he'd seen the Join us for Sunday brunch sign in front of Mama's Diner, he'd laughed. Then he'd decided what the hell.

As for how he'd ended up back in Coyote Ridge, he wasn't sure.

Okay, that wasn't necessarily true.

After checking out of his hotel, Jack hadn't known exactly where to go. So, he had shoved his crap in his car, hit the rural highway, and found himself right back where he'd been last night. Only instead of going to a bar to drown his sorrows in whiskey, he'd stopped in for brunch at the first place he'd come to.

Was it a risk coming back here? Probably.

Did he care? Not even a little.

After last night, Jack felt like an entirely different man. And he wasn't talking about the lingering euphoria from the amazing orgasm. Or the slight hangover, either.

Nope. Jack had a new lease on life. From the moment his eyes opened and he felt the slight discomfort from the night before, he hadn't been able to wipe the smile off his face. Last night had been...

Eye-opening.

And since he hadn't felt this damn good in years, he figured what the hell. Might as well make the most of it.

So, here he was, sipping coffee and skimming through his phone, ignoring the dozen or so messages he'd received from Tina last night. He remembered turning off his phone at some point. Good thing, too. The woman was in a state, each message longer and more tense than the previous one. Apparently, she wanted to apologize.

"A little late for that," he whispered to himself, glancing around to ensure no one heard him talking to himself.

"Here you go, handsome," the waitress purred as she set a plate on the table. "Sunny side up with a side of whole wheat toast."

"Thank you," he said kindly, shifting his phone to the other side.

"Need anything else?"

Jack shook his head, grabbed his fork. Before he could dig in, the bells over the door chimed and people were suddenly piling into the restaurant. The conversation seemed to precede the group and he found himself staring. There were a few faces he recognized from the bar last night, a whole bunch he didn't, but it wasn't until the last cowboy stepped inside that Jack's heart skipped a beat or two.

Holy shit.

His cowboy was there.

No, wait. He didn't belong to Jack.

Familiar brown eyes lifted, locked right onto Jack's face, causing his breath to halt in his lungs momentarily. There was a glitter in the mocha brown for a brief second, but then it was gone and so was the cowboy.

Jack managed to pick up his fork, even shoveled a few bites into his mouth. He kept his eyes pinned to the table while his mind spun with all the memories of the night before.

Had it been a mistake coming back here? Was he going to make a fool of himself?

"Probably," he muttered to himself.

Did he care?

Well, it wasn't like he could make more of a mess of his life at this point.

Right?

Forty-five minutes later, Jack was walking down the sidewalk through what appeared to be the center of town. Main Street—aptly named since it was, indeed, the main street through town—was dotted with various businesses on one side, what appeared to be a city park and a few large, older homes spaced quite a distance apart on the other side. On the business side, there were cars and trucks tucked into the angled spots all along the street. It was the epitome of those made-for-TV romance movies that his exes had liked. Jack had never been a big fan.

While he much preferred the wide city streets with the chain restaurants and large retailers, Jack couldn't deny there was a charm to this town. He'd passed a bookstore, heard the jingle of a bell when someone walked into the hardware store, and smelled the delicious aroma drifting out from the bakery. Farther down, he could see a toy store tucked between a real estate office and the *Coyote Ridge Gazette* office.

Quaint. That was what it was.

And while the street wasn't bustling with tourists and noise, there were quite a few people wandering about, going in and out of the small shops, stopping to chat, despite the frigid temperatures.

Since he had no plans for the foreseeable future—being that his entire world had been upended last night, in more ways than one—Jack did a little window shopping in an attempt to pass the time. Not really his thing, but seeing as he had nothing better to do, he figured why the hell not.

After stopping in the bookstore and perusing the comic book section, he realized he was being silly. It wasn't like the cowboy from last night was going to come searching for him. His fantasy that it might happen had already gone up in smoke about ten minutes into his trek.

And since the minutes were ticking by, Jack figured it would make more sense if he tried to find a place to stay for a few days. Perhaps some of the hotels he'd passed on the way into town would have some vacancies now.

"Come back to see us, now," the pretty young woman at the counter said cheerfully as he made his way to the door.

"Thanks." He nodded, then stepped outside into the cold.

As he turned up his collar and started toward his car, Jack came up short when someone cleared their throat. He lifted his eyes in time to see his cowboy coming toward him.

"Not mine," he muttered under his breath.

"Well, if it ain't the city boy," the sexy man said, his deep voice sliding over Jack's skin. "If I didn't know better, I'd think you were stalkin' me."

Flustered, Jack shook his head. "No. Not at all."

The cowboy grinned.

"I … uh … just…" He had nothing.

"Hey, wait up!" a woman hollered, her boot-clad feet carrying her quickly in their direction. When she reached the cowboy's side, she smiled up at him, then tucked her arm into his.

"What's up?" the cowboy asked her.

Feeling awkward and, yes, slightly like a stalker, Jack stood tall, cleared his throat. "Excuse me." He squeezed past the couple, his legs moving as though his ass was on fire.

"Who was that?" the woman asked, her cheerful voice drifting on the cold air.

"Tourist," the cowboy said, making Jack cringe.

"Stupid, stupid, stupid," Jack muttered, tucking his hands into his pockets as he raced to his car.

Definitely time to find a place to stay for the night. Maybe for the next month. Then, perhaps if he gave himself enough time, he'd forget all about the sexy cowboy from last night.

"And your cheating ex-fiancée," he reminded himself.

Yes. Her, too.

After all, she was the reason he was here in the first place.

Seven

BY THE TIME EVENING ROLLED AROUND, REX couldn't sleep. He should've been exhausted after last night, but sometime during the day he'd gotten his second wind, driven mostly by the enthusiasm from his family that morning.

Instead of being tucked into his bed, he traipsed through the big, drafty house, Duke on his heels. He wasn't sure whether the adrenaline fueling him was due to excitement over the plans and the fact that he was moving forward or if it was because he'd seen the city boy lurking earlier in the day.

"What do you think, Duke?" he asked his snoozing dog. "Maybe a little of both?"

Duke didn't answer. No surprise there.

As he moved through what used to be the kitchen, Rex stared at the old stove, wondering why he hadn't tossed it out yet. He'd managed to rip out everything in the house except for that damn stove and the farmhouse sink that had definitely seen better days. It wasn't like the kitchen was functional in any way. There were no countertops, no cabinets save for the one still holding up the sink. The old linoleum floor had been ripped out, the original hardwood dusty and rotted in many places. The bright yellow wallpaper had come down first, followed by everything else. But for some stupid reason, he couldn't part with that damn stove. Perhaps that was because he could remember his mama cooking at it, making him and Rafe dinner every night, laughing with them as she moved around the small space.

His gaze drifted to the window. "Damn it, Rafe," he muttered. "It's time to come home."

Knowing his wishful thoughts wouldn't help, Rex turned his attention back to the kitchen, imagining what the space would look like when it was finished. The gleaming appliances, shiny countertops, and weathered-white cabinets would make the area homey. At least that was his plan. After all, a bed-and-breakfast did insinuate that a meal would be served during a stay.

Not that Rex was much of a cook. He could hold his own, sure. Toast, cereal, the occasional omelet. It wasn't exactly the highlight of his day, which meant he would have to come up with a plan for when he had guests. Right now, it didn't matter. The kitchen was gutted. Luckily, he had the means to feed himself in the third-floor apartment. The small kitchen was more than enough for him. And when he wasn't up for making a meal for one, he could always hit up the diner.

Perhaps that was where he should go now. Over to the diner, grab a piece of pie and some coffee, chat with some of the night owls. They rarely closed up early, not even on Sunday.

Or if he had the energy to do that, he could simply start working. He had shit to do, and the more he stalled, the worse it would be. It was driving him crazy to have things in such disarray here.

That was one of the reasons it had taken him so long to get this far. It wasn't that he was a slow worker. He wasn't. However, Rex was a stickler for organization, and when things were chaotic, his brain shut down, so he had taken his time clearing things out, coming up with designs for each room as he went. Never did he start something he couldn't finish, and to be honest, his methods had worked well for him. After all, the apartment had come along nicely, and from what he could tell, his new investors had been impressed with the work he'd done there.

Even his best friend was now on his side.

Not that Bristol hadn't been there for him from the beginning. She had. In every way. Bristol supported his dream, even if she'd thought he was crazy back in the beginning. And while she was supportive, always rooting him on, Bristol liked to give him shit simply because she could.

When his mama had first told him the property would belong to him when he turned eighteen, Rex hadn't thought much of it. Why would he? A thirteen-year-old kid had no use for an old house and a bunch of dry grass. Then, once the idea of building a resort rooted, he'd thought of little else. As he got older, Rex realized his dream had a few flaws. Such as there wasn't much to draw people to this backwoods town in the first place.

Sure, there was the lake ripe with fishing tournaments, but that was all it was good for. It drew a few folks in, most of them shacking up in the big hotels that now surrounded it, but that didn't seem like a vacation to Rex.

Then there was Alluring Indulgence Resort, not too far down the road. They had a nice spread, but it catered to a specific type. Since they were by invitation only, they didn't draw too many tourists.

But there weren't any other bed-and-breakfasts in the area. Not that he knew of, anyway, and Rex knew almost everything there was to know about Coyote Ridge and the surrounding small towns.

In that regard, there was hope for this place yet, even if it wasn't as fancy as the dude ranch a half hour away. But he still needed to come up with something that would draw people to him. Because, aside from heat and temperamental weather patterns, there wasn't much else.

Rex still remembered the conversation he'd had with Bristol when he decided to really set his plan in motion a year and a half ago.

"A bed-and-breakfast, Rex?" Bristol asked, confusion and more than a little amusement injected in her tone. "You're sure this is what you wanna do with the house?"

"Yeah. Why?"

"Well…" Her gaze dropped. "I just figured since you'd waited this long…"

"That I'd forgotten about it?"

Her eyes lifted and there was a sadness there. "Actually, yes."

"I didn't forget," he assured her.

She seemed to consider her words. "Well, I can understand why you want to do it, but I'm not sure I understand how you'll do it."

"Easy. I'm gonna tear it down and build it back up again."

Bristol laughed. *"That's not what I mean. Physically, I get it. You're capable of demolishing it and rebuilding. But…"*

"But what?"

"But how do you plan to run it?"

"It's not like it's rocket science," he said, trying to figure out where she was going with this.

"Maybe not."

"Why do you say it like that, Bristol?"

"Well, for one, you're not really the hospitality type. You might be good with power tools and you might've gotten the decorator's touch that seems to be common with boys who like boys, but you didn't get the gene that allows you to interact well with others."

Okay, fine. Maybe she had a point there.

"To be honest, Rex, I just don't see you serving breakfast to guests. Nor do I see you on your hands and knees scrubbing toilets."

No, it wouldn't all be glitz and glamor, but it was the dream he'd had since he was a kid and he was going to see it through. And that was his end goal. To make a place for him and Rafe, a place where they belonged.

"Most importantly, it means…" Bristol sighed, all amusement disappearing. *"Come on, Rex. You know people around these parts… They're not gonna make it easy for you. They've formed their opinions and they'll fight you tooth and nail."*

She was right. He couldn't deny it. Which was one of the reasons he didn't mind that fourteen years had slipped by since the scandal that had rocked this little town. People remembered what had happened, but they were finally getting past it. Despite the occasional rowdy redneck who took pleasure in making Rex's life hell, there were a lot of people who supported him. Some who were even willing to help.

These days, Rex was focused on moving forward, not dwelling on the past. And fine. Maybe he had failed at a few things in life. Namely, taking care of his brother like their mama asked and his college education. But he was trying to make up for it all now.

Of course, there was nothing he could do about a college education. His career had been mapped out at an early age because of his dream, not to mention, by the time Rex had graduated from high school, he was so damn tired of everyone breathing down his neck that he hadn't wanted to spend another minute in a classroom. Apparently, having a four-point-oh GPA was a big deal. Even if you were a redneck kid with a tarnished reputation and only one dream.

Just to appease his uncle, Rex had considered college for a bit, but eventually decided to stick with his original idea. He'd even turned down the baseball scholarship, which had pissed his uncle off in the beginning.

So what if he hadn't gotten a degree? He'd still managed to make good money. Well, *decent* money. But Rex had never been the sort who needed a lot. Plus, he'd learned the skills he needed to learn. That was what mattered.

His thoughts drifted to the city boy. What would he think if he knew the details of Rex's life? Would he have let him fuck him last night? Would it matter that Rex didn't have a degree or that he felt responsible for his brother running away from everyone in his life? What would he think about Rex's dream to build this place up?

"Why do I care, Duke?" he muttered, knowing his dog wouldn't respond. "I didn't even get his name and number."

Rex sighed.

Perhaps if he had, he wouldn't be sitting idly by, contemplating the status of his life.

Oh, well.

You live and learn.

JACK HAD BEEN DRIVING FOR THE PAST hour, wandering aimlessly in big circles, trying to steer clear of the bar he'd gone to last night and the small town that surrounded it. While he was pretending to know what he was doing, Jack had no choice but to admit he didn't have a plan.

While he was hoping to find a secluded place to spend a little alone time—a seemingly good idea when he had stuffed his shit in his car and left Tina with her boy toy last night—Jack had come to the conclusion that he should've planned this out better.

"If you'd done that, last night would've never happened," he said to his steering wheel.

There was something to be said about spontaneity.

And that was the only thing he could think about. Had he not walked in on Tina, not hopped in his car and run far and fast, he wouldn't have ended up in bed with the sexiest man on the planet. Never mind the fact he hadn't gotten the guy's name, or that Jack couldn't stop thinking about him today, even if the cowboy had referred to him as a tourist. He wouldn't regret it. No matter what.

However, since he left Coyote Ridge that morning, he hadn't known what to do. He'd even gone so far as to drive back to his apartment, convinced he could simply kick Tina out, but he had changed his mind at the last minute, driving right on through without stopping. He couldn't handle seeing Tina right now. She'd been blowing up his phone all damn day and he wasn't ready to talk to her. Not yet.

So, he'd had an early dinner, called Shawn to discuss where they'd left off with their current work in progress, then had gone to the mall of all places. For a coat. If that had been all he'd gotten, he would've been fine. However, he'd spent more money than he should have on shit he didn't need, but it had soothed some part of his soul, albeit temporarily. Once that was done, he'd ended up at a Starbucks, drinking coffee and absently downing a blueberry scone he hadn't wanted, while scrolling through social media on his phone, wishing like hell he'd gotten the cowboy's name.

Hadn't helped his mood one bit.

And now he was driving around aimlessly, trying to talk himself out of going to Moonshiners to see if the cowboy might be there, but fearing that was exactly what he was going to do. That bordered too much on the stalker-ish side and Jack refused to be that guy.

It was a few minutes before eleven, and no matter how much coffee he downed, Jack was too damn tired to continue driving. Every hotel he'd stopped at was full. Apparently, there were a couple of conventions going on, one in Round Rock, one in Austin. They were the reason for the lack of rooms at any of the respectable hotels, so there wasn't much Jack could do about it. Rather than risk being carjacked while sleeping in his car, he'd decided to go the nontraditional route. Airbnb was looking good right about now, but until he got a call back from the owner, he was stuck in limbo.

"Fuck this day. Fuck this week. Fuck this year."

Jack took a deep breath, let it out slowly.

"I'm ready to start over."

Hence the need for a place to sleep.

After traveling down the dark, two-lane road for what felt like an eternity, he'd apparently gone from civilization to no-man's land. Obviously, he had drifted a little too far off the beaten path.

Figuring it was time to fuel up, Jack stopped at the first place he came to that still had lights on inside. It appeared to be a gas station, although the rutted parking lot had certainly seen better days.

He got out, went to the pump only to find it didn't work.

"Fucking shit," he grumbled as he stalked toward the small convenience store.

Jack opened the glass door and a long, slow whistle sounded from inside.

"Fancy car ya got there," a raspy male voice laced with a thick twang hollered from somewhere inside. "You lost?"

"Something like that." Jack peered around as he nodded, letting the door close behind him. He couldn't see anyone, so he wasn't sure who he was speaking to, but he let the question come anyway. "This isn't a gas station?"

"Nope." An older man with thinning gray hair and a weathered face appeared from behind one of the counters. "Got some sodas and cold beer, plus all the jerky you could want." He motioned toward the parking lot. "Those ol' pumps are from the last owners. Couldn't afford to tear 'em down, so I left 'em."

Great. A sign would've been nice.

"Ain't got no gas," the older man continued as he glanced at the clock on the wall, "but I got a special runnin' on live bait. You'll hafta make it fast 'cause I'm closin' up here in a few minutes."

Live bait and beer? What more could Jack want?

For fuck's sake.

"I'm good. Thanks. Do you happen to know of anyone who might have a room for rent for the night?" Jack asked, doing his best not to breathe through his nose. The place smelled like dirt and … and he didn't even want to make a guess at what the other smell was.

"A room?" The man appeared confused. "Like a hotel?"

Jack nodded. "Yes. Exactly."

The man scratched his chin. "You stop at Bobby's Motel 'bout a block back?"

No, Jack had *not* stopped because he did not consider Bobby's Motel an appropriate place to spend the night. He'd already had the displeasure of seeing it from the street. The place looked more like a Quonset hut than a motel, and the three vehicles in the parking lot—two of which were lacking any tires—had made him skip right on by.

"Do you know of anything else?" Jack asked.

"You ain't lookin' for that fetish place, are ya?"

Jack frowned. "Uh … no."

The old man nodded. "There's a big, fancy dude ranch about an hour north."

An hour? Yeah, no. No way would he last that long. He shook his head.

"You'd probably have better luck in the next town."

"How far's the next town?" he asked, fearing the old man would tell him he still had miles in front of him. As it was, Jack didn't really know where he was.

He motioned toward the front windows. "'Bout two minutes."

Two minutes? Really?

Jack frowned. "Are there some hotels out that way?"

"A few on the lake, yeah."

"Tried those," Jack admitted with a disappointed sigh. "No vacancies."

"Hmm." The guy scratched his salt-and-pepper beard. "I know there's a small motel about half an hour out. But I heard the owners were shuttin' down for the holidays, so not sure they're open right now. 'Nother little place not too far down, but they only have a coupla rooms in their barn they rent out." He smiled, showing a missing front tooth.

A barn? Yeah. Jack was *not* sleeping in a damn barn.

Shit. He was running out of options and going back to his apartment was not something he was contemplating. Not until Tina left.

The man's eyes widened. "Wait. Heard there's a bed-and-breakfast bein' built, but it's two towns over. About eight minutes, I'd say. Figure it'd be openin' soon. Maybe they've got a room."

A bed-and-breakfast? Probably not quite the solitude Jack was looking for, but it would do in a pinch, sure.

Until Jack could get Tina to move out, he was homeless, so his plan was to find a place to hide out for a little while. A week or two, maybe. Long enough for her to pack her shit and go.

In the meantime, what Jack needed was some time to process what was going on in his life. And to be fair, it wasn't only Tina's infidelity that had him running. He'd spent months trying to figure out which way was up only to end up feeling trapped every single time.

Except last night. You didn't feel trapped then.

Jack shook off the crazy thought and held the old guy's stare. "Could you point me in the right direction?"

The guy crooked his thumb toward the parking lot. "When you head out, take a right. Once you come to the old high school—it's bein' torn down now that they built a new one—you'll turn left. Once you pass the big oak tree, you'll take the fork to the right. Follow that road—it's only wide enough for one car, so keep an eye out—until it dead-ends."

Jack wasn't sure he caught any of that, but he figured it couldn't be too hard. Worst case, he had Google Maps, so surely, he'd find where he was supposed to be.

"Does it have a name?"

"Not that I know of," the old man said. "But it's right in the middle of town. Can't miss it."

Well, Google Maps probably wouldn't help then.

"Thanks." Jack turned toward the door.

"Sure you don't need some bait?" the old man called after him.

"Not much of a fisherman, but thanks." He pushed open the door and headed for his car. "Turn right, then left, then right again," Jack mumbled as he pulled out of the parking lot. "Shit. Or did he say left, then right?"

Roughly two minutes later, when he came upon what appeared to be the remains of an old school building—complete with a few portable buildings outlining it—Jack took a left. He knew it was the correct way to go, considering it was the *only* way. A few yards ahead was a fork in the road. He assumed he was to take a right because a downed tree blocked the road on the left. And sure enough, it put him on a one-lane road that looked just wide enough for his car to ease down. If someone was coming at him, they'd both end up in the ditch. Heaven forbid a deer come strolling out of those trees.

"Welcome to the backwoods, y'all," Jack mumbled under his breath.

It was pitch-black with no lights, other than what beamed off of his car, which was lending a spooky air to his surroundings. From what he could tell, there wasn't a damn thing out here. Nothing more than trees, anyway.

"He was fucking with me, wasn't he?" Jack laughed, but there was no humor in it. "He sent me out to the boondocks, and now he's sitting in his bait/beer store laughing his ass off."

Jack sighed but kept driving, the music from all those scary movies he'd watched sounding in his head.

He continued to drive a little more until...

"Finally." He huffed out a relieved sigh. Jack could see lights in the distance. They were dim, but from what he could tell, there was something up ahead.

Of course, about that time, he came to the end of the road, forcing him to make another decision. Did he go left or right? He was on the verge of panicking, wondering what the hell he was going to do now when he saw a truck coming down the road. When it passed, he decided to follow, hoping like hell he'd end up back in civilization.

A sign appeared and he squinted until it came into focus.

"Welcome to Coyote Ridge." Jack's eyes widened. "What the fuck?"

He'd already been through here once today and he knew there were no hotels. Well, aside from Alluring Indulgence Resort. Which, he'd learned, after a quick perusal on the internet, was *not* what he was looking for.

He drove until he came to the one stoplight on Main Street. He glanced to the left and the right. The businesses were all closed down for the night, and except for the big farmhouse that sat closer to the street than the others, there were no lights on.

That was when he saw the sign in front of the house.

"Coming soon," Jack read aloud. "What? What's coming soon? Would it've been too hard to list that out?"

It wasn't like he had a lot of options at the moment. With a sigh, he turned into the circular driveway.

"Please be the bed-and-breakfast." If it wasn't, it was highly likely he was going to get shot.

To the left of the huge white house with the wraparound porch, he could see the outline of another structure. The sodium lamp between the two gave enough light to make out what appeared to be a huge metal building that he assumed was either a barn or some sort of workshop.

"Great. This very well could be a horror movie in the making," Jack groused as he shut off the engine and opened his door.

A gust of chilly air made him stagger but jolted some of the exhaustion from his fuzzy brain. He snagged the new coat he'd bought and quickly shrugged into it. Shoring up his nerve, Jack headed for the stairs, plastering on his best smile.

Despite the lights, the house looked abandoned and in desperate need of repair. The porch squeaked beneath his shoes and he dodged a rotted piece at the last second, keeping himself from plunging into the ether.

"Well, here goes nothing," Jack whispered as he pulled open the screen, the squeal of the hinges making him cringe. He rapped his knuckles on the wood door, then let the screen shut as he stepped back out of the way.

Tucking his hands into his coat pockets, he sent up a silent prayer that someone was awake. And that they'd have room for him. At this point, Jack was willing to sleep on the floor if he had to.

His cell phone rang, but he didn't bother to look at the damn thing. Tina had called at least a dozen times over the course of the day. He knew it had to be her, and Jack had absolutely no intention of talking until he could get some sleep.

That was, if he could find a place that would allow him to do that.

Eight

THE SOFT RAPPING ON THE FRONT DOOR had Rex glancing over his shoulder. Duke's ears were perked up and his eyes were locked on the spot the sound came from.

"You heard it, too, buddy?"

Rex backed away from the boards he was prying off. He should've been in bed, saving this part of the work for tomorrow, but he'd been restless and eager to get started, so here he was, working well into the night. Rather than move, Rex waited to see if he'd actually heard a knock or if his overtaxed mind was playing tricks on him. He couldn't imagine anyone paying him a visit this late.

Another knock sounded and Rex frowned at the same time Duke let out a raspy bark. It was as though the dog wanted to know who was there, but he wasn't sure he really cared.

Rex placed the hammer down on the table before grabbing the towel and wiping his hands. He maneuvered toward the front door slowly.

"Who is it?" he hollered.

There was no response.

He picked up the shotgun he kept in the corner. Visitors were rare because he wasn't open for business. More so, those who stopped by at… Rex glanced at his watch. It was 11:22 p.m.

Who the fuck was making house calls at this time of night?

Turning the knob, Rex pulled the door open, keeping the shotgun out of sight but accessible.

"Yeah?" he prompted, his eyes scanning the sexy city boy standing on his porch. "Well, I'll be damned. Twice in one day."

Rex was tempted to pinch himself because this seemed far too much like some of his fantasies as of late.

No, wait. Not *his*. The city boy did *not* belong to him.

"Is … uh…" The city boy glanced both ways down the porch, then back to Rex. "Oh, God. Please tell me this is a B and B and I don't look like a crazed stalker?" The guy swallowed hard. He looked nervous. Definitely not the same as he'd been writhing and moaning beneath Rex in the wee hours of the morning.

Leaving the shotgun safely hidden, Rex leaned his shoulder against the doorjamb and studied the city boy through the screen. Duke came to sit by his feet. He seemed far less interested in their visitor than Rex was.

"Not yet," he admitted.

The city boy frowned, his eyes rounding as though he couldn't believe Rex had said that. His gaze dropped down to Duke briefly, then back up to Rex's face. "Not yet?"

Rex waved his hand behind him. "Mostly gutted. Probably won't be open for business for six months or so." If he was lucky.

The good-looking city boy sighed heavily. "I knew that old man was fucking with me."

"Huh?"

"Guy at the bait/beer shop a couple of towns over sent me this way. Said there might be a room."

Looked like good ol' Andy Dobbs was still trying to be helpful.

"Funny," Rex said with a smirk. "I recall seein' you doin' a little shoppin' this mornin'. Figured you'd know we don't have any vacancies."

"I was…" The man sighed. "Fine. I was bored. I was trying to pass the time. It had nothing to do with you. But this… It really is a coincidence."

Rex stared at him, trying to determine whether or not he wanted the city boy to know he believed him.

"I swear it."

Yeah. Rex knew it to be the truth. No way would the city boy have known where Rex lived, much less that he was in the process of remodeling for the bed-and-breakfast.

"Well, you're forgiven for stalkin' me, but that doesn't change anything. Still not open for business."

He peered over Rex's shoulder into the house. "Perhaps I could speak with the owners."

"You've got him."

The city boy stared, uncertainty gleaming in his eyes. "I'm … uh… My name's Jack Cunningham."

"Jack, huh?" Rex smirked. "Couldn't have said that last night?"

Jack's eyes slid over him and he frowned when it was evident Rex wasn't going to introduce himself. "And you are?"

"Busy." It was true.

"Fine." Jack sighed. "Have it your way. Do you happen to know where I can get a room for a few hours? I just need to sleep for a bit."

"Probably have better luck closer to Austin. Or there's a motel couple of towns over," Rex suggested, standing tall once more as he reached for the door. While he wanted to let the city boy in, he knew better.

"Bobby's Motel?" Jack scoffed. "Yeah, I'd rather take my chances in my car."

Rex grinned, then took a step back and started to close the door. "Good luck with that."

"No." Jack moved forward. "Please. Wait."

Heat slammed into Rex at the all-too-familiar words. Jack had said the same last night when Rex had tried to leave the hotel.

"I know this is weird, but I swear I'm not stalking you. I really do need a place for a few hours."

"Last I recall, you had a pretty comfortable bed to sleep in."

The groove in Jack's forehead deepened. "Only had the room for one night. They're all booked up." He sighed. "Hell, everyone's booked up. Sounds like they've got some huge convention in Round Rock," Jack explained. "I figured it was overflow from Austin, but I was not-so-kindly corrected at the last chain hotel I stopped at."

He had no idea why he did, but Rex stood motionless, his hand on the door, ready to close it. Something in Jack's tone had Rex pausing. Or maybe it was something about him overall. Last night had been memorable to say the least. And while he hadn't considered having a repeat, there was no denying he was damn tempted. Worst case, maybe if he gave himself a chance, Rex could look enough to be able to make him the star of tonight's five-fingered fantasy.

Rex purposefully gave him another once-over, inspecting him from head to toe. Beneath all those fancy clothes, Rex knew firsthand the guy was a solid dime. Probably would've been off the Richter scale if he was gay and not merely curious.

Yep. Unfortunately, Rex pegged the guy to be straight with enough curiosity to scratch an itch but not go any further than that, which was just his fucking luck. Stranger showed up on his doorstep looking for a place to crash and there was no chance Rex would get to blow off a little steam.

"I just need a room for the night," Jack repeated.

"So you said." Rex considered him for a moment. As much as he wanted to let him in, Rex knew this would be a mistake. Last night was one thing. Two nights in a row…

Jack didn't move, his eyes locked on Rex's face as though willing him to give in.

For fuck's sake.

"One night?" Rex narrowed his eyes.

Rex should've shut the door and gone about his business. For some stupid reason, he felt the strange urge to help Jack. He'd been battling those feelings lately, and it seemed they were growing stronger every day. He blamed it on the solitude. Way too many hours alone in this house. Definitely wasn't some connection they'd made last night when they'd been naked and Rex had been lodged balls deep in the guy's tight fucking ass.

Fucking hell.

"Well, technically, I need it for longer," Jack said, "but if that's all you've got, I'll gladly be out of your hair when the sun comes up."

He considered it for a moment. Technically, he had a spare room on the third floor.

However, he wasn't ready to stop the fun just yet. "What's in it for me?"

Jack's eyes widened slightly, and his gaze scanned Rex from head to toe, then back again. He couldn't help it, Rex peered down at himself, unable to remember what he was wearing. The black T-shirt wasn't in the same class as the city boy's. He'd picked it up down at Walmart. His Wranglers had seen better days, but they were decent, the work boots worn but intact. The ball cap he had on—backwards, mind you—ensured his hair wasn't an issue. Rex looked like he'd put in a hard day's work, no doubt.

"I can pay," Jack said on a rush of air.

"That's a given." Rex smirked, wondering whether the city boy would be interested in round two.

Realizing he was seconds away from putting a move on him, Rex shook off the lust that was quickly becoming his single-minded focus.

The guy was in luck. Rex was feeling rather … hospitable. He would have to remember to tell Bristol about this. About the hospitable part. Not about Jack.

"Come in," Rex grumbled, turning away from the door as he grabbed the shotgun and carried it with him. "I've got a room you can have for the night."

The screen door squeaked when Jack pulled it open. Rex added oil to his mental list of things to get at the hardware store in the morning.

"Hey, boy," Jack said softly. "I promise, I'm not here to cause any harm."

Rex glanced over his shoulder to see Jack rubbing Duke's furry head, his dog's tail wagging excitedly. Rex rolled his eyes because Duke suddenly seemed over the moon to have a stranger in the house.

"So, how much do I owe you?" Jack asked when he straightened. His eyes darted from Rex's face to the gun.

He shrugged and turned away once more. "We'll discuss it in the mornin'."

"Okay."

Without looking back at the man, Rex pointed toward the stairs. "Third-floor apartment."

"Is that where you're sleeping?"

Turning around slowly, Rex's gaze zeroed in on the sexy man. Perhaps he *was* in the mood for round two? Or maybe this really was a dream.

"I… *Damn*. That did not come out right," Jack said, flustered. "I just didn't want to be an inconvenience."

Rex tossed the towel onto the table. "Two bedrooms. You'll have your own. Mine's the one with the unmade bed."

The frown that grooved Jack's forehead was actually kind of sexy. Okay, fine. Every damn thing about this dark-haired city boy was sexy. Especially the way he begged and pleaded for Rex to fuck him harder.

Mind outta the gutter, Sharpe.

"Do you mind if I get my suitcase?" Jack asked, his tone slightly hesitant.

Rex cut a quick look at him as he picked up the hammer. "Whatever you need to do, city boy."

Jack's eyes rounded and he continued to stare at him, seemingly waiting for something, but Rex had no idea what. He could think of a dozen things he'd like to give him. Round two definitely at the top of that list. And round three. Because if Rex got him naked again, one round wouldn't be enough. Not by a long shot.

Yeah. It was time for bed.

"Good night, Jack," Rex finally said, turning and heading for the kitchen. He needed to put his tools away and go to bed.

He damn sure didn't need to stand there and make this situation worse.

And that was exactly what he'd do if given the opportunity.

WELL, THAT WAS DEFINITELY AWKWARD.

Jack made a beeline for his car, wanting to grab his suitcase before the surly cowboy changed his mind and locked the front door. As it was, the man made him nervous. Not in the *I'll likely be buried in the backyard beneath the old oak tree* kind of way. More in a *he wants to ravish me until I can't think straight* sort of way.

As in, one night wasn't enough.

Jack knew the feeling, although he wasn't going to push his luck. As it was, he did look like a stalker, showing up on the cowboy's doorstep not even twenty-four hours after their hotel romp.

"I need sleep," Jack grumbled. "Not to contemplate having that cowboy fuck me stupid two nights in a row."

His dick thickened despite his brain's insistence that it would never happen again. One night was all he got.

Fuck, he needed sleep.

Grabbing his suitcase and his art case from his car, Jack returned to the house, glad to find the door was still unlocked. Without thinking, he closed the door, locked it up tight, then stared at what he'd done. Did they lock their doors out here in the country? Figuring it wasn't going to do any damage for it to be locked, Jack headed for the stairs.

After huffing his stuff up two flights to the third floor, Jack paused at the top, opened the only door.

The first two floors had been ridiculously empty and in desperate need of repair. As in no walls, shitty floors, and no furniture aside from a table he'd noticed on the main floor. While the downstairs appeared to be under construction, this part looked as though it was finished and ready for guests. Directly in front of him was an open space with vaulted ceilings, ivory walls, enormous windows, a flat-screen television, a dart board, and rows of empty bookshelves. Bachelor's pad, for sure.

A hallway extended to the right, a kitchen and breakfast nook to the left. Jack could see three white doors down the hallway, only one of them closed. Figuring the guest room would be obvious, Jack started down the hall. The door on the left proved to be a bathroom. He kept going. The door on the right led to a room with a rumpled bed. He did his best not to think about the cowboy sleeping in that bed.

Jack opened the last door, straight ahead, and stepped inside, flipping on the nearest light switch. A rustic ceiling fan clicked on and three white bulbs lit up the room. He took a moment to scan the space as he closed the door behind him.

The décor was nicely done. Surprisingly, despite the cowboy accents, it wasn't overdone, which was something he'd noticed people tended to do when they liked something specific.

"A far cry from a cabin in the woods, though."

In fact, the only thing this place had in common with a cabin was the wood. It was rustic and masculine with its oversized dark furniture, stone fireplace, and wood floors. Dark brown curtains were pulled back to reveal a single French door on the back wall, which he assumed led to a balcony. A dark walnut dresser stood on the wall with the door. Two matching nightstands flanked the king-size bed, which was decorated with a few fluffy pillows and a brown suede comforter that appeared to be lined with … fur?

Jack moved closer and touched the blanket.

"Not real fur, thank God."

Jack quickly flipped on the lamp beside the bed, then retreated and headed for the bathroom. Perhaps he could take a shower and be asleep before the cowboy came upstairs.

"Holy shit."

Quite frankly, he was surprised to see the shower took up nearly half the room. There were no glass doors or glass walls, only a square, tiled enclosure that was just a hair too tall to see over, with a small gap opening to get into it. On one side of the shower was a claw-foot soaking tub, on the other a pedestal sink. Another door led to the toilet.

The guy had gone all out in an effort to make this a homey space, that was for damn sure.

"Shower." Jack stretched his back and yawned. "Then sleep."

He needed to turn off his brain for a little while. As it was, thoughts of Tina's infidelity were creeping in on him, making his stomach churn. On top of that, he had memories of last night overwhelming him. After all, a man had to come to terms with things he learned about himself. Especially when those things altered the entire course of his life, including everything he thought he knew up to that point.

Jack flipped on the shower, then grabbed one of the dark brown plush towels that were folded neatly on a shelf beneath the sink. He laid it over the shower wall, then headed over to take a leak.

Less than a minute later, he was standing beneath the warm water with his eyes closed. He could feel the heat stirring inside him. He wished the cowboy would come upstairs and join him, let Jack disappear beneath the onslaught of lust he stirred in him.

That thought reminded him of what Max had said, the way he'd so casually sat in Jack's bed while Tina pranced half-naked around the bedroom after she'd been fucked in the ass by the guy. His gut twisted, thoughts of Tina invading, snuffing out all the heat the cowboy had instilled. Thankfully, the anger was stronger than the hurt. At least right now.

Jack had spent the majority of today trying his damnedest to understand how they'd gotten to this point. So much so that he'd replayed several conversations he'd had with Tina over the past month. One stood out more than the others. Although, *conversation* wasn't the most appropriate description. More like argument.

"We need some spice in our lives, Jack," Tina said, interrupting him for the third time in thirty minutes. "Remember how you were talking about…"

Jack looked up when she trailed off. "About what?"

"About bringing another guy in?"

Jack frowned. "What the fuck, Tina? I told you I was drunk. I'm not into that shit."

"But it could be fun," she huffed. "Just one night. A little experimenting."

"By experiment, you mean cheat?"

"No!" Tina frowned. "I'm talking about you, me, and … another man. You could see if you enjoy it or not."

For fuck's sake. Was she crazy?

"Not going to happen," he insisted. "Besides, I've got too much shit going on right now. The wedding coming up, plus, I have a deadline, Tina."

"You always have a deadline."

"Because I have a job."

"Fuck you, Jack. You think you're hot shit because you draw comic books. I'll have you know, you're not the only artistic one here. In fact, I've got someone interested in my writing. He says it's good."

"He?"

Tina waved him off.

"I didn't know you were writing again," Jack admitted.

"How would you? You've got no time for anyone but yourself and your stupid drawing crap. You don't even know what's going on with me."

Jack stared at Tina. Her blond hair was pulled back in a ponytail and she was wearing yoga pants and a thin tank top that showed off her sports bra. It was similar to the outfit he'd seen her in that first day at the gym. He remembered thinking she was fucking hot. For whatever reason, she didn't look the same to him anymore.

"Enlighten me then. Who's the guy interested in your work? Maybe I know him."

"You don't. And it's not important." Tina frowned. "We're supposed to get married in a few months, Jack, and you never have time for me. It's almost like you want me to go away."

He sat up straight, his defenses falling into place. "I don't want you to go away." Jack knew there wasn't much conviction behind the words, but he wasn't in the mood to argue.

In all fairness, things between him and Tina had been bad for a while. Well, not necessarily bad, but they certainly hadn't been good. Although she had been moving forward with the wedding plans, they both knew there was a problem. For one, they'd lacked the intimacy their relationship had been full of in the beginning. Now that he thought about it, maybe that was because Tina had been getting it on the side.

"Bitch."

Then it hit him. Was Max the guy interested in her work? Was that why she was fucking him?

He choked out a laugh, but it burned with anger. "So, when he says her work's good, did he mean her writing? Or her ability to take it in the ass?"

Realizing he'd forgotten his toiletries in his suitcase, Jack reached for the bottle on the shelf. He sniffed it, his eyes closing as he remembered the way the cowboy smelled last night. Spicy, sexy…

"No," he demanded. "Shower and sleep. That's all."

Jack went through the motions of cleaning up while he forced himself to think about Tina, about her infidelity. Despite the fact that he hadn't exactly been in love with her, it still hurt that the woman could do that to him. Jack should've confronted Tina, insisted she tell him exactly what he'd done to deserve this. Instead, he'd run like he always did. Worst part, the other man had still been there—in *his* apartment—still naked in *his* fucking bed.

Rubbing his chest over his heart, Jack swallowed down the anger, the hurt, and the hatred. He poured body wash into his hand, quickly washed up, then shut off the water and dried off. Wrapping the towel around his hips, he headed back to the bedroom. He closed the door, flipped off the light and the lamp, then crawled naked beneath the blankets and the sheet, pulling them up to his head before closing his eyes.

He needed sleep.

Maybe after that, some of this shit would start to make sense.

Unfortunately, that was the moment his cell phone rang.

Nine

REX WOKE THE NEXT MORNING JUST AS the sun was coming up and his first thought was about food. Shockingly, it had nothing to do with being hungry, either.

No, he had a bigger problem. Rex knew he didn't have a damn thing to make his guest for breakfast. He should've had some sort of meal on hand, even if it was just cold cereal. Too bad he didn't have any milk. Or eggs. Or bread. He needed to go to the store. If his guest was relying on him, the man was going to go hungry. Unless he could make do with a protein bar and beer. Rex had plenty of those.

Not that Jack Cunningham was really a guest. He was more like a stranger who was camping out in Rex's guest room uninvited.

So why was he so damn worried the guy would be disappointed with his stay?

"Because this is your livelihood," he said aloud, waltzing into the bathroom and turning on the shower water.

Okay, total lie. He was worried because his thoughts were consumed by the city boy. Was it a sign that Jack had showed up on his front porch? Or merely an awkward coincidence?

Hell, he didn't know. Nor did he have the brainpower to think about it anymore.

After a quick shower, Rex pulled on jeans and a T-shirt, then tugged on his boots, grabbed his ball cap before stepping out of his room, not bothering to close the door behind him. So what if Jack didn't like that Rex hadn't made the bed. Or picked up his dirty clothes from the night before. It wasn't like he was trying to impress the city boy.

When he reached the end of the hallway, Rex was hit with the smell of freshly brewed coffee. Slowly, he made his way through the den, past the small breakfast bar and into the kitchen. He peered over at the coffeemaker, his eyes coming to rest on the man standing here, his back to Rex.

He noticed Duke was lying on the floor, his attention darting between him and Jack. He looked content to be chilling, probably waiting to go out and do his morning business.

The city boy wasn't looking at Rex or Duke. In fact, Jack wasn't looking at anything that Rex could tell. His head was hanging down, palms flat against the granite countertop, shoulders hunched. Although he'd been intimate with the man, he hadn't had a chance to fully enjoy the view up to this point. He probably shouldn't have, but Rex took a second to admire Jack's muscular physique outlined nicely in a pair of Levi's and a snug charcoal-gray Henley.

Jack was relatively tall. Right at six feet, if he had to guess. And damn did he make every inch look good. Jack's dark brown hair was short on top, tapered on the sides and back. Not nearly as unkempt as it had been when he arrived late last night. Rex could see the corded muscles in his shoulders and neck, and he fought the urge to stare for too long.

When it became clear that Jack hadn't heard Rex join him, he walked over to let Duke out. When he'd built the apartment, he'd wanted to have a way for the manager to come and go privately if necessary. So, he'd built a small deck off the back of the house with a stairway that led down to the ground. Once Duke had started down the stairs, Rex let the back screen door slam shut.

That got Jack's attention.

The city boy spun around, his eyes darting to Rex's face.

That was when Rex noticed he looked like hell. Oh, sure, he was still handsome, even if his eyes were red-rimmed and his jaw was lined with a couple of days' worth of dark stubble. He wasn't sure if he preferred him this way or the clean-shaven pretty boy he'd met at the bar. Both ways tripped his trigger, he figured, so it didn't really matter.

"Mornin'," Rex greeted, moving toward the coffeepot.

"Morning."

Reaching for a mug in the cabinet, Rex cast a quick glance over his shoulder. "Sleep well?"

"Not too bad." Jack's voice was raspy, as though he'd just rolled out of bed. Or perhaps been up most of the night.

Which he had, Rex knew. It hadn't been easy to ignore the conversation coming from the guest room last night. Eventually, Rex had covered his head with a pillow, refusing to nose his way into Jack's business. Based on Jack's tone, Rex figured Jack had been talking to whoever he was running from. Girlfriend? Wife? Hell, it could've been his mother for all he knew.

Rex poured a cup of coffee. After taking a sip, he turned to face Jack while he leaned against the counter to keep his eye on him.

"I'll be out of your hair in a minute." Jack sounded defeated, his speech slurred somewhat. He hadn't even touched the steaming mug sitting in front of him. "Just need a little caffeine."

Rex didn't respond. He wasn't asking him to leave.

Jack stood up straight and swayed on his feet.

"Whoa." Rex set his cup down and reached for Jack's arm.

Okay. Bad idea. That simple touch sent shockwaves down Rex's arms, the tremors heading due south.

He probably shouldn't be touching the city boy—too damn much temptation—but he got the sneaking suspicion Jack Cunningham was dangerously close to face-planting into the floor. Probably better to touch than to have to call an ambulance.

"You all right?" Rex asked, trying to keep his touch light as he kept Jack upright.

"I … uh…"

Jack's eyes crashed into his face and Rex found himself getting lost in the swirling gray. Like storm clouds on a spring morning, despite the fact they were bloodshot. He had thick, dark eyebrows and a perfect nose. Nice lips, too.

Not helping, Sharpe.

"I didn't sleep last night," Jack admitted.

Rex released his arm and took a step back, hoping the distance would cool his libido. "Problem with the bed?"

"No. I just…" Jack shrugged, then turned toward the door. "Thanks for giving me a place for the night. I'll go get my shit."

"Hold up. You hungry?"

He had no clue why he was even talking. Rex should've let Jack head out. He wasn't Rex's problem and there was plenty of shit he needed to take care of, especially since the place wasn't going to fix itself. Last thing he needed was someone hanging around, getting in the way.

Jack's gaze swung back around to Rex. Once again, he swayed on his feet.

"What the fuck?" Rex lunged for him again, grabbing hold of his arms and steadying him. He felt the play of Jack's muscles beneath his fingers. "You didn't sleep *at all?*"

"No. Had some … shit to deal with." Jack shrugged.

Whoever he was talking to on the phone, no doubt.

Rather than boot him out, Rex turned him toward the hallway. "Go back to your room and sleep."

"I should—"

"It wasn't a request," he growled, glaring at Jack. "Go."

Although he appeared to want to argue, Jack finally sighed, then turned around and headed out of the kitchen. Because he could, Rex followed, watching until Jack disappeared down the hallway.

Stubborn man.

Rex's dick twitched in his jeans.

"Dumb ass," he chastised the unruly appendage as he poured some kibble into Duke's bowl and set it on the floor before letting him back in.

Once his dog was happily chowing down, Rex dug his truck keys out of his pocket.

He needed to run to the store and grab some food and supplies. More accurately, he needed a distraction from the sexy man who'd invaded his thoughts since he walked into Moonshiners.

Three hours later, Rex returned to the house, oddly happy to see that Jack's fancy little sports car was still parked out front. He'd briefly wondered if the city boy would disappear while he was gone. For whatever reason, Rex had been hoping he wouldn't.

"Don't get attached to the city boy, Sharpe. Not gonna happen," Rex chided himself as he opened his truck door and stepped out.

As Rex was approaching the third-floor patio from the exterior staircase, the screen door opened, and Jack stepped outside. The guy instantly shielded his eyes from the brutal morning sun.

It was humid today, which took off some of the January chill. The temperatures would hover in the fifties, but they were predicting snow in a couple of days, something that wasn't all that common for his neck of the woods.

"Are there more?" Jack asked, stepping aside and opening the screen door.

Rex shook his head. "Shouldn't you be asleep?"

"I did sleep."

Before Rex could set the last bag down, Jack began emptying the other bags on the counter. A little taken aback, Rex stood stone-still and watched as Jack placed the eggs and bacon in the refrigerator, the bread in the pantry. Appeared the guy had made himself at home.

Rex fought the urge to chuckle.

"So, you've got a lot of remodeling to do downstairs, huh?"

Rex didn't answer. He didn't need to. It was obvious.

Jack turned to face him. "What?"

"I can unpack my own groceries."

Rather than apologize, Jack stared at him. The gleam in his gray eyes seemed almost like a dare. As though he didn't mind helping out in the kitchen and wanted Rex to know that.

Okay, do not go there.

This guy is not going to let you play house with him, no matter how tempting the notion.

And there it was. Those hopeful thoughts that had plagued Rex's mind since the instant he'd secluded himself in this big old house. The idea of finding a man who was eager to give him every part of himself had become a near obsession. Not one he was acting on, more like something he thought about endlessly. Fantasized about. In return, Rex would give everything he was to a man because ultimately, he was looking for a happily ever after.

Yeah.

Jack Cunningham was not his happily ever after. Perhaps he could've been if he wasn't running from his demons. Rex had enough of his own, didn't need to pile more on top.

Rex turned his attention to the other grocery bags, quickly emptying them and placing the contents in their appropriate places. He hadn't bought much since cooking for one didn't require an awful lot, but he'd gotten enough to get by for a couple of days in case Jack decided to stay longer.

Like he said … hopeful.

"You hungry?" Rex asked, mainly to make the awkward silence go away.

"You don't have to feed me," Jack stated, closing the pantry door. "Now that I've slept, I feel much better."

"Three hours isn't sleep," Rex objected, watching the other man closely.

Jack nodded. "Can't get my brain to shut off."

Great. And now the guy was going to tell Rex his life story. If he did, Rex might actually give a shit and that was what worried him the most. The last thing he needed was a reason to want to keep this guy around. For one, Jack wasn't gay. And even if he was trying to come to terms with it, he wasn't there yet. Curious, absolutely. Out and proud, definitely not.

Which meant Rex could fantasize all day long, but in the end, it wouldn't change Jack's sexual preference. And two, Jack was obviously going through something, hence the reason he had shown up on Rex's doorstep in the first place. The safe bet would be to send him on his way so Rex could get back to doing what he'd been doing.

And that would be?

He hated that damn voice inside his head. The little fucker never had anything nice to say.

Rex's stomach rumbled, reminding him that he hadn't eaten that morning. Without looking at Jack, Rex said, "I'm gonna make bacon and eggs. If you want some, stick around."

"How much do I owe you?"

Rex shook his head. "Nothin'."

"For last night?"

"Nothin'," he repeated.

"For the room," Jack clarified.

This time Rex did turn to look at him. "Am I not sayin' it right?"

They stared at one another for a few tense seconds. Rex was trying not to be an asshole, doing his best to remember it was his job to be hospitable. But it wasn't easy.

Probably had a lot to do with the fact that Rex was having those weird fantasies about the city boy. Had been since he walked out of Jack's hotel room on Sunday morning. Hell, aside from knowing how tight the guy's ass was, how fucking good Jack felt beneath him, Rex didn't know the first thing about him. Yet he'd been obsessing. So much so, he wondered if that was what had drawn Jack to him. Maybe the universe had put Jack in Rex's path for a reason.

He really needed to get out of the house more. Maybe pick up another hobby.

Rex walked over to the fridge, retrieved the eggs and bacon without looking at Jack. He opened the egg carton and turned his attention to the stove. He wasn't sure when the last time he'd actually cooked on that stove was. If at all. It was brand new and most of Rex's meals were nuked if they had to be cooked.

He thought about the stove on the main floor, the last time he'd used it to make spaghetti for his old man. The night... A shiver raced down Rex's spine and he shook off the memory. The last thing he needed was the past invading his present. He'd built something for himself and he refused to go back to a time that was best left buried with the old bastard.

"You all right?" Jack asked from behind him.

"Fine."

Rex glared at the stove, then peered back at Jack over his shoulder. "If you don't mind, I prefer not to have an audience when I cook."

Jack chuckled, but thankfully, he took the hint.

JACK STILL DIDN'T KNOW THE GUY'S NAME.

The man had driven his car, dozed in the same bed, fucked him, given him a room for the night, cooked him breakfast, and Jack still didn't know his name. Hell, he didn't know anything more than the fact the guy made him feel things he'd never felt before, made him contemplate his entire life, question himself and all the things he'd thought he wanted.

Sure, there was some definite heat, perhaps even a few sparks between them. The kind that had the hair on the back of Jack's neck standing on end, his body priming for a repeat of the other night. As much as he wanted to pretend it wasn't there, he couldn't. However, he was getting rather good at ignoring it. Okay, so ignore was a strong word. He couldn't ignore it. Not entirely. The cowboy had an intimidating presence. Even when they weren't in the same room, Jack could still feel him. It was weird.

But not entirely off-putting.

Or perhaps there was no interest and he was merely plotting a way to get Jack out of his hair.

"No," he muttered. "Probably not." Jack figured if the cowboy wanted him out, he would simply tell him to go. He didn't seem like the type to beat around the bush.

"So, how long've you lived in Austin?" the cowboy asked when Jack brought his plate to the kitchen after they ate.

"All my life."

The cowboy frowned. "If you live there, what had you searchin' for a hotel in the middle of the night?"

"Spur-of-the-moment vacation," Jack said, not making eye contact.

"You're a shitty liar," the cowboy said with a smirk. "I'd lay my money down on you runnin' from somethin'."

"Yeah. Something like that."

The cowboy cocked his head to the side, studied Jack momentarily before turning back to the sink, but before he could launch another question, Jack asked, "What's your name? I kinda feel at a slight disadvantage since, you know, we've been naked together and all."

The cowboy peered over at him, those dark, devastating eyes surveying him momentarily as though he was searching for something.

Jack held up his hands in a show of innocence. "Not gonna steal your identity or anything. I just don't know what to call you."

He didn't immediately respond, and Jack was starting to think he wouldn't when he finally sighed and said, "Rex Sharpe."

Rex. Hmm. Some people's names suited them. That was certainly the case with Rex.

"And the dog? Does he have a name?"

"Duke."

Rex and Duke.

"Does this place have a name?" Jack inquired when it was obvious Rex wasn't going to contribute any more to the conversation than he had to.

"Not yet."

"But you do plan to turn it into a bed-and-breakfast?"

"That's the plan," Rex stated.

"Soon?"

"No."

Jack started to open his mouth, but quickly closed it when Rex glared over at him.

"This is startin' to sound like an interrogation."

Jack chuckled. "To me it sounds like conversation, but whatever."

Jack got the impression Rex wasn't big on talking. He tended to say as few words as possible. During breakfast, neither of them had said anything. Which had been just fine with Jack. It wasn't like he was looking for a friend. Rex had diligently eaten everything on his plate, but he hadn't appeared to be in a rush. Jack had tried to mirror his pace, not wanting to look like a complete jackass.

But admittedly, he did enjoy conversation, so the longer Rex went without speaking, the more awkward he felt.

While Rex went back to washing the dishes, Jack secretly admired him. Rex's dark hair was almost military short, the top a tad longer than the sides. The stubble on his jaw was obviously intentional. Not quite long enough to be considered a beard, but it was the same length as his hair. Wide shoulders, narrow waist, long legs. He had the build of a man who got his exercise by working. Probably got quite the workout simply by doing what he was doing around there.

For the first time in a while, a spark of inspiration hit him. He wanted to use Rex as his muse for a character he'd been thinking about. A somewhat dark, sexy superhero—like Batman—who had an issue getting close to people because he insisted on closing himself off. Not exactly good, but not evil, either. He wondered about Rex's upbringing. Had his childhood been good?

Not that Jack was big on digging into details of someone's past. He was the sort who shared more information about himself than he tended to get from others. Jack figured that was part of his flaw. He didn't quite know what he was getting into because he didn't bother to do the research. Not when it came to life, anyway.

Maybe if he had, Jack wouldn't be in this position. The one that had him contemplating his recent decisions, his spur-of-the-moment choices. Such as sleeping with the sexy cowboy. What happened between them had been … a spur-of-the-moment thing. Totally against his norm. An anomaly. Maybe an experiment. After all, Rex wasn't Jack's traditional type. Jack's interests tended to lean toward petite blondes. Petite, blond females to be more specific.

Keep telling yourself that.

Although, after Tina's deceit, Jack was starting to wonder if maybe he should give up on women altogether.

A ludicrous thought.

It wasn't like one night with this sexy man could possibly lead to something more. Could it? Would it be possible to explore something deeper with Rex?

Oh, for Christ's sake. Relationships are not your strong suit.

Sleep deprivation. That was what this was. His temporary insanity could be blamed on his lack of sleep.

Fucking hell.

Time to think about something else.

What Jack should've been doing instead of having these off-the-wall thoughts was figuring out what his next move would be. Where was he going to go? What was he going to do? It wasn't like he could sit around this place forever. He should probably hop in his car and head farther north, away from Austin. Find a hotel he could hole up in for a few weeks. Perhaps Tina would be out of his apartment by then.

"What do you do for a living?" Rex asked.

His question caught Jack off guard because Rex still wasn't looking his way.

"I'm an artist," he explained. "I contract with comic writers, do the artwork for their stories."

"So you draw?"

"To put it simply, yeah." Jack grinned. "You've read comic books, right?"

Rex glanced at Jack over his wide shoulder. "Maybe when I was a kid. So someone writes the thing and you draw it?"

"For those I contract with, yes. I've also written my own. Although my own work is better described as a graphic novel."

"Where do you work? Where's your office?"

Jack leaned against the counter. "No office for me. I work out of my apartment. I can meet with the writers virtually or, for those who're close, we'll schedule times to get together at coffee shops, bookstores."

And that was the reason he had the flexibility to stick it out here for a while. After Rex had commanded him to go back to bed, Jack had taken a few minutes to check out the view from the balcony. He'd felt some inspiration while he was out there. The lack of city noise, the cattle he could see grazing on the dry, brittle grass that went on for miles, the solitude that seemed to shroud the place. He could see himself working here for a while.

Which wasn't an option because this place wasn't open for business.

"So, if you've got an apartment in Austin, what are you doin' hoppin' from hotel to hotel?"

"I'm ... uh ... having it exterminated."

"Ah." Rex didn't seem convinced.

Jack turned his attention to Duke, hating that he was going to have to leave but not exactly sure why. He peered over at Rex one more time, then stood tall and cleared his throat. "Well ... Rex. Uh, thanks for letting me stay. And for breakfast. I guess I should be on my way."

With his back still to him, Rex reached for a towel, then used it to dry his hands. "You can stay here if you need to."

Jack frowned, confused. "What was that?" He wasn't sure he'd heard him correctly.

"You heard me, city boy."

"Actually, no." Jack moved closer. "I didn't."

Rex turned, and suddenly, Jack was overwhelmed by Rex. All of him, so close. Sparking delicious memories of their night together. His thoughts raced, his mouth went dry. He wanted to close the distance between them, to remove the clothes that would keep Jack from touching all those glorious muscles.

Thankfully, Rex's voice broke through his ill-timed fantasies.

"I said you could stay here if you need to."

Jack swallowed hard, forced his eyes to focus on Rex's face. Then his words registered.

Need. Not want.

Jack's first inclination was to decline and tell Rex thanks but no thanks. He wasn't looking for any handouts. However, the logical side of his brain was shouting that this was exactly where he wanted to be and Rex had a spare room, so why put up a fight? It was obvious Rex wasn't interested in a repeat of what had happened, so Jack didn't have to be concerned he'd go and do something stupid like fall for the guy or anything.

"I ... uh..." Jack sighed and took a step back, hoping the move appeared casual. "I'd... You know what? Yeah. Okay. That would be great."

"Good." Without another word, Rex walked around him, heading toward the living room.

His arm brushed Jack's, and they both paused. Jack's entire body went stone-still as he processed that casual touch. The weird sensation that coursed through him was similar to the one he'd felt the other night, when Rex had been thrusting inside him, making him beg and plead for more.

Their eyes met, held for a second before Rex turned and left the room.

Jack shook off the thought and followed him out of the kitchen.

"Think maybe we could settle on a per night fee?" Before Jack got too comfortable, he needed to ensure he could afford the place.

"How long do you plan to stay?" Rex turned to face him once again.

Jack shrugged.

Rex held his gaze. "A couple of days? A week? How long until your apartment is *exterminated*?"

Jack was suddenly at a loss for words. Rex was offering to let him stay long enough to give Jack time to think. He could take advantage of the seclusion, get his thoughts in order, and not have to worry about dealing with Tina.

Before he could respond, Jack's cell phone rang. He tugged it out of his pocket.

Speak of the devil.

Tina. Again.

Jack hit ignore, then shoved the phone back into his jeans.

"I honestly don't know," Jack stated when he met Rex's dark eyes once more. "A couple of weeks, maybe?"

"Then how about we make a trade," Rex said.

Jack's body flashed hot. "Sex?"

The smile that split Rex's face came on slowly, as though he hadn't thought about it, but he wasn't opposed to the idea.

"You offerin', city boy?"

Jack's throat was too dry to speak.

Rex chuckled. "But no. Not that kinda trade, city boy."

"Oh." Was that disappointment that trickled through him?

"I was thinkin' more along the lines of you helpin' out downstairs. Maybe assist with some of the work. For room and board, of course."

"I'm not much of a … handyman."

"Anyone can learn," Rex stated, his smirk growing wider. "Plus, you'll have to help out with meals," Rex added. "I'm not all that big on cookin'."

Jack considered that for a moment, then grinned. "I'll take it."

"Good."

"I'm serious, though, Rex. I'm not all that handy with tools, but I'm a fast learner. Show me once and I'll usually master it."

As soon as the words were out, Jack realized the innuendo in them. He fought back the heat creeping up his neck and maintained steady eye contact with Rex.

"I'd say it doesn't take you long to catch on, no."

The heat intensified, but neither of them moved. Jack's cock twitched, lengthening as his mind raced back to Saturday night, to the warmth of Rex's body above him, the intensity of their joining, the way Jack had come completely apart that night. Sensations churned through him, but he fought them back, refusing to act on them.

Before Jack had come up with something—*anything*—to say, Rex pivoted and walked out of the room.

Then right out the door.

Two hours later, Jack was sitting in his room when his cell phone rang. His gaze darted down to his phone and his breath rushed out of his lungs when he noticed it wasn't Tina.

"Thank Christ," he huffed, snatching up the phone and tapping the screen to take the call. "Hey, Shawn. What's up, man?"

His response was a heavy sigh followed by, "So, I was thinking…"

"Uh-oh. That's never a good thing." Jack pushed to his feet, went to the balcony door, and stared out at the gloomy gray sky. He already knew where this conversation was headed, because only a couple of days ago, he'd spent two hours of his life arguing with Shawn about it.

Had it really been just a few days?

It seemed like a million years ago.

"This is serious, Jack. I don't want you making jokes right now."

"Okay, fine. I'm listening."

There was silence for a few seconds, followed by a rustling of paper and then Shawn's scratchy voice. "I'm worried this isn't the direction we should be going. You know, with the heroine. She doesn't feel right to me, Jack."

Yep. Just as he'd thought. They were picking up right where they'd left off.

"You worry too damn much," Jack told him, stepping out onto the balcony. He bent over, rested his elbow on the rail, his gaze scanning the yard below. He noticed the pool and a hot tub. The hot tub wasn't attached to the pool. It was one of those fancy ones. Probably had a hundred jets and boiling water. It was currently covered by a brown mat, the kind used to keep the heat in.

Shawn snorted. "No, you don't worry enough."

Little did Shawn know but Jack's life was a fucking merry-go-round of worry. Especially these days.

"Seriously, Jack. I think we need to spend a little more time on the design."

"You haven't given me time to perfect it," Jack countered.

"But that's the problem. I'm not on board with the direction you're taking her. She's not how I envision her."

"I get it." Jack sighed. "I do. But, Shawn, it's good. *Really* good. All of it. Your storyline, the characters. I promise, when we're done, it's going to be *exactly* what you envision." Once Jack ever got around to working on it again. He wanted to relax, try to rationalize the shitty turn his life had taken.

"I disagree. I don't like her look," Shawn argued. "I was thinking more along the lines of Wonder Woman. You know, long black hair, tiny waist, sparkling blue eyes, and maybe a stronger chin."

"Not gonna happen." Jack was not about to piggy-back off of another idea, no matter how successful it'd been. Originality was key as far as he was concerned.

As an artist who'd contracted with many writers over the years, Jack had dealt with more than his share of novelists who wanted to do just that. But he would argue to the ends of the earth that Wonder Woman was already taken. So were Harley Quinn, Batgirl, Captain Marvel, Black Widow, Supergirl…

"We need to talk about it some more, Jack. I'd like to meet, hash it out. I'll even give you a rough design of what I'm thinking."

"You're not the artist here," Jack reminded him as he moved back into the room, closing the door behind him.

"No, but you're not the writer on this one."

That was true, Jack was not contributing to the storyline on this particular novel. But they'd worked on plenty together, so Jack expected some respect in this regard. Jack hadn't let the man down yet. Truth was, Shawn was one of the most stubborn men he'd ever met, but Jack genuinely liked the guy. Plus he had some serious talent, which was why they'd co-authored four novels thus far.

So Jack relented. "Fine. But I'm not in town right now. Won't be back for a couple of weeks. In the meantime, you work on the storyline. Leave the drawing to me. I'll catch up with you in a few days."

Shawn huffed but then agreed and the call disconnected.

Jack tossed his phone on the bed and glanced out the window again, realizing for the first time in a long time…

He had absolutely no desire to draw.

Ten

REX SPENT MOST OF THE AFTERNOON WORKING in his workshop. Technically, it was a large metal building he'd added to the property back before he started working on the house, but it could function as almost anything. Once he'd begun converting the attic, he had started using the extra space as storage to house the various deliveries, as well as the furniture he was accumulating.

During his procrastination periods, Rex spent quite a bit of time out there. Usually building something. Dressers, rocking chairs, beds, tables, various decorative pieces. Anything to keep his hands occupied while he put off the inevitable. His goal was to outfit the entire house with his designs, the things he could make with his own two hands.

Today, he hid in the workshop mainly so he could get some space from Jack. Not that Jack was bothering him. Not yet, anyway. He was merely proving to be a distraction Rex didn't need. With the potential investors waiting for the next steps to be completed, Rex really needed to focus on the tasks at hand, not sitting around fantasizing about bending the city boy over the kitchen table and fucking him blind. Because that was what he wanted. He wanted to get his hands on Jack again, to run his lips over all those lean muscles, to grip Jack's hips and drive deep into the blazing depths of Jack's body. Thinking about it was driving him mad. He'd never been so consumed with thoughts. Not a single man in his past had caused Rex to lose control quite so easily.

But he had shit to do. And that didn't include *doing* the city boy.

However, since Rex couldn't start checking off his to-do list until he met with Kylie to go over the design and finalize the blueprints, he figured it only made sense to work on furniture.

So, after putting his headphones on and finding a country music station, he got to work.

As he sanded what would be the top of one dresser, he stared into the grain, wondering where Rafe was. Maybe in Dallas. Rex didn't know for sure and it pained him not to. He wanted to ensure his brother was safe, healthy. Rex blamed himself for his brother's disappearance, but that didn't stop him from wanting to hear from Rafe. And once he did, Rex wanted to make amends.

While he worked and tried to focus, Rex's mind still drifted to Jack. He couldn't help but wonder what he was doing right at that moment. Was he bored? Was he sleeping again? Or was he on the phone with whoever had caused him to run from his life in Austin? Admittedly, Rex was curious. He wanted to bombard the guy with questions, figure out what made him tick.

There was no denying the chemistry between them. It was there, thick and potent, lingering in the air anytime they were in the same room. Rex could see the curiosity in Jack's eyes. He was thinking about that night, too. Perhaps even about a replay.

Not that it mattered. Jack would be gone in a week, maybe two, and he would no longer be Rex's problem. The one night they'd shared together would become a distant memory. And that was what he needed to remember. Jack wasn't a permanent fixture and Rex wasn't interested in temporary. He'd done that for too long.

He forced his mind to clear of all thought and focused on the task at hand. He didn't take a break until Jack appeared in the doorway holding a paper plate and a bottle of water. Rex had no idea how long Jack had been standing there before Rex finally pulled his headphones out of his ears and turned to face him.

"Thought you might be hungry." Jack raised the plate toward him.

"You cooked?"

"Don't get excited," Jack said with a grin. "It's not hard to make grilled cheese."

No, it wasn't. However, it was more than Rex usually had. Most of the time he settled for a protein bar. When he was feeling wild, he would head over to the diner. Of course, he was always offered a Sunday dinner at his aunt and uncle's, but as of yet, he hadn't accepted the invitation. While he loved his aunt Lorrie, Rex still felt slightly uncomfortable around all the Walkers.

Rex peered up at the clock on the wall. Holy shit. Where had the day gone? It was already four o'clock. He'd burned away more hours than he'd intended.

"Yeah, thanks." Rex nodded toward one of the tables near the door. "You can set it down there."

Jack placed the plate and the bottle down, surveyed the space before turning and walking out. While Rex wouldn't have minded having dinner with the city boy, he figured it was in his best interest to steer clear of the man for a bit. Considering he'd spent most of the day fantasizing about him, it wouldn't do either of them any good if he pursued him.

Until Rex could convince himself that Jack was off-limits, he would have to keep his distance.

Another hour and a half passed before Rex put down the paintbrush and decided to call it a night.

After he made a mental note of what was next on his agenda, he went to the house for a shower. Once he was clean, Rex realized he wasn't ready to settle in for the evening, so he pulled on jeans and a T-shirt, then made his way downstairs to check on things. Duke trotted along beside him, clearly looking for some attention.

Rex generally took advantage of these times when he was restless. If he wasn't in the mood to relax in front of the television, Rex would fiddle with something until he found himself focused. That was the process he'd followed for clearing out the house, tearing out the linoleum flooring, the carpet, some of the rotted hardwood, the Sheetrock, a few of the walls. It had been slow going, but it worked.

"No manual labor tonight, Duke." Rex peered up at the ceiling, tipped his chin upward. "Considering our guest up there, logical to keep the noise to a minimum, huh?"

Duke stared at him like he was lost.

"Okay, so that's another excuse. So what?"

Rex marched into the space that would one day be the kitchen again, then the dining room, the old parlor, the formal areas that were now nothing more than wood and air. He headed for the stairs, slid his hand along the banister, and paused on the bottom step as he surveyed the room.

Rex peered across the open foyer and into the parlor. He would have to get creative when he was designing the downstairs. Since the house had originally had four bedrooms and eight seemed to be the new magic number, he would have to make some concessions to deal with space constraints, not to mention ensure he could accommodate any guests with physical limitations. Since an elevator wouldn't be feasible, Rex knew that meant having some guest rooms on the main floor.

Maybe he could widen the living area, make it more of a community area. The front section of the house didn't have a second floor, which would allow him to keep the tall, vaulted ceilings. Rex wanted to install wood beams, drop a large ceiling fan from the center post, and perhaps place two oversized leather sofas in front of the stone fireplace. The giant flat-panel television over the mantel would work nicely for football or whatever the guests might be inclined to watch.

But would it be enough space? And what about the dining area? How many tables would he need? Did everyone congregate at one? Or would he need to build a few smaller ones? Those were all questions that he needed to have answers to.

In an effort to get a little inspiration, Rex took a trip upstairs with a notepad in hand to make a list of what would need to be focused on once they got the essential upgrades out of the way. After the electrical and plumbing were completed, he could start on the guest rooms. Maybe if he had enough help, they'd be able to knock the Sheetrock out in a week or so. That was probably his best bet. Then again, he would likely need to get the central heat and air installed. That was logical. Then the Sheetrock could go up.

He paused to take a look at the wide space he intended to turn into a game room. Rex wanted to elevate the room slightly, make it into a prominent area, a place guests would want to hang out. He envisioned it, the far wall holding the flat-screen television, the pool table that would sit in the center, maybe some bookshelves.

No, he'd save those for the library. But where would that go? Did he need to rethink the entire space, shuffle a few things around? There was more than enough square footage, he knew. However, Rex wasn't sure what the best layout would be.

Okay, so he really needed to nail down the design.

Rex's gaze shot to Duke, who was lying in the middle of the floor. "I guess I should call her, huh? Meet with Kylie, put it all on paper?"

Duke didn't acknowledge him.

Rex headed down the hallway to the left, stared at what used to be his bedroom. That night came flooding back in a deluge of memories. He could still feel the way the metal had bitten into his wrists, the hard hands holding his ankles. Jolene's face flashed in his head, and for a moment he swore he could smell the stench of pot and booze on her breath.

Forcing his feet to move, Rex went to the back windows. While there wasn't much to see, aside from the acres of grass and the groupings of trees on the southwest side of the property, there was a spectacular view of the sunset from these spots. Back when he'd started tearing things out, Rex had found himself designing the balconies where people could sit and watch the sun go down.

One day.

Swallowing hard, he moved to the other end of the floor. He planned to have a couple of rooms facing the front of the house. They wouldn't have a phenomenal view, but he imagined they would be cozy enough. In an effort to entice people to rent them, Rex had decided they would be larger suites with a small kitchenette complete with microwave and sink. Rex wanted three of those rooms in the house, one downstairs and two up, just to change things up a bit, give the guests a few options. At the very least, he could get more money per night for the larger rooms.

"Yep, one of these days, Duke. It'll be all done, and I'll look back on this with a smile."

He heard footsteps moving overhead, wondered what Jack was doing up there. Watching television? Taking a shower? Calling it a night?

Figuring he might as well give in himself and relax for a while, Rex made his way to the third floor. When he opened the door, he was greeted with silence. The den was empty, the television off. He stepped into the hallway, peered at the closed guest room door. Was Jack already asleep? Or maybe he'd napped more during the day and he was as wide awake as Rex was.

Not that he cared. He didn't.

Turning to go to the kitchen, Rex paused when he heard the deep rumble of Jack's voice.

"No, Tina. I've already told you. That's not gonna happen."

Hmm. Who was Tina? Girlfriend? Wife?

"You were fucking another guy in our bed, damn it. I think it's safe to say the wedding's off."

Ouch. That had to fucking hurt.

"That's bullshit. Your boy toy offered to have a go at me, remember? I told you that shit in confidence."

Hmm. That sounded interesting. Perhaps the city boy had been conflicted prior to their one-night encounter.

"No, I don't want him fucking my ass, Tina. I was drunk when I said that."

Rex grinned to himself. He'd learned that most of the time people tended to speak the truth when they were intoxicated. Jack had seemed quite content to have Rex doing the honor of taking his virgin ass.

Heat slammed into him, had him damn near stumbling. While he'd strongly suspected Jack hadn't previously been with a man the night they met, Rex hadn't thought about it much. He was the only man who'd ever had the pleasure of thrusting into his body, driving them both higher and higher until…

"Fuck," Rex hissed.

"It's over, Tina," Jack declared. "I'm done."

Knowing that man's problems weren't any of his business, Rex turned and traipsed into the kitchen, leaving Jack to deal with the fallout of that relationship on his own. But it did explain what he was running from. And another reason Rex needed to keep his distance from the guy. The last thing he needed to deal with was someone else who was planning a quick getaway when things got rough.

He sighed. His fascination was simply because he'd been alone for so long. That had to be it. Perhaps a few hours of sleep would do him some good. He could start first thing in the morning. Meet with Kylie, come up with a timeline. Move forward.

And be that much closer to opening the doors to the public.

"NO, TINA. IT DOESN'T WORK LIKE THAT." Jack huffed, pacing in front of the balcony door. It was dark outside, so the only thing he could see was his own reflection.

He'd been on the phone with Tina for the past hour. The term *hell on earth* came to mind when he thought about all the bullshit she'd tried to feed him. He would've avoided her like the plague, but Jack figured he'd give her the time she felt necessary to hash this thing out. Although they'd spent hours on the phone Sunday night, that had been mostly spent with Tina reminiscing, discussing how they'd met, the good things that had happened to them during their time together. Tina had needed it and Jack had been hopeful it would allow them both to move on.

Apparently not, since Tina was now blowing up his phone with text messages and voicemails, pleading for Jack to take her call so they could work this out. Figuring he could keep them on the straight and narrow, he'd decided to give it one more shot.

The conversation, that was. Not any sort of reconciliation. That wasn't even an option where Jack was concerned. Listening to her pledge her love for him, insisting she would never cheat again wasn't helping. Jack was *not* going to change his mind. He was done with Tina. Forever.

"What do I tell the guests, Jack? What reason do I give them for why we're calling off the wedding only a few weeks before? Can you tell me that much?" she asked, her voice soft, almost remorseful.

"I don't care what you tell them. Maybe start with the fact that you're fucking another guy?"

Tina snorted. "I am *not* gonna tell them that."

"Well, then make something up. You could always tell them we're breaking up because of irreconcilable differences. You want to fuck other people and I don't want you to, so our goals don't exactly align."

"God, Jack. I said I was sorry. What more do you want?"

"Well, for starters, I want the woman I'd intended to marry *not* to be fucking other people. It's not like I was asking for a whole helluva lot, Tina."

They'd already been over this at least a dozen times. After the intense phone call last night, Jack had asked her to give him some time. Her idea of time was evidently a few hours. And they were back to going around in circles, getting absolutely nowhere.

"I'm really sorry, Jack."

He didn't respond. For one, he didn't believe her. And two, an apology didn't matter at this point.

"Jack?"

"Hmm?" He wondered if it really would snow. It was a rare thing here, but not unheard of. While the cold wasn't something high on his list of things he appreciated, snow would be a sight to see.

"I said I was sorry," Tina repeated.

"Yes, you did." He wasn't going to accept her apology.

Tina was surprisingly quiet for a moment, and Jack wished like hell she would hang up. Put an end to this bullshit once and for all. He didn't care what she said or how much she groveled, whatever they had between them was over. He merely needed her to move out of his apartment so he could go home.

Which brought him back to the topic he'd tried to keep it on. "When can you be out, Tina?"

She sighed. "You're really asking me to move out?"

"I really am."

"That's not fair, Jack. You want me out on the street?"

Jack laughed, a bark that erupted from his chest. "You haven't been on the street a day in your life. Your daddy will rent you an apartment in a second. You just have to tell him."

"Whatever. He's already forked out the money for the wedding. I can't just go and tell him you called it off and then expect him to get me a place to live. He'll want reasons."

"Well, for one, your father hasn't forked out anything. I've covered all the deposits. If you cancel now, perhaps I'll even get some of that back. And if not..." He sighed long and loud.

"I don't want to cancel," she whispered. "And I still have to give my father reasons."

"Then tell him the truth. You like being fucked in the ass by Max and you need a place so you can do it."

He heard her growl, the same sound she made every time he brought it up.

"Are you seeing someone else, Jack? Is that what's going on?"

Jack pulled the phone away from his ear and stared at it, shocked by Tina's question. "*What?* Why the fuck would you ask me that? You're not gonna pin this on me, Tina. You're the one fucking other people."

Jack put the phone back to his ear to hear her response.

"Maybe so," she said quickly. "But you did admit you have fantasies about men. Is there a man you've been lusting after, Jack?"

He was not going to dignify that question with an answer. And he damn sure wasn't going to tell her that he might have become slightly infatuated with Rex in the short time he'd known him. It wasn't her business. And it certainly had nothing to do with the end of their relationship.

"I said I was sorry," she snarled. "But I don't think this is only about me. Is that what happened, Jack? You left and found someone else? Cheated on me as payback?"

He laughed, but there was no humor in it. "It wouldn't be cheating since we're broken up, Tina."

"So you *did* sleep with someone else? Was it a woman or a man?"

"No, for fuck's sake, Tina. I didn't sleep with anyone." He figured there was no sense telling her the truth. It would only make this worse, have her blaming him for everything.

Not that she didn't already.

"Then where are you?"

"It doesn't matter."

"It does to me."

For whatever asinine reason, Tina wanted to know where he was. No way in hell would he tell her. If he did, she would likely show up on Rex's doorstep.

His thoughts drifted to Rex. More specifically, wondering what he was doing. Aside from brief glimpses of him working, Jack hadn't seen much of him throughout the day. It was as though the big cowboy was steering clear of him for some reason. More than once, Jack had thought about seeking him out, asking what he could help with. After all, that had been their trade-off. Maybe if Rex put him to work, Jack wouldn't feel like such a burden.

"Jack? Do you think we can work this out? I can give you all the time you need. Maybe in a week you'll be ready to come home. The wedding's just over a month away. I know we can work this out if you'll give it time."

Damn, but the woman didn't listen. He'd already told her no several times.

"Please, Jack? I promise I won't cheat on you again. But you'll have to put more effort into giving me what I need, too."

Oh, for fuck's sake.

"And what do you need, Tina? A stranger fucking you in the ass? Or a threesome? Because as fun as that sounds"—it didn't sound fun at all—"I'm not good at sharing."

"I just … I thought it was what you wanted, Jack. I thought you were interested. Max is bisexual. He was willing to experiment. I never thought…"

A sob sounded and even Jack could tell it was fake.

"Oh, bullshit, Tina. You're not gonna pin this on me. You fucked Max for you, not for me." He sighed heavily. "I have to go. And no, there's no chance of us reconciling. Trust is important and as you can imagine, there's no way I could ever trust you again. If you aren't going to cancel the wedding, I will. And I won't lose a wink of sleep over telling everyone what happened. And I do need you out of my apartment. Soon. I can stay gone for a couple of weeks, but you'll need to be out by the first of the month, at the very latest. That's the best I can do."

"Fuck you, Jack. You're—"

He hung up before she could go into a tirade. Honestly, he was surprised she hadn't already, but Jack knew it was only a matter of time. The woman did not want to take responsibility for this. And sure, perhaps he was at fault for some of the issues they'd had as of late, but that didn't make it okay for her to sleep around on him.

As for what Tina was going to tell the people she'd invited to the wedding, he honestly didn't give a shit. It wasn't like he had any family coming. His mother had disappeared when he was five. She'd just up and walked out on him and his dad. Not that they had missed her.

Unfortunately, his father had passed away three years ago, so he wasn't around to see Jack get married. If he ever did get married, that was. At the rate he was going, Jack would never stand at the altar and accept any woman as his wife. He'd tried and failed three times. Trying again would be the definition of insanity.

Sighing, Jack flopped onto the bed and stared at the ceiling.

Perhaps this was the way things were meant to be. He was supposed to be alone. If he gave it a chance, he wondered if he could end up enjoying the solitude. And wouldn't that be a nice change of pace? Living the single life out here in the boondocks. No one bitching and moaning, no one wanting anything from him.

Granted, it did seem a little lonely. This huge house was so empty. For all intents and purposes, Jack had the place all to himself. It was a little weird at times, but not altogether awful. The only thing he'd do to change it was to have a little more time with Rex. To talk, of course. He liked the guy, enjoyed the few conversations they'd had.

Jack sighed again, but this time it was lighter.

Relief?

Yeah. That was exactly what it was.

For the first time in a long time, he felt some of the stress he'd been burdened with easing out of his muscles. Perhaps in time, he'd be ready to go back to his life.

Of course, he wasn't ready to think about that.

Not yet.

Eleven

"SO?" KYLIE STARED AT HIM, SO MUCH hope in her eyes. "What do you think? Do you love it? Hate it?"

Rex wasn't sure what to say. And though he was generally a man of few words, he didn't tend to get tongue-tied. Yet here he was, sitting at the small table in Kylie's kitchen, staring at the screen before him, and his mind was completely blank.

"Oh, God." Kylie groaned. "You do hate it. I am so, so—"

"I certainly don't hate it," he assured her, flipping to another picture, this one of the design for the kitchen. "It's..." He lifted his gaze to her face. "It's amazing, Kylie."

He thought for a moment she was going to jump out of her chair. Being as pregnant as she was, he didn't think that was a great idea.

"Really? There's nothing you have an issue with?"

This time Rex grinned. "I didn't say that. But in general, it's very close to what I've envisioned. I'm just confused as to how you could be so spot on."

"Well, the blueprints helped," she admitted, resting her hand on her rounded belly. "Not to mention, I did a little research of the period that the house was built. Taking both into account, along with technology from today and some of your personal interests, I think it's a great mix of old and new. Modern farmhouse, if you will."

That it was. And she'd thought of everything. "Which brings me to the question of how much is this going to cost me?"

Kylie grabbed the iPad, tapped the screen a few times before turning it to face him.

"I've got figures for you here. We can easily punch in any changes, taking into account the labor that we'll save if you're doing a significant amount of the work yourself. And I took a look at your business plan. As solid as I've ever seen. I adjusted a few things to align with your goals. As far as materials for the decor, I assure you, I'll get the best prices possible. I do a lot of research prior to purchasing anything." Kylie smiled. "And my husbands have advised me to get your final approval as well. You know, before I go on a shopping spree."

Rex chuckled. He still couldn't believe what he was seeing. He wasn't sure what he'd expected, but this wasn't it. He thought for sure they'd spend half the day making major changes to her design because he doubted she could come close to what he wanted. That didn't seem to be the case.

"Are you okay?" Kylie reached out and touched his hand, her concern palpable. "I know I threw a lot at you at one time."

"It's not any more than I've been thinking about for the past decade," he assured her. "And I'm fine. Really."

She sat up straight, clapped her hands together. "So we're a go?"

Rex nodded. "Definitely."

She squealed, making him laugh.

"All right. Now let me get some hard copies of these few things and we'll walk through it in detail, change what you know you want to change initially. Then we'll meet routinely as the project moves along to ensure I don't go off half-cocked."

Three hours later, after Rex and Kylie had shuffled through pictures on the screen, a 3-D software rendering, and a handful of paper copies, modifying the overall design, adding a few details, deleting others, his head was spinning from so much detail. Which wasn't exactly a good thing since Rex was heading over to the diner to meet Travis and Gage. However, he was happy he'd met with her first. Certainly made him hopeful that whatever Travis presented would be something that would benefit them all.

When he arrived, he was happy to see Travis and Gage were the only two there. He hadn't been sure whether the entire crew would show up or not, but he figured when it came to business, these two were the best to talk numbers with. Not to mention, he wasn't sure he wanted to deal with the ideas and suggestions from so many people at one time.

After shaking both men's hands, Rex took a seat across from them. The waitress appeared promptly, and Rex went with iced tea, figuring now was not the time for a beer. Maybe after they'd finalized the paperwork.

"Let me preface this by saying I had Tristan draw this up," Travis began, motioning toward a stack of papers on the table.

Rex nodded. Tristan Walker, Travis's cousin on his father's side, was a well-known lawyer. While Rex didn't know him all that well, he'd heard plenty of good things, even seen him a time or two over the years.

"I figured he'd have all of our best interests at heart," Travis continued.

Rex didn't know about all that, but since this was the first time he was seeing the information, he figured he could hold his opinion until he reviewed their proposal.

The waitress delivered his iced tea and left them to their business. Travis passed over the paperwork, giving Rex time to skim through it. He would go over it with a fine-tooth comb later, but for now, he wanted to see what their investment offer was. He scanned the information, moving from page to page until he got to the last one, which listed those who wanted to invest, how much they were willing to contribute, as well as the interest rate they were requesting in return.

Rex's eyes shot up to Travis. He wasn't sure his heart was beating. "Are you serious?"

"Very," Travis assured him, a self-satisfied grin on his face.

"But..." Rex glanced at the paper once more, then back to Travis. "You're not asking for interest."

"No, we're not. You're family, Rex. We only want to help you out, not take money off the top."

Rex laughed, looked over at Travis's husband. "You know if he does business like this, y'all aren't doing too hot."

Gage laughed, put his hand on Travis's shoulder. "Trust me, business is fine."

"Holy shit."

Rex couldn't quite believe what he was seeing. Not only the dollar amount that was being invested—which would easily cover the cost to fully renovate the old farmhouse—but also the number of people who'd contributed.

"Why?" he finally blurted, staring over at Travis. "Why so much interest?" He leaned forward. "And don't tell me it's because we're family, Travis. We've spent very little time together over the years."

"True," Travis said, leaning back and regarding Rex. "I guess you could say I've already got a vested interest in the place."

Rex's eyes narrowed as realization dawned. "You're the one leasing the property."

"I am," Travis stated simply. "I'm also the one who kept the taxes paid on the house until you could claim it."

Fucking hell. Rex should've known. Then again, he hadn't considered Travis. He'd thought one of his uncles was leasing the land, not a cousin.

"Why'd you do it?"

Travis smiled. "Because I could. And because I knew it would help you and your brother." A hard gleam came into Travis's blue-gray gaze. "I've got no ulterior motive here, Rex. Never have. You're family. It's as simple as that. Don't look for issues where there aren't any."

Easier said than done. It was difficult for Rex to trust most people, although he had to admit, his family had never let him down.

"And before you ask," Travis said, pulling another sheet of paper out, "should you decide to proceed, the only signature that's needed is yours."

Rex stared down at the paper. There were so many signatures scrawled on it, he wasn't sure it was real.

He took a deep breath, turned his attention back to Travis and Gage. "Okay. What's the catch?"

Travis glanced at Gage, smirked. "I told you he'd ask that."

"Yes, you did."

Rex sat waiting.

"Okay, there are a couple of stipulations," Travis said, leaning back in his chair.

Expecting as much, Rex nodded for him to continue.

"Every person on that list has requested that they be allowed to stay at the B and B for free—for as long as it's open to the public—provided there is a vacancy, of course." Travis pointed at the paper. "You'll see the rules around that. We have no intention of bombarding you with our presence. It's simply a way to get some enjoyment out of it."

"Sure." Rex understood.

This time Gage sighed. "And the other stipulation is that we get it fully renovated within nine months, open to the public no later than October fifteenth of this year."

"Nine months?" Rex was sure he was hearing things.

"Yes," Travis stated. "You'll have the full backing of Walker Demolition, including our equipment as well as employees as they can be loaned out. Tomorrow morning, I've got a meeting set up down at the bank for you and me to open an account. The investment funds will be there for you to use however you see fit and we've established a repayment schedule as well. It's listed out in the paperwork."

Sounded fairly straightforward, but Rex flipped through the pages to see the schedule, wanting to get a feel for how quickly they expected their money back.

"And the only stipulation where the funds are concerned is that should you have an issue repaying once the B and B is open, you agree to come to me. We'll work on it together, determine the best course of action." Travis sat up straight. "This is yours, Rex. I don't want you to think I'm stickin' my nose in. You'll find everything outlined in that document. Should you change your mind and decide not to use Kylie's design, there'll be no hard feelings."

Still slightly off-kilter, Rex simply nodded. "I'll read through everything tonight. If I have any questions, I'll call you."

Travis grinned, held out his hand. "Me or Tristan, either one. He can answer anything from a legal standpoint. And if you prefer, we can push off the bank meeting for a couple of days if you want to meet with him personally."

"Sounds fair," Rex agreed, shaking Travis's hand firmly. "I'll let you know."

"And if you read through it and decide you want to move forward, meet me at the bank in the morning. I'll have Tristan meet us there to witness the signing of the final document. Otherwise, let me know what your next step might be."

Rex couldn't stop the smile. "And thank you. Seriously."

"That's what family's for," Travis said, pushing to his feet. "And no matter the past, Rex, we're all still family."

Unable to speak, Rex remained seated, watching as Travis and Gage left the diner. He sat there for the longest time, staring down at the paperwork.

His dream was about to come true.

He only wished he had someone to share the good news with.

JACK WAS SITTING ON REX'S LIVING ROOM sofa, staring at the muted television. He'd taken it upon himself to pour a glass of whiskey.

That was two hours ago.

Since then, he'd poured several more. One after the other.

The liquor coursing through his bloodstream hadn't dulled the pain and anger that slithered through him like an oily film, coating every inch of his mind with a haze of hatred. In fact, Jack was pretty sure it had confounded it. Every passing minute, the haze thickened, blurring his thoughts, until he was focused solely on the shit Tina had put him through.

He'd received numerous texts from the bitch since he hung up on her, each one nastier than the one before.

It took everything in him not to pick up the phone and call her, tell her exactly what he thought about her. The words that came to mind were vicious and vile. Hell, Jack even considered giving her the juicy details of his tryst with Rex. He could practically see her face when he told her how good it had felt when Rex kissed him, the way the man's hands had worked over his body, bringing him to life, giving him the most intense orgasm he'd ever experienced.

Luckily, the whiskey hadn't pushed him over the edge.

Not yet, anyway.

The door opened, drawing Jack's attention away from the television. Rex walked in, a stack of papers in his hand and a confused expression on his face. He considered asking what they were, but then realized it was none of his business. He wasn't friends with Rex, he was a guest in his house.

"Guest," he grumbled. "Sort of like a tourist."

"Somethin' wrong, city boy?" Rex asked when he stepped into the living room. His gaze instantly shot to the bottle of whiskey on the table.

"Not a damn thing," he muttered. "I'll buy you another bottle."

Rex's steely stare implored him, but Jack didn't move. "I'd appreciate it."

With that, Rex turned and left the room, disappearing down the hallway to his bedroom.

"Well, so much for adult conversation." Jack glared at the empty space, his anger intensifying.

The rational side of his brain—the part not completely drowned in alcohol—told him to leave Rex out of it. The cowboy owed him nothing. However, the irrational side, along with the whiskey, was telling him to push his limits. If he played his cards right, perhaps he could get Rex to fuck him again.

That was all he needed. Something to obscure the pain, something to focus on other than the hatred he felt for Tina. Just a few hours of amazing, meaningless sex.

"Nope. Not smart," he whispered on a groan. Closing his eyes, Jack let his head fall back. The instant he did, the room began to spin.

Fucking lovely. Tina had reduced him to a pathetic drunk. A man who was willing to indulge in casual sex in an effort to set his world to rights although he knew it wouldn't help.

Nothing would help.

Jack forced his eyes open, glared down at his cell phone. "Maybe *something* will help."

Before his better sense could change his mind, Jack pulled up Tina's contact info, tapped the call button.

"Jack?"

"You know what, Tina? Remember how you said—" Jack's words dropped off when Rex appeared before him, shaking his head.

"Hang up the phone," Rex commanded, his tone hard.

Turning away from him, he vowed he would tell Tina exactly what he thought of her and her cheating ways. "Tina," he began again. "Remember how you—" The phone was yanked from his hand before he could complete his sentence.

"I'm sorry. Jack will have to call you back," Rex said into the phone before disconnecting the call.

Jack went toe-to-toe with Rex. "Who the hell do you think you are?"

"The guy who's gonna save you from explanations tomorrow." Rex's words were rough, a raspy whisper that had Jack staggering back.

"I don't have anyone to explain anything to," he insisted, although he knew Rex was right. The worst possible thing he could do was unleash on Tina. If he told her how he really felt about a man he'd known for only a couple of days, Jack would look like an idiot.

"Why don't you call it a night," Rex suggested. "I'll keep this until tomorrow." He waved Jack's cell phone in front of him. "And when you can make good decisions, I'll give it back."

"Good decisions?" Jack snorted. "Are you saying I can't make good decisions when I'm drunk?" He stumbled slightly. "How the hell would you know? You don't even know me."

"I know more than you might remember," Rex countered.

Another snort escaped. "Ha! I remember every single detail," Jack countered, his voice dropping to a whisper. "The way you touched me, the way you kissed me." He closed his eyes momentarily. "How fucking good it felt to have you inside me."

Rex cleared his throat and Jack's eyes flew open.

Shit. Had he really said that out loud?

"Sleep it off, city boy."

"Fuck you," he snapped. "Why do you get to boss me around? Why? Because you fucked me?" Jack barked a laugh. "Is that how you treat all the guys you fuck, Rex?"

"You're itchin' for a fight, Jack. And I'm not gonna give it to you. Sleep it off."

When Rex reached for him, Jack spun away. "Fuck off."

Despite the alcohol haze, Jack knew he was being petulant, but he couldn't help himself. He was hurting. Not only because Tina had been fucking other men while they were engaged, but also because he wanted Rex. He wanted five minutes of the man's time but knew he wouldn't get it. For whatever reason, Rex had stayed gone all day and Jack got the feeling he was doing it so he didn't have to look at him.

"Was I that bad, Rex?" Jack asked, not really wanting to know the answer.

Rex's dark eyebrow lifted, followed by the corner of his mouth.

That smirk only pissed Jack off more. "Fuck you."

"You keep makin' the request, but it's not gonna happen, city boy."

Jack squared off with him. "See, that's where you're wrong."

Rex frowned. "How so?"

"'Cause I'm not askin' for it. I don't *need* you to fuck me. I can find some other desperate cowboy who'll take advantage of the drunk guy."

The instant Rex's expression went from cool to heated, Jack knew he'd fucked up.

"Let's get a couple things straight, city boy," Rex snarled, stepping right up to him. "First, I'm as far from desperate as a man can get. Two, you were *beggin'* me to fuck you. And thirdly, I didn't take advantage of you."

Although Jack knew that was true, he couldn't seem to stop arguing with the man. "Whatever helps you sleep at night."

"I sleep just fine," Rex growled, moving in until Jack was crushed between him and the wall.

Jack had a million words that wanted to tumble off his tongue, but he suddenly couldn't think, couldn't breathe. The lust burst in his veins, an inferno erupting in every nerve ending.

"Prove it," Jack whispered.

"Prove what?"

"That it wasn't as bad for you as I think it was."

Rex smirked. "Doesn't work that way, city boy. I'm not gonna fuck you so you feel better about yourself."

It was Jack's turn to smile. "Okay, then. Tell me why you *will* fuck me."

Twelve

WELL, THAT CERTAINLY WASN'T WHAT REX HAD expected Jack to say.

Forcing himself back a step, he glared into the man's handsome, chiseled face and reminded himself he was not going to get caught up in whatever drama Jack was immersed in.

"I'm not gonna fuck you," Rex declared.

There was a flash of hurt in Jack's eyes, which had Rex pausing. As much as he wanted this man, as many times as he'd replayed their night together over in his head, he knew this was the moment he had to put the brakes on. Giving in was far too easy and Rex wasn't one for easy. And he damn sure wasn't one to allow a man to use him for his own entertainment.

Jack pushed off the wall, stepped closer. Rex didn't move, continued to maintain eye contact. He was in control here. Not Jack.

"I need you to kiss me." Jack's voice was a rough, raspy plea.

Rex shook his head, but his gaze dropped to Jack's lips. He remembered how the man tasted, how soft and eager his lips were, how they'd glided so firmly against his own. His entire body relived that first kiss, the heat that had consumed them, the anticipation. Finding a man who could kiss as well as Jack wasn't easy. Not in his experience, anyway.

"You want to," Jack stated, although he didn't sound all that sure of himself.

Rex forced himself back another step. "Actually, I don't. You need to go to bed, Jack. Sleep it off. We'll talk in the mornin'."

Jack didn't move. His gaze never wavered. "I might be drunk, but I know exactly what I want."

"Yeah?" Rex snorted. "Is that what you say to all the guys?"

"You're the only one, Rex."

A spark of anger lit in his gut and he stepped forward. "Yes, I am. And just like the last time, you're plastered. That's the only way you can seem to bring yourself to give in to your desires, to accept the fact that you might possibly be gay."

Jack's eyes widened. "That's not true."

"Isn't it?" Rex nodded toward the bottle of whiskey on the table. "Seems to be a staple of yours right before you indulge in a little man-on-man action. Do you do that with the ladies, Jack? Do you have to get plastered to fuck a woman?"

Jack swallowed hard. "No."

"I didn't think so."

Knowing this was not going to go anywhere pleasant, Rex turned and headed for his bedroom. He thought for sure Jack would stay back, let it go. Of course, he shouldn't have been surprised. From the moment Rex had stepped through the door, he'd felt Jack's anger, knew he'd spent a significant amount of time stewing over whatever problems he had. Since Jack had downed almost half the bottle, Rex figured the city boy was drifting on liquid courage and disappointment, using both to ask for what he wanted.

"Don't you walk away from me!" Jack snapped.

Rex didn't stop, continued walking toward his bedroom. "Or what?"

A firm hand gripped his arm, spinning him around. Rex followed the momentum. He shoved Jack back against the wall, then slammed his palms down beside Jack's head, moved in nose to nose.

He glared down into those storm-cloud-gray eyes, used his anger and frustration to keep himself from doing something stupid. "Don't do somethin' you'll regret here, city boy."

The tension eased out of Jack's shoulders immediately, his eyes going soft, his expression sobering. "I don't regret it," Jack whispered. "I think about you all the fucking time, Rex. Every single minute."

Damn it. That wasn't the shit he wanted to hear from Jack.

Rex realized how close he was to Jack's mouth. It was right there, centimeters from his own. He could feel Jack's labored breaths, feel the warmth of his body.

"Please, Rex."

Fucking hell. What was it about this man? Why the fuck couldn't he simply walk away? It would be the smart thing to do. For both of them.

Rather than do the smart thing, Rex slammed his mouth over Jack's. He wasn't gentle when he cupped Jack's head with both hands, aligning their lips so that Rex could own the kiss, so he could show Jack exactly who was in charge here. Their tongues dueled and Jack's whimpering moans had Rex's control shattering.

Somehow, Rex managed to stumble down the hall, never breaking the kiss as he guided Jack to the guest room. He shoved the city boy down on the bed, moved over him. Without finesse, he jerked Jack's shirt off over his head, ran his palms roughly over warm skin as he continued to devour him. The kiss was brutal, fueled by adrenaline and a pure burning need that Rex was absolutely positive he'd never felt before.

When Jack tried to speak, Rex kissed him harder. He didn't want words. Jack wanted him. He wanted Jack. They would leave it at that for now.

Their hands fumbled as they somehow managed to remove clothes until they were skin to skin. To keep Jack from talking, Rex didn't stop kissing him, bruising his own lips in the process. He didn't stop until he needed to catch his breath and grab a condom and lube.

"Don't say a fucking word," Rex hissed as he rummaged through the nightstand. He knew there were condoms in there. Lube, too.

When he turned back, he found Jack staring at him, stroking his cock firmly while he panted. It was clear what Jack needed and although Rex knew he was being used, knew Jack wouldn't be doing this if he were sober, he couldn't help himself. But Jack wasn't the only one making bad decisions. Rex was onboard that train alongside him. And because of that, Rex had to pretend he wasn't taking advantage here. Otherwise, he couldn't go through with it.

"Roll over," Rex ordered. "On your knees."

When Jack moved, Rex fell back on the bed, spread out long. Propping his head on a pillow, he settled in, got comfortable as he rolled the condom on, lubed himself up. All the while watching Jack.

Rex used his finger to mimic a circle. "Turn around. Face the door."

Once Jack's back was to him, Rex reached over, grabbed the man's hips, then urged him to straddle his thighs. "You're gonna ride me," Rex told him. "Sit on my dick and take what you need."

"I—"

"No talking," Rex commanded.

Rex showed Jack a little mercy as he guided him down on his cock. He allowed the city boy to take control, to ease onto him. Since Rex couldn't see his face, he had no idea what Jack was thinking. Nor did he care. This was what Jack wanted. He wanted to be fucked, needed Rex to accommodate him.

So he would.

Doing it this way, the man could get what he wanted, and Rex could go on pretending that Jack wasn't using him, that he wasn't some fucking experiment for the guy who was confused about his own sexuality.

And this way, Rex could pretend he didn't give a shit that the city boy didn't want him the way he wanted Jack.

"CHRIST ALMIGHTY," JACK HISSED, PLEASURE GLIDING THROUGH him as he inched down slowly, allowing Rex's thick cock to stretch his ass.

He wasn't sure if the alcohol was dulling the pain or if taking Rex's cock like this was easier, but the discomfort was manageable, perhaps even pleasant.

"No, it feels good," he mumbled to himself. "So fucking good."

Initially, Jack had been confused by Rex's request for him to turn around and face the door. He hadn't been sure what the man was wanting from him. But then when he realized he was going to mount Rex, Jack had been both anxious and nervous. He'd never thought about sex like this. Considering his experience was limited since he'd only been with a few women and, for the most part, missionary had been the position of choice, Jack hadn't considered what it would be like to explore.

Then again, he'd never given much thought to sex with a man before. Well, nothing more than the position he'd experienced in the hotel. That was usually how his fantasies went. Him facedown on the bed, a man plunging into him from behind. Very little intimacy, mostly pure need.

Although the intimacy was lacking here, there was something that made this moment memorable. Jack knew he would forever have this time with Rex imprinted on his brain, and he hoped like hell he could use these memories to fuel him for the remainder of his life because this … *this* was perfect.

Planting his palms on Rex's legs, Jack used the position to brace his upper body while lifting and lowering himself on Rex's cock, taking him deep, reversing, over and over. The pace was steady, not too fast, not too slow. It was amazing. He felt so in control, as though Rex was allowing him to draw out his own pleasure.

The only thing missing was that he couldn't see Rex's face. He wanted to see him, to touch him, kiss him, to know that Rex was right there in the moment with him.

He moaned softly as he eased down onto Rex, remembering that Rex had told him not to speak. It wasn't easy. He found himself wanting to verbalize how incredible this was.

Figuring he could test the waters, Jack moaned again, whispered, "Christ, you feel so good."

He could feel Rex tense beneath him, but he didn't say a word.

"Fuck," Jack groaned as he dropped down, increasing his speed. "Oh, yes."

While this was amazing, Jack couldn't help but wonder if Rex was enjoying himself. He hoped that was the case because, holy fuck, Jack wasn't sure he'd walk away from this unscathed.

"Oh, fuck, Rex…" Jack squeezed Rex's thighs. "I've never felt anything—"

"I said no talking!" Rex shouted.

Right.

Apparently, Rex was sticking to it.

Going back to his moaning and groaning, Jack continued to ride Rex's cock, taking all the pleasure he could.

Jack could hear Rex's occasional grunt and groan, and he took those as sounds of pleasure, focusing his attention on the way Rex gripped his hips, guiding him up and down. It was delectable torture. He wanted it to go on forever, but his cock was so fucking hard, aching for release. He knew he wouldn't last forever. Neither of them would.

"Rex… oh, fuck…"

"Take all of me, dammit," Rex growled, jerking Jack down onto him.

Pain and pleasure collided then exploded deep inside him, obliterating all thought, making his body hum. "Fuck yes. *That!*" Jack's body lit up, a warm energy shooting through him. "Just like that, Rex. Harder. Fuck."

With Rex's help, Jack continued to drop down onto him, taking the full length of him until he couldn't stand it any longer. He grabbed his cock with one hand, jerking roughly as Rex took over, holding Jack just above him while Rex fucked him from beneath, driving his hips upward, filling him. They were both moaning in earnest when that telltale tingle erupted in Jack's spine.

"Gonna come, Rex," he warned. "Oh, fuck, yes."

Rex slammed into him over and over, harder each time until Jack's eyes crossed, his mouth falling open. He gripped his cock hard as his orgasm ripped through him. It was all he could do to ensure he didn't shoot all over the bed and the man beneath him. And the instant Jack let himself go, his cock spurting all over his chest, he felt Rex pulse inside him, the man's body going completely still.

It took what felt like an eternity for Jack's breaths to return to a semblance of normal. When they did, he shifted, wincing as Rex pulled from his body. He fell back onto the bed, careful not to get his cum on the sheets.

"Rex, that was..." He was just about to reach for Rex when the man launched up out of bed.

With absolute horror in his eyes, Jack watched Rex grab his clothes and walk right out of his room. A door slammed a moment later.

Jack closed his eyes, took a deep breath in through his nose. The air around him was tinged with alcohol, sweat, and sex, plus Rex's distinct, intoxicating scent. Time stood still as his brain replayed the event, his sated body relaxing as his breaths deepened. He found himself smiling, reaching for Rex again only to remember he wasn't there. It was then that Jack realized the room was spinning.

He was drunk.

So drunk.

It would've been easy to fall asleep, but Jack needed to do something about the mess he'd made on himself.

A shower went a long way toward cleaning him up, but it did little to clear the fog from his brain. When he stepped out into the hall, he hesitated at Rex's door. Jack considered knocking, wanting to talk through this, needing to apologize. He'd asked for this, sure. And Rex had given in. They'd both been there in the room, but Jack felt the weight of what they'd done.

It was quite similar to that first night. They'd both been eager and willing then. Except tonight ... well, it was almost as though Rex had merely been a body for Jack to use.

Was that how it felt for Rex? Was that what he thought? That Jack was using him?

Unable to bear thinking that, Jack rapped his knuckles on Rex's door. There was no answer.

Jack pressed his forehead against the wood. "Rex?"

No response.

Feeling unexpected emotion churning inside him, Jack fought it back, choked it down. Forcing himself to back away from the door, he turned and went into his room. He gently closed the door behind him, tumbled into the bed facedown.

For the longest time, he thought about Rex, wished the man was curled up against him. He hadn't expected this … this feeling of abandonment. Granted, Jack couldn't necessarily blame Rex. As he played back what had happened in his head, he could see how Rex might feel as though Jack had been thinking only of himself tonight.

Was it true? Was Rex right when he'd said Jack couldn't be with a man unless he was drunk? He didn't think that was the case. Hell, he hadn't been intoxicated when he'd been thinking about the man endlessly since he arrived. Yet he hadn't had the nerve to confront him until he was liquored up.

"Fucking hell," Jack muttered.

He needed to sleep it off. Perhaps tomorrow it wouldn't be as bad as he felt it was now. Maybe Rex merely needed to sleep, too.

Yeah. That was it.

"Whatever you gotta tell yourself," he mumbled as he drifted off.

Thirteen

Friday, January 11, 2019

HAVING A GUEST WASN'T QUITE WHAT REX had expected. Not this guest, anyway.

While technically Jack wasn't a guest of the B and B, that was the way Rex was attempting to look at things. Whatever had transpired between them in recent days was now in the past, and moving forward required Rex to view their situation in a different light.

So, Rex had decided he would move into roommate/guest mode. Pretend that was the case for the time Jack was there.

To be fair, over the course of the past few years, Rex had wondered whether or not he'd be able to hack it as a B and B owner. To actually deal with the hassle of having people traipsing through his house, eating his food, sharing his living space. And yes, Rex was the one who had decided to open a bed-and-breakfast, which was the ultimate test for a man who enjoyed his solitude.

Which was why Rex decided to view Jack's visit as somewhat of a test run.

As for how he would rate the interaction … Well, despite the unavoidable tension, it wasn't entirely pleasant.

Their temporary cohabitation certainly had its challenges. For example, Jack's hissy fit last Monday night. From the moment Rex had stepped through the door, he'd been able to feel the animosity coming off the city boy. The conclusion Rex had come to was that Jack wasn't dealing—not well, anyway—with whatever had happened to him, whatever had him skipping out of Austin looking for something to distract him from real life.

And of course, there was the subsequent sex that had accompanied said hissy fit. Not that Rex was placing all the blame firmly on Jack's shoulders. Rex had given in, allowed himself to be used. And though he'd gone to sleep that night pissed off, Rex had woken with a new outlook, one he'd maintained for the past few days. It was done, behind him. He had to move forward.

For the past four days, Rex had only encountered Jack briefly. Neither of them had acknowledged what had happened. In fact, it seemed they were both pretending it hadn't. Whether that was because Rex had walked out after they'd fucked or because Jack felt like an ass for his behavior, he wasn't sure. Whatever the reason, Rex was hoping to get back on an even keel with the man. After all, Rex harbored no hard feelings. He understood that Jack was going through a rough time and the situation wasn't going exactly the way either of them had probably figured it would. His positive outlook told him that he should make the best of it.

Rex smirked. For the record, positivity was a difficult outlook to maintain when it came to Jack Cunningham.

Luckily, he had plenty to do to keep his mind off their … issues.

Now that Rex had signed the papers and opened the account with Travis, things were getting underway at the farmhouse. It hadn't taken long to realize that Travis Walker was a man who wanted to see results quickly. Thankfully, Rex was the type of guy who could make things happen with a little incentive. Since he considered all the investors the kick in the ass he needed, they were both going to be happy.

To his surprise, Jack had asked if he could pitch in to help out. Although Rex was passing him small, mundane tasks such as clearing out the debris and ensuring the water cooler remained stocked, Jack did so with a smile.

Of course, Jack also wasn't making eye contact with Rex. Hadn't since he'd woken the morning after his whiskey-induced tantrum.

Admittedly, Rex was doing his best to stay out of Jack's way while attempting to not make it glaringly obvious. Not because he didn't want to be around him. Even though the man frustrated him beyond measure, Rex still enjoyed his company. Far more than he should. Jack was smart, funny, and so fucking sexy it irritated the shit out of Rex to have to look at him for long periods of time.

Probably didn't hurt that Rex was over his desire to fuck him. Twice was more than enough. Especially since he had realized Jack's need to be fucked up in order to get fucked. That had been a hard pill to swallow, but at least it had given Rex a little perspective.

It seemed Jack had changed as well. Gone was the haggard man who had shown up on Rex's doorstep a week ago. In his place, a guy who had found his footing. Jack moved around the apartment like he'd been there his entire life. Every now and then, Rex would find him cleaning stuff. Sweeping, vacuuming, dusting. Even hosing off the back deck. And no matter what, when lunchtime rolled around, Jack ensured Rex had something to eat. Usually grilled cheese, but it was the thought that counted.

Rex hadn't bothered to tell Jack it wasn't necessary. He was more than willing to maintain his living space and feed himself. He'd managed to do so this far. He could continue even while Jack was in his space. But Jack kept everything clean. And he was efficient, too. Last night, Rex had gone into the laundry room to find both the washer and dryer running. Two hours later, he'd gone back in expecting Jack's laundry to have gone unfinished. Nope. Everything was spotless.

Jack was making it easy to have him around.

"Perhaps too easy," he muttered to himself. Now that he thought about it, Jack was pretty much the perfect tenant. As far as Rex went, perfect was always too good to be true.

But that didn't stop Rex from falling for the ruse. He found himself gravitating back toward Jack a little more each day, wanting to interact, although he was the type who didn't care much for conversation. Yet Rex was looking for reasons to talk to him. The easiest way was when Duke was around. Jack and Duke had become fast friends. Rex even found Duke sleeping in the hallway, just outside the guest bedroom.

"So, what's on the agenda for today?" Jack asked when he joined Rex in the kitchen after breakfast. "I heard they were going to start installing the HVAC today."

"That's the plan." And they wouldn't be there soon enough. The weather had taken a turn and the big farmhouse was cold as hell. The weatherman was still predicting snow, but it had yet to be seen.

"What can I help with?" Jack turned to face Rex.

"Well, Kaden and Keegan are comin' over. Why don't you check in with them, see what they might need?" Rex turned back to the sink, finished rinsing the last of the dishes.

"Suit yourself. If you wanna pass me off to your friends, who am I to argue?" Jack chuckled, his voice low, cheerful. "But if you're so inclined, you're welcome to use me any way you'd like."

Rex's hands stopped moving, his shoulders tensing. He stared down at the running water, a silent fury churning in his gut. How could Jack say something like that? Every so often, he would make some sort of innuendo, as though building on what had happened between them.

In fact, Rex wasn't even certain Jack remembered what had happened on Monday night. The way the sexy city boy had ridden his dick until Rex's head had nearly exploded off the top of his body. While the situation hadn't been ideal, Rex would admit the sex was still some of the best he'd ever had.

Sure, it would've been easy to take Jack up on the offer now. Perhaps ply him with a few beers, talk him out of his clothes again. Except that wasn't going to happen. No way was Rex going to fall into that trap. He was not going to be some confused guy's play toy.

"I … uh…" Jack coughed. "Sorry. That came out wrong."

Rex finished the dishes, waited until he heard Jack's footsteps retreat from the room before he turned around, drying his hands. He stared at the empty doorway, wondering if that was Jack's plan. Was he looking for a cheap affair? Perhaps some experimentation while he avoided the real world?

"This is my *real* world," he muttered to himself.

And that was something Rex couldn't forget. This wasn't a game for him. He lived here, he worked here. This wasn't a temporary getaway for him the way it was for Jack. He had to stay focused, not let himself get caught up in something that would never go anywhere.

Rex figured he could chalk their first encounter up to circumstance. It had been wild, spontaneous, and not at all disappointing. But their second encounter … that was an entirely different story.

As much as Rex wished things could be different, Jack Cunningham had showed his true colors that night.

"ENOUGH'S ENOUGH."

Jack couldn't take any more of this. He was slowly going insane sitting in his room, staring out at the gloomy sky, willing the clouds to dump the snow they were threatening.

He needed to do something productive. At this point, he was even willing to learn how to use some of those intimidating power tools that had moved into the house below. Everyone else seemed to know how to use them. Everyone except for him. Instead of getting a little schooling, Jack was relegated to delivering water and relocating tools to various spots. Rather than Rex show him how to do something, the man would have someone else take Jack under their wing, leaving him to wish like hell he could come up with a plan to fix what he'd so obviously broken.

Yeah, it was true. He was embarrassed about what had happened, how he'd approached Rex, used him for sex in an effort to ease the frustration his life was causing him. The good news was, he had sworn off liquor for the time being. He decided he would prove to himself, and to Rex, that he didn't need liquor to feel whatever it was he was feeling for Rex. Problem was, Rex was avoiding him.

Rather than addressing their issues like men, Rex had passed him off to Kaden and Keegan, and Jack had let him. And rather than put him to work, the rowdy twins made him their errand boy. But there was only so much he could do when there really wasn't anything *for* him to do. While it was obvious they were getting this massive project underway, it didn't seem to be moving all that fast. Then again, from what he'd heard, most of the work was being done by electricians and plumbers. For now.

So, rather than wander around aimlessly, waiting for someone to throw something his way, Jack had completed his minuscule assignments, then attempted to focus on the artwork he was supposed to be completing for Shawn. Not so surprisingly, Jack hadn't made a lick of progress on the heroine for Shawn's book. Then or now.

Tossing his sketchpad on his pillow, Jack stood and headed for the door.

"You just have to ask," he mumbled as he slipped out of his room and marched toward the living room. "The worst he can say is no."

Jack could hear Rex in the kitchen, knew this was the perfect time to talk to him. He'd been avoiding a confrontation with the man for no good reason. Nothing more than the ridiculous notion that Rex deserved to have a little time to deal with the shit Jack had thrown at him. Then the weekend had come along, and Jack managed to make more excuses. While Rex had disappeared for several hours on Saturday night, Jack had remained in the apartment, wondering where the cowboy was, who he was with. Those thoughts only made him edgy, so he'd forced himself to focus on work.

But now that another Monday had rolled around, Jack couldn't think of any more excuses. So, he ventured into the hallway, made a pit stop at the bathroom, wasted as much time as possible before forcing his feet to carry him to the kitchen.

He found Rex—shirtless, of course—standing in the kitchen, staring down at his open laptop while drinking water.

When Rex didn't acknowledge him immediately, Jack cleared his throat. Rex lifted his head, his eyes slowly scanning Jack from head to toe, then back up. Warmth pooled in every part of his body that received the intimate caress of Rex's gaze.

"Did you need something?" Rex prompted.

Jack realized he'd been staring at him, his eyes fixated on Rex's bare chest. Forcing his gaze up to his face, Jack cleared his throat, willed his mouth to work. "I … uh … I need something to do," he admitted. "And by that, I don't mean passing out water bottles or filling the cooler with ice. I mean, I may not be mechanically inclined, but surely there's *something* I can do."

"I thought you were an artist." Rex leaned back against the cabinet, the muscles in his abdomen flexing in a manner that had Jack's throat going dry.

"I am," Jack admitted, yanking his gaze back to Rex's face.

"So, what is it you think I do around here?"

"I'm trying to focus on work but can't. I just … I need something to do to take my mind off it."

Jack stared at Rex, fighting the urge to let his eyes trail down his chest. The man was ridiculously built, his muscles defined. He found himself fascinated every time Rex moved, his lean body shifting, muscles flexing. Hell, every time he closed his eyes, Jack remembered the short time he'd been allowed to experience that body for himself. And if that wasn't enough, he would then fantasize about all the ways he would've changed both encounters. All the things he wanted to do to Rex. Touch, taste, explore.

"Well, we've already established you can't handle power tools."

"No. Not really." Jack was sure he could learn, but he figured it was rhetorical.

"Electrical, plumbing?"

He shook his head. "No."

Rex glanced around as though looking for something. "I'm runnin' out of ideas here, city boy."

Jack honestly hadn't expected him to be so open to the idea. He was at a loss.

"Do you paint?" Rex asked when Jack didn't respond.

"I do." Jack could definitely paint. "I'm good at it, too."

Rex chuckled, probably amused my Jack's enthusiasm. He hadn't meant to sound quite so exuberant about the notion, but hell, it sure beat passing out water and sandwiches.

"I'm talkin' about paintin' furniture, city boy, not the Mona Lisa."

"Oh." He felt his face heat. "Well, yes, I can wield a paintbrush. I'm sure painting furniture isn't all that hard."

"All right." Rex stared at him for a second, then pushed away from the cabinet. "If you're bored, I've got some furniture that needs to be stained."

"Perfect." Jack peered around the room. "Where are the supplies?"

Rex nodded toward the back door. "Down in my workshop. You'll find the stain on the table by the door, and just grab anything you see. It's all gotta be done."

"Awesome."

Without hesitating, Jack stomped to the door, slipped out, then practically ran down three flights of stairs. He flipped on the workshop light, found the bucket of stain and a brush. With a smile, he carried them over to what appeared to be a couple of nightstands.

Considering the path he'd taken in life, Jack had never seen himself doing something like this. It wasn't beneath him by any means, he simply hadn't considered it. But it would give him something to do, and perhaps if he let his mind blank for a little while, he'd be able to focus on the WIP.

He dipped the end of the brush in the stain bucket, swiped it over the edge of the can to keep it from dripping, then slid it over the wood, keeping in the direction of the grain. He did it again and again until he realized he was smiling.

Maybe there was hope for him after all.

Fourteen

Friday, January 18, 2019

"HEY, CITY BOY!" REX CALLED AS HE made his way down
the hall toward the kitchen. He tapped on the bathroom door.

"Yeah?"

"You wanna hit the nursery with me today?"

The door swung open, and Jack appeared wearing nothing
but a towel around his lean hips. Unable to help himself, Rex's gaze
slid slowly down the man's muscular chest, over the chiseled six-
pack before he forced them back up to Jack's face.

"A nursery?" Jack's head cocked to the side.

"Yeah."

Jack's forehead creased. "Are we talking plants or babies?
Because I draw my line at kids."

Rex laughed. "Plants."

"Oh." Jack grinned, sliding his hand through his wet hair.
"Sure. Just let me get dressed."

Rex stepped back so Jack could come out of the bathroom.
"Take your time," he muttered, watching the sexy city boy walk
down the hall, the muscles in his back shifting with every step.
"Damn."

"I heard that." Jack turned around, grinned, then shut the
bedroom door.

Rex noticed he didn't close it all the way.

It was a move that seemed relatively bold for the city boy. Ever since their last encounter—nearly two weeks ago—there'd been a bit of innuendo on Jack's part, more than a little sexual tension building between them, but no moves being made. Rex was trying to pretend he didn't want to get Jack naked and have his wicked way with him because he knew it was a dead end. Nothing good could come out of them fucking each other again.

And while he was horny, and it would be so easy to march down the hallway, peek into the room, and ogle Jack while he dressed, he knew better. It might take more control than he possessed, but Rex was not going to do that to either one of them. As far as he was concerned, their history in that department would remain exactly that. Behind them.

Half an hour later, Rex was weaving through the back roads, making his way out of downtown Coyote Ridge with Jack riding shotgun.

"I've lived in Austin all my life, but I never knew there were so many small towns up this way," Jack stated, staring out the window.

"Quite a few," Rex confirmed. "Although they're growin'. Round Rock exploded several years back, and it's pushin' farther and farther out. And now, all these master-planned communities are chokin' out the farmers."

"And I assume Round Rock grew because Austin expanded."

"Exactly."

"But you like it here?" Jack questioned. "Living in a small town?"

Rex could feel his gaze, but he kept his eyes on the road. "I do. Couldn't imagine livin' anywhere else."

"It's not hard to see the draw," Jack stated softly. "Have you lived here all your life?"

"I have."

"In that house?"

"Yep." Rex didn't see the point in specifying that he'd lived with his aunt and uncle for a bit.

"And your parents?" Jack peered over at him.

Rex glanced over at Jack, considered how much he was willing to tell the guy. He wasn't the type to share his life story with anyone. In fact, there were only a select few who really knew what it had been like for him and Rafe growing up. He'd learned that not everyone had the stomach for the life Rex had been immersed in. Most of the men he'd spent time with over the years didn't want to hear about the devil that was Rex's father, or the reasons for the nightmares that still plagued Rex on a weekly basis.

But for some insane reason, he wanted to trust Jack, wanted to talk to him. More importantly, he wanted Jack to listen.

"They died," Rex blurted, pulling into the parking lot of the nursery.

"I'm sorry."

Rex heard the sympathy, wished he could take the words back. Instead, he shut off the engine and climbed out of the truck. Jack joined him as they walked toward the front entrance.

"Were they sick?"

Knowing Jack would continue to pelt him with questions because Rex hadn't given him any details, he slowly turned to face the city boy. He met those captivating gray eyes. "My mother died when I was sixteen. My father hit her hard enough it killed her."

"Oh, man. That sucks." Jack didn't look away. "Your father?"

"Just before my seventeenth birthday, my brother shot and killed him."

Yes, Rex had delivered the message for the shock value. However, it didn't work the way he'd intended.

"I can only imagine how hard it was for your brother. No doubt he had a good reason."

Rex narrowed his eyes. "And you figure this how?"

Jack's head tilted slightly to the side. "Deductive reasoning. If your father killed your mother, it wasn't like he was a pillar of the community. I figure there was a reason for your brother to do what he did."

His throat felt tight. Rex had never gotten that sort of response from anyone. For the most part, people were quick to assume Rafe was homicidal and it had all been a tragedy. Jack's response made Rex like him all the more.

"I know I'm not your favorite person," Jack said softly. "But if you ever want to talk about it, I've heard I'm a good listener."

Rex nodded. He wasn't sure he was ready to share all the details with Jack. The story would surely send the man running for the hills and he'd grown quite comfortable with having him around.

"What about your parents?" Rex asked, walking across the parking lot.

Jack fell into step with him. "My mother left when I was a kid. Never heard from her. No idea if she's even still alive. My father passed away a few years back."

Rex heard the sadness in Jack's tone. Clearly, he missed his old man. "Sorry to hear that."

"Thanks."

"Any brothers or sisters?"

"Only child."

"Sounds lonely." Rex opened the door to the small square building that housed the office. He stepped back, allowed Jack to walk in front of him.

"Wasn't too bad, I guess. I had my Dad. And you? You've just got the one brother?"

"Yeah. His name's Rafe."

"Older or younger?"

Rex walked out into the fenced area where they kept the rows of plants and flowers. "Younger."

"He live in Coyote Ridge?"

Rex glanced over at Jack, kept walking. "No. Disappeared when he was eighteen. Set out for greener pastures, I figure."

"Do you see him at all?"

Rex shook his head. "Every day I pray he'll come back. So far, no one upstairs seems to be listening."

They walked in silence for a moment. Rex pretended to be looking around, secretly hoping the conversation wouldn't end. This was the most they'd talked about their personal lives since the night they met.

It wasn't long before Jack broke the silence with, "How long have you been planning to open a bed-and-breakfast?"

Rex grinned. "Since I was thirteen years old."

Jack chuckled. "Quite some time ago, huh?"

Rex couldn't help but smile. "If you're insinuatin' that I'm old, I assure you, I'm only thirty."

"Ouch. The big three-oh already. Gotta be tough."

Rex smirked. "I take it you're not that far behind me, city boy."

"Twenty-nine and holding."

"Yeah?" Rex peered over at a row of plants. As much as he wanted to start getting the front fixed up, he had to wait. Until they had the front porch replaced, a flower garden would simply get in the way. "Until when?"

"July. The *end* of July."

Rex laughed. He liked Jack. A hell of a lot more than he thought he would. They truly didn't have much in common, but the guy was easy to be around. Plus, everyone seemed to get along with him. Even Bristol had had great things to say about Jack. Considering Rex hadn't known the two of them had spent any time together, he found it interesting.

"So, what are we here for?" Jack asked, fingering the leaves of a large plant.

"Gravel."

Jack frowned. "Gravel?"

"For the ground. With all the crews moving across the yard, I need to shore it up, keep it from being trampled too much. Figured I'd make a decent path using that and some plywood."

"So, why come to a nursery and not a hardware store? Don't they usually have gravel to go with their plywood?"

"They do." Rex turned when he heard footsteps heading their way. "But they don't have *this* guy."

"Well, I'll be damned," Byron Cartwright said with a crooked grin. "Didn't expect to see you 'round these parts."

When Rex reached for Byron's hand, the man jerked him forward, offering a back-slapping hug. Rex returned it, then stepped back. "Byron, I'd like you to meet Jack Cunningham. Jack, this is an old friend of mine, Byron Cartwright."

"Nice to meet you," Jack said, holding his hand out.

"Same." Byron's gaze slid over him slowly, his smile never dimming. "Never imagined you'd start datin' a city boy, Rex."

"Oh, we're not dating," Jack blurted.

Rex merely nodded, gave Byron a crooked smile. He'd known Byron most of his life, had spent a few years fucking the man to pass the time. It had been a discreet relationship that had ended amicably. They were still close, but only friends these days.

"Rex is letting me stay at … uh … the B and B."

Byron pursed his lips, nodding. "The B and B?" His dark brown eyes shot to Rex and he belted out a laugh. "Last I heard, that place was gutted. Where you got him sleepin'?"

"In my guest room," Rex assured him.

"I'm helping out with the construction," Jack inserted.

"Is that so?" Byron's assessing gaze slid over him again, his megawatt smile still in place.

Rex laughed. "He's tryin', anyway." Turning his attention to Byron, he smiled. "So. You got someone to load the gravel, or should I?"

"I'll have Spencer bring it over."

"Spencer? My cousin Spencer?" Rex asked.

"One and the same." Byron must have noticed Rex's concerned look because he grinned. "Don't you worry about him. Not my type."

Rex wasn't so sure about that, but he let it go. For now.

Knowing Byron would give him shit for the rest of the day if he allowed it, Rex turned his focus on the business at hand. Figuring now was not the time to dredge up the past or to put too much attention on the city boy who was quickly pulling Rex into his orbit, he set out to get shit done.

GRABBING THE BEER HE HAD SNAGGED FROM Rex's refrigerator, Jack walked out onto the third-floor deck just off the kitchen, the cool night air a welcome relief to the dry heat inside the apartment. It was cold out tonight, but the wind had died down somewhat. He'd opted for the deck off the back of the house so he didn't have to watch the goings-on in town tonight. As it was, Jack felt all alone but he wasn't sure why that was. It had been a good day. One that had given him some surprising insight into Rex Sharpe.

After Rex had introduced him to Byron Cartwright, it hadn't taken Jack long to pick up on a few of the looks that passed between the two men. If he wasn't mistaken—and he didn't think he was—those two had been in a relationship previously. What Jack wanted to know was whether or not that had been jealousy in Rex's tone when he asked about his cousin working for the nursery owner.

Then again, he knew it shouldn't matter. What Rex did in his spare time wasn't any of Jack's concern. They were simply two men sharing an apartment temporarily, working alongside one another from time to time.

Jack had spent the afternoon helping Rex shovel the gravel out of his truck and spread it across the side yard. Hadn't taken too long, but it had required more of his muscles than he'd thought. So, he'd taken a hot shower, hoping to ease some of the aches and pains. Now he simply wanted to relax with a beer and clear his head.

The sound of a door opening below had Jack glancing down at the yard as he eased into one of the rocking chairs. A chair leg scraped against concrete, drawing his attention. He watched as a shadow grew out of the light, getting longer and longer until Rex appeared with a towel in one hand, a beer in the other. He set both on one of the tables dotting the concrete decking around the pool before glancing left, then right. Jack followed his gaze.

Despite all of the acreage, there wasn't much seclusion for the house itself. It sat close to the street in the heart of downtown Coyote Ridge and had a narrow lot until the point where it broke open and seemed to go on for miles. Jack had spent a little time wandering the property, getting some fresh air, and trying to learn a little more about Rex. He'd noticed the remains of what he assumed had been a barn, as well as the rotted shell of a small shed. Everything was old, with the exception of the pool, hot tub, and the workshop.

The pool area was framed by the farmhouse, Rex's workshop, a six-foot fence, and acres of pastureland. For the most part, the hot tub offered as much privacy as one could ask for outside unless someone was sitting on one of the decks like Jack was. He wasn't sure what or who Rex was looking for, but a second later, he figured out *why* the cowboy had been scanning the horizon. Rex quickly discarded his T-shirt, then shucked the jeans he'd been wearing.

Holy.

Fucking.

Shit.

Jack's breath lodged in his throat as he stared down at a very naked cowboy. Damn. Admittedly, he did enjoy the sight of that body.

Although he knew it was wrong to be eyeing Rex—for a number of reasons—Jack couldn't seem to tear his eyes away from the sight.

Rex's wide back was layered with muscle just like his chest. There wasn't much marring his smooth, bronzed skin. No tattoos, only a few small scars. He watched intently as Rex moved toward the stairs that would lead him to the water. Jack swallowed hard as Rex stepped into the tub, his feet disappearing, then his calves. For whatever reason, Rex paused there, and Jack willed him to keep going, to remove the temptation from view, because damn it all to hell, Jack's dick was hard as iron.

He remembered the warmth of Rex's skin, the way it had felt beneath his hands. As Rex stood there, partially immersed in the water, Jack held his breath and tried to force all the erotic thoughts out of his head.

"This isn't helping my cause," he whispered. "Not at all."

Jack could admit he'd been trying to convince himself their time together had been a mistake. Mostly because he had a hard time accepting that he'd fucked up so royally where Rex was concerned. Sometimes it seemed as though it was merely a dream, a figment of his imagination. Then he would catch a whiff of Rex and it would slam into his brain, a flash of memory vivid in the details.

Of course, Rex hadn't brought up the subject, so neither had Jack. They were both doing well to pretend it never happened.

Until now.

Seeing Rex like that … Jack wanted to stroll down there and jump into that boiling water with the man. He wanted to feel— even just one more time—what Rex had made him feel. He'd spent his entire adult life looking for something to sate the ache inside him. Little had he known he was looking in the wrong direction all this time.

Jack's hand inadvertently went to his cock, rubbing absently through his sweatpants.

He jerked his hand away and stared down at his traitorous dick. What the fuck was going on here? He was supposed to be moving on with his life. After the last incident with Rex, Jack had made a pact with himself. No relationships in his future and certainly no sex. Those things always complicated matters.

Suddenly, Rex turned toward the house. His eyes shifted to the balcony Jack was on, and he knew there was no way he could hide from view. Jack did his best to keep his eyes on Rex's face and not allow them to drift down his torso to the thick erection bobbing out proudly from his body.

He failed. He was a voyeur, damn it.

Jack's body heated, his ass clenching as though remembering the way Rex had stretched him, then filled him so perfectly. He'd never experienced anything like it. Jack swallowed, his hand once again pressing against his cock. He glanced right then left to ensure no one was paying any attention to him. He couldn't see anyone, forced himself to believe no one cared, that they were all going about their business, too caught up in their own lives to worry that Jack was slowly coming apart at the seams.

Jack turned his attention back to Rex, watching as he leaned against the contoured chair, the jets causing bubbles to form, obscuring Jack's view.

"No," he mumbled. "No, no, no. I want to see." The lights only allowed for Jack to see distorted bits and pieces under the moving water.

Long seconds passed. Hell, it was probably more like minutes as Rex relaxed in the hot tub while Jack held his breath and stared down at him, willing those damn bubbles to stop.

And then they did.

As though the universe heard him, the night silenced once more, the jets in the hot tub stopped, revealing a very naked, very erect cowboy relaxing right before his eyes. The silence was almost deafening.

Jack discreetly slipped his hand inside his sweatpants and palmed his cock. He had no idea what spurred him on or why he was compelled to watch this man while he jacked off. He'd never had this sort of reaction before but something deep inside him told him that this was exactly what he'd been looking for all along. Jack had prided himself on being a good, decent man. He always treated people well. He held doors for women, always paid for dinner. He helped the elderly when they needed help, tried to keep to the straight and narrow.

But right now, he wanted to let that all go, to do something taboo. Something to prove to himself that he had a wild side. A side that was worthy of a man like Rex, because whether he liked it or not, Jack couldn't deny he'd developed a connection with Rex Sharpe, and he wasn't ready to let go of it yet.

No relationships, no sex.

Yeah, yeah, yeah. He shrugged off his subconscious. Right now he didn't have the willpower to stick to that plan.

With his beer in one hand and his cock in the other, Jack watched Rex.

After a few minutes, Rex moved, leaning over and setting his beer in one of the cup holders. He returned a few seconds later and leaned back, this time his attention focused upward. Jack stared, wondering if Rex could see him.

"No way," he whispered, his hand fisting his cock more firmly. "Too dark." There were no lights aside from the one in the kitchen, so Jack knew Rex could see his silhouette, not what he was doing. But even if he could, Jack wasn't sure he could stop.

Rex leaned his head back and his eyes closed about the time his hand slipped beneath the water to fist his cock. The hot tub lights highlighted what he was doing even if his movements were slightly distorted as the water shifted around him.

Jack's breaths came in sharp pants as he jacked off watching Rex do the same.

He couldn't believe he was doing this. For one, he wasn't the sort who enjoyed public displays of ... well, anything. Never in his life had he jacked off while outside, nor when someone else was watching. That wasn't in his nature. He tended to prefer privacy.

He had no idea what the fuck it meant, but it didn't feel wrong. Different, sure, but not wrong.

Jack's fist worked his cock faster, tighter as he kept his eyes locked on Rex. He was a sight to behold with his eyes closed, the muscles flexing in his arm as he stroked his dick, his chest rising and falling as he succumbed to the pleasure.

A soft moan escaped Jack, and Rex's eyes opened, once again fixed on where he was sitting. Rex never stopped jerking his cock and neither did Jack.

It felt like hours passed, but he knew it was only minutes.

Jack moaned again, unable to help himself.

"Fuck." Rex's voice drifted up to the balcony, his body jerking.

It was that exact moment when Jack lost control, coming hard at the same time Rex did.

As he struggled to catch his breath, Jack expected to feel shame for what he'd just done, but it never came. Confusion, embarrassment, sure. He was outside, where anyone could see him, and he'd just rubbed one out by watching a man.

But there was another emotion churning through him. One he'd never felt before. Something that felt a hell of a lot like ... freedom. As though this was where he was meant to be, *how* he was supposed to be. Carefree, open. Perhaps honest with himself for the first time in his life.

"I think it's safe to say I'm gay," he muttered to himself, his chest tightening.

Talk about a revelation.

The bad news was that Jack had absolutely no fucking idea what he was supposed to do with that information.

Fifteen

Monday, January 21, 2019

REX AWOKE EARLY ON MONDAY MORNING FEELING better than had in a long time. He'd taken some downtime over the weekend, keeping an eye on the plumbing and electrical, but opting not to do anything that would get in the way of progress. Not the sort who enjoyed being sidelined, Rex was eager to get the day started and to jump into the next phase of his project.

With a renewed sense of purpose, he showered and dressed, then headed to the kitchen to make coffee, grab a protein bar. The new windows were being installed today and Rex wanted to be ready and available for when they showed.

All was quiet when he sat at the breakfast bar while the coffee brewed, so Rex did his best to keep the noise to a minimum, figuring Jack was asleep.

Although he suspected it was a fluke and not a sign of things to come, Rex couldn't stop thinking about Friday night. About the way Jack had watched him in the hot tub. Although neither of them had mentioned what happened, Rex was very aware that it had. Despite the distance between them, something had connected them to that moment.

Granted, Jack probably hadn't realized it, but the light on the front of the workshop had been left on, which had cast the perfect glow over him, allowing Rex to see exactly what he was doing, even from down below. And there was no denying Jack had been stroking himself as he watched Rex do the same.

Rex hadn't expected it. Not the incident and certainly not the way it made him feel. With every passing second, Rex found himself growing tired of pretending nothing was going on between them. Sure, he knew it could merely be curiosity on Jack's part. He'd even considered that he might be curious, too. After all, Rex had never been with a man who hadn't known who he was, what he wanted.

Jack might be merely curious, but Rex sensed there was an underlying need that had never been sated. It seemed the longer he was there, the stronger it got.

As for whether or not that could lead to something more, Rex wasn't sure. And he knew he couldn't waste any more time worrying about it, either.

By the time seven o'clock rolled around, Rex had downed two cups of coffee, finished off the protein bar, and skimmed an update to the design that Kylie had emailed him. She had gladly incorporated a couple of ideas he had regarding the guest bathrooms without pause. He appreciated that she was holding true to her word, allowing him to design but providing him with the vast experience she had. Their partnership seemed to be working well.

Rex glanced over at the hallway. He hadn't seen Jack yet and he was starting to wonder if the man intended to sleep all day.

Rex's cell phone buzzed in his pocket and he pulled it out as he made his way to the coffeepot, figuring he could finish it off before he headed downstairs. He smiled at the screen as he tapped to take the call and put it to his ear.

"Yeah?"

"You know you can't answer the phone like that, right? You'll never get any business that way."

Rex laughed. "You called my cell phone, Bristol."

"I know that," she said testily. "Still. A pleasant hello wouldn't kill you. You're grumbly enough."

"Grumbly?" Rex pulled the coffee carafe off the warmer and poured the rest into his cup.

"Yes. It's in your voice, young man. You growl when you speak."

"Young man?" Rex laughed. "I'm older than you, remember?"

"Only by three months," Bristol countered. "And since *I'm* young, that makes *you* young."

His gaze shot to the hallway again. He *was* young, wasn't he? And so was Jack. Why couldn't they experiment for a little while? It wasn't like he was looking to settle down with the city boy or anything. Perhaps he could expound on what had happened the other night, seduce Jack, take him to bed, and get lost in him for a while.

"Rex Sharpe, what are you doin'? Besides ignoring me?"

"Huh?"

"That's what I thought. I think we're gonna have to do somethin' about your phone etiquette."

"Since when are you worried about my phone etiquette?"

"Since it sank in that you're opening a bed-and-breakfast. It's just one of the things we have to work on before you can open the door to the public."

"We're a long way from that," he reminded her.

"It'll be here before you know it, believe me. That means we have to come up with something."

"Are you applyin' for the job of answerin' phones, Bristol?" Rex countered.

"It probably wouldn't hurt." She sighed. "So, how's it comin'? I heard you've got windows and doors comin' today."

"I do. AC should be finished today, too."

"So you'll be focusing on the interior next?" Bristol's voice had risen, excitement slipping out. "I cannot wait until it's done, Rex. Can't wait until you've got people beggin' to stay there all the time."

He still had too much shit to do before he could even begin to think about that. On top of getting the house finished, he probably needed to do some marketing to get people interested in staying there. He honestly figured he'd spend the first month he was officially open with his thumb up his ass.

Not that he would let Travis know that.

"Quit doubting yourself," Bristol stated firmly.

Rex wasn't sure how she could read him so easily, but his best friend had always been that way.

"So, when are we gonna hang out?"

He smiled. "You're welcome here anytime. You know that."

"Sure, sure. But I figure since you've got company and all… I wouldn't want to be a third wheel."

"What are you talkin' about?"

"The incredibly handsome Jack Cunningham, the man currently sleepin' in the guest room. He *is* sleepin' in the guest room, right?"

Rex laughed. She was always fishing. "He is most definitely sleepin' in the guest room. We're just friends. You should come hang out, see for yourself."

"I have. I've seen for myself that Jack has eyes for you. And bein' that I am your best friend and all…" Bristol laughed. "Don't want to put a damper on your sexy times with Jack."

Rex barked a laugh as his face heated. He wasn't sure why, but he tended to get embarrassed when Bristol teased him. "It's not like that," he countered. "There are no sexy times, B."

He and Bristol were close. She'd always been his rock. Always trying to talk him off one ledge or another. It was safe to say he'd been rebellious in his younger years. While he had accepted the curve balls life had thrown his way, Rex had had a difficult time accepting who he truly was. Partly because it had altered his and Rafe's lives in an irreparable way. Yet Bristol hadn't let him hide out. Even when Rafe had left and Rex had fallen apart, blaming himself for everything, Bristol had stood beside him, holding his hand every step of the way, ensuring he knew she was there to support him.

And he appreciated her for that. She was the one he knew he could always turn to.

"But you want there to be," Bristol noted. "Sexy times, that is."

Rex felt compelled to argue his case more. "There's nothin' goin' on between me and Jack."

"I didn't ask you that. I was merely makin' an observation. You, Rex Sharpe, want somethin' to be goin' on with Jack."

"No. *Yes*. Maybe." Rex sighed.

"So why not take a chance? I mean, what more could you want than a super cute guy who's hiding out from the real world?"

Rex sighed. That *was* what Jack was doing and he'd be smart to remember that. Jack wasn't here because this was his plan in life. He was hiding from his problems.

She must've taken his sigh for something else because Bristol said, "But I'm not pushin' you, Rex. If Jack's not what you want, then ignore everything I've said."

Forcing some cheer into his tone, Rex said, "Trust me, I always ignore you."

"I *know*," she said with another laugh. "But seriously. I actually called to see if you wanted to grab lunch one of these days. I've got a new teacher coming in, but I'm confident I've got her training covered this time, which means I won't have to fill in so much."

"Whenever you want," he told her. "I'm always up for lunch."

"Hmm. What about dinner?"

Rex chuckled. "Just like you to change your mind although it was your suggestion."

"I know, right? But I was thinkin' I could stop by tomorrow night, we can watch *The Masked Singer* and chow down on Chinese."

"Make it pizza," he suggested, "and you've got yourself a date."

"Pizza it is. I'll see you tomorrow night."

After agreeing, Rex disconnected the call and stared down at his phone. He really should take some time to talk to Bristol about Jack. Perhaps if he told her what was going on, she could give him her perspective. From the outside looking in, maybe it wasn't as bad as Rex continued to make it out to be.

Then again, perhaps he was merely trying to come up with another excuse to get into bed with the guy.

JACK COULD ADMIT HE WAS A CHICKENSHIT.

Yep. He said it.

To prove it, he'd spent most of the weekend avoiding Rex. He even waited until he knew Rex had left the apartment before he snuck out of his room for food. He would slip into the kitchen, grab a few things he could snack on during the day before disappearing into his room once again. He had avoided breakfast and coffee, along with lunch simply to keep from running into him.

Of course, Jack knew that wouldn't last forever. At some point, he had to suck it up and look Rex in the eye. After what had happened on Friday—the mutual masturbation show—Jack couldn't seem to stop blushing. Every time he thought about it, he felt his face heat and his ears flame.

And still he felt no shame for what he'd done. Merely embarrassment. He had jacked off while he watched Rex. He knew Rex couldn't see what he was doing, but that didn't mean he wasn't aware of it. For all Jack knew, the man went down to the hot tub and jacked off every night before bed.

Jack's cock swelled and throbbed just as it had every damn time he thought about the incident.

But he had to leave his room at some point, otherwise he wouldn't be holding up his end of their deal. Jack was supposed to be helping out with the work being done on the house. Even if there wasn't much he could do, it was only right for him to offer. Which he would.

Tomorrow.

For now, he was starving. Since it was dinnertime, he had more incentive to come out. If he was lucky, Rex wouldn't say anything about it. Maybe he was as embarrassed as Jack was.

The thought made him smile. For some reason, he didn't think Rex was the sort of guy who embarrassed easily.

Forcing himself to his feet, Jack took a deep breath and decided to get it over with.

Like a kid trying to sneak past his parents' bedroom in the middle of the night, Jack slipped out of his room and down the hall. Surprisingly, Duke wasn't lying on the floor the way he had been for the past week. He paused at the mouth of the hallway, listening for any sounds that would tell him whether Rex was in the apartment or not.

Nothing.

He took a deep breath and stepped into the living room. Slowly. Quietly.

He felt like an idiot.

Hell, he *was* an idiot.

He was a grown man. A man who was capable of taking care of his own basic needs. So what if he'd found pleasure in watching Rex? That didn't make it a bad thing.

Just as Jack was about to go into the kitchen, the front door swung open. He nearly jumped out of his skin when Rex stepped inside, a bag in his hand, Duke trotting in behind him.

Their eyes met, held.

He wasn't sure he was even breathing.

A barely discernible smile pulled Rex's lips upward. However, Rex didn't say a word as he closed the door and headed for the kitchen.

For a moment, Jack debated on whether or not he should go back to his room. Hide out until Rex went to bed.

Chickenshit.

Damn it.

Forcing his feet to move, Jack followed Rex into the kitchen. He stopped abruptly when he noticed all the food sitting on the island.

"Wow." Jack took in fresh vegetables, potatoes, and slabs of meat. "You're … making dinner."

"That was the plan." Rex began poking holes in the potatoes. "I figured I'd grill steaks tonight, force you to come out of your hiding place for a bit."

Well, hell. So much for thinking Rex had been too busy to notice.

"Can I—" Jack cleared his throat and tried again. "Can I help?"

"There's a bag of charcoal in my workshop. Meet me on the back porch."

"Got it." Without waiting for Rex to say anything more, Jack made a beeline out of the kitchen, down the exterior stairs, and right to the metal building.

It didn't take long to find the bag of charcoal. He picked it up and carried it back toward the house, where Rex was now standing by the grill on the main-floor wraparound deck. He noticed two beers sitting on one of the small tables.

"Thanks." Rex took the charcoal and motioned for one of the chairs. "Grab a beer, have a seat."

Desperately wanting to go back inside and hide out, Jack fought the urge. He was not going to run away. Not when there was nothing to run from. So, he grabbed one of the beers and plopped into one of the chairs while Rex got the grill going. A few minutes later, after the steaks were sizzling over the coals, Rex grabbed the other beer and took a seat.

"You must've been tired these past couple of days," Rex said as he crossed his ankles and tipped back his beer.

"I ..." What the hell was he supposed to say to that?

"Figured that was why you hid out in your room."

"Yeah," Jack lied, then felt bad for it. "No, actually. It wasn't sleep. I was ... working." Okay, so maybe he was a chickenshit.

"So, the creativity's flowing once again?"

"Mostly." Not exactly the truth, but there had been a little progress.

The two of them stared out at the endless acres of grass, neither of them saying anything for the longest time. Jack felt bad sitting there when Rex had put forth the effort to invite him to dinner.

"What made you want to open a bed-and-breakfast?" Jack blurted when he felt the silence begin to suffocate him.

Rex's eyes shifted over toward him. "Nothin' better to do, I guess."

"Really? Just a spur-of-the-moment decision?" Jack chuckled. "When you were thirteen?"

Rex shrugged and Jack knew there was more to the story.

"Tell me. I'd love to hear it."

Rex sighed, took a long pull on his beer, and stared out at the field once more. "When I was a kid, my mother took me and Rafe to a lodge. Great big place. I fell in love with it. Not only the look, but the feel of it. Rustic and quaint, lots of people, plenty for everyone to do. We never got bored. In fact, I remember begging my mother to stay forever." He motioned toward the house with his hand. "Sort of the same feel here. That's what I'm going for, anyway.

"So when my mother told me that my grandfather was handing the house over to me when I turned eighteen, I had an epiphany. I could see the transformation in the house, visualize what it would look like. From that moment onward, I'd imagined exactly how it would be one day."

"I'm glad it could come to fruition for you," Jack told him, making a point not to look at Rex. He got the feeling the man felt vulnerable merely sharing that story. "What'd you do before this?"

"Construction."

That made sense. Certainly explained how he knew the ins and outs of what needed to be done.

"You're making all the furniture for the house?" Jack asked.

"Hobby of mine." Rex's attention turned to the grill, then back toward the setting sun. "Something I do to pass the time."

"You're quite talented." Although that was a completely innocent comment, as soon as the words were out of Jack's mouth, his mind took a hard left turn, directly into the gutter. He knew he was blushing, hated that he was.

Son of a bitch.

"So, you married?" Rex asked, a hint of amusement in his words.

"What? No. Why would you ask that?"

Rex shrugged. "Can't help but overhear some of your phone conversations. Small place and all."

"Oh." Jack took a long pull on his beer. "No, I'm not married. Never made it to the altar." He stared out. "I was engaged though. Three times."

"Wow. Three, huh? That's quite the effort."

Thinking of it that way had Jack laughing. "A lot of effort. Unfortunately, none of them worked out."

"Why not?"

Jack shrugged and tipped his bottle to his lips. "Irreconcilable differences."

"Or maybe you were simply playing for the wrong team?"

Jack couldn't help but laugh. "Or that."

And as he snuck a peek at Rex relaxing in the chair, Jack was starting to question just how much truth there was in that statement. Not one of the women he'd dated had ever made him feel the way Rex did. Never had he enjoyed the physical intimacy—or any intimacy for that matter—the way he did with Rex.

Considering how turned on he was simply sitting here with Rex, Jack was starting to wonder if he was personally responsible for all the failed engagements.

Perhaps those women hadn't been what he was looking for after all.

Sixteen

"I'M TELLING YOU, THAT'S GOT TO BE Cameron Diaz," Bristol exclaimed when the character on screen finished singing.

"I disagree," Jack argued. "I think it's Paris Hilton."

Bristol sighed sharply. "Seriously? What makes you even think that? No way does Paris Hilton have a voice like that."

Rex's eyes volleyed back and forth, following the conversation that had been going on for the past half hour as the three of them downed pepperoni pizza and watched *The Masked Singer*. Rex didn't much care for the show, but he knew Bristol loved it, so generally, he didn't mind downing a beer while she rambled on and on about who she believed was hidden behind whatever ridiculous costume they'd come up with.

Now that Jack was here, it didn't seem as though Rex was needed. Or any of the judges on the show, for that matter. Bristol and Jack had that part covered, too.

"Now that you mention it," Jack said, tapping his chin, "maybe you're right."

Bristol's smile widened.

"But…"

Bristol's smile fell.

"I don't think it's Cameron Diaz," Jack told her.

Bristol turned to Rex, her eyes wide. "What do you think?"

Rex chuckled. "I think I need another beer."

Pushing to his feet, he escaped to the kitchen while the argument ensued. The two of them were getting along like they'd known one another their entire lives. It was actually kind of fascinating.

"Hey, Rex?" Bristol hollered. "You mind bringing the cinnamon sticks in here?"

He snatched a beer from the fridge and the box of cinnamon bread things from the counter and joined them in the living room. It was then that he noticed Bristol had moved from sitting on the sofa near Jack to sitting in the armchair Rex had been occupying.

When he handed over the box, she grinned wide. "Thanks."

Rex dropped onto the sofa, ensuring he kept some space between himself and Jack.

"So, do you like the show?" Bristol asked Jack when it went to commercial.

"I do. I'm surprised, but I do."

Rex frowned. "You've never watched this before?"

"Not until tonight, no. I don't tend to watch much television." Jack twisted, turning so he faced Rex at an angle. "You?"

Rex nodded his chin in Bristol's direction. "She's in love with it. I simply watch to make her happy."

Bristol laughed. "It's true. He does. And that's why I insist on watching it every week if we can. I make him record it for the times we miss."

"So you like punishing him?" Jack reached for his beer.

"I do. It's so much fun."

"How long have you two known each other?" Jack asked, his head swiveling, eyes darting between the two of them.

"All our lives," Bristol told him. "I grew up only a couple of streets over. Rex and I were in the same class every year in school."

"And you've been friends all this time?"

"I know," Bristol said dramatically, scrunching her nose at Rex. "You're wonderin' how I survived."

Jack laughed but didn't glance Rex's way.

"Until she got married," Rex said, then closed his eyes. Why had he brought that up?

"You were married?" Jack asked, his eyes wide, his tone shocked.

"For a little while," Bristol said, her gaze dropping to the floor. Rex knew she did not like to talk about that time in her life.

"When did you figure out you were gay?" Jack questioned Rex.

Based on his tone, it sounded as though Jack was attempting to redirect to get the heat off Bristol. While he didn't care to discuss this, he appreciated that Jack could see she'd been bothered by the line of questioning.

Not looking at Jack, Rex answered. "I've known I was gay since I was a teenager."

"Oh."

"What about you?" Bristol asked Jack. "At what point did you know *you* were gay?"

Rex nearly fell out of his chair laughing when Jack's eyes widened the size of dinner plates.

"What?" Bristol asked, horror reflecting on her pretty face. "What did I say?"

"Jack's not gay," Rex said without enthusiasm.

Her gaze shot to Jack. "Oh, I'm sorry. I didn't mean to insinuate. I just thought…"

"What?" Jack asked, his voice low, tone curious.

Bristol glanced at Rex as though seeking his permission to continue. Knowing it wouldn't matter at this point, Rex nodded.

"Well, I've just seen the way you look at Rex."

Jack's eyebrows shot downward. "How do I look at him?"

Bristol sat up. "You know what? Never mind. I need to learn to mind my own business."

Jack reached over, touched her arm gently. "No, please. I mean, I don't think you're entirely wrong. It's just…"

Rex waited along with Bristol for Jack to continue. Rex wasn't sure where this was going, but he found himself riveted.

"It's just that I didn't realize I was even interested in men until recently."

"Really?" Bristol asked.

Jack leaned back, his attention solely on Bristol as he spoke. "I've practically been engaged since I was nineteen. To three different women."

"Oh, wow. That's a lot of … engagement rings."

Rex laughed alongside Jack as he got comfortable. He propped his feet on the coffee table, rested his beer on his stomach, and watched the two of them.

"True."

"What caused them to fall apart?" Bristol questioned. "If you don't mind me asking."

Jack seemed quite content to share his life story with Bristol. "I'm not sure I can pinpoint any one thing. Well, not until this last one. With Tina … I came home and found her in bed with another guy."

"That fucking sucks," Bristol snarled. "How could she do that to you?"

"According to her, she was only fucking him because she thought I would be interested in a threesome. The guy she was with is bisexual. Evidently, she thought I wanted to experiment with the two of them." He cleared his throat. "In fact, when I walked in on them, he offered to have a go at me."

"He *said* that?" Bristol's eyes narrowed.

"He did."

"Wow. How … romantic." Bristol rolled her eyes. "What a douche."

Jack laughed. "I turned him down, then left. Tina was yelling at me as I walked out the door. We've talked a few times since. She's a little irate at the moment. Tried to turn it all back on me."

"Did you tell her you wanted a threesome?"

Jack set his beer on the table, and Rex focused on what he would say next.

"No."

"Then where'd she come up with the idea?" Rex found himself asking, needing to know how this had come about.

"On occasion," Jack said, speaking mostly to his lap, "I would get drunk, and Tina and I would talk about some of our fantasies. I might've mentioned having fantasized about men a few times."

"But not about a threesome?" Bristol asked.

"No. Never. I'm not the type of guy who's interested in sharing."

Bristol's eyes darted over to Rex momentarily.

Jack must have thought he'd offended her, because he clarified with, "Not that there's anything wrong with a threesome. I mean, I totally get it. We love who we love. It's just not something I could do."

"Evidently, Tina thought differently," Rex whispered softly.

"What a bitch." Bristol shook her head. "I mean, it would be one thing if she'd gone about it the right way. But she was with you. It wasn't her place to go testing out the merchandise if she was looking to hook you up with a guy."

Rex laughed. Bristol did have a way with words.

"In her defense," Jack stated, "I wasn't supposed to be home that night. I'd intended to stay gone for a little while longer, finish working on a project."

"Oh, well, *that* makes it okay." Bristol threw up her hands and rolled her eyes, making Rex smile.

He loved to see her when she was so animated.

"I know, right? But yeah, instead of staying gone all weekend," Jack continued, "I got the crazy idea to make amends with her because I felt as though I'd been running away from my problems for too long. Came home and found her in my bed, the guy's dick in her ass." His eyes flared. "Oh, God. I am *so* sorry I said it like that. Totally inappropriate with present company."

Bristol waved him off, her smile flashing. "Oh, you don't have to mind your manners around me. You should hear what me and my girlfriends talk about."

"You're gay?" Jack asked her.

Rex snorted and Bristol burst into a fit of laughter.

"What's so funny?" Jack asked once the noise level returned to normal.

"No, sorry. I'm not gay. I mean my friends, who are girls. While Rex is my best *boy* friend, I have several really close *girl* friends, too. I'm very much straight."

"Ah." Jack's cheeks had more color. "Gotcha."

JACK HAD NO IDEA WHY HE WAS so chatty tonight.

Bristol was one of the nicest women he'd ever met, and from the second she stepped into the apartment tonight, she'd gone out of her way to make him feel included in their obvious plans for the evening. Initially, Jack had tried to excuse himself, but she hadn't allowed him to go running for his room.

So, they'd settled in to watch *The Masked Singer* and somehow, they'd ended up on this topic.

"So, what is it that you do?" he asked her, hoping they could ignore his blunder and the way his face heated from embarrassment.

"I own a daycare center," Bristol explained.

"Oh, wow." Jack knew he looked sincerely horrified, but he couldn't help it.

Bristol's smile never wavered. "You don't know how many people have that same reaction. But honestly, it's the best job in the entire world. I mean, sure, there are moments when I want to pull my hair out, but I wouldn't trade it."

"She's a saint," Rex noted with a smirk.

"I'd say so."

"And you?" Bristol prompted. "What do you do?"

"Artist."

"Like paintings?" she inquired.

"No. Like comic books."

Bristol's blue eyes rounded. "Shut the front door!" Her eyes narrowed suddenly and then her mouth fell open. "Oh. My. God. You're *the* Jack Cunningham?" She shot to the edge of the cushion, her hands vibrating. "As in the Jack Cunningham who writes *Thunderstone?*"

"The one and only," he admitted shyly. Although he'd been to plenty of Comic Cons over the years, Jack couldn't seem to get used to fans having this sort of reaction.

"Writes?" Rex asked. "Or draws?"

Jack smiled but couldn't quite meet his gaze. "Both. A few years ago, I went out on a limb with an idea I'd come with. It's the only thing I've written, though."

"Rex!" Bristol stood, then sat, then stood again. "You didn't tell me that was who he was."

"Well, that's because I didn't know," he said, watching her with an amused gleam in his eyes.

"How could you *not* know?" Bristol's gaze shot to Jack's face once more. "How could anyone *not* know who you are?"

Rex obviously considered the question rhetorical because he didn't respond, and Jack wasn't sure what he was supposed to say, if anything.

"Well, how 'bout we don't make a big deal of it," Rex suggested.

For a moment, Jack wondered if Rex could read his mind.

"Yeah. Yeah, you're right." Bristol couldn't seem to sit still. "I can keep my mouth shut. I can."

Rex laughed. "I've heard that before."

"Oh, hush it, Sharpe," she snapped without heat. "I will. I'll be quiet." Her eyes remained on Jack's face. "But could I get your autograph? I mean, I've got every comic you've done."

"Really?" Jack wasn't sure why this surprised him so much.

"Really." Bristol's attention shot to the television screen. "Oh, my God! They unmasked the pony. Was that…?"

"Okay, I think you've had enough for one night," Rex stated, clicking the television off.

"Hey, wait! I need to see that."

"Well, you can catch it on Hulu and go through it one more time. I know how you are when it comes to surprise endings."

Bristol huffed a breath, then got to her feet. "You're right." She smiled shyly at Jack. "I'm not all that fond of surprises."

"Amongst other things," Rex stated, grabbing the empty pizza box and taking it to the kitchen.

Jack remained where he was, watching Bristol and listening to Rex rummage around the kitchen. He couldn't remember a night he'd been this content in quite some time. Nothing to do but hang out. It was nice.

Too bad he didn't have friends like this back in Austin. Most of the people he interacted with had been Tina's friends. And since the demise of their relationship, he figured they wouldn't be coming back around.

"Okay, I'm gonna head out," Bristol said, pulling Jack from his thoughts.

Jack pushed to his feet.

"Do you know how long you'll be staying, Jack?" she asked when Rex came back into the room to walk her to the door.

"I'm not sure yet. I'm waiting for Tina to vacate my apartment. Until she leaves, I can't go home."

"No, you can't," Bristol said adamantly. "You don't need to be anywhere near that vicious woman."

Jack secretly liked that Bristol was coming to his defense. He didn't have much of that in his life, either. Since his father had died, Jack didn't have anyone who was there just for him.

"You're not gonna kick him out, are you?" Bristol asked Rex as he helped her into her coat.

"No. Jack can stay as long as he needs to."

Bristol's blue eyes shot over to him and Jack could've sworn there was a hint of mischief there, as though the woman had a plan.

"Say good night, Jack," Rex stated.

Jack jerked himself to attention, focused on the two of them standing with the apartment door open. "Oh, sorry. Good night, Bristol. Thanks for allowing me to intrude on your evening."

"No intrusion whatsoever. I look forward to hangin' out again."

When the door closed behind them, Jack simply stared.

Seventeen

Saturday, January 26, 2019

REX FLIPPED ON THE SHOWER, THEN WENT over to the sink to trim the scruff on his face.

He glanced at his reflection and smiled. He was happy to say that he was entirely focused on the house. There were a few more windows to install on the second floor, but with the subcontractors he'd hired, things were going much more smoothly than he'd anticipated. He knew they would be able to handle the job as would any of the other subcontractors he'd brought on board. The problem was, Rex was beginning to think he was scheduling himself right out of the very jobs he was hoping to complete.

Then again, he didn't much care for most of what was underway at the moment. Windows, doors, roofs, air ducts … the labor was intense. Better left to those who specialized in it. He preferred to keep his hands in the cosmetic side of things. So once it was time for the flooring, tile, bathtubs, sinks, etc., to go in, he'd have more than his fair share of things to do.

Rex clicked on his razor, scraped his palm over his face as he studied himself in the mirror.

No, he certainly wasn't above using the help he'd been given, either. Travis had come through, sending people every day, someone eager to earn their portion of the sweat equity that went into a place of this magnitude. There was more than enough work for everyone, and Rex had to learn to delegate the things he could. He had even considered teaching Jack a few things. The guy seemed more than willing to learn, and what could it hurt? Plus, it would allow them to spend a little time together.

Whoa, cowboy.

He instantly pulled the electric trimmer away, glaring into the dark eyes peering back at him in the glass.

"Probably ought to let the city boy stick to what he knows best."

Rex knew that if he put too much of an investment of time into training Jack, it would all be a waste when Jack went back to the city. On top of that, he knew he didn't really have time to walk Jack through some of the more difficult processes such as cutting tile or installing a backsplash. Not that they were even close to doing those things, but if they were…

"Eye on the prize, Sharpe." It was the same thing he told himself every time he got off track, his thoughts drifting to Jack. Always Jack.

He knew the man was temporary. As Jack had told Bristol, he was simply waiting for his ex to vacate his apartment and then he would be leaving. Based on Bristol's over-the-top reaction to the guy, apparently Jack was good at what he did, writing comic books. Or drawing them, whatever went into the process. Which meant Jack couldn't be absent from his life for too long.

Maybe Jack could help him with a name while he was there, though. Being that Rex was in the middle of several small towns, most people never traveled to these parts. Those who did lived there. Which meant something catchy and clever would likely help bring people their way. With Dead Heat Ranch not too far away, equipped with cattle drives, horseback riding, cabins, and dinner with the cowboys, Rex would have to have a real draw to get people to even think about this place. And he wasn't sure the idea of a romantic couples' getaway would be enough to keep the rooms occupied.

Rex clicked the razor off, then set it on the charging base. He then stripped off his sweatpants and padded naked into the shower. The warm water pelted his skin, making him sigh.

If Jack had been looking for a romantic place to stay, what would've been his criteria? Rex had a pool and a hot tub. He had a couple of grills. Eventually he'd have an outdoor gazebo or something where people could congregate if they chose. The kitchen would be fully equipped, the rooms nice, beds comfortable. Lots of places to chill. Fireplaces, nice view. But other than that?

What was he going to have? Horseback riding? Perhaps. Eventually. But what else?

Shit. Maybe he should find a way to spice things up a bit. He knew Alluring Indulgence was a huge hit with those who visited. Kink and BDSM seemed to be the draw. Rex had never been, but he'd checked it out on the internet just to get ideas. They had some fancy spa, rooms that ranged from standard to presidential, plus a handful of playrooms and popular nightclubs. Definitely not the sort of place Rex was going for, nor was it a place he even cared to visit. He wasn't into all that kinky shit. Being tied up…

No fucking way.

Granted, it had been a long fucking time since Rex had had any spice whatsoever. Hell, until Jack, it had been a long fucking time since he'd had sex of *any* sort. After he'd moved out of his uncle's house, Rex had dabbled in the serial dating lifestyle a little but found it wasn't all it was cracked up to be. Rex really wasn't the type who enjoyed small talk, so getting to know people wasn't something he was good at. First dates scared the shit out of him.

Then there'd been the fling with Byron.

Byron had been phenomenal in bed, but not once during all their interactions had Rex felt the sort of connection he'd felt with Jack in the couple of short, awkward trysts they'd had. While their sexual fling had lasted a little over a year, it had never been serious. They'd used one another to scratch the itch, no feelings, no complications.

But that had dissolved a long time ago.

That didn't mean Rex wasn't interested in meeting someone. Getting to know them. Dinners, dates, nights spent chilling in front of the television, then rolling around naked for a while. Sure, Rex was all for meeting the person he could do that with.

If that someone was like Jack.

Rex closed his eyes, dipped his head under the hot water. He hated that he continued to have these thoughts. It had been two weeks since the night when Rex allowed Jack to use him, and nearly three weeks since Rex drove the intoxicated city boy back to his hotel room. And though Rex remembered everything about their encounters, including the anger and frustration he'd felt toward Jack for treating him so callously the last time, Rex still wanted the man.

Hell, his cock was practically roaring for release, desperate for some attention, for someone else's touch. As stupid as that might be.

Not for the first time in the past two days, Rex wondered if Jack would be interested in another sexual encounter. Perhaps Rex could allow Jack to use him again, to figure out exactly what it was he enjoyed about being with a man. Because Rex knew Jack enjoyed it. He merely needed some time to adjust to his recently acknowledged desires.

Fucking hell.

Rex scrubbed shampoo into his hair, then rinsed it quickly. He needed to get out of this damn shower while he had some sense left. He poured body wash onto the puff and scrubbed roughly, his mind threatening to derail once more.

Maybe he should start on one of the house projects. Perhaps it was a little soon, but if he could get focused, there was a better chance he could spend his days working, doing something that would tire him out, so he only had enough energy for sleep.

His soapy hand went to his cock.

It wasn't working. Thinking about the house, the projects. None of it. The only thing on his mind was Jack. More specifically, getting the man naked and fucking him into oblivion one more time.

Rex stroked his dick.

When Jack was around, he distracted Rex in the worst fucking ways. The thought of having him underfoot didn't help, either. The guy made him feel slightly off-kilter. And yes, that was saying something because Rex wasn't the off-kilter type.

Which was the very reason he was standing in the shower, the hot water sluicing over his skin while he tugged roughly on his dick. Rex kept his eyes closed, thoughts of Jack spurring him on. The mental image was one he couldn't seem to shake. Jack laid across his bed, his body eager and waiting for the pleasure only he could give.

"Fuck," Rex groaned, jerking himself harder, faster.

He had no idea what he was even thinking. Jack Cunningham would be going home soon, out of Rex's life for good. Rex had no business entertaining ideas of any sort of interaction with the man. Temporary or otherwise.

Again, that seemed to spur Rex's fantasies further, which only made his fucking balls draw up tighter to his body, electricity buzzing in his spine as his release hovered just out of reach. He fell back against the tile, his hand squeezing, stroking faster and faster.

Damn. He wanted nothing more than to pound that guy's ass, to fuck him until neither of them knew what day it was. Only this time, Rex wanted Jack to be sober, to offer him his vulnerability and trust. He wanted it so fucking badly he could practically taste it.

Rex's hips tipped forward as his orgasm slammed into him, his cock jerking in his hand. He was out of breath, gasping for air, his entire body loose.

And to think, that had been from mere thoughts.

He had to wonder what the fuck it would be like if he ever did get Jack spread out before him again. Not that he was going to worry about that, nor was he going to pursue it. Jack wasn't ready for what Rex wanted from him, and since Rex wasn't looking for temporary, he knew it was better left alone.

Hell of a nice fantasy, though.

WILDLY INAPPROPRIATE.

That was Jack's first thought when he paused by the bathroom door on his way back to his room. He'd gone to the kitchen for a cup of coffee, and upon his return, he'd noticed Rex hadn't closed the door all the way. Of course, that would've been no big deal had he not caught the sight of Rex toweling off, the perfect angle of the mirror giving Jack an unobstructed view.

He wasn't sure how long he'd been there but figured it could've only been seconds. His brain was telling him to move on, that he wasn't a peeping Tom. However, his feet weren't moving, and his eyes were locked on the image in the reflective glass.

Right up until Rex's dark gaze paused, his eyes, too, on the mirror.

Shit.

Busted.

Feeling slightly ashamed that he'd been ogling Rex like that, Jack stumbled forward, heading for his bedroom. Unfortunately, he came up short of safety when Rex's deep, booming voice sounded behind him.

"Enjoy the show, city boy?"

Swallowing hard, Jack turned around. "I ... uh ..."

Rex cocked one dark eyebrow, evidently waiting for Jack to explain.

Since there really was no excuse that he could come up with— nothing that would sound rational, anyhow—Jack settled on apologizing.

"It was inappropriate, and I'm sorry," he whispered, his eyes glued to Rex's handsome face.

To his surprise, Rex took a step closer, then another until only a foot or so separated them.

"I've noticed you like to watch."

Instinct had Jack shaking his head. Guilt had him nodding. He wasn't sure if there was a right or wrong answer here. The fact was, he had violated Rex's privacy. Worse, his cock was rock hard, and he knew his sweatpants were doing a lousy job of disguising that fact.

When Rex's gaze dropped, Jack's stomach muscles tightened.

"I guess your body speaks for you."

The heat from Rex's perusal flushed out the embarrassment he'd originally felt from being caught, but Jack wasn't sure what to say, what to do. They'd been circling one another enough, the mutual attraction undeniable. However, from what he could tell, neither of them were open to repeats of their past nights together.

Jack understood mostly. When he rationalized their last night together, he couldn't help but feel guilty for how he'd gone about it. And since he hadn't had a drop of liquor since, he was proving to them both that the booze wasn't fueling his lust. It pained him to know he'd hurt Rex, more so when he saw it flash in Rex's eyes.

Now was not one of those moments.

For one, Rex didn't look at all pained by what was happening here. Two, Jack's cock continued to swell, throbbing more insistently the longer they faced off.

"What do you think we should do about this?" Rex asked, his words and the raspy tone of his voice surprising Jack.

"How do you mean?"

One of those thick brows lifted, those dark eyes penetrating Jack.

Yeah, okay, fine. He didn't need Rex to explain. He knew what was happening here. He even knew what would happen should either of them push for a replay. The chemical reaction would be combustible should they give in to their lust. No doubt about it.

Before he could say anything more, his cell phone sounded behind him. Jack dropped his head.

"Important?"

Jack nodded. The ring tone belonged to his agent. "I have to take this."

Rex smirked, then, without another word, walked into his bedroom and kicked the door shut. Before Jack turned away, he noticed it was slightly ajar.

Thankfully, the shrill sound of the phone jerked him out of his haze. He went to his room, shut the door behind him, ensuring it was closed all the way so there was no chance of him doing something stupid.

"So, tell me what's goin' on with you, Jack," his agent said in greeting.

"Not a whole lot." Jack dropped onto the bed, leaned against the headboard, and stared at the door.

"So, how's your WIP coming along?"

"Slow going," he admitted. "But I should be able to have something to you by the end of the month."

"In less than a week?" Herbert Miller sounded both shocked and thrilled.

Jack frowned. "What do you mean?"

"Well, since today's the twenty-fifth..."

"Oh, shit." Jack sighed. "Already?"

"Yep."

"Okay, so maybe not the first of *next* month."

"So you meant the first of March?" Herb chuckled. "You always were a kidder, Jack."

He wasn't kidding, but he figured Herb didn't need to know that. While he'd spent some time the past couple of days working on Shawn's new heroine, Jack hadn't had any time to dedicate to the solo he was working on. And in all fairness, he owed Shawn a completed project before he launched into another one of his own.

"What else is going on, Jack? You getting ready for your wedding? Twenty days and counting."

"The wedding's off," he said, still staring at the bedroom door.

"What?" Herb exclaimed. "Since when?"

"Since Tina cheated on me."

"Holy shit, Jack. I had no idea. I'm so sorry."

"Don't be. Things are looking up for me."

"How so?"

Realizing he was about to launch into a topic that was definitely not something he would share with his agent, Jack jerked his attention to the balcony door. "Got a lot going on right now," he told Herb. "I've been on vacation, taking a little time for myself."

"A vacation? Like the Caribbean?"

Jack chuckled. "A little closer to home."

"Good for you. Hopefully somewhere relaxing."

Relaxing wasn't exactly the word he would use. "I'm actually staying at a bed-and-breakfast in Coyote Ridge, Texas."

Herb laughed. "Sounds ... rural."

Jack smiled. "It is. I'm finding I like that about the place. Was even thinking about moving this way when my lease is up on my apartment."

"Really?" Herb sounded distracted.

"Yeah. Thought maybe a change of scenery would do me some good."

"I just pulled it up on a map," Herb said. "You're gonna give up the glitz and glamor of Austin for small-town USA, huh?"

It was Jack's turn to laugh. "I forget you haven't been to Austin. It's not New York City, Herb. No glitz or glamor. Mostly starving musicians."

"I remember you mentioning that." The smile was evident in Herb's voice. "Well, I guess you can give me a call when you get back home. Do you know when that'll be?"

"I told Tina she needed to be out by the first of February. Provided she follows through, I'll be going home then."

Or at least, that was what he was telling himself. Truth was, Jack wasn't ready to leave, but he feared he was overstaying his welcome.

Eighteen

Sunday, January 27, 2019

THE FOLLOWING EVENING, REX WAS SITTING ON the chair in front of the television. He had tried to focus on the furniture he had lined up on his schedule but had lost his interest early on. Rather than fret that he wasn't getting anything accomplished, he had come up to the apartment to relax. After all, it was Sunday— the only day of the week he didn't schedule subcontractors—and he deserved a little downtime, too.

For the past half hour, he'd been trying to come up with a name for the B and B, using it as a distraction mostly. He was still stuck, and that had sent him stumbling along various other mental avenues until he found himself trying to determine the best way to answer the phone. He was hoping that by envisioning it happening, something would click, and he'd come up with the perfect name.

Easier said than done.

Not that he needed to worry about how to answer the phone this soon in the process. Until the damn thing rang, it wouldn't matter anyway. If the damn thing *ever* rang. Although Rex was well on the way to getting the place fixed up, that didn't mean anyone was going to want to stay there when it was completed.

That was the other issue he was running into. For some stupid-ass reason, Rex was being super critical about the entire project. As though he was setting himself up for failure. All the positivity he'd been latching onto lately had dissipated, leaving him feeling ... mopey.

Yes, that was a good word for it.

He figured most of it had to do with the restless energy. He needed to burn it off, but he wasn't sure what would help.

Well, that wasn't *entirely* true.

Rex's gaze swung over to the couch.

Jack was reclined, watching whatever was on the TV. Rex had no idea because he couldn't get his mind out of the gutter. When he wasn't forcing himself to think of pleasant ways to answer the damn phone, he had mentally stripped the guy where he lay about a half dozen times already.

He was beginning to fear it was becoming an obsession.

"So, have you thought about a name for this place?" Jack asked, his attention still on the television. "I was talking to Bristol yesterday. She stopped by to see the progress."

"Where was I?"

Jack waved his hand. "Hardware store, I think. Anyway. She mentioned you hadn't figured out what to call this place."

Evidently not needing an answer, Jack continued, "I think it needs to be something catchy but not cliché."

Rex knew that. However, he had no idea what to call it. He had a few ideas, but nothing that he was married to. It would probably help if he knew how he wanted to market the place. A couples' retreat or a romantic getaway. Perhaps great for businesspeople. Or simply as a bed-and-breakfast—a place to rest your head with an early-morning meal to boot. The only thing he didn't want to do was end up being a random motel.

The issue was, he wasn't looking to be a motel. He didn't want businesspeople to be the only ones dropping in for a night to sleep and then expecting something warm in their bellies before they hit the road. He wanted this to be a retreat. A place people wanted to vacation to, to get away from the big city. Couples, families, single people. It didn't matter. Everyone was welcome.

"What's your hook?" Jack asked.

Rex's gaze swung over to him. "Hook?"

"Yeah." Jack waved his hand. "You know. The draw of this place. I mean, sure, it's a bed-and-breakfast, and people who need to sleep will likely stumble upon it. Maybe. But you are pretty far out here. And the directions from the beer-*slash*-bait store guy weren't all that easy to follow. I mean, what happens when the oak tree gets struck by lightning or the old high school gets torn down? Then how will they direct people here?"

Rex chuckled. He could only imagine what ol' Andy Dobbs had said to get Jack out this way.

"Plus, that guy mentioned some dude ranch. Isn't that a big thing? People want to ride horses? Milk cows? I don't know. I'm not sure what goes on at those places."

"Dead Heat Ranch," Rex told him. "That's the name of the dude ranch."

Jack's head swiveled. "Oh, really. So, he was serious?"

"Very."

He frowned. "And people stay at a place with *dead* in the name?"

Rex grinned. "Not *dead*," he clarified. "*Dead heat*."

"Ah." Jack nodded. "Like a race. Got it now." Jack turned back to the TV. "So what do you have going on that will make people want to stay here and not there? I'm finding it hard to imagine this place once it's open."

It was true. Rex wouldn't have much to do unless someone wanted to sleep, swim, play pool, or read.

He shrugged, unable to answer.

"You'll have eight rooms, right?" Jack inquired.

"Yeah."

"And a game room?"

"Yep."

"A library?"

He nodded. Kylie seemed insistent on a library.

"What about a meeting room? Bristol said that was a possibility." Jack shifted his position on the couch, getting comfortable. "A place for the townspeople to gather. After all, you are right here, in the heart of it all. Don't use that, by the way." Jack mimicked quote symbols, his voice deepening. "Deep in the heart of Texas. Yeah. Don't use that in your marketing. Very cliché." He waved another hand. "Anyway. You could charge for that, you know. A meeting room. Maybe host a few events." He waved a hand. "I'm not talking weddings or anything, but smaller events. Baby showers, bridal showers. That shit. If you had a room that was convenient, people could get together there. Maybe on the main floor. Easy access."

No, he didn't know. Rex hadn't thought much about that stuff. Not until Kylie had brought it up, that was. It was just another thing he would have to worry about once the interior work started.

"You do have a pool and hot tub," Jack continued. "That's a good draw, especially since both are heated. You can keep them open year-round."

Rex didn't say anything. He didn't know what *to* say.

"What else? Are you aiming to get families out here? What do you have for kids?"

"Like what?"

"I don't know. Maybe some summer activities. A slide in the pool. Hay rides in the fall. Some sort of Christmas events in the winter. Activities. The kids want to play games. The parents want them to be worn out so they sleep all night. Or so Bristol tells me, anyway." Jack sat up, dropping his feet to the floor. "There has to be some sort of draw."

"I honestly wasn't thinking about kids," Rex admitted.

"Why's that? You plan to have some risqué stuff going on here?" Jack chuckled. "Because to be fair, what're couples going to do all day when there's nothing here for them? You can only get in the hot tub so much. Trust me, I know." He reclined, rested his head on the couch arm. "There is the town. They could always do a little shopping. Maybe another town close by? Add that sort of thing to the brochure, give them options. But what if they don't want to leave? What can they do here?"

"Fuck," Rex said, locking his eyes with Jack's. "I really don't have a clue."

"Okay, let's brainstorm. If you market it well, you'll have people coming simply because it's a B and B in a small town and there aren't that many around. So you'll have the charm factor. It's different from a chain hotel. But you'll want to entice return visits. What will have them coming back for more?"

Rex frowned. "Same answer. I don't know. My cousin owns a fetish resort here in Coyote Ridge. It does well for itself."

Jack's eyes widened. "Seriously?"

Rex grinned. "Yeah. Alluring Indulgence Resort. Ever heard of it?"

"Holy shit, yes. I've heard of it. The opening of that place was a big deal, even in Austin. They've got all kinds of kinky shit going on there."

The blush that stole over Jack's face was hot.

Rex turned his attention to the television, needing this conversation to steer itself back to neutral ground.

"So, what if you did that? BDSM or something, maybe?" His gaze swung back to the television. "I could see it. A red room of pain, some decorative handcuffs on the walls, chains, sex swings. You know, that shit's quite popular these days. Are you into that stuff?"

"No." Rex was not about to have this conversation with him. He was too worked up to delve into a topic such as this one, but the mere thought of chains and handcuffs made his stomach churn and not with anticipation, either.

"So, maybe you could be a little more low-key. Just have a playroom? Something that's got whips and sex swings?" He grinned. "I do write and draw comic books for a living. I can come up with some off-the-wall ideas if you'd like. My imagination knows no bounds. Perhaps you could do the whole bondage thing. Being tied up—or better yet, handcuffed could be hot, right?"

Rex's body went cold, a chill slithering down his spine. The memory of that long-ago night when that bitch had handcuffed him to the bed took root. He fought it back, but not before he started to sweat.

"Did I say something wrong?" Jack asked, his tone concerned now.

"No. But none of that shit."

"Okay, so no bondage. Maybe dressing up. Parties." His eyes widened. "Fetish parties."

Rex stared at him. Where the hell was this coming from? For the past couple of weeks, Jack had barely been able to look him in the eye. Yesterday, when Rex had boldly challenged Jack about him watching him in the bathroom, the man had turned a dozen shades of crimson. Tonight he was asking about whips and handcuffs and fetish parties?

"You could convert the workshop."

"No." Rex forced his gaze back to the television. "I'm not into that shit."

"What *are* you into?"

"Hell if I know." That was the truth.

"When you're not working, what do you do?"

"I'm always working."

Jack cocked his head, his disagreement showing. "You're not working now."

Rex sighed. "Fine. The rare times I'm not working, I…" Rex had to think about it. He rarely did anything these days aside from shower, eat, grab a quick workout in his personal gym, and of course, chill in the hot tub.

"I work out," he admitted.

"For fun?" Jack made it sound like a ludicrous idea.

"Yeah."

"Where?"

"The workshop."

"You have your own gym?"

Rex nodded, stared at the television. "Have to. Not one in this town."

Jack got to his feet. "Show me."

Rex's gaze cut to Jack. "What?"

"Show me," Jack repeated.

"Show you?" He wanted to see his gym? Seriously?

"Not like you've got anything better to do." Jack motioned toward the television. "We've been watching HGTV for the past hour and I know you're not interested in tiny houses."

Rex could think of something better to do. *Someone*, in fact.

"I've been jonesing for a gym, Rex. I may not be some big burly guy who spends hours with weights in his hands, but I do happen to enjoy some cardio. That was the one thing I could use to work off the frustration. Show me. Please."

"I can think of a few ways to work off the frustration," Rex grumbled, keeping his voice low.

"What's that?"

"Nothing." Knowing his thoughts were straying where they didn't belong, Rex got to his feet, headed into the kitchen, and grabbed a bottle of water. He heard Jack's footsteps behind him.

"I was also thinking about your marketing for this place. Do you have a website? You know, for your bed-and-breakfast?"

Rex grunted an affirmation as he took a long swig of water, then put the bottle back in the refrigerator.

"What's the web address if you don't have a name?"

Rex spun to face Jack. "What?"

"You know. Like www dot something or another."

Rex frowned.

"How will people find it?"

"They don't." Because Rex hadn't thought about that. Without a damn web address no one was going to ever find him. Sure, Rex had a website designed, or mostly designed. He'd started it, but without an address, it wasn't visible to anyone. "Shit."

Jack chuckled. "Show me your gym, because like I said, I'm jonesing to work out, and maybe if I'm nice, you'll let me use it. And while I do, I might be able to help you come up with a name for this place."

Rex stared at the man for a second, then shrugged. Nothing wrong with a little bartering now and then.

Of course, Rex preferred to barter a little differently, but only time would tell whether or not Jack was open for something more interesting than a leg press.

"I THOUGHT YOU SAID THE GYM WAS in your workshop," Jack said when Rex headed for his bedroom. He hadn't intended to follow the man around like a puppy, yet here he was.

"Gotta get the key."

"Separate key for the gym?"

"No, but I had to lock up the workshop last night."

Ah. Okay, then. "So, I was wondering about this apartment. Bristol mentioned you built this yourself. Like, all by yourself?"

Rex nodded as he opened his bedroom door. "Not too difficult to convert an attic space."

Jack huffed a laugh. "Not too difficult, he says. Only installing … *everything*. And you plan to live here when the place opens?"

Rex sauntered over to one of the two nightstands. "Ultimately, it'll be for whoever manages the place."

Without hesitation, Jack followed him inside. The room was dark, the blinds drawn. The hardwood floors were the same dark walnut as what was in the rest of the apartment, some of the decor similar to the guest room.

There was a small sitting area and, like the guest room, this one had its own balcony.

Jack had to admit, he was curious about the man and he wanted to know what his personal space looked like, so he walked around, took it all in. It was very similar to the room Jack was staying in. A lot of brown/wood tones, ranging from dark to light. It was simple, clean, despite the bed being unmade. It suited Rex.

Not wanting to let the conversational ball drop, Jack asked, "Where will you stay if you're not living here?"

"Thought about building behind the house."

"Well, you've got the land for it. Bristol mentioned you owned a couple thousand acres." Jack peered out the blinds, checking the view. Feeling Rex watching him, he turned back to survey the room. "So, does this room see a lot of action?"

Rex's dark eyes widened as he shot a brief look his way, closing the nightstand drawer.

Jack was trying to get a rise out of him, but still his face heated. He had absolutely no idea why he was venturing down this path because he knew exactly where it would go. Ever since yesterday's incident in the hallway, Jack had been trying to figure out how to get back to that moment. He knew he had let an opportunity pass him by and it bugged the shit out of him that he had.

Rex paused on his way to the door, turned back to the bed. "Not nearly as much as you'd think. But if you'd like to check out the mattress, I'm more than happy to show it to you."

Jack's stomach dropped to his toes, a strange sensation coming over him. He wanted to take Rex up on that offer simply because he could. One more night wouldn't hurt, would it? One last roll in the hay? Jack could indulge in Rex. For old times' sake. Although, he doubted a couple of weeks ago would qualify as old times, but whatever. What could it hurt?

Fuck. What was he thinking? This was stupid. He was leaving in less than a week.

"Yeah, I'll have to pass, but thanks." Jack turned away quickly, not wanting Rex to see the disappointment he knew was visible.

"Suit yourself. But if you're ever in the mood…"

Jack spun back around, put his hands on his hips. "Would you really? I mean … I was teasing you like you teased me yesterday. I didn't think you'd really be interested—" Hell, he needed to shut up while he was ahead.

For a moment, they squared off from across the room. Their eyes were locked, but neither said a word. Jack held his breath, waiting for a signal. Any sort of sign that this might happen, because damn it, he so wanted it.

Rex cleared his throat, laughed. "I'm just fuckin' with you, city boy."

Jack breathed out and it felt as though he exhaled broken glass. The pain was sharp and fierce. "Yeah, I knew that." Forcing cheer he didn't feel, he said, "It's a nice bedroom, though. I mean … apartment. This'll be cozy for a manager. Do you know who you'll hire?"

"No," Rex replied, following Jack back into the hallway.

"Will you hire someone as soon as you open?"

"Probably not until I'm turnin' a profit."

"Oh." Jack started toward the apartment door, leading the way to the workshop. "What happens if you meet some guy? Fall in love? Would you ask him to move in here with you?"

As they navigated the narrow stairway, Rex's woodsy scent consumed him. He had no fucking clue why he didn't run down the stairs.

"I can't predict the future, Cunningham. And why are you so curious?"

"No reason." Jack kept walking, made it down to the main floor.

Once they hit the foyer, Jack didn't stop. He knew the way to the workshop. And if by chance Rex decided not to keep following, Jack would've been okay with that, too. An irritating sense of rejection had consumed him. He didn't like it one bit, although he knew he probably deserved it after what he'd done to Rex.

Jack allowed Rex to move in front of him. He watched the ground while Rex unlocked the door. Once inside, Jack pretended to be interested in the furniture lying around while Rex unlocked a single door that Jack had just assumed was some sort of storage closet.

Rex flipped on another light and Jack's eyes widened at the sight of Rex's home gym. The guy had downplayed it, no doubt. Jack was surprised to see how big it was. Much bigger than he'd anticipated. For whatever reason, he had expected maybe a treadmill and a weight bench, perhaps a handful of free weights.

This wasn't your average home gym, that was for sure. There was all sorts of equipment. One of those fancy cycles and a state-of-the-art treadmill, an area for stretching, some free weights, a bench, a Smith machine, as well as a dip rack and a leg press.

"Do you use this much?"

"Mostly the weights."

Jack moved closer to the fancy stationary cycle. "This is amazing. I would kill to have a place like this in my house."

"It does the job."

"What job's that?" Jack asked, curious about the statement, the odd tone of Rex's voice.

"It ensures I'll never be the weak one in the room."

Jack stopped for a moment and met Rex's gaze. He was dead serious. And something in that statement made Jack believe there was a story behind it. Maybe it was related to what happened with his brother and his father?

Knowing it wasn't the right time to ask those personal questions, he forced his attention back to the equipment.

"Would you mind if I used it sometime?"

Rex glanced around the room, then back to him. He smirked. "What's in it for me?"

There was definitely innuendo in his tone. Jack forced himself to stay focused on the gym and not drift back to Rex's bedroom. His bed. Feeling the weight of him.

He inwardly sighed, swallowing his disappointment. He knew Rex was joking.

Rex laughed, clearly taking Jack's lack of response as embarrassment. "Yeah. You can use it. Anytime you want."

"That would be awesome. Thank you." In fact, he needed to work off some frustration right now and this would be the best place for him, except he wanted to ensure he didn't have an audience.

Jack peered back at Rex, then past him toward the outer door. "Well, okay then. So…" He moved toward the exit. "Show me the website."

Nineteen

REX MANAGED TO RELEASE THE BREATH HE'D been holding.

Now that they were back in the apartment, some of the tension had faded. The *sexual* tension. Mostly.

From the moment Jack walked into Rex's bedroom a short while ago, Rex had felt the emotions churning inside him. It was a mixture of feelings. Anticipation, fear, anger, and yes, disappointment.

Jack was the only person Rex had allowed into his bedroom. As a rule, he didn't invite people into his personal space. Not even Bristol.

A therapist would likely tell him his need to keep people out was due to the trauma he'd experienced as a kid. Rex figured that was likely the reason, but he didn't like to think about it. Rex had never shared his bed with anyone. He didn't have a problem getting into bed with men, just not his own. And as a rule, he didn't sleep with them, either.

Any time he'd ever considered it, he found himself consumed with a sense of fear. Since that fateful night, Rex found it nearly impossible to trust others.

Until Jack.

From the moment Jack stepped into Rex's bedroom, he hadn't felt anything negative whatsoever. It hadn't bothered him to have Jack discreetly snooping around. In fact, he would go so far as to say he'd liked that Jack had taken the time to do so.

Not that Rex had been *entirely* okay with it. Having Jack that close had dragged out a sense of longing he'd been trying to avoid. Rex had already crossed a line he never should've crossed by getting close to the man. And it was getting harder and harder to come up with valid excuses. Back in the beginning, Rex had believed it would only be one night, that he would never see Jack again after that, so that had made it all right.

Unfortunately, Jack had appeared on his doorstep, and the interactions they'd had since then taunted him with every breath Rex took. They'd become friends in a strange way, and Rex wasn't sure Jack was interested in a repeat of their night together. One minute Rex would think so, the next he questioned himself. The guy confused him, to say the very least.

"So, what should the focus be?" Jack asked, pulling Rex from his thoughts. "Do you want to cater to families? Try that angle? Or did you decide to go the romantic route?"

"Yes. That's—" Before he could get the sentence out, the phone on the desk rang.

He looked at it as though it had grown legs and walked. No one even knew that phone number. It was for the bed-and-breakfast, something Rex had set up back when he'd decided he needed motivation to get started on the place.

"Are you going to answer it?" Jack's gaze darted between him and the phone.

Rex moved toward the desk, snatched up the receiver. "Bed-and-breakfast," he answered, since he had no idea what to fucking call the place.

"Yes, my husband and I were looking for a quiet getaway, and before he has a chance to change his mind, I wanted to get a room reserved. That way he can't back out on me. Do you have anything available for the middle of March?"

Rex stared at the wall, let the request sink in. "I'm not open yet," he told the woman, not remembering his manners in time to sound even remotely hospitable.

"Oh." Her disappointment was clear. "I got your number from a friend and she said you'd be opening soon."

The only friend he could imagine who could've given out his information would be Bristol, but he had no idea how she'd have gotten the number.

"If, by *soon*, your friend meant October, then yes."

"October? Oh, no. That definitely won't work."

Rex's gaze shot to Jack, who was staring at him intently. He realized he needed to say something to this woman, something that would leave her with a good impression even if he wouldn't be open for business for months.

"How about I take down your information." Rex rummaged in the drawer for a pen. "That way, once I have a firm date on the opening, I can give you a call. Perhaps you and your husband would like another vacation toward the end of the year."

"Oh, that would be wonderful," she said, a smile in her voice. "Two getaways in a year. I'm not sure that's happened since we were first married."

Rex took down the woman's information, then disconnected the call.

"This is new for you, huh?" Jack asked, his ass perched on the arm of the couch, arms crossed over his chest.

"What makes you say that?"

"We need to work on getting you more comfortable with speaking to potential guests."

"*We?*"

Jack glanced around dramatically. "Considering there's clearly not much for me to do aside from getting coffee and passing out water, I figure maybe there's a better way for me to contribute to the room and board you've so kindly given me. Perhaps I can give you some helpful tips."

"Tips, huh?" Rex was interested in hearing this.

Jack offered a pleased grin. "I might be an artist, which I will admit is a very lonely job at times; however, I'm not a stranger to interacting with people."

"Fine. What're your suggestions?"

"Well, for one, don't sound so eager. You want people to think you're booked up. That way they'll assume the place is in high demand. It's all about perception."

Rex glanced around dramatically. "In case you didn't notice, the house is in shambles and this apartment is the only thing functional."

"Maybe. But … well, that won't always be the case. Once, you know, you have walls and furniture, you'll be that much closer. Perhaps some bathrooms to use."

Rex cocked an eyebrow. Jack was clearly being a smartass.

"Oh, and more importantly, once you come up with a name. Maybe finish the kitchen, too." Jack stood.

Rex couldn't argue. A name and a working kitchen were ideal.

"So, what if we try to narrow the scope?" Jack suggested. "Focus on one aspect that will draw people here."

"Like what?"

"Marketing it as a romantic couples' getaway. Initially. That's likely the demographic that'll be the most interested. Especially during the holidays. You mentioned opening at the end of the year. Then, once you get some additional activities planned, you can gear it more toward families." Jack grinned. "With couples, you could offer packages."

"Packages?"

"Yeah. For instance, themes. Holidays are a good marketing ploy. Christmas and New Year's. Especially New Year's. Other themes work, too. Halloween, maybe. Come up with events or something."

Rex shook his head. "I doubt that's something I'll be able to sustain."

"Okay, so what is it you want?"

"I want … people to be happy. And fine. Maybe some romance to go along with it." Yeah, he might've blushed when he said it aloud.

"In an effort to get a good feel for what your intentions are, let's pretend I'm here for a romantic getaway," Jack suggested. "Walk me through the place and explain what it is you think me and my significant other might get out of our time here. That way I can get a feel for what you're really going for."

Rex's gaze slammed into the man as he tried to hide his surprise. "You want me to pretend … what … that you're a guest?"

"Yes."

"And that you've brought your lover?"

"Yes."

"Is your lover a man or a woman?" Rex questioned.

Jack's response was instant. "A man."

Okay, his heart jumped into his throat. He hadn't expected Jack to say that. Although he wasn't sure why not. The guy did not seem to be questioning his sexuality from what he could tell. Still, he expressed his incredulity. "A man? Seriously?"

That seemed to put Jack on the defensive. "Why do you say it like that? Like you don't think I'm capable of accepting it?"

It wasn't that he didn't think Jack was capable. It was that he didn't want to think about Jack with another man. He wanted to show Jack exactly what *he* could offer *him*. Not what his bed-and-breakfast could offer him and his fictitious lover.

Jack moved closer, his eyes zeroed in on Rex's face. "Do you have a problem with me accepting who I am?"

This was a bad idea. No matter how intrigued he was, there was no way this would end any way but badly if he allowed Jack to taunt him.

"No."

"I'm not sure I believe you." Jack's gray eyes had gone cold. "If you don't have a problem, then let's pretend."

"No," Rex stated firmly.

"Why not? It's not like either of us has anything better to do." Jack glanced around. "Everyone has the day off, and I have nowhere to be."

"No," Rex repeated, keeping his tone brusque.

"Why?"

Rex stood to his full height and stared down at Jack. "You wanna know *why*?"

Jack nodded, a defiant gleam in his pretty gray eyes.

Rex took a step forward, moving into Jack's personal space. He had to give the guy credit, at least he didn't back down.

"Because I'm not looking for make-believe, Jack," Rex growled, leaning in, lowering his voice as he continued. "We've been skating around this shit for weeks. Pretending nothing happened, acting like I don't want more. I'd much rather kiss you and feel you go weak beneath me. Then I want to lower you to the fucking floor and drive so deep inside you, you'll never forget exactly what I can make you feel."

His blunt admission apparently surprised Jack. Hell, it surprised Rex, too. He'd been fighting this for too fucking long. The games had to end now.

"I can't give you what you need." Jack sounded as though that was the most ludicrous thing in the world.

"You coulda fooled me, city boy," Rex snarled. "I got everything I needed when I was lodged deep in your ass as you were begging me to make you come. Both times."

Jack's face flamed red, but he didn't back down and neither did Rex.

"That was a mistake," Jack said softly, his eyes hard. "I was coming out of a bad relationship."

Rex laughed without mirth. He hated fucking excuses and that was the most ludicrous one he'd ever heard. "So, because you were on the rebound, it was a mistake?"

"Yes, it was. I was drunk and vulnerable."

"And that means it was a mistake?" Rex narrowed his eyes, doing his best to hold in his anger.

"Yes. I need to work on myself, Rex. In order to do that, I have to abstain from … everything."

"Everything meaning sex?"

Jack's shoulders tensed. "Everything meaning everything. Sex is all great and fine, but what comes after?"

"What's supposed to come after?" Rex countered hotly. "Some cuddling, maybe breakfast. Then everyone goes on their merry way."

"That's not what I'm looking for!" Jack snapped. "I don't want to be someone's cheap fling."

Rex felt his temper burst free. "Like I was for you the last time?"

Jack swallowed hard, but surprisingly he didn't look away. "Rex. I…"

Rex waited. He wasn't going to let Jack get out of this so easily. They'd been taunting one another for days. It was time they figured out what direction they were headed.

"I have to go back to my life soon. And as much as I want to … to experiment—"

"Experiment?" Rex barked a laugh. "That's what you call it?"

Jack didn't say anything, but his face softened.

It was then Rex realized Jack already had one foot out the door.

"Whatever." Rex was done pretending this could've been something more. He turned away, paced to the other side of the room. He wanted to walk out, but something kept him there. He needed to get some closure here.

"But that doesn't mean I don't want to be friends," Jack said softly. "I can still help you out. We can pretend—"

Rex cut him off before he could finish. "I don't want to pretend with you."

Jack huffed a laugh and his expression went dark. It was the first time Rex had seen true frustration in the man.

"Oh. So what, Rex? You want the real thing? You find me attractive?" Jack threw up his hands. "I'm so fucking out of my element here, no way could you find anything appealing about me, Rex. I'm a fucking mess. Have been since I stepped onto your porch."

Rex shook his head, took one step closer, then lowered his voice. "Trust me, there's plenty appealing about you. You've been here what? Three weeks? Do you know that I've fantasized about you every fucking day since you arrived? Even after that night, after you got drunk and used me. I still fucking want you, Jack. Sure, I hate myself for it, but it doesn't make it less true."

Jack opened his mouth, closed it. No words came out.

Didn't matter. Rex didn't want to have this conversation anymore. This was going in the absolute opposite direction of where it should be, and this time, Rex was the one to blame.

"You're wrong," Jack stated.

Rex grinned, but he didn't find this at all amusing. "Am I?"

"Yes." Jack's tone was adamant. "You are."

"About?"

"About me using you. I didn't use you."

Rex exhaled slowly. "Whatever you have to tell yourself."

"It's true." Jack moved closer, his voice lowered. "That night was amazing for me. But I wanted to touch you. To kiss you. To see your face, Rex. Like I said, I'm out of my element when it comes to you."

"You mean when it comes to *men*?" Rex couldn't seem to let this go.

Jack's eyes narrowed. "No, that's not what I meant." He took a step back. "But I'm done here. There's no sense making this harder on either of us."

When Jack started toward the hallway, Rex's anger got the best of him. "Keep runnin', Jack. That seems to be your MO."

Jack spun around to face him, stomped back over. "I'm not running from you, Rex. I just can't do this with you. Not anymore."

This time, when Jack started to step back, Rex lifted an eyebrow. "Don't. Move."

The other man froze.

And for the first time in days, Rex knew exactly where this was going.

JACK HAD BEEN READY TO WALK OUT until Rex barked the order. Now, against his better judgment, he found himself mesmerized by those dark eyes, the way they seemed to peer down into his soul, to know what he wanted, what he needed.

The feeling was disturbing, yet it was accompanied by a sense of relief mixed with confusion. To admit what he wanted would be easy, but he knew it wasn't the same as what Rex wanted. Not at the moment. While Jack was all for falling in love and living happily ever after, he wasn't ready. Wasn't sure when he would be. He had too many bad relationships in his past haunting him, reminding him that he was a bad bet when it came to things like this. Why would he want to put Rex through that? Or himself, for that matter?

"What do you want from me, Rex? Are you looking for more than one night? Or simply friends with benefits? Perhaps a quickie every other week? Or God forbid, eternity?"

"Why does it matter?" Rex countered.

"Because it does. If you're looking for more than one night … well, that changes the game altogether."

"I didn't realize we were playin' a game," Rex hissed, his eyes locked on Jack's.

Jack wasn't sure why he wasn't bolting to his room and locking the door, trying to get away from the confrontation. He hated these heated moments when everything threatened to come to the surface. These were contributing factors to the fallout of his entire life. Every time he was met with confrontation, something bad happened.

He breathed in slowly, let it out, tried to center himself. Explaining this was going to take effort, restraint. Another deep breath in… "For the first time in my life, I know what I want, Rex. But I also know what I *need*. And that freaks me out, especially after what's happened between us."

Although he could come up with a million excuses as to why he needed to avoid any sort of relationship, Jack knew that what he wanted was right in front of him. Even if it would've been better for everyone if he went back home, put this all in the past, he couldn't deny that he was so damn tempted to see where this might go. Didn't even matter that Rex could be thinking a quick roll would be ideal, Jack was almost willing to give him that because he didn't want to miss out on being with Rex one more time.

"Keep goin'," Rex urged.

Jack kept his voice low, his words even. "I have a history of hopping from one relationship to another and this is no different. Hell, I don't even know if my ex-girlfriend is out of my apartment yet."

"Why does that matter?"

"*Why?* Because I haven't even bounced back from what she did. She betrayed me, Rex. Fucked some other guy in my bed. And the same night I found out she cheated on me, I ended up in bed with you." And if that wasn't enough, it mattered because his heart was pumping fiercely as he tried to deny that what he felt for Rex was real. But Jack couldn't tell him that, couldn't admit that in the short time they'd known one another, he had fallen for the guy.

"So, you were with the wrong person," Rex said with a gruff snort. "Suck it up, city boy. We all go through it at some point."

"Sure. Fine. I'll give you that. But when's the last time you fucked a man and realized—"

Rex motioned for Jack to continue. "Realized what?"

Jack exhaled in a rush. "Never mind. It doesn't matter."

"But it does," Rex insisted. "Stop fuckin' runnin', Jack."

Jack glared at the man standing before him, the man who was purposely trying to piss him off. He could feel it in the way Rex stared at him. The man was trying to get Jack to trip himself up. And if he wasn't careful, Jack was going to walk right into the trap.

But he wasn't running from Rex, so he considered that a good start. He was glued to the spot, unable to look away from the handsome cowboy who had his thoughts and his emotions tied up in knots. Was that because Jack was lonely? Hurt by Tina's betrayal? Angry that she'd fucked another guy in his fucking bed? That would make this a rebound, and Rex didn't deserve that because Jack had proven he couldn't sustain a relationship.

His mind instantly conjured up images of Tina with that naked asshole. "Just thinking about her pisses me off, Rex. Don't you get that? Not because I love her. I don't. Not sure I ever did. But she hurt me. She betrayed me. And the memory alone makes me want to go against every principle I've ever had."

"Such as…?"

"Such as I'm not into casual sex. Never have been. I value commitments, relationships, monogamy. The one night I had with you at the hotel … that was my first one-night stand. *And* my last. I have no intention of turning into that guy. The one who tries to compensate with cheap sex. That's not me."

"Maybe that's the problem," Rex stated.

"What?"

"Well, for one, that you think what we shared was cheap sex."

So, it seemed Rex did have a trigger and evidently Jack had pulled it.

"And two," Rex continued, the muscle in his jaw bunching. "That you think you have to be committed. You said you've been engaged three times, right? You're twenty-nine, for Christ's sake. You haven't spent all that much time alone since you were old enough to *be* in a relationship."

"You're right. I haven't." At least Rex understood. "Whenever one girlfriend jilted me, I merely searched for the next. When I grew tired of one, I moved on to the next. And so on and so forth." Jack sighed. "Three times I thought I was in it for the long haul, but I'd clearly been fooling myself."

"My point exactly. Perhaps some *cheap sex*, as you referred to it, is exactly what you need."

"Trust me, it's not," Jack demanded, hating that he was getting so emotional over this.

There was one thing he knew with absolute certainty. Never had he dwelled on a breakup for more than a few days. Which likely said something about the nature of his relationships. Regardless, Jack wasn't looking to get caught up in another. Not romance or commitment. Not even meaningless sex. He didn't have the energy for either.

Rex smirked, but it wasn't as playful as Jack suspected it was meant to be. "Perhaps some naked playtime'll keep your mind off the other shit. You should give it a shot."

"It's not my thing," Jack insisted. He could see by the look in Rex's eyes that he wasn't buying the shit he was selling, but Jack figured he'd humor him anyway. "And even if it was, how does it help, Rex? Tell me that much."

"Why don't I just show you?" Rex sidestepped him, moving around behind him.

Jack's body tensed, but it wasn't his fight-or-flight instinct kicking in. It was more like self-preservation. It would be too damn easy to let this happen, to allow Rex to seduce him. Hell, he'd been hoping the man would for the past two weeks.

Jack started to pivot, but Rex snapped a deep, rumbling, "I said don't move."

"Rex…"

"Let me talk now."

Jack wasn't sure that was a good idea, but he didn't move, and he didn't speak. When Rex's warmth pressed up against his back, a tremor raced down his spine and his cock twitched.

"Have you ever had someone lay you out on the bed and take their time running their mouth over every inch of you?"

"I've only ever been with women," Jack said.

Rex chuckled, his warm breath fanning the back of Jack's neck. "I might be gay, but I don't think foreplay is restricted to gender, city boy."

"That's—"

"No talking," Rex demanded softly. "Have you always had to be in control when you were with a woman?"

"Yes," Jack confirmed.

Rex's chest brushed against his back. "But you weren't in control when you were with me."

Jack shook his head. No, he wasn't.

"You were at my mercy when my cock was lodged deep in your ass, weren't you?"

He nodded, his breaths coming in pants now.

"Even when you were riding my dick, I was in control."

Jack nodded once again.

"And before me, you merely fantasized about being with a man."

"Yes."

"Did I live up to your expectations?"

Jack shook his head. "You exceeded them. In every way."

"Really?" He sounded pleased. "Well, that was nothin', city boy. Absolutely *nothing* compared to what I *want* to do to you," Rex crooned. "I want to take my time. To feel your mouth on me and have mine on you. To have you writhing and moaning as I sink deep inside you." Rex appeared in front of him. "Face-to-face."

It wasn't a question, so Jack didn't feel the need to answer. His brain was geared to argue, but he figured what was the point. He wanted that more than anything.

Rex's expression turned serious as he tilted Jack's head back, forcing him to look him in the eye. "Was I really your first?"

Jack shook his head, then nodded. "Yes. But it doesn't matter." This was pointless. Jack couldn't give in. He couldn't afford to fall for someone else only to have it all come crashing down.

"But it does."

The air escaped Jack's lungs in a rush when Rex's hands brushed against the fronts of his thighs. It was only a slight touch, but it felt ridiculously intimate.

He could deny it all day, but what he wanted was everything Rex had mentioned. He wanted someone who put him first, someone who wanted to take care of him. Not financially. He had that part covered. Emotionally, though. He had longed for someone who was looking to give and take in equal measure. Unfortunately, he'd never found that.

But he knew Rex wasn't offering that, and even if he was, Jack couldn't do this. He was going home in a week. Less than. He had a life to return to and he knew once he was out that door, he would be an image in Rex's rearview. He wasn't even sure he could move forward knowing that. If he allowed something more to happen, Jack feared he would fall all the way.

When Jack met Rex's gaze again, he saw him watching him intently. He knew Rex was waiting for Jack to tell him that it could be only about sex, but it couldn't. It just couldn't.

"I thought we were gonna look at the website." Jack's voice came out in a rough whisper.

His abrupt subject change seemed to stun Rex momentarily. It took a moment, but Rex finally nodded, then took a step back. Jack suddenly wished he'd kept his damn mouth shut, because, just like that, whatever had transpired between them was gone.

Rex moved toward the desk, retrieved a laptop from the top drawer. He opened the lid, then, with deft fingers, strummed over the keys until the screen changed.

"It's all right there," Rex said before turning and walking out of the room.

Then right out of the apartment.

Jack dropped his head and sighed.

He was going to have to stop making the man do that.

Twenty

REX SPENT THE MAJORITY OF THE AFTERNOON working in his workshop.

He would've preferred to be outside, but the weather had taken a turn. The highs were in the twenties and a few flurries had started to come down. Nothing that would cause more than a few traffic hazards, but enough that it kept Rex from getting fresh air and attempting to clear his mind. The hot tub was even off-limits right now.

So, he had busied himself staining the rocking chairs he'd finished, utilizing the heaters he'd installed. Not because he needed to. The furniture could've waited a few more days. Hell, a few more months, even. However, Rex needed to keep himself busy. Needed to focus in order to avoid asking Jack to indulge in something he was evidently fighting tooth and nail. As it was, keeping his hands to himself was becoming a serious challenge.

Rex wasn't sure how he felt about that. Or even how he'd gotten to this point. For the better part of the afternoon, he had tried to figure out just when he'd gotten so attached to the city boy. That certainly hadn't been his plan, yet here he was.

The biggest issue was that Jack would be leaving soon. No, wait. That *wasn't* the biggest issue. The award for that went to the fact that Jack was confused. Just when they both seemed to know what they wanted, Jack was coming up with excuses as to why he had to avoid it. Why did they have to put some asinine label on sex? Couldn't they simply have it for the sake of having it? Rex knew it would make them both feel a hell of a lot better.

Rex sighed. Unfortunately, he doubted that was the case.

Jack hadn't backed down to Rex's argument, hadn't given a quarter. The man was hell-bent on keeping his distance, when not too long ago, he was practically begging for Rex's dick. And today, he'd come up with all sorts of excuses as to why it wouldn't work out.

So what? Why did there have to be an end game? Rex wasn't understanding. He'd lived his life one man at a time since the day he accepted himself. Why did Jack insist on changing the rules? It had worked just fine up to this point.

And that's why you're single, Sharpe.

Oh, who the fuck was he kidding? It hadn't worked at all.

Regardless, Rex had absolutely no business trying to inch his way into Jack's life mere days after meeting him. It was obvious Jack was looking for some solitude, an escape, maybe even a do-over after the shit storm that ex-girlfriend had rained down on him. The last thing Rex wanted was to be the rebound, as Jack had already referred to him.

Been there. Done that.

Rex remembered the days back when he'd first accepted himself. Back in his early twenties. He had been dating unsuccessfully for months and had all but given up on finding something to satisfy him. He'd actually met one guy who had piqued his interest, but it never went anywhere. Several dates had followed, but things had fizzled quickly. It didn't take long for Rex to realize his standards were too damn high.

Until finally, Rex had met Rick. They had clicked instantly. Granted, it wasn't the sort of clicking that had the world spinning ridiculously fast or anything like that, but Rex had felt a connection. They'd enjoyed the same movies, listened to the same music, had a fondness for working with their hands. They'd had plenty in common, had never run out of things to talk about. So much so, Rex had thought there was something there. Until one day, about two months in, Rex saw his new lover with another man. From that moment onward, Rex pretended not to know the guy. Didn't take his calls, didn't answer his texts. Nothing. He damn sure wasn't looking for that headache in his life.

It was then that Rex had known he wasn't the type who would be able to handle serial dating. Too much risk involved, not nearly enough reward. That was where Byron had come in. Having been friends for so long, they'd already built trust between them. Communication had been a key factor in their relationship, too. They'd agreed up front to be monogamous and quiet about what they were doing. It had suited them both, but neither of them had been looking for more.

And when it had ended, it had ended. No hard feelings on either side. Truth was, they'd grown bored of one another.

So, rather than get caught up in another pseudo-relationship, Rex had spent his time keeping busy, focusing on working toward his future. If love was meant for him, he had no doubt it would find him.

Oh, sure, Rex knew he was past kidding himself about the type of man he was looking for. He was done playing games, wasting time, chasing men who merely wanted to be chased. He had no real interest, no true attraction to a man who only pretended to be looking for a happily ever after.

Granted, he doubted most people knew what that even looked like. Rex damn sure didn't. Or, at least, he thought he didn't. But then Jack Cunningham had stumbled right into his path.

Not that it would go anywhere, but a guy could dream, right?

Rex might've been alone, but that didn't mean he was unhappy. The house was underway with the backing of his family and friends. He had everything he needed right here. He was a little lonely, sure. But that was by his own choice. He damn sure didn't want to admit—not to himself or anyone else—that Jack filled a void that had been plaguing him for a long time.

A friend? Potentially more?

Rex didn't know, nor was he going to think too hard on it.

The sharp rap of knuckles on metal had him turning.

"I cooked dinner," Jack stated in a matter-of-fact tone. "Thought maybe you'd eat something."

"How?" Rex had no food in the apartment. Nothing that would make a decent dinner.

"You're not the only one who knows how to drive. Or work a grill."

Unsure what to say to that, Rex nodded. He glanced down at his watch. It was six thirty. Which meant he'd skipped lunch and his stomach was all too aware of it.

Without waiting for a response, Jack turned and headed back to the house, leaving Rex to stare after him. And stare he did. As he watched him walk away, Rex realized just how hungry he was. But it damn sure wasn't for food.

Shaking off the thought, he glanced back at the rocking chair now drying with the heat lamp and a fan. The furniture certainly didn't need Rex to babysit it, so he made his way up to the apartment, opting to wait on a shower as well. Once he ate, Rex could wash up, then retire to his room and pretend today hadn't happened.

Then again, he really did owe Jack an apology. He shouldn't have acted the way he had, shouldn't have come on to him, much less been disappointed when Jack turned him down flat. It was inappropriate if nothing else. They had ventured onto a topic that was completely irrelevant, yet Rex had allowed it to play out because, deep down, he wanted Jack to want him, to feel something.

Unfortunately, even if Jack did feel something for him, he wasn't willing to accept it, and Rex had to live with that.

"So, I've been giving it some thought," Jack prompted when Rex was washing his hands at the kitchen sink.

"About?"

"The name for the place."

Disappointment flooded him, but Rex ignored it. Or tried to. For some dumb-ass reason, he had secretly hoped Jack had given more thought to what had transpired between them earlier. He obviously wouldn't be so lucky.

"I was thinking you should go all in on the romance theme," Jack continued. "Something to get some traction on the place." Jack didn't look at him as he spoke. "You can snarl and growl at me later if you want, but I took it upon myself to design a website that would appeal to … that demographic. Rather than families, you know. Your design was very … tailored. To the perfect family. And let's be honest, the perfect family doesn't exist, Rex."

Jack turned the laptop toward him while Rex dried his hands.

"This is the home page. Feel free to do whatever you want with it. I was bored, so——"

Rex cut him off by pulling the laptop toward him and leaning down to survey the screen.

Wow. This was … impressive. Jack had found a picture of a gay couple standing on a balcony at sunset. The two men were staring back at one another, obviously in love.

"You said you were an artist, huh?" Rex found himself asking.

"Yeah." Jack grinned as though he knew Rex approved of what he'd done. "You can click through the other links. I've set up a price list, although the numbers are blank. I wasn't sure what your structure would be. I also left spots for pictures of the rooms. That way, when they're finished, you can just drop them in."

What had taken him nearly six months had taken Jack less than six hours and his version was professional quality. Plus it held a certain appeal that Rex had definitely been lacking.

"Where the hell were you back when I was doin' this the first time?" Rex muttered to himself as he clicked on another page.

"More than likely, I was trying to figure out how to stop feeling trapped," Jack said under his breath.

That got his attention and Rex stood up, staring the other man down.

Jack shrugged, as though it didn't matter. "Dinner's on the table."

Once again, Jack gave Rex his back as he retreated out of the room.

Rex's alpha instincts were blazing. He wanted to demand that Jack come back, that he not walk away during a conversation as deep as that. However, he managed to keep his mouth shut. Jack wasn't his. The man was a guest and Rex had to figure out how to respect that.

Mine.

For whatever reason, that word stuck in his head as Rex stared at the empty doorway.

He wanted Jack Cunningham to be his.

That was what it was. This wasn't about sex. Rex wanted the man with a passion he hadn't felt in … maybe not ever. And he wanted him all to himself.

Fucking hell. This was not going to end well.

Rex gave the website one more cursory glance before he joined Jack at the small kitchen table.

"You had three phone calls this afternoon," Jack told him as he took his seat. "I answered. Two of them wanted details about the B and B, and the third one was a reviewer. Said he'd be interested in coming to stay for a weekend, and if he enjoyed his stay, he would highlight the place on his travel blog."

"Where are these people gettin' the number?" Rex asked.

"From what the reviewer said, Travis Walker referred him."

Rex nodded, then chuckled. Of course Travis was starting to spread the word. Rex sobered, glancing over at Jack. "What did you tell the reviewer?"

"I asked for information about his blog, then checked it out. From what I could tell, he's big on romantic getaways. Apparently, he's a traveler, enjoys staying at various places all over the world. With his husband."

Rex hadn't expected Jack to do that much research, but he appreciated him for it.

"I told him you wouldn't be opening until the fall, but to expect availability to be very limited because of the overwhelming interest. I informed him you'd be getting back to him once you had a date for the opening."

Cocking an eyebrow, Rex waited to see if there was more.

Jack didn't look his way when he said, "Oh, and Bristol called."

"Oh, yeah?" Rex shoveled potatoes into his mouth. "What did she want?"

A smirk pulled at the corners of Jack's mouth, but he still didn't look at him. "No clue. Said she tried your cell phone, but you didn't answer. However, she was very impressed with the way I answered the phone and wanted to know if you had come to your senses and hired me to handle that for you."

Rex grinned to himself.

Of course she had.

JACK WASN'T SURE WHY, BUT HE COULDN'T seem to stop talking. "I told her no such luck. Said I was temporarily helping out, but that I already had a full-time job."

Granted, Jack wasn't going to mention what else Rex's nosy best friend had asked. As it turned out, Bristol was quite curious as to what was going on between them. She had rambled on about how Rex never let anyone stay in his personal space. Certainly not for lengthy periods of time. And she'd been thrilled when she thought Jack was more than merely a guest. Her argument had been that Jack had stayed far longer than a normal guest, so surely there was something more between them.

It was then that Jack realized he had likely overstayed his welcome. She'd sounded disappointed when he mentioned he would be leaving soon.

Grabbing his fork, Jack proceeded to eat, hoping that by filling his mouth with food, he would stop rambling unnecessarily. Yes, he'd spent the majority of the day working on Rex's website, hoping to help him out just a little. They had agreed in the beginning that Jack would work in return for room and board. Aside from slapping some color on a few pieces of furniture, rarely had Jack done anything of value. Until today. He simply wanted to help. After all, Rex had given him a place to stay when he had no reason to do so.

"So'd you come up with a name?" Rex asked between bites.

Jack grinned. "Not anything you'll probably go for."

"Hit me."

Lifting his head, Jack looked at Rex, noticing he was watching him intently.

"Well … for starters, Sinner's Seclusion." Jack chuckled. "Although, as I say it out loud, it sounds ridiculous."

"Won't hear me argue," Rex mumbled, grinning.

"Okay. How about Romance Retreat?"

Rex grunted. "How about not?"

"Backwoods Bed-and-breakfast?" Jack suggested.

Rex's eyebrows lowered even more.

"Hospitality House?"

"Sounds like a clinic."

True. It did.

"Seduction Manor?" Jack laughed at his own absurdity and scooped mashed potatoes onto his fork. "Back-Country B and B?"

A subtle shake of his head was all the answer Rex offered.

Obviously, Rex wasn't going for any of those, but Jack had been kidding, anyway. They were ridiculous, but he was enjoying myself. However, he now had a better understanding of why the man hadn't come up with a name. It wasn't nearly as easy as it sounded.

"Okay, seriously," Jack said, sitting up straight. "The only real one I could come up with was…" He paused as he waited for Rex to look at him. "Serenity. That would be the name of the place."

"Serenity? Doesn't make you think of a day spa?"

Good point.

Jack stared at Rex for a moment, stumped. He had been working the couple angle, and it was obvious Rex was going for more of a family retreat. He thought about the picture of Rex's brother sitting on the small desk in the living room. Jack had asked him about it once, but he'd seen the way Rex's face had transformed when he talked about Rafe.

Jack's eyes widened and he smiled. "The Double R Retreat," he blurted.

Rex's eyebrows reversed their path, lifting toward the ceiling. Jack took that as a good sign.

"The Double R Retreat, huh? I kinda like it."

Jack watched him, waiting to see if he would say something else. When Rex continued to eat, Jack wondered if he'd failed at this task. Sure, Rex seemed as though he liked it, but did he really?

Rex started nodding. "I like it."

"Which one?"

"The Double R Retreat." Rex pointed his fork at Jack. "I'll see if the domain name is available."

Jack snatched his phone off the table, pulled up the site he'd been looking at earlier. He tapped in the new name and smiled. "It is."

After a few more keystrokes on another search engine, he checked a few more things. "And there aren't any other hotels, motels, lodges, ranches, or inns in the state named the same. I can get it all set up, so all you have to do is submit the request for the name."

Rex nodded. "Then it sounds like we're in business."

Jack knew Rex wasn't really incorporating him in the overall scheme of things. It was merely a phrase. That didn't stop the glow in his chest from bursting wide open at the thought of being included.

Not that he was going to think too hard on what *that* meant.

After dinner, Rex insisted that Jack go do something else because he didn't want him cleaning the kitchen since he had cooked.

Feeling slightly shunned, Jack retreated to his room. He considered sitting on the balcony for a bit, but the wind was blistering cold and every so often he heard sleet pelting the windows, which squashed that idea quickly.

As he sat on his bed, Jack considered calling Tina. He hadn't talked to her since he hung up on her the other night, but she had left at least a dozen messages. According to her last one, she wanted to talk about the logistics of her moving out. Jack didn't necessarily want to talk to her; however, he really did want her to move out of his apartment. Until she left, he wasn't going to go home.

The mere thought of talking to her turned him off the idea.

Falling back on the bed, Jack stared at the ceiling, his mind drifting to thoughts of Rex. More accurately, to their interaction earlier in the day. His dick stirred to life within seconds of remembering the man's gruff tone when he'd been talking about how he'd thought of Jack.

Trust me, there's plenty appealing about you. You've been here what? Three weeks? Do you know that I've fantasized about you every fucking day since you arrived?

"You're wasting time," Jack muttered to himself.

He was simply confused. That or just horny. This was normal. His dick had a mind of its own, and it didn't really give a shit who offered it relief.

He barked a laugh.

So not true. He was actually rather finicky, which was why he'd only been with a handful of women in his life. And while he wished it weren't true sometimes, his heart did care if he was in a committed relationship or not. Jack wasn't the fling type and he honestly didn't want to be.

A firm knock sounded on the bedroom door.

"Come in," he called out, not bothering to move.

The door opened and Rex remained in the doorway. The tall, handsome cowboy leaned against the doorjamb, his dark eyes taking everything in.

Before he even realized he was doing it, Jack was looking the man over from head to toe. Rex had showered, his hair still wet. He was wearing a black long-sleeved shirt that hugged his chest and a pair of dark blue jeans. His feet were bare. The man had really nice feet.

Jack forced his eyes up to Rex's face. "What's up?"

For a second, he didn't think Rex was going to answer. Not with words, anyway. He seemed to be considering something. But then his eyes cleared, and his dark gaze swung to Jack's face.

"I wanted to thank you for dinner. And for handlin' the website." His gaze dropped to the floor. "And apologize for my actions earlier."

Jack frowned, trying to figure out what he was referring to without questioning him outright. They'd already had one deep conversation that day, he wasn't sure he could handle another so soon.

Rex's gaze lifted and there was a wealth of emotion churning in the darkness. Part of him wanted to inquire as to what was on his mind, but he knew better. They'd said all they needed to say earlier today. It was time to move on.

"I'm happy to help out," Jack told him, addressing Rex's first statements only.

"How long were you engaged?"

The question surprised him almost as much as the apology.

"To Tina?" He shook his head. "Eight months. Together for a year and a half."

Rex's head cocked to the side. "You said there've been three?"

"Long story." Jack put his hands beneath his head, trying to appear casual. "Let's just say I made a few irrational decisions in my youth."

Rex stared back at him for what felt like an interminably long time before he nodded. "This comic book business... You been successful at it? Like Spiderman and shit?"

A lot of success, actually, but Jack wasn't going to mention that. Although he'd footed his and most of Tina's bills for the past eight months, plus put down the deposits for the wedding, Jack had still managed to save money. He had more than enough to sustain him for a while. Along with a couple of additional advances that would be coming in once he signed the most recent contract he'd agreed to.

"I can hold my own," he admitted.

"And the ex-fiancées?" Rex shifted on his feet, appeared genuinely curious.

Jack held Rex's gaze. "The first, Michelle, she was a kindergarten teacher. The second, Janine, an administrative assistant. And Tina was a bartender."

Just when Jack thought Rex was bored with the conversation and was about to turn around and leave, he stepped into the room. *Stalked* would be a better way to describe it.

Jack held his breath, watching as the bigger man moved closer. Closer still.

His heartbeat picked up speed and strength, thumping heavily against his chest. He couldn't seem to move, his hands still tucked under his head. He felt almost vulnerable as Rex came to stop at the edge of the bed.

When the man leaned over, Jack inhaled sharply, keeping his eyes locked with Rex's. One big hand reached up and settled on the pillow beside his head, the other against the headboard as Rex leaned down.

Jack only closed his eyes when Rex was too close for him to focus. Or so he told himself. The warmth of Rex's breath fanned his mouth and his insides coiled tightly. He felt himself sinking deeper into the mattress. Not from Rex's physical weight but from his presence.

His stomach spiraled, but not in a way that reflected any trepidation whatsoever. Rex's nearness certainly didn't turn him off. In fact, it made him want things he knew he wasn't supposed to want. They'd been through this already, but even Jack had a hard time remembering exactly why he was putting a rift between them.

The air exploded from his lungs when Rex closed the few inches between their mouths, pressing his lips down softly. Jack started to move his hands, but Rex immediately grabbed his forearms. He didn't forcefully hold him down, but he applied enough pressure to keep Jack in place as his probing tongue slid over his lips.

Instinct had Jack's lips parting. The kiss deepened and the room started to spin as he was engulfed by a heat he'd only ever experienced with Rex. His dick hardened, his muscles tensing, his brain going off-line.

Rex's tongue slipped against his. The kiss was familiar yet foreign at the same time. Jack hadn't realized how much he'd wanted Rex to kiss him again. He was firm, insistent, yet gentle. He tasted like mint and man, a heady combination that had Jack wanting him to continue.

That was the moment Rex pulled back and stared down at him.

"I haven't forgotten what you said earlier," Rex whispered. "Doesn't mean I like it, but I understand it. If you change your mind…"

Unable to do anything else, Jack nodded. He could deny it all day long, but he wanted everything Rex was offering.

The heat engulfed them both, a conflagration of energy and emotion that they were both clearly denying. Jack knew he should let Rex leave, to simply let it be, but he couldn't.

Before Rex could pull away completely, Jack mumbled, "Wait. Just … one more kiss."

Their eyes connected, searching, seeking. They both wanted this, it was obvious. As for whether it was smart, that was yet to be seen, but Jack couldn't seem to make the right decision. Having Rex that close did all sorts of crazy shit to his head and heart.

When Rex leaned in again, Jack kissed him back, lifting his head from the pillow to get closer, despite the fact that Rex was still holding his arms down.

It allowed him the ability to simply feel. No thinking, no worrying. Rex offered him a lifeline, something to cling to in the chaos racing through his brain.

Unfortunately, Rex pulled back and that lifeline was disconnected long before he was ready.

Twenty-One

REX WASN'T SURE WHAT PROMPTED HIM TO kiss Jack, but now that he had, he didn't know how he would resist going forward.

The way the man responded was exactly as he'd hoped. Jack might claim he had no interest in whatever was going on between them, but his actions belied his words. And yes, Jack might be the take-charge kind of guy in his day-to-day, but he was certainly looking for someone to take the reins, to lead the way, to make the decisions when it came to this. Which, of course, made Rex want him all the more.

Reluctantly, Rex released Jack's wrists, then started to stand tall. Before he got far, Jack's arms banded around him, jerking him closer, their mouths crashing together.

Putting a knee on the bed to keep from crushing Jack, Rex held himself back, knowing that if he gave in, he would likely take this too far. It had been a long damn time since he'd had his hands on a man before the city boy walked into his life, and Jack was pushing Rex's limits. Rex wanted more from him. Hell, he wanted everything, and that was more than a little terrifying to acknowledge.

Warm hands slipped beneath Rex's shirt and his body hardened as Jack's palms caressed his abs, his ribs, then slowly slid higher. He hadn't been touched in so damn long, Rex found it difficult to breathe while Jack's hands were on him.

"We're gonna take this slow," Rex whispered. "Very slow."

Jack nodded.

Inching closer, Rex pressed his thigh between Jack's legs, grinding against the hard ridge of his dick. Oh, yeah. Jack was definitely turned on by this. The man could deny it all day long, but this was what he needed.

"Oh, fuck…" Jack hissed, his hips undulating as he used Rex's thigh to increase the friction.

Somehow Rex managed to get Jack's hands in his grip again, holding them above his head while he encouraged Jack to dry hump his leg. He knew he couldn't let this go too far. Rejection wasn't his strong suit, and right now, Rex wasn't sure how he'd react if Jack sent him out of the room.

Rex nipped Jack's lower lip before thrusting his tongue into his mouth. He wanted to strip them both, to slide deep into the delicious heat of Jack's body, but he knew he couldn't. If this was going to go anywhere at all, Rex had to follow this new plan, to take things slow, to ease them both back into it.

Didn't mean he couldn't remind Jack of how good it was between them.

"I wanna make you come," Rex growled softly, his lips brushing against the pulse in Jack's neck. "Right here. Right now."

Jack moaned, bucking against him.

Pulling back so he could watch Jack's face, Rex admired him. The long, thick lashes that brushed his cheeks as his eyes remained closed. When Rex took him the next time, he would insist that Jack keep his eyes open, watch him. Face-to-face.

And he was pretty damn sure there would be a next time. Just not yet. For now, he could give Jack this.

"Keep going, baby," Rex urged. "Let go."

Jack's body tensed as he rocked against Rex's thigh. It was the sexiest thing Rex had seen while being fully clothed. He was assaulted with the memories of how fucking hot the man was as Rex was lodged deep in his ass, fucking them both into oblivion.

Jack moaned loudly. "Oh, fuck … oh, fuck, Rex … I…"

God, yes. He wanted to hear Jack moan his name over and over again.

When Jack began moaning in earnest, Rex leaned down and sucked on his neck. Hard. That earned him a cry as Jack's body jerked and twitched and then went eerily still.

Jack was breathing hard when Rex leveraged himself up onto his hands, stared down at Jack's beautiful face, the bewildered look in his eyes.

"You okay?"

Jack nodded, then shook his head, his eyes glassy as he stared back in silent wonder.

Confused was what he was.

Taking one more kiss, Rex forced himself to release Jack, getting to his feet and keeping his eyes on the sexy man. What he wouldn't give to strip him down and ravish him for hours. It wasn't going to happen, but the fantasy would be something he could jerk himself off to tonight.

As he turned to leave, Rex glanced back at Jack. The city boy was staring at him, his expression one of wonder, his breaths still choppy. He had enjoyed that even if he needed time to process what it meant. For him. For Jack. For them.

Because without a doubt, they were going to explore this further. The only question remaining was when.

"Good night, city boy," Rex said softly before closing Jack's door behind him.

He glanced down at Duke, who was sleeping soundly in the hallway.

"You wanna make a pass through the house?" he asked the dog.

Duke got to his feet, following close behind, his nails clicking lightly on the hardwood.

Knowing he wouldn't be able to sleep, Rex slipped out of the apartment and wandered the main house.

"I hate leaving him, Duke."

A soft doggy sigh was the response.

"But I have no choice."

There was a soft snort and he wondered if Duke disagreed or if he simply wanted Rex to shut up.

"If I'd stayed," he continued talking to his dog, "I would've done something neither of us is ready for." Rex wasn't prone to self-recrimination; however, he was starting to worry about his own intentions.

What exactly *did* he want from Jack? "One more night? Two? A week? A month? Forever?"

He peered down at Duke, noticed the dog's eyes were closed. Clearly, he wasn't going to get any advice from him.

"Or should I back off entirely and forget this ever happened?" he mumbled, this time to himself.

In a few weeks, Rex would be so immersed in work, he wouldn't have time to entertain anyone. He fully intended to dive in. He wanted to surprise Travis, to be ready to open the B and B before October. He figured if he worked hard enough, hired the right people, perhaps the summer wasn't looking too bad for a grand opening. That would keep him busy for a little while.

Rex sighed. "Come on, Duke. It's time for bed."

Being as loyal as he was, Duke simply got to his feet and followed.

After flipping off all the lights and ensuring the house was locked up, Rex forced himself back up to the third floor. The apartment was dark, just as he'd left it. Without making a sound, he slipped into his bedroom, closed the door before dropping into his bed.

Staring up at the ceiling, Rex couldn't help but wonder what Jack was doing. Was he sleeping? Sated from their too-brief interaction? Was he trying to come to terms with the fact that he'd given in to his desires? Again? Was he thinking about him? Did he wish that Rex had stayed? Or was he in denial, refusing to accept that there was something between them?

Memories of those few minutes had Rex reaching beneath the blankets and lightly palming his cock. He stroked slowly, not looking to get himself off but wanting to feel some of the pleasure he'd gotten from merely watching Jack come.

Closing his eyes, Rex shoved the blankets down his hips, imagining Jack was with him. When the cool air caressed his overly warm skin, Rex tightened his grip on his dick. He wanted to feel the suction of Jack's mouth, the warm rasp of his tongue. Rex wanted to hold Jack's head in place while he fucked his mouth, watching his cock tunnel between those sweet lips.

Rex hadn't had fantasies this vivid in a long time.

Truth was, he hadn't met anyone who'd even remotely interested him in years. Being single had suited him. It allowed him to do things his way, to live his life how he wanted.

And how would that be? Alone and lonely?

Ignoring the annoying voice in his head, Rex reached down and palmed his balls, kneading them while he tugged roughly on his cock. He spread his legs wider, inching closer to release as his mind was filled with thoughts of Jack. And only Jack.

JACK AWOKE TO THE SUN SHINING IN through the balcony door, the bright light beaming right on his face. He glanced around, trying to remember where he was.

Then it all came back in a rush of memories.

Rex kissing him. Him kissing Rex. Touching him, feeling the warmth of his skin against his palms. Rex getting him off with nothing more than friction against his cock while they were both fully clothed.

"Like a damn teenager." Jack groaned and rolled over.

Something was seriously wrong here. With every step forward, Jack seemed to be taking one step back. He was supposed to be focusing on getting his life together, not coming apart at the seams.

He had no fucking clue what had happened last night. "Why?" he whispered. "Why the hell do my good intentions go right out the window whenever Rex is near?"

Worst part was that his cock was hard again, desperate and aching, ready for more of what the man had to offer. Which didn't make a lick of fucking sense. Okay, fine. It made a little bit of sense. After all, he'd never met a person he was attracted to the way he was Rex. Never. Male or female. Still, there was something more. Something deeper. A connection, maybe?

"No. No connection. Can't be a connection. It's too soon." Jack groaned again.

Admittedly, Jack was driven by emotion and he considered that his downfall. The very reason he'd been engaged three times. Yet after Tina's betrayal, Jack had vowed to ignore his heart, to allow logic to win out. Which was the very reason he was thinking things to death. And he'd certainly been doing that ever since Rex slipped out of his room last night. He'd thought about that kiss, the way Rex's tongue felt, how his body had responded to him. The way his heart beat faster, harder in anticipation. It wasn't just physical, either. Of course, Jack couldn't forget the incredible nights they'd spent together, or even the night he'd masturbated on the balcony while Rex was in the hot tub.

Ignoring the ache in his balls, Jack forced himself out of bed. None of this was going to make sense if he spent too much time dwelling on it. Before he fell asleep last night, Jack had considered hiding out from Rex for a while, but he knew that couldn't happen. He was tired of running from everything, tired of pretending. Jack had been with women because it seemed natural, only it never felt as good as it did when he was with Rex. And when he thought about it, he wasn't confused. There was no shame when he accepted how he felt about Rex. Sure, he was slightly disappointed that he'd spent all these years not knowing who he truly was, what he wanted.

Jack figured he had two choices. Leave and never look back or let things progress for the short time he would be there. Maybe Rex was right. A little naked playtime could be exactly what he needed. And if it was meant to be, perhaps they could build a relationship off of that. It wasn't like Austin was a million miles away.

He opted for a quick shower, then made his way to the kitchen to start coffee. Glancing around, Jack realized Rex wasn't there. Neither was Duke. While he filled the coffee carafe with water, Jack peered out the window. Rex's truck wasn't in the driveway.

"Made quite the impression on the guy," Jack mumbled to himself. "Dry hump his leg and he disappears on you."

Not that he was disappointed that Rex wasn't there. He wasn't. He was just…

"What?" Jack snorted in disgust. "You thought because he gave you a fucking orgasm that he was going to have breakfast with you?"

"Talk to yourself often?"

The gruff voice startled him so much, Jack emitted a high-pitched squawk at the same time he dropped the carafe in the sink. He grabbed for the glass, thankful it didn't shatter against the porcelain.

"Shit," he barked when he realized he'd soaked the front of his shirt with water.

After shutting off the faucet, Jack tugged the soggy material away from his skin and turned only to come face-to-face with the ridiculously handsome man who was staring him down.

Rex smirked. "So, were you more interested in breakfast or another orgasm?" His deep, rich baritone glided around him, keeping Jack from moving an inch. "'Cause I'm open to either," Rex added, stepping closer until they were almost toe-to-toe. "Or both."

"I…" Jack had no fucking clue what he was going to say.

Rex inched forward and this time Jack did take a step back, only for his ass to bump into the counter.

Strong hands gripped his sides. He didn't even inhale as Rex removed the soggy T-shirt by lifting it over his head and tossing it into the sink. The man's dark eyes scanned Jack's chest while he continued to hold his breath, willing Rex not to stop this time, not to give Jack an out.

"Breathe," Rex whispered, his voice a dark rasp against Jack's senses. "We'll both feel better if you do."

Jack took a deep breath, trying to keep his chest from expanding. As it was, Rex was too close.

"I see you've given last night some thought."

A jerky nod was the only response Jack could offer. He was stunned into silence, scared to move, scared to breathe. He had no idea what he wanted right now, but breaking this spell wasn't on the list.

Rex leaned in a little more, his voice still soft. "You came so easily. And I bet it's safe to say you wanna come right now, don't you?"

Jack didn't answer. He couldn't. Logic dictated that he move away from Rex, that he not let himself be seduced, because no matter what, it wouldn't end well. For either of them.

Fucking hell.

He wanted to be seduced by this man. He wanted to seduce him, too. Wanted it more than air.

Rex closed the gap between them, his breath fanning Jack's ear. "I wanna take your dick in my mouth. Lave you with my tongue." Rex pulled back and met his gaze. "Suck you until you come down my throat."

The shiver that wrenched Jack's body nearly had him stumbling.

"I thought..." Jack tried to shake off the overwhelming feeling.

"You thought what?" Rex shifted back an inch.

"I thought you would expect a little in return. Something to make up for last night," Jack said, hoping he didn't sound too much like an idiot.

"And why would you think that?"

"Uh ... I thought maybe ... you wanted to find a release. Isn't that how it works?"

"You think it's all about getting something in return?" Rex's grin was sexy. "You've certainly been with the wrong people, city boy."

Jack frowned.

Rex leaned in, cupped his face. "Can I not just want to make you feel good?"

Jack shook his head at the same time he said, "Yes?"

Rex chuckled. "There's no points system here, city boy. I get plenty of pleasure from giving you pleasure. And the idea of making you come again…" Rex cupped him through his jeans, his voice dropping several octaves when he said, "I want that too fucking much."

Jack swallowed hard, his hips involuntarily shifting, forcing Rex's hand more firmly against his throbbing dick.

Rex's thumb brushed over Jack's lip. "Doesn't mean I won't want you on your knees, my cock tunneling in and out of your pretty mouth, though."

Pretty? No one had ever called him pretty before. He wasn't sure how he felt about that.

Rex kept his finger on Jack's lower lip. He was tempted to suck the digit into his mouth, but he refrained. He was confused. This wasn't supposed to be happening. More importantly, Jack wasn't supposed to want this to be happening. They'd already discussed it, hashed it out.

Before he could activate the filter from his brain to his mouth, Jack blurted, "I want to feel your mouth on me."

Rex smiled again. "I thought you'd say that."

Now that he'd mentioned it, it was the only thing Jack could think about. Feeling Rex's lips wrapped around his cock, sucking him dry. Jack groaned and realized Rex was still grinding the palm of his hand against his cock. If he wasn't careful, Jack was going to come in his pants like he had last night. It wouldn't take much.

"Do you want me to stop?"

Unwilling to rationalize his thoughts, Jack shook his head.

That was the last damn thing he wanted.

Twenty-Two

IT WAS CLEAR TO REX THAT JACK did not want him to stop. He didn't even need the man to clarify, but for his own peace of mind, Rex would insist. This was far too important to rely on instinct. It was obvious Jack was hard, but Rex needed to confirm that this was mutual. He wouldn't have it any other way.

"Tell me," Rex stated firmly. "Say, 'I don't want you to stop.'"

Rex could see the confusion in Jack's eyes. There was a battle brewing there. The more he thought about it, the more uncertain he became even if his body ached for what Rex was willing to give him.

"Say. It."

Jack swallowed hard.

Rex pulled his hand back.

"No. Please, Rex. Fuck." Jack hissed. "I don't want you to stop. Don't fucking stop. Please."

The need in his tone had Rex reaching for Jack's hips, sliding his fingers into the waistband of his sweatpants. He didn't waste any time, freeing Jack's cock from the confines of the loose fabric, never taking his eyes off the city boy's face. Rex wanted to see everything the man was feeling.

And he was feeling something, all right.

Lust, anxiety, confusion.

It was all there, all reflected in his expression.

Wrapping his fist around Jack's cock, Rex stroked slowly.

"I'm done playin' games with you, Jack," Rex stated firmly. "Done bein' your experiment. If you want more, you're gonna have to accept everything."

Jack sucked in a breath when Rex pumped his cock, squeezed gently. "Everything?"

"No more runnin'. You take what I'm offerin' this time, you're stuck with me."

Rex realized as soon as the words were out that they sounded like some sort of declaration. He could see it in Jack's eyes that the man recognized it as well. Worse, it appeared to be having the opposite effect on Jack.

"Not like that," Rex clarified, suddenly uncertain about his intentions. "I'm talkin' no more one-time thing. If you want me to fuck you, I'm gonna fuck you. A lot. No more back-and-forth, no more hidin' from this. Do you understand?"

Rex continued to stroke him, watching the pleasure that contorted the man's features. Damn but he loved watching Jack like this, accepting what Rex could and would give him.

"Do you understand?" Rex repeated, wanting to keep Jack in the moment.

Jack's lips parted. He managed a nod, but Rex wanted more than that.

"Say it."

"I understand."

Rex stroked him more firmly, teased the sensitive head of Jack's cock.

"Oh, fuck…" Jack moaned softly. "Your hand … it feels good. *Please*, Rex."

Rex loved the way Jack said his name.

"I happen to like the way you beg," he told Jack with a self-satisfied smirk. "Is that what you want, city boy? For me to make you beg?"

"Yes." Jack inhaled sharply when Rex brushed his thumb over the sensitive head again.

"Beg me."

"Please." Jack swallowed hard. "Please, Rex."

Rex yanked Jack's sweatpants down his legs, then pulled them off, leaving him standing naked in the kitchen.

"Please what?"

The guy had a phenomenal body. He wasn't body-builder thick, but he was damn near perfect. The hard planes and angles of his chest, narrow waist, muscular thighs, and a fucking beautiful cock. Rex was going to have fun getting to know this body inch by delicious inch. With his mouth, his tongue, his teeth. And yes, his cock. He wasn't going to satisfy Jack by merely getting him off. He was going to ensure Jack enjoyed every delirious minute.

"Suck me, Rex. Put your mouth on me. Please."

Rex maintained his firm grip on Jack's cock, tugging him forward. He would've preferred to perch Jack on the countertop, but he needed a little more space, so he would have to find another place to lay him out. The bedroom was too damn far.

Leading Jack by his dick, Rex steered him to the kitchen table, then released him.

"Lie down."

Jack frowned.

"It wasn't a request," Rex clarified.

Still seemingly uncertain, Jack shifted so that his ass rested on the wooden table top. It took a second, but he finally managed to get into position, laid out like a Thanksgiving feast.

"Very nice." Rex could definitely get used to this.

Jack might've been hesitant, but his body certainly wasn't. His cock bobbed eagerly between his legs, the swollen head slapping against his abdomen as he shifted.

Rex stood on Jack's right side. Using one hand, he cupped Jack's balls, kneading them gently as he stared directly into the soft gray of his eyes, watching as they darkened with lust.

Jack hissed in a breath.

Unable to help himself, Rex placed two fingers on Jack's lower lip. "Suck my fingers."

Those stormy gray eyes widened as Rex pushed the digits inside Jack's mouth.

"Suck."

Rex imagined his fingers were his cock, feeling the warmth of Jack's mouth as it closed around them, the rasp of his tongue caressing the swollen, sensitive head, the suction engulfing him, eradicating all thought. His would be the only dick those lips had ever touched, and Rex fucking liked that more than he could explain.

"Harder," Rex commanded. "Suck my fingers the way you want me to suck your cock."

Jack's chest was heaving, his legs trembling. It was obvious he was fighting this. And sure, Rex understood that. It was easy to come up with reasons as to why they couldn't go down this path, but it was far more difficult to deny the urge when it was so fucking powerful.

When Jack applied the right amount of suction on his fingers, Rex slid his right hand up, circling Jack's cock with his fist. He stroked, keeping the hand job in perfect rhythm with the way Jack was sucking his fingers.

"I want you to remain still," Rex ordered. "And I want you to remain quiet."

Jack nodded.

"Do you want my mouth on you?"

Jack nodded again.

Rex pulled his fingers back. "Tell me."

"I want your mouth… Fuck, Rex. Suck me."

Leaning over, Rex took the head of Jack's dick in his mouth, swiping his tongue over the velvety smooth skin.

"Holy fuck," Jack groaned.

Rex lifted his head.

"I said quiet. No sound." He met Jack's eyes. "Or I stop."

Jack nodded curtly, obviously understanding him.

Rex swiped his tongue over the wide crest, lapping up the pre-cum forming, teasing, tormenting. He paused momentarily. "How many men have sucked your dick?" He already knew the answer, but he wanted to hear it from his lips.

"None," he said on a rough groan when Rex took him to the back of his throat. "Only you, Rex. Oh, fuck."

Being that he was his first, Rex decided to give Jack a little leeway with the noisy part. While he worked him with his lips and tongue, Rex allowed Jack's breathy moans to fuel the heat in his veins.

Mine.

That word reverberated around in his head over and over as he had Jack begging and pleading.

"Christ, Rex… That feels so fucking good. I've never… God, don't stop."

He didn't intend to. While Jack continued a litany of praise, Rex continued to suck and lick, his own cock so fucking hard it hurt.

Only when Jack's breaths became rapid did Rex pause, lifting his head to look at Jack. "You wanna come?"

"Yes."

"In my mouth?"

Jack's mouth fell open and his eyes rolled back, a deep growl erupting in his chest. "Yes, Rex. I wanna come in your mouth."

Fuck. Rex loved hearing that.

As a reward, Rex lowered his head again and sucked him deep. He worked Jack's cock fast, then slow, drawing out his pleasure until he knew Jack was hanging by a thread. While Jack was busy writhing and moaning, Rex slipped his index finger into his mouth, lubing it with saliva before sliding it between Jack's ass cheeks. When he took Jack to the back of his throat again, Rex inched his finger into his ass. Gently, slowly.

He added another finger, continuing to lave Jack's dick, sucking firmly. He searched until he found that one spot that would—

"Oh, fuck!" Jack cried out, his hips bucking. "That feels… Oh, shit! I'm—"

Hell yeah.

Jack responded so fucking beautifully as Rex teased his prostate. His cock jerked and twitched, then pulsed as he came in Rex's mouth, his body drawn up tight.

While he gave Jack a second to catch his breath, Rex stared into his eyes.

Once again, the only word that came to mind was…

Mine.

THAT WAS AN ORGASM THAT JACK WOULD never forget for as long as he lived.

It seemed, at the hands of this man, Jack always came harder than he ever had in his entire life. And with every single release, it only became more intense, nearly impossible to ignore, to pretend it wasn't as earth-shattering as he knew it was. The moment those fingers brushed that spot inside him, Jack saw stars. Everything coiled into a ball of warmth and energy, then released in a blaze of ecstasy.

And now, as he fought to catch his breath, the only thing he could think about was returning the favor to Rex. He wanted to explore, to learn every inch of Rex's body, to have his turn.

"I want to touch you," Jack whispered when he could finally form words.

Rex's dark eyes pinned him in place.

Jack was still flat on his back on the table. He wasn't sure he could move. That had been earth-moving, soul-shattering. Intense. Far more than anything he'd ever expected to feel, even. And now he wanted to give the same to Rex, to allow him to come apart the same way.

Rex stood tall. "I'm at your mercy."

Forcing himself to sit up, Jack dropped his feet to the chair. He scanned the room, wondering if they should move this to the couch or relocate to the bedroom.

The couch is closer.

Yes, yes it was.

Clearly realizing what Jack was thinking, Rex took his hand. Jack hopped off the table and allowed Rex to lead him into the living room, where he stopped. Being naked in this man's apartment should've felt awkward, but his brain couldn't process it at the moment.

"I've never done this before," Jack admitted, feeling nerves flutter anxiously.

In a surprisingly intimate gesture, Rex cupped his cheek and moved in close. "I know. And I fucking love that about you."

When Rex leaned in and kissed him, Jack kissed him back, unable to resist. He tasted himself on Rex's tongue and it surprised him momentarily. He liked it, enjoyed it even. There was something innately sexy about the act, knowing Rex had swallowed him down. And when Rex's hand remained on his face, Jack felt something. A strange stirring deep in his chest, or maybe it was in his soul. He wasn't sure, but it was something he was fairly certain he'd been seeking his entire life.

The intimacy was shocking but not unwelcome. He simply hadn't expected it. For whatever reason, Jack had never truly considered what it was like between two men. Sure, he'd had some thoughts. But his fantasies had always leaned toward the physical. He'd always imagined the man he would be with was masculine, in control. No weakness, no vulnerability. He realized his fantasies had been superficial because this ... whatever this was ... it felt powerful.

More importantly, it felt real.

When they broke apart to catch their breath, Rex pressed his forehead to his. Jack let his hands wander down Rex's chest, then beneath his shirt. He wanted him naked, wanted to feel Rex's skin against his.

"Keep touchin' me," Rex urged when Jack's hands drifted higher, forcing the cotton upward.

Before Jack had a chance to get Rex's shirt off, there was a knock on the door.

Instinctively, Jack jerked away from Rex as though they were teenagers busted making out. He stared at the door, suddenly too aware of how naked and vulnerable he was.

Rex moved over and peeked out the security hole, then turned back to him and smiled. "I think it's safe to say the roofers are here."

Yeah. Okay. Great.

Jack managed to nod, then raced into the kitchen to grab his sweatpants. He tugged them on and grabbed his wet shirt out of the sink. Rex must've slipped out because he wasn't at the door when Jack returned.

The next thing Jack knew, he was hauling ass straight for his room. He shut and locked the door, then leaned against the wood, breathing hard.

"What have I done?" he whispered as his brain processed all that had taken place in the past hour. Rex finding him in the kitchen, Rex blowing him on the table, the most incredible orgasm ever. Well, maybe not the most incredible. All the orgasms Rex had given him had been mind-blowing, each one more powerful than the last. But it had been news-worthy, no doubt about it.

Holy shit.

If the roofers hadn't shown up, what would've happened? Would Rex have let him explore? Would they still be there now? How far could he have gone? Was Rex willing to let Jack fuck him, too? Or merely suck him?

"Fuck," he breathed out roughly. He had no idea how this was supposed to play out, but he suddenly had the overwhelming urge to drive his dick deep into Rex's ass.

His cock jerked at the thought.

"No," he snapped, pushing off the door. "This is not supposed to happen. It's going the wrong direction."

But what if he caved? Gave in to the undeniable lust?

"It would be amazing," he whispered even as he shook his head.

But where would he be then? Back in the same situation where he tried to turn a casual relationship into something more? He knew Rex was okay with a one-night stand. Naked playtime, as he'd referred to it. That first night had been … well, it had been one night. A memory. They weren't supposed to ever see each other again. Then the second time… That had been a mistake. Jack had manipulated the situation, allowed his out-of-control emotions to lead him. It had been amazing, but a mistake, nonetheless.

But this…

Rex's words rang in his head: *If you want me to fuck you, I'm gonna fuck you. A lot. No more back-and-forth, no more hidin' from this.*

Damn.

Could he do it? Could he seriously consider having something with Rex?

Funny how it didn't even matter that Rex was a man, that this was an entirely new thing for him. No, that actually felt normal. As though he'd finally accepted who he was, what he wanted. Accepting that he was gay was easier than he'd expected. Jack was more worried about his shitty track record with relationships and how, no matter what, he was going to get his heart broken in the end.

And this time, Jack knew he wouldn't simply move on. In fact, he wasn't sure he would be able to move on after Rex. The man would wreck his heart and leave him in shambles.

Which meant he was running purely on emotion. Perhaps that was the only reason he was even entertaining the idea of a relationship that was based on sex. He'd never felt anything even remotely similar to what he felt when he was with Rex. Hell, he knew for a fact he'd never felt this way about any of the women in his past.

Did it mean he'd wasted his entire life searching for something he would never find because his focus had been too narrow? Or was this happening because Rex was offering him something he'd fantasized about? Perhaps Jack was extra needy because of Tina's infidelity.

Fucking hell.

He was so confused. More so than he'd ever been in his life.

Jack took a deep breath, headed for the closet. He needed clothes. Dry clothes. Warm clothes. He needed to get out of there for a little while. His gaze strayed to the balcony door overlooking the pasture.

After yanking a pair of jeans off the hanger, followed by a T-shirt, Jack grabbed a pair of socks out of the dresser. Hurriedly, he pulled everything on, snatched his shoes, then grabbed a sweatshirt and wrestled into it before snagging his leather jacket for good measure. It was fucking cold outside, but at the moment, Jack didn't care. While Rex handled the roofers, Jack would take a walk, clear his head. Maybe it would bring him some clarity, allow all of this—or hell, even *some* of this—to make sense.

And if not, perhaps Jack could figure out his next move, because one way or another, he had to come to terms with whatever was going on with him. Before Jack allowed this to go any further with Rex, he had to figure out what he wanted.

Otherwise, they were both going to end up doing something they'd likely regret.

Twenty-Three

IT DIDN'T TAKE LONG TO GET THE roofers going. Rex had talked to them, ensured the shingles they'd brought were the ones he'd purchased, then let them get started.

On his way back into the house, he'd run into Kylie, who'd stopped by to talk about the fireplaces. She'd wanted to know if he would be discarding any. He had agreed to keep them all, changing the layout a little to accommodate them, as well as get someone out there to clean them out.

So, rather than sneak back upstairs to pick up where he'd left off with Jack, Rex had called a few places, found a reputable company who could come out within the next couple of days. It was during that phone call that Rex had watched Jack sneak out the back door.

Although Rex would've preferred to ignore everyone and everything in lieu of getting back to what he and Jack had been doing prior to the roofers interrupting, the instant Jack ran out the back door, Rex felt the disappointment deep in his bones. He tried to shrug it off by pretending Jack was merely coming to terms with who he was, accepting that he was gay. Only, Rex wasn't sure that was the reason Jack had disappeared. He didn't seem to have an issue accepting his desires for a man. He seemed to have a problem accepting there was something between the two of them and that it was more than simply sex.

Not that anything would come of this. Rex suspected Jack was going to go through a lot before he ever figured out what he truly wanted. And more than likely, he would be doing that when he went back to Austin. Rex only hoped that wouldn't be soon because he'd been truthful when he told Jack he was done playing games. He didn't want a one-and-done thing here. They deserved to enjoy one another for a while. Maybe once they'd fucked each other out of their systems, Jack could go back to life as he knew it. It would likely be a long time before Jack was ready for something serious, anyway.

As for Rex … well, he wanted long-term. He wanted commitment. He was ready for serious. He wasn't looking for a fling, no matter how attracted to Jack he was. He needed more. A whole lot more than one or two nights.

Did he want more with Jack? It was possible.

What he knew of Jack, he admired. No, he didn't know the ins and outs of the man's life, but that was all right. Jack didn't know about the hell Rex had been through, either. However, Rex did know that he wanted to explore this with him. And he was even willing to do temporary just to spend some time with the man. They didn't have to make decisions for the rest of their lives now. Sex was supposed to be fun, and from what he could tell, they both deserved a little of that.

Or Jack would come back from wherever he went and realize their morning escapade had been a huge fucking mistake.

The thought made Rex's gut twist. He didn't want to be the cause of Jack's uncertainties. And since thinking about it wasn't going to fix the situation, Rex decided he had better put the minutes to good use.

So, after grabbing a bottle of water, checking in on the guys who'd started painting the exterior, Rex called for Duke, then headed for his workshop. He had things that couldn't be put off any longer. Rex fully intended to get this place open because that was something he *did* have control over.

By the time four o'clock rolled around, Rex started to get worried about Jack. He hadn't seen him come back, and if he'd been walking all this time, he was going to be in a world of hurt come morning. It was too fucking cold to be exposed to the elements for long.

After putting his tools away, Rex locked up the workshop and headed to the main house. He took a lap around the exterior, noticed the painters had evidently quit early due to the weather. Same with the roofers, but they had gotten all the shingles up onto the roof. They'd assured him they could get the job done in three days, provided the weather held out. He could only hope they would still be on track.

Rex headed up to the third floor, stepped into the apartment. When he peered down the hallway, he noticed Jack's door was closed. There was a twist in his gut, but he fought it off, marching right up to the door. He rapped his knuckles on the wood, fully expecting to be met with silence.

When Jack's abrupt "What?" sounded, Rex took one step back. Evidently, he'd snuck back inside the same way he'd snuck out.

"You okay in there?"

"Yeah."

"You hungry?"

"No."

His tone was clipped, and he obviously didn't want to talk, so rather than bother him, Rex headed to the kitchen. He had prepared himself for this. In fact, he felt responsible for pushing Jack to this point. Except he didn't quite understand Jack's need to run from everything. It reminded him of his brother, of the way Rafe had skipped town without a word to anyone. Although he could rationalize the reasons, it still pissed him off. Rex fully believed you faced your issues head on, otherwise they were simply going to fester.

If Rex had to guess, Jack had spent the entire day questioning himself. Their interactions that morning had gone against the entire argument they'd had the day before. He'd been thinking about it himself, only Rex wasn't curious as to *why* it happened. He merely wanted it to happen again.

However, Rex knew when to leave well enough alone. Jack had to figure it out for himself.

After grabbing a beer from the fridge, Rex headed toward the back door. Since he wasn't necessarily hungry, he braved the hot tub before he took a shower. This time, rather than get naked, Rex discarded his shirt and jeans but kept his boxer briefs on. The other night he'd done it to see what reaction he would get from Jack. Now that he knew, it was up to Jack to make the next move.

If there was a move to be made.

Forty-five minutes later, Rex forced himself out of the hot water. The wind chilled him straight to the bone, but he ignored it as best he could, wrapping a towel around himself. As he was grabbing his clothes, he peered up at the third-floor balcony. Jack was standing inside, staring out through the glass door. Rex held his stare for the longest time despite the fact his ass was freezing. His chest ached, but he wasn't sure why. Was it for Jack? Or for himself? Or perhaps both?

Unfortunately, Rex couldn't ease anyone's pain but his own, so he gave Jack a quick nod and then started for the house. He would have to face Jack soon enough. When he reached the apartment, he was met by Duke. The dog circled him twice, then went right for his food bowl.

"Sorry, man. It's past suppertime, huh?" he mumbled as he grabbed the food from the pantry, then scooped kibble into Duke's bowl.

Once Duke was settled in with his evening meal, Rex headed toward the bathroom. He tried to ignore the fact that Jack's bedroom door was closed, which he took to mean the man had nothing to say about what had transpired between them.

Rex sighed. He really was getting tired of this. His understanding and patience had a limit.

Still, he fought the urge to break down Jack's door. Instead, he took a quick shower, then retreated to his own bedroom for the night.

If Jack wanted him, he knew where he was.

If he didn't…

Well, Rex wasn't sure he wanted to think about that just yet.

Tuesday, January 29, 2019

JACK HAD MANAGED TO AVOID REX FOR more than twenty-four hours.

Yesterday, he'd ventured out of the house, wandering through the woods while Rex played contractor and handled everything going on at the house. When he'd gotten bored with that, Jack had taken a trip along Main Street, stopped and had lunch at the diner, spent a little time wandering through the various stores without buying a thing. And this morning, when he woke to find Rex already downstairs working, he had taken advantage of the extra time to think.

And walk.

And walk some more.

His face had the windburn to prove it, but he didn't care. Jack had needed the time to gather his thoughts and come up with a plan of action. And when he thought he was finally going to confront Rex that afternoon, to tell him what he wanted, he'd found the man holed up in his workshop. So, what did he do? He decided not to bother him, of course.

"Does that make me a chickenshit?" he mumbled under his breath.

Yeah, it did. But so what? It wasn't like he was running. He wasn't. Rex was simply busy. They hadn't been able to connect since their last encounter.

"Yeah, right," he muttered.

Rather than worry about it, Jack had come upstairs, slapped a sandwich together, then eaten in his bedroom. He had heard Rex come in, but not too long after, the door had closed again. That was the moment Jack realized that Rex was avoiding him, too.

For some reason, that bothered him. Sure, Jack knew why *he* was spending so much time thinking, but he didn't know what reason Rex would have to avoid him. Maybe he wasn't interested anymore? Maybe he never really had been, and he was glad Jack hadn't confronted him?

Whatever it was, Jack wanted to know. And that meant he had to suck it up and talk to him.

Jack was standing at the door overlooking the back patio when he saw Rex come out to the hot tub a little before seven. That was a fairly consistent routine for him, Jack had realized. When he wasn't busy managing the subcontractors or working alongside them, Rex would work in the shop, then lock up the house, spend an hour in the hot tub before going to his room for the night.

Part of him had expected Rex to seek him out, to confront him. Surely Rex was pissed. Every woman he'd ever dated had found an issue with Jack seeking seclusion. Didn't matter if he had a good reason or not.

Not Rex. He didn't seem to give a shit one way or the other.

Secretly, Jack had been waiting for him to come up to his room or to corner him in the kitchen. In fact, Jack had been hoping. Hell, he'd turned the man away the only time he'd come up here, hoping to engage Rex in an argument, but it hadn't worked. Rex had turned right around and left.

"Admit it," he told himself. "You're being childish."

Okay, fine. He was. He wanted Rex to chase after him, to force him to make a decision about what it was he wanted. To convince him that Jack wasn't rushing headlong into something without giving it the appropriate amount of thought. Instead, Rex had left him to his own devices, and Jack was no closer to figuring himself out.

But Jack was definitely going stir-crazy, and to be fair, he was fucking tired of thinking so damn much. He had managed to work on the character Shawn was all up in arms about and somehow even impressed him with it. Since he'd avoided Shawn rather than meeting with him like he'd promised, Jack had put more effort into ensuring he captured what Shawn was looking for in the character. They had talked on the phone yesterday evening, and since Shawn was over the moon with the new design, Jack agreed to do another mock-up to ensure he was happy before Jack started working on the graphics for the book.

All the while, Jack had spent every minute thinking about Rex.

"Fuck it. Stop being a chickenshit," he growled. "It's time to fight this out."

Jack waited for Rex to get into the water before he headed downstairs. He paused on the second-floor landing, debating on simply going to bed and pretending nothing had ever happened. Eventually he would be going back to Austin. Jack did have a life there. He simply needed Tina to move out so he could get on with it. Six months from now, Jack would likely be remembering his first kiss with Rex, their amazing nights together, that mind-numbing blow job, and Rex probably wouldn't even remember him.

"Fuck that," Jack grumbled as he stomped the rest of the way down. No way would he ever forget Rex. And Jack damn sure wasn't going to let Rex forget him.

Rex didn't look up from where he was relaxing as Jack pulled off his shirt and tossed it on the table. The wicked January breeze slammed into him, making him rethink his actions for a brief moment. Getting in the water wouldn't be a problem. Getting out … well, that was another story.

"Don't be a chickenshit," he whispered as he unsnapped his jeans, then stripped them off.

Rex still didn't look up when Jack took the steps down into the tub. Even when Jack got closer, Rex didn't pay him a lick of attention. The moment Jack leaned back against one of the contoured seats, sinking down so that only his head remained above the water, Rex pushed to his feet as though he was going to leave.

What the fuck?

Seriously?

It pissed Jack off. So much so that he grabbed Rex's arm. Rex stopped suddenly, then slowly turned to face him, jerking his arm from Jack's grip. His dark eyes didn't show a hint of what he was thinking.

"What's your problem?" Jack asked, narrowing his gaze as though that would help him see into Rex's brain.

Rex frowned. "Last I checked, I wasn't the one with the problem."

When he turned to get out, Jack reached for him again. He'd never done that before. Never felt the need to confront anyone. He was the type who preferred people to walk away so he could pretend things never happened.

Rex sank back into the water. Probably not because he wanted to hang out, more so because his nuts were going to shrivel up if he didn't.

"What do you want, Jack?"

Jack backed up at the growl in Rex's voice. He obviously didn't appreciate being manhandled.

"I want to know why you're avoiding me," Jack said truthfully.

Rex smiled, but it wasn't a good thing. He looked dangerous. Definitely irritated.

"Me?" Rex glanced around, then turned his attention back to Jack once more. "I'm not the one who's been hidin' for two days."

"Thanks for noticing," Jack snapped. That made him feel marginally better.

"How could I miss it?" Rex snapped, his tone rough, his eyes flashing with frustration or anger. Perhaps both. "Did you get your thoughts in order?"

"What?"

Rex moved toward him as Jack sank deeper against the seat, trying to maintain some distance between them. Unfortunately, he had nowhere to go.

"That wasn't what you were doin'?" Rex continued, getting right up in Jack's personal space. "Takin' walks, avoidin' the issues? Runnin'?"

"I wasn't running," Jack insisted. "I just needed time to think."

"Two days?" Rex scoffed. "You spend an awful lot of time thinkin', no time takin' responsibility for your actions."

Jack couldn't deny that stung even as he recognized the truth in the words. Still, it pissed him off.

"I'm sorry if I'm not like you, Rex. I can't simply indulge in something and walk away without—"

Rex cocked an eyebrow. "Without what?"

Jack stared at him for a moment. He noticed the way Rex's gaze slid to his mouth once or twice.

"Without feeling guilty."

"Guilty?" Rex snorted. "Trust me, city boy, I don't feel guilty."

Yeah, well, that made one of them.

"Did it work? Your avoidance? Did you at least figure out what you wanted?"

Jack swallowed hard because, no, he had not. He couldn't seem to rationalize what was going on no matter how long he thought about it.

"It's not that easy," Jack told him.

Rex inched closer. "As far as I'm concerned, it's pretty damn simple. You either want me or you don't."

Yeah. Little did Rex know, there was nothing simple about that. He did want Rex, but he wasn't sure if he *should* want him.

Rex's chest pressed up against his and Jack knew he was going to kiss him. He wanted to push him away, he wanted to pull him closer. It was so fucking confusing.

"Tell me, Jack. Do you want me?"

"Of course."

Rex pulled back, held his gaze. "Then what's the problem?"

Jack stared into Rex's dark eyes.

"Because let me tell you something, Jack," Rex whispered, not missing a beat when his hands curled around Jack's neck. "I want you with every fucking breath I take."

Holy fuck. The conviction behind those words shocked him. Jack reached for Rex then, cupping the back of his head and jerking him forward, their lips slamming together. The kiss was explosive. Rex crushed Jack between his big body and the side of the hot tub as their tongues dueled. Jack ran his hands over him, acknowledging every hard angle of his body with his palms.

In that moment, there was no confusion. Jack knew exactly what he wanted. Rex. Everything Rex was willing to give him, for as long as he was willing to give it. One night, two. Or hell, even a lifetime. He'd never felt like this and he was starving for it, desperate to explore, to see just what was in store for him.

"I already told you, I won't play this game with you," Rex said when he pulled back. Rex's hands remained in place, curled around Jack's neck, his thumbs pushing under his chin as he forced Jack to hold his gaze. "I have no desire to be your toy, the one you toss onto a shelf when you're tired of it. I'm not askin' for commitment, but I'd like to know we're on the same page."

No commitment? Was that what Jack needed? Naked playtime? Yes. His cock seemed to think so. Nothing serious. No relationship, commitment, no chance of betrayal. Then he could walk away afterward, go back to his life in Austin, forget Rex Sharpe even existed.

Sure, it was the exact opposite of what Jack knew deep down. He would never forget Rex. If he did allow this to go further, walking away would be damn near impossible. Leaving indefinitely … yeah, Jack wasn't sure that could happen.

Suddenly Rex released him and moved back. His eyes were locked on Jack's for a second before Rex stood tall, spun around, and walked away. He didn't even bother with a towel as he made the trek up the stairs to the third floor.

Jack was left staring after him, wondering how in the fuck Rex had read his mind. Because surely that was what had happened. Otherwise, he wouldn't be quite so pissed.

The question was, which did Rex dislike more? The thought of Jack using him and walking away? Or the idea of Jack falling in love with him?

Twenty-Four

AFTER SHOWERING, REX MADE A SANDWICH, SCARFED it down, then fell into bed.

He was so damn tired.

And pissed.

He was angry at Jack for playing this game, more so at himself for allowing it to happen. After all, he had instigated it. And he'd thought it a good plan. Right up until he realized that was Jack's intention. He'd seen it in his eyes. Jack had been contemplating a quick roll again, one more chance to succumb to the overwhelming lust that was undeniable. But Rex knew Jack was going to run away or hide, just as he'd been doing for the past couple of days. Probably feeling ashamed that he'd given in to his baser urges.

Hell, he wouldn't put it past Jack to go back to his life and pretend Rex didn't exist.

Rex was no longer willing to do that with him.

It wasn't that Rex was opposed to one-night stands. He'd had more than his fair share in his lifetime. But he could no longer go down that road with Jack. Somewhere along the way, his heart had gotten involved. The last thing he wanted was to fall in love with Jack only for him to walk away, claiming this was all a mistake.

Rex wasn't going to be his mistake.

Not now. Not ever.

With a sigh, he flipped off the lamp and closed his eyes.

Tomorrow was a new day. A day that included a conversation with Jack. They would sit down, hash it out for good, and determine…

When the man was going back to Austin.

Because, as far as Rex was concerned, it was time.

A sharp rapping on Rex's bedroom door woke him. It took a second to realize where he was. He scrubbed a hand down his face and glanced over at the clock. Two in the morning.

What the hell?

Suddenly worried something had happened, Rex launched himself out of bed and clicked on the lamp before rushing to the door, yanking it open. There, standing in the hallway, was Jack. The dim light from the single bulb cast his face in shadow as he stood there looking like every gay man's wet dream.

"Somethin' wrong?" Rex asked, peering around him to look down the hall. No flames coming from the living room, so he considered *that* a good thing.

"No," Jack said, his shoulders square, gaze still locked on Rex.

Rex narrowed his eyes and frowned. "Then what do you want?"

Their eyes met, held, and Rex suddenly knew. There wasn't an emergency he needed to tend to. Jack was there because he wanted something from him.

"Sorry, Jack. Not interested."

Rex reached for the door, intending to close it on him, but Jack moved forward. Before he could order Jack to get out, the man's arms wreathed Rex's neck and he was kissing him like a starving man.

Damn. The man could kiss. His lips were pliant yet impatient. His tongue insistent as it pushed into Rex's mouth. Jack devoured him, consumed him. For the most part, Rex had been the instigator in their rendezvous. Not this time.

For a brief moment, as he stood in the doorway of his bedroom, he was overwhelmed by Jack. There was a hint of panic at Jack's aggressive response, but Rex managed to push it back, remind himself where he was, who he was with.

Jack.

The natural fear abated, leaving him breathless and overwhelmed. He wanted this man with a desperation he'd never known before.

Only…

This wasn't supposed to happen.

When he came to his senses, Rex tried to push him away, desperate to get this thing resolved before it went too far, but Jack was persistent. He used his body to force Rex backward. He stumbled, wrapping his arm around Jack as he fought to keep upright.

As he stumbled, Jack never released him, holding on tight as though that was the only thing he could do. Rex's body took over, the desire to claim this sexy man overwhelming in its intensity. Rex pushed him up against the wall, kissing him roughly as he twined his fingers in Jack's hair and held him there.

When he came up for air, Rex let his mouth trail over Jack's stubbled cheek, down his neck.

"Is this what you came for?" Rex questioned, his voice a rough growl in his throat. Part lust, part anger.

"God, yes, Rex. This is what I want. What I need. You. Me."

Rex tried to ignore the way Jack's words stirred something in his chest. He wasn't looking for more. He wasn't.

"You came to me," Rex told him. "You better remember that the next time you think about runnin'."

"I'll remember," Jack whispered hoarsely. "I don't want to run. I *need* you, Rex."

Yeah. He was a sucker, Rex knew it. But he gave in, anyway. It had never been a question whether he would or not. He'd wanted Jack since the night he'd seen the man at Moonshiners. That hunger had only intensified with every passing minute since.

Somehow, they ended up on Rex's bed, Rex flat on his back before he realized what they were doing or how fast this was moving. He managed to flip their positions, kissing Jack like a starving man. He started to get off the bed, ready to move this to Jack's room because he didn't want to do this here. Not in his room. Not in his bed. Not since that night had he ever allowed himself to be vulnerable in his bedroom, his only safe space. It brought back too many memories.

"Where are you going?" Jack asked, his lips sliding over Rex's neck as he moved with him.

"Your bed," he moaned softly, trembling from the need overwhelming him.

Jack pulled back, met his gaze. "What's wrong with your bed?"

Rex took a quick look around, shaking his head. He didn't know how to explain it. Wasn't sure he even could.

"Rex? You okay?"

Their gazes collided once more, as Rex managed to get his footing. He reached for Jack, helped him to stand, then led the way to Jack's room. Once inside, he shut the door, then spun Jack around and pressed him up against the wood.

In an effort to redirect, to get Jack's mind off the reason Rex had bolted from his own room, Rex glared down at him. "If you're fuckin' with me—"

"I'm not," Jack said, his concern evident, his voice stronger than before, his hands gentle as they slid up Rex's chest. "Why did we come in here?"

Not intending to go into the details, Rex shook his head. "The way it has to be."

Jack's eyes bounced over his face momentarily but then settled. When he didn't say anything more, Rex took a step back, then moved over to the bed. Knowing Jack was the type who wanted someone else to be in control, Rex decided to give it all up to him.

He dropped onto the mattress, then fell back, tucking his hands beneath his head in a move he hoped was casual. He was still fighting back the panic, reminding himself that Jack would not hurt him.

"What are you doing?" Jack asked, uncertainty lacing his words.

"You came to me. It's your turn to take charge."

Rex turned his head to stare at him, wondering how Jack would handle that. His gray eyes sparkled in the soft glow from the lamp. His hair was tousled from Rex's fingers, his lips red and swollen from his kiss. He looked like every fantasy Rex had ever had.

Jack eased onto the bed, lay beside him, then propped himself up on one elbow and faced Rex. His fingers trailed over Rex's chest while their eyes remained locked. When Jack finally looked away, Rex noticed he was watching as his hand glided over Rex's skin.

"I want to take my time," Jack said softly. "I want to explore you."

Jack's fingernail scraped over Rex's nipple and he sucked in a breath.

Jack's eyes shot up to his. "Did that hurt?"

"Not even a little," he rasped.

"Do you like it?"

Rex held his gaze. "Very much."

Jack continued to explore, making Rex hiss and moan. When Jack paused one too many times, Rex reached for his wrist, curled his fingers around it, and dragged Jack's attention back to him.

Bringing Jack's hand to his mouth, Rex kissed his knuckles. "I'm all yours, Jack. Whatever you need. Whatever you want. I promise, you won't disappoint me, so do your worst."

Rex would probably regret that decision come morning, but right then, he wasn't going to back down. Jack had made the first move. It was time to see if he was man enough to see it through.

To his utter shock, Jack didn't hesitate. The city boy leaned in and kissed Rex. Hard and thorough. Rex remained at Jack's mercy for the longest time. Jack explored him with his hand while their tongues danced and dueled. Rex kissed him back but kept his hands to himself. He wanted to touch, but he had to refrain. It was the only way to maintain his control.

When Jack finally snaked his hand into Rex's boxers and curled his fist around his cock, Rex groaned, lifting his hips to drive his rock-hard dick into Jack's hand.

Jack's eyes shot to his again, but Rex kept his mouth shut. He wanted Jack to suck him, but he wasn't going to give him the command. It was imperative Jack make the decision on his own. Rex would not allow him to put the blame back on him if he regretted this when the sun came up.

It didn't take long before Jack managed to remove Rex's boxers, but he didn't do anything more than fist his cock while his lips moved over Rex's chest. Jack was killing him slowly, but there was nothing he could do about it. He was at Jack's mercy by sheer force of will.

Every so often, Jack would look at him, his eyes searching, seeking. Rex wasn't sure what he was hoping to find. Permission, maybe? The fact that Rex was naked was all the permission he was going to get from him.

"Ah, Christ!" Rex growled when Jack's mouth finally descended on his cock.

He couldn't help it, his hand darted to Jack's head, holding him in place as the warm rasp of his tongue made Rex lose his breath. He watched him because he wanted to remember this moment forever. Rex knew this was the first time Jack had taken a cock in his mouth, and the sight was something he would never forget.

Jack's movements were hesitant, but his eyes blazed with heat. Rex could tell he wasn't sure whether he was pleasing him or not. And because this was his first time, Rex wasn't about to let him wonder.

Tightening his grip in Jack's hair, Rex urged him to take more of him. "Just like that, baby," he whispered. "Oh, fuck, Jack. Your mouth feels so damn good."

His words seemed to bolster Jack's courage. His mouth became more urgent, more certain, sliding up and down Rex's shaft while his hand remained wrapped around the base. While Jack blew him, Rex continued to ramble incessantly, urging him to continue, ensuring Jack knew how much Rex loved every fucking thing he was doing. But when Jack tried to push him to the brink, Rex jerked his hair to pull him back.

Wary eyes shifted to Rex's face and he pulled Jack toward him by his hair. "Not yet, city boy. I'm not finished with you yet."

"No?" Jack grinned as though he knew he'd done something right.

"Kiss me, damn it."

When Jack moved over him, Rex banded his arm around Jack's torso and took his full weight on top of him, holding him there as he kissed him roughly.

It would take some time, but Rex would realize he didn't feel suffocated by the weight on top of him. There was no panic, no fear that he wasn't in control. Rex relished the warmth, allowed it to seep deep into his soul as Jack continued to kiss him. He could've allowed it to go on all night, but he knew Jack was capable of shattering his control and he was already dangerously close.

Rex had to take a moment to rein himself in or this would be over before it even got started.

And since he'd learned that was a real possibility with Jack, Rex decided then that it was time he took the reins once more.

JACK THOUGHT THAT BY CONFRONTING REX, HE would see the man and figure out what it was he wanted. With every step that led him from his room to Rex's, he'd thought about what it meant, what it would lead to, where it would leave them. Even as confusion racked his brain, he had decided to go with his gut. Whatever his first thought was upon seeing Rex would be how he proceeded.

Yeah. That felt like an eternity ago and there was no questioning what it was he wanted. Evidently, Jack wanted Rex because he'd practically jumped the man as soon as he opened the door.

And now…

Even though he'd been confused over the quick change of venue, Jack figured that was a story better left for another time. So he'd pushed it out of his head. Now, there were no thoughts other than all the things he wanted to do to Rex, all the ways he wanted to pleasure him, starting by sucking his cock one more time.

"I'm not finished yet," Jack whispered as he broke the kiss and moved back down Rex's long, lean body.

From the moment Jack wrapped his lips around Rex's cock, he didn't want to stop. The feel of his velvety smooth shaft against his tongue... Jack wanted to pleasure him for hours. Admittedly, he'd never been much for oral sex—giving or receiving—but that was because he'd never really enjoyed it.

That certainly wasn't the case now.

Unfortunately, Rex seemed to have other ideas, because his fingers were once again tugging on Jack's hair, sending sparks of electricity straight down his spine.

"In a minute, baby," Rex whispered as he pulled Jack's mouth back to his. "Right now, it's my turn."

When Rex flipped their positions so that Jack was lying beneath him, he was overwhelmed with his heat, his strength, the sheer power Jack saw in his eyes. The man unhinged him, made him delirious with need. Jack wanted to be closer. And when Rex kissed him, he wanted to feel every part of Rex on him, in him.

"Rex..." He couldn't verbalize what he needed, but whatever it was, Jack suspected Rex already knew.

"I promise, baby," Rex whispered, staring into his eyes, "I'm not goin' anywhere."

Was it weird that Jack liked how Rex called him baby? He'd said it numerous times since Jack barged in his door, and he wanted to hear him call him that again and again.

"Stay right there," Rex insisted as he got to his feet.

The next thing Jack knew, his sweatpants were gone, and Rex was back. He had a condom and lube in his hand, his eyes trailing a heated path over Jack's skin.

When Rex sprawled out beside him, Jack reached for him, pulling his mouth to his. And once again Jack was surrounded by all things Rex. His heat, his hunger ... they mixed with his, turning the kiss into an inferno.

Rex never stopped kissing him, even as he positioned Jack's legs, spreading them wider. Rex paused every so often to tug on Jack's cock, making him moan, eager for more. With one foot on the mattress, Jack's knee resting against Rex's hip, Rex shifted Jack's other leg so that he was completely vulnerable.

And then everything seemed to slow down.

Rex's kiss became gentler, his hands not quite as urgent. Rex teased him relentlessly, stroking his cock, kneading his balls, but he wasn't in a rush. This time wasn't like the others. Just as intense, sure. But more controlled, as though they had all the time in the world.

When something cool dripped onto his leg, Jack broke the kiss and peered down his body. Rex was lubing his fingers, still watching him as Jack observed what he was doing with his hand.

"I won't hurt you," Rex said softly.

Jack nodded. He knew that. Rex had never hurt him, always putting his pleasure first. He trusted Rex, knew he would take care of him. He'd proven that the first night they were together. Even when they'd agreed to only one night, Rex had been gentle with him.

"I'm gonna tease you," Rex whispered.

"Not necessary," Jack countered. "I'm ready."

Rex chuckled. "But I'm not."

"Oh." Jack's gaze shot to Rex's rock-hard cock.

"I didn't mean it like that," Rex mumbled softly. "Trust me, I just have to look at you and I'm ready. I'm simply gonna take my time." He smiled. "Because I can."

Okay. That made sense.

When Rex stroked him, Jack's dick jerked, eager, desperate. He wanted to feel Rex inside him, to hold him close. He wanted to spend the rest of the night locked in this room, just the two of them, no worries in the world.

When one finger slowly inched inside his ass, Jack moaned softly. He dropped his head back to the mattress and closed his eyes as the sensations overwhelmed him. It felt good. Too good. His dick throbbed.

"God, you're tight," Rex said on a soft groan.

With his eyes still closed, Jack smiled. "Practically a virgin."

Rex chuckled. "There's no such thing as practically." Rex brushed his lips against Jack's. "This ass belongs to me. And only me."

Another groan from Rex had Jack opening his eyes. Heat was blazing in the dark brown depths.

"Only me," Rex repeated.

Jack nodded, unsure what he was responding to, but it seemed necessary somehow. Those words felt important. Impactful. As though Rex had spoken directly to Jack's soul.

Rex's lips returned to his as Rex continued to finger his ass. He didn't rush and every second felt like an eternity. Jack wanted more. *Needed* more.

Just when Jack thought he would lose his mind, Rex added another finger, pushing in deep. The slow glide and retreat had his balls drawing up tight to his body. And when Rex stopped, his fingers lodged all the way inside him, Jack sighed.

Rex shifted his hand and suddenly Jack was jerking, moaning, nearly coming out of his skin. Oh, God! He was doing that thing with his fingers. It felt—

"Holy shit, Rex... Oh, fuck... Don't... Don't... You'll make me... Oh, fuck."

"Feels good?"

"God, yes." Jack's hips bucked. "So good. What are... What... Oh, *fuck*."

"Don't come yet," Rex growled, the deep timbre of his voice making it difficult to follow his instructions.

The pressure on that spot disappeared, and Jack could breathe again, his stomach muscles unclenching. Rex continued to finger-fuck his ass, and when he added a third finger, the pressure became too much. Jack grunted, the pain intense.

"Relax, baby."

Rex's lips returned and Jack focused on the kiss as Rex stretched his asshole with three fingers. Jack breathed through the pain, focusing on his kiss, the way his tongue leisurely danced against his. Jack's body was rock hard, and his cock swelled more. The pain morphed into pleasure, and once again, Jack wasn't sure he was going to last.

"You want to feel me inside you?" Rex whispered against his lips.

"Yes."

His finger found that spot again and Jack moaned in earnest.

"Rex ... fuck ... please." He groaned long and low. He couldn't take any more. He needed to feel him. "Please, fuck me. Now. Right now. Oh, fuck."

Jack had never known pleasure like this. This never-ending, all-consuming intensity that made his body come alive in a way that sent his mind spiraling.

Unable to resist, Jack reached for Rex's head and held him there, his mouth inches away. "Please … fuck me."

A devilish smile curled Rex's mouth and heat flashed through Jack's body.

"It would be my pleasure, baby."

"I love when you call me that." Jack didn't mean to say the words aloud, but they tumbled out anyway. The way Rex stared at him had Jack tensing, hoping like hell he hadn't just fucked this up.

Long seconds passed as Rex watched him. It became difficult to swallow. Rex never stopped fingering his ass, continuing to stretch him gently. Jack's breaths were rapid, his heart pounding way too fast.

And another smile tipped Rex's lips as he said, "You're gonna love a lot more before I'm done with you."

Jack got the feeling he was right.

In so many ways.

Twenty-Five

MINE

That was the only thought Rex had as he stared down at the sexy man spread out before him. He could see the pure need in Jack's gaze. The heat. The desperation. Even the fear.

Jack had given himself over to him in every way possible, and Rex was hard-pressed not to take what he was offering. He'd known there was an undeniable chemistry between them from the first night at the hotel, and then again, the morning in the kitchen when Jack nearly face-planted on the floor. The instant Rex had touched him, he had felt it. And every time since.

Still, something deep inside clanged in warning. This man was dangerous. He was a threat to Rex's heart and soul. Jack's uncertainty could backfire in his face. And when Jack left, where would that leave him? If Rex fell for him—which he feared was a real possibility—what would that do to him when Jack was gone?

Yet he couldn't bring himself to let this opportunity go. To feel Jack beneath him, surrounding him. It was the only thing he wanted. Even if it was only one more time.

"Open the condom," Rex instructed as he leaned his hips back.

Jack fumbled with his hand until he found the foil packet on the mattress while Rex leveraged himself up onto his knees, remaining beside Jack, his fingers still buried in his ass. A minute later, Jack was rolling the latex down Rex's cock while Rex continued to finger him, stretching him wider, preparing him to take his cock. He knew when he fucked him, he was going to lose control. The last thing he wanted was to hurt Jack, but he needed him in a way that terrified him. He enjoyed teasing the man, listening to his soft moans and groans, watching the way his eyes would roll back when Rex massaged his prostate. Rex would've been content to do this for hours, but in order for things to progress, he had no choice.

Reluctantly, Rex pulled his fingers from the hot depths of Jack's body.

"Give me your hand," Rex insisted. When Jack offered it to him, Rex put a generous amount of lube in his palm. "Stroke me."

Jack fisted Rex's cock, lubing him up as they both watched what he was doing. The vise grip of Jack's fingers around his dick was heaven and hell at the same time. It wasn't enough, but it was too much. This man threatened his very control.

Rex maneuvered between Jack's spread thighs while Jack's hand continued to work his dick.

"Your turn," Rex said, shifting out of Jack's reach. "Let me watch you stroke yourself."

Jack's eyes never left Rex's face as he relaxed into the mattress and stroked himself. Rex alternated between watching his face and the sensual movement of his hand. Jack's cock was thick and long, and Rex couldn't wait until the day he felt him inside him, fucking him, taking the control he was so willing to give up.

While Jack jerked his own cock, Rex aligned the head of his dick to Jack's anus, pushing forward as he leaned over him. With one hand beside Jack's head, Rex guided his cock home.

Jack paused, his breaths choppy, his eyes wide.

Sensations pummeled Rex, flooding his bloodstream with heat. "Don't stop," Rex growled. "Stroke yourself and look at me."

Jack's eyes shot up, locking with Rex's, while his arm began moving faster. Rex could see the strain around his mouth. He didn't want to hurt Jack, but he knew from experience the pain would ease, morph into something he would come to crave. It had been a while; otherwise, he wouldn't have been able to hold back. The need to claim Jack in the most predatory way was damn near overwhelming.

Rex took his time, inching deeper inside him while Jack's movements became jerky, his breaths labored. In an effort to distract him, Rex crushed his mouth to his. Jack grunted but kissed him back. His tongue thrust into Rex's mouth and he could taste his desperation and the fear.

"Relax, baby."

"Can't."

"Pull your legs up."

Jack shifted, his knees tucking closer to his chest, which changed the angle and allowed Rex to push in deeper. Jack's ass gripped him, tight and hot. So fucking hot. He felt too damn good.

Rex kissed him again and fought the urge to plunge all the way inside. He only wanted to give him pleasure. It took several long minutes, but finally Rex was seated all the way inside him. When he retreated and pushed forward, Jack cried out.

Rex bit Jack's lower lip. Not hard enough to draw blood, but enough to get his attention.

"Put your arms around me."

Jack did. His breaths were rough now, his body strung tight.

Using his arms to hold most of his weight, Rex rocked his hips forward and back. Slowly at first, shallow thrusts as Jack's ass stretched around him. Unlike the other times they'd come together, Rex allowed himself to get lost in Jack. This wasn't a fast fuck. It was more and Rex wanted to feel, to enjoy the way Jack shifted beneath him, the way his moans echoed in the room, his deep, labored breaths, his soft pleas for more.

Rex kissed him, working Jack's lips and tongue with the rhythm of his thrusts. It wasn't long before Jack's arms tightened around him and his kiss became frantic.

Rex pulled back then, but he didn't stop fucking him.

"You okay?"

Jack nodded, smiled, his eyes glassy with arousal. "Yeah. Feels…" His eyes darted down between their bodies. "I need more, Rex."

"Then hold on, baby. 'Cause we're just gettin' started."

This time when Jack pulled Rex to him, Rex retreated slowly, pushed in deeper. Harder, faster. It didn't take long before Rex was fucking him relentlessly, Jack's breathy moans fueling the fire. Their bodies slid together, sweat coating their skin. Rex couldn't remember the last time he'd felt this fucking good. Jack surrounded him in every way. He was all Rex could feel, all he could see, all he could smell. He wanted to remain like this forever, sliding deeper into Jack's body, hearing him beg and plead for more.

He went as long as he could before even that wasn't enough. Rex broke away from him, straightening up on his knees. Wrapping his hands around Jack's hips, Rex jerked Jack toward him, changing the angle once more as he pounded into him. Jack's hand instinctively went to his cock and he began jerking himself roughly.

"Fuck, Rex. I … I can't… I need…"

"Tell me," Rex urged.

"I'm gonna come." Jack's eyes closed and his back arched as his cock twitched and pulsed, a long stream of cum shooting out over his chest and belly. The sight sent Rex over the edge. He slammed into Jack one last time as he gave in to his release.

Rex fought for air and stumbled forward when Jack pulled him down. He was surprised by Jack's response, but not at all disappointed. His lips were soft, warm, his kiss so damn sweet.

He knew then that this was going to hurt when it came to an end. Jack might be confused about where he was in his life, what he needed. Rex had long ago passed that point. He knew what he wanted, and he honestly had never thought he'd find it.

Until this stranger showed up at the bar.

Until this city boy stumbled onto his doorstep.

Until this man got under his skin.

Until Jack made his way deep into his soul.

And right up to that moment when Rex's soul claimed Jack as his.

Knowing he couldn't sleep with Jack, Rex worked up the energy to crawl out of bed. It pained him to leave, but he knew if he didn't, the nightmare would be back. Although he could deal with those, he couldn't deal with the possibility that he would hurt Jack. If he woke up, not knowing where he was, there was a real possibility he'd become violent. It had happened before, but luckily, he'd never had anyone in his bed.

"Where're you going?" Jack mumbled sleepily.

Rex leaned over, kissed Jack's shoulder. "I can't sleep in here."

Jack opened his eyes, frowning. "Why not?"

Rex didn't want to explain, so rather than do so, he said, "I need a shower."

"Can I join you?"

For a moment, he considered telling Jack no, but he couldn't. In fact, he didn't want to. When Jack crawled out of bed, Rex took his hand, led him into the bathroom. The hot water was instant and for the next twenty minutes, they stood under the spray, soaping one another while making out.

When they were squeaky clean, Rex turned off the water and grabbed two towels.

"Rex," Jack whispered, moving up behind him as Rex stared at himself in the mirror. "Stay with me tonight. I want to hold you."

"I can't." He didn't want to hurt him.

"You can. Please. I need this."

Although he knew it was a mistake, Rex couldn't deny Jack his request. It was what he wanted, too. To spend the entire night holding him.

"Okay," he finally conceded. "But give me a minute."

"Sure."

Jack slipped out of the room and Rex continued to stare at himself in the mirror. He silently willed the nightmare away, to give him this one chance to enjoy the moment, to relish the time he had with Jack. Knowing he couldn't control his subconscious, Rex sent up a silent prayer before slipping back into bed with Jack.

It only took a few minutes before his eyes drifted closed and he found himself wrapped in Jack's warmth.

Rex had no idea how long it was before the nightmare came upon him, but once it did, he was trapped, suffocated, reliving that hellish night.

"Told Jo ain't no boy of mine gonna be a queer," his father snapped.

Jolene giggled, but it sounded slightly hysterical. "I told him you weren't queer. You're just a confused teenage boy. I've seen the way you look at me." She leaned forward, cupping her breasts near his face. "You'd like to see these wouldn't you?"

Ah, Christ. Rex was going to throw up.

"Yeah, you do," she said with a snort. "I can see it in your eyes. Can't know what you want until you've had a woman's touch, right? I bet you'll like it just fine."

Rex jerked at the restraints. "I ain't gay," he insisted. "I ain't never said that. Now let me go."

"We're just here to make sure, handsome," Jolene crooned. "Once we do, we'll let you go. But don't you worry, Rexi boy, I'll make this feel good."

Bile rose in Rex's throat, the bitter taste threatening to choke him as Jolene set her hand on his stomach. Rex was still wearing his jeans and his T-shirt. He'd been sleeping fully clothed since his mama died. He hadn't trusted his old man not to burn down the house with his cigarettes and he'd wanted to be prepared to get him and Rafe out if necessary.

Rex jerked away from her touch.

The slap from his father was hard and instant, making his ears ring. He hadn't even seen the man move, didn't realize he was now standing over him.

"Be still, boy!" the old man bellowed. "Jo's gonna fix you and that's that."

Fix him? The old man was going to stand by while this crazy bitch touched him?

"Fix me how?" he asked, his voice trembling.

"I'm just gonna make your dick hard, Rexi boy. Show your daddy that you like women and not boys. And as a reward, I'll even make you come." She cackled again. "If you're really nice, perhaps I'll climb on up here and ride you like a stallion."

Oh, fuck. He really was going to vomit.

When Jolene's hand slipped down to the button on Rex's jeans, he jerked again, trying to keep out of her reach. He thrashed like a wild animal, shaking the bed, the handcuffs digging painfully into his skin as he tried to free himself. To no avail.

A hard fist made impact with his jaw, shooting Rex's head to the side, making him see stars. He tasted blood and a tear streamed from his eye. He focused on breathing, fire lancing through his face from the punch.

"Last chance," his father snarled. "You be still, or I'll snatch your brother outta that closet and force him to watch this. Or maybe I'll let Jo prove the snot-nosed shit ain't queer, either. You want that?"

Rex's chest heaved, the pressure building inside him, the need to get away stronger than anything he'd ever felt before, but he fought it back, forced himself to remain still. He couldn't let them touch Rafe, couldn't let his brother be subjected to this.

"Oh, you don't have to worry about Rafe," Jolene said with a giggle, peering up at Billy Don as her fingernail ran over Rex's stomach. "He's not queer, baby."

"How would you know that?" Billy Don asked, his tone more curious than upset.

Jolene licked her lips. "He lets me play with him."

"The hell he does!" Rex screamed, jerking his entire body, causing the bed to come off the floor on one side. "You touch him and I'll—"

Jolene gripped his face between bony fingers, forcing him to look at her. "You're a little late for that, Rexi boy. Rafe likes it." Jolene's eyes remained locked on his face while her other hand tucked into his waistband. "We can bring him out here and I'll show you how much if you'd like."

Rex swallowed hard and remained completely still. He wasn't going to let this crazy bitch touch his brother again. No fucking way.

"Now be still. This'll be over before you know it." Using two hands, Jolene worked open the button on Rex's jeans, then lowered the zipper.

Rex held his breath, stared at the ceiling, willed her to have a heart attack and die.

"Don't worry, Rexi boy," she whispered. "I promise, I'll make it feel real good. You'll like the way my lips feel on you, just ask your daddy. He's always sayin' I'm the best he's ever had."

"Don't," Rex snarled.

Jolene giggled. "I like when you play hard to get."

His stomach churned, bile inching up his throat. "Don't." He sucked in air, let it out. "Don't touch me."

While the need to protect Rafe was great, Rex couldn't let her do this. He couldn't let her touch him. Not like that. God, not like that.

Rex attempted to kick free again, praying the bed would break apart, but it was sturdier than he gave it credit for. He was growling, anger fueling his muscles, making him crazy. He had to get away. Had to.

"Hold his legs, Billy Don! Keep him still."

His father moved to the end of the bed again, his rough hands circling Rex's ankles, the grip harder than he'd expected. Pain shot up through his shins and he stilled at the same time Jolene reached into his underwear, wrapping her hand around him.

"Stop." The snarl turned into a sob. He couldn't believe this was happening. "Don't! Don't do that." Angry tears fell unbidden as Rex fought to get away from her. His father's grip sent pain radiating through his legs, but he ignored it. He had to get away. "Stop! Don't touch me!"

Her hand tightened around his flaccid cock, making him cry out in pain, humiliation and horror consuming him. How could she do this? How could his own father do this?

"My hand feels good, don't it?" Jolene's eyes were crazed, staring down at what she was doing. "I'm gonna make your dick hard, Rexi boy. It won't take long. Let me show you what it's like to be pleased by a woman. You just need to relax. Enjoy it."

"Don't... God, don't..." Rex sputtered and coughed, crying uncontrollably, willing her not to touch him.

She didn't listen. Instead, Jolene leaned over, her mouth closer to his dick. He could feel her breath and his stomach revolted.

"Don't!" Rex yelled, no longer caring if he woke Rafe. "Don't fucking touch me!"

Another laugh followed and she inched closer, her lips brushing against his cock. Rex pulled at the restraints, tried to break the cuffs. He could feel the blood dripping down his fingers from where the metal was digging into his wrist.

She sucked him and his stomach revolted.

"Fuck! Stop!" He didn't care how loud he was now. Fuck it all. He had to get her off him.

Billy Don took a step forward. "Be still, you—"

The bifold closet doors flew back. "Stop it right now!"

Rex's head shot over at the sound of his brother's voice, followed by the telltale rack of the rifle Rex had hidden in there with him. It was their grandpa's gun. Rex had hoped they'd never need to use it, but he'd kept it all the same. Just in case.

"Let him go right now, I said!" Rafe yelled, the barrel of the gun aimed directly at Jolene. "Let him go or I'll shoot you. I will. Let my brother go!"

"Get yer boy, Billy Don!" Jolene screamed at their father, her hand still wrapped around Rex's dick. "Take that gun and get him outta here. You promised me, Billy Don. Promised I could prove it."

"Goddamn it, boy," Billy Don growled at Rafe.

"Take him outta here," Jolene demanded. "I got a job to do and I ain't leavin' till it's done."

Rex couldn't look away from his brother. He couldn't believe this was happening. The tears came, the shame so overwhelming he could hardly breathe with it. Rafe's eyes met his and Rex saw exactly what Jolene had done to him in the sorrow reflected there. The bitch had really done it. She'd molested his kid brother.

Billy Don moved and Rafe took one step back, but he didn't lower the gun, he merely swung it so the barrel pointed at their father.

"Come closer and I'll shoot you, old man. I'll do it," Rafe snarled, teeth bared. "I will do it."

Not listening, the old man closed the distance between them, stumbling once but righting himself.

"Don't you come closer, you asshole," Rafe warned, his voice eerily calm, his dark eyes focused on their father.

Billy Don took one more step, his arm rising, and Rex saw Rafe's finger shift on the trigger.

"Rafe, no!" Rex shouted, but his voice was drowned out by the unmistakable sound of a shotgun blast followed by Jolene's scream.

"REX," JACK MUMBLED SOFTLY, NOT SURE HOW to wake him without startling him. He was thrashing in the bed, clearly trying to get away from someone or something. "You're safe, Rex. Wake up. I'm here."

A hard hand flew out, banded around Jack's throat, squeezing as a guttural cry tore from Rex's throat. "Don't fucking touch me!"

"Rex! Wake up," Jack shouted. He clawed at Rex's wrist, urgently trying to remove the death grip cutting off his air. "Rex! Wake up! Fuck!"

The grip loosened instantly when Rex sat up, his chest heaving, his body covered in sweat. Jack took a moment to breathe, to slow the pounding of his heart.

When Rex turned to look at him, Jack saw his terror and his remorse.

"Did I hurt you?" His voice was a gravelly rasp, barely audible.

"No," he lied, sliding his hand over Rex's arm. "You didn't hurt me. Come here."

Rex shook his head. "I can't. I can't sleep in here."

Unwilling to let Rex run from him, Jack gripped his arm tightly, pulled him back down. "Stay, Rex. Stay right here with me."

He could feel the reluctance in Rex's body, but he didn't bolt immediately. Jack considered that a good sign. He laid his hand over Rex's chest, inched closer so his head rested on Rex's shoulder. "You're safe, Rex."

No response.

"Want to talk about it?"

"No."

"Okay." Jack wasn't going to be offended by that. Whatever terrorized Rex enough that he knew he couldn't sleep in the same bed with someone, it had to have been horrible. Jack wasn't going to push him. "Stay with me, Rex. Let me watch over you."

To his utter shock, Rex turned toward him, burying his face in Jack's shoulder. There was a silent sob that damn near broke his heart. Jack didn't move, he simply wrapped his arms around Rex and held on. He remained like that until he felt Rex's body relax as he slipped back into sleep.

Only then did Jack close his eyes.

Jack woke up in his bed, Rex's warm body spooning him from behind. Every one of Jack's muscles ached but not in a bad way. He was sore, yes. But not to the point he was concerned or even put off by the thought of feeling Rex inside him again.

Rex.

He still couldn't believe what had happened last night, how eager he'd been to feel Rex consuming every part of him. In many ways, it had been no different than the other times they'd been together. And in other ways, it had been so much more.

Jack wasn't sure if Rex had woken again during the night. If he had, Jack had slept through it. Considering the position they were in now, he didn't think that was the case. The thought made him smile. He wanted to be Rex's safe place, prayed that he could be.

He tried to ignore the uncertainty that clawed at his mind. He didn't want to worry that they were rushing things, that he was falling too hard and too fast. Now was not the time, and the truth was, Jack was tired of thinking. He was tired of trying to fight the feelings he'd already developed for Rex. They were strong, powerful, and unlike anything he'd felt before.

Did that scare him? Sure. But surprisingly, there was no overwhelming urge to bolt. He didn't feel the need to run from Rex. For the first time in forever, Jack wasn't bombarded by doubts or confusion. He tended to overthink things, but right now, Jack simply wanted to feel Rex's body against him, his heavy arm draped over his stomach. He didn't want to move because he didn't want this moment to end.

Rex stirred behind him, his arm tightening, pulling him closer. "Mornin'."

"Good morning," he whispered. Rex's stubble tickled Jack's neck as Rex's warm lips slid over his skin. A tremor shot through him, lust building again.

Feeling bold, Jack allowed his hand to drop behind him, his fingers seeking the hard ridge of Rex's cock.

"Tease," Rex whispered.

A soft moan escaped Rex as Jack began stroking him slowly. He wanted to taste Rex again, to feel his cock on his tongue. In fact, he wanted it so badly he managed to free himself from Rex's grip. When he turned over, Rex shifted to his back. Jack quickly tossed the sheet down to the end of the bed.

"What're you doin'?" Rex asked, his voice rough.

"I need room to work."

Rex chuckled. "Is that right?"

"Absolutely."

Before Jack could reach for him, Rex picked up where Jack left off, his fingers curled around his shaft, squeezing, stroking. When Jack shifted, eager to take over again, Rex put his other hand on Jack's thigh. "Just watch."

Swallowing hard, Jack focused on the way Rex palmed his dick. There was something distinctly hot about seeing him like this. Sleepy and vulnerable even as his body hardened, his muscles tightening, his brain coming online.

"I saw you watching that night," Rex said, his voice raspy. "When I was in the hot tub."

Jack's gaze drifted up to Rex's face. His eyes were closed, his face relaxed. "Yeah?"

"Yep. I was watching you, too."

Jack's eyes widened. "You could see me?"

Rex smiled, that mischievous grin that had caught him completely off guard the first time he saw it. "I could definitely see you. I could hear you, too. It's the reason I came so fast."

Jack dropped his gaze back to Rex's cock. His mouth watered to taste him. He licked his lips. "Let me suck you."

Rex's eyes slowly opened, and his smile instantly vanished.

"What's wrong?" Jack asked.

Rex sat up, reached for Jack's neck. "I hurt you. You said I didn't." His big hand caressed Jack's skin. "Holy fuck. Did I strangle you?"

Knowing any response to confirm that would send Rex into a spiral, Jack redirected. He took Rex's hand, eased him back down to the bed, and pressed his lips to Rex's.

"I want you thinking about this," Jack insisted. "About me. About my mouth on your cock. Let me taste you, Rex."

Their eyes met momentarily, and it took a few seconds, but Jack saw the instant Rex relented. They might have this conversation later, but for right now, they were here. In this moment.

Jack reached for Rex's cock, stroked him until he was hard again.

"Tell me," Rex groaned softly. "Tell me what you wanna do to me."

"I want to suck you," he replied, watching as Rex's hand glided up and down his shaft, tormenting Jack.

"In detail," Rex stated. "Explicit detail."

Jack's breath lodged in his chest, his body tightening. "I…" This wasn't easy for him, but he wasn't going to disappoint Rex now. "I want to suck your cock. To feel you in my mouth. To lave you with my tongue." He fought the urge to reach for Rex's cock. "I want to explore every inch of you, to find out what you enjoy."

"If you put that sweet mouth on my dick, I'm gonna come." Rex's free hand curled around Jack's wrist, guiding him closer. "In your mouth."

A strange tingling ignited in Jack's spine. The thought of Rex coming in his mouth made his body burn hotter.

"You'll have to swallow."

It was definitely a warning, but it wasn't necessary.

"I want to," Jack assured him. "I want to suck your dick until you come down my throat."

Rex's eyes flashed with heat, pre-cum glistening on the tip of his cock. And when he moved his hand, his cock standing proud and tall, practically begging for Jack's attention, Jack positioned himself between Rex's thighs, then leaned down and took him in his mouth. He watched Rex's face as he did. He would take his cues from the man's expression. Last night, Rex had spurred him on with his commentary, and Jack had loved it. He'd never had a lover who was vocal, never had anyone assure him that what he was doing was what they needed.

"Wrap your lips around my dick," Rex growled. "Suck me hard."

Jack did as Rex instructed, sucking as he bobbed up and down. When Jack went to grip the base of Rex's cock with his fist, Rex growled.

"No hands. Put them on my thighs. I just wanna feel your lips and tongue."

Jack pressed his palms against Rex's thighs, the hard muscle shifting as Rex thrust his hips upward.

"Don't move but keep sucking."

Rex began fucking his mouth, driving his hips up, then dropping them back to the bed. When Rex's fingers twined in his hair, Jack's cock pulsed. He liked that Rex was forceful. Jack enjoyed the way he used him for his pleasure.

Those fingers tightened in his hair and guided his head lower until the head of Rex's cock pushed too deep, causing Jack to gag. Rex's hold relaxed, giving Jack the opportunity to catch his breath.

"Try again." Rex guided him back down. "I want you to take all of me."

The man was far too big to fit entirely in his mouth, but Jack did his best. The next thing he knew, Rex jerked Jack's head down and his cock lodged in Jack's throat. He gagged but didn't pull away. Rex repeated the movement twice more before his hand fell back to the bed. Jack continued to deep-throat him, taking control, giving Rex everything he had.

"Suck harder, baby," Rex urged. "I'm so fucking close."

Jack hollowed out his cheeks, applying as much suction as possible as he bobbed his head, his hands pressing into Rex's thighs as he worked to make him come.

"Oh, fuck, Jack … yes. Just like… Fuck, baby." His hips thrust upward as he grunted and groaned. "Swallow me."

Rex's cock pulsed in his mouth, cum splashing against his tongue. Jack focused on his taste, the salty essence of him. It didn't freak him out or make him panic. It felt natural and damn near perfect. Jack swallowed and proceeded to lick Rex clean. When Jack sat up, Rex reached for him, pulling him so that he was draped over his body.

Rex crushed his mouth to Jack's, his tongue licking inside, exploring. Jack knew Rex could taste himself, and it seemed he enjoyed knowing Jack had done that for him. When they broke for air, Rex settled Jack on top of him, his hand curling around his head. Jack's ear pressed against Rex's chest, the rapid thump of Rex's heart beating against his cheek. Jack found himself relaxing, shocked by the intimacy of this moment.

Like everything else he was experiencing, this was new for him. Rex was showing him things he'd never imagined, and for the first time in his life, Jack was … content.

And he knew then that this was what he wanted.

Twenty-Six

BY THE TIME REX MANAGED TO CRAWL out of bed, the sun was high in the sky. It had taken some effort to get up this morning. Pulling himself away from Jack was damn near impossible.

However, after Jack blew him and they fell back asleep for a couple of hours, Rex forced himself out of bed.

He'd felt Jack's eyes on him when he headed for the bathroom. Rex wasn't sure what the man expected, but while staying in bed all day sounded damn good, it wasn't something Rex was capable of. He had shit to do if he wanted to get this place open for business.

Not to mention, he needed a little time to come to terms with what had happened last night. The part where he'd gone to sleep, relived that horrible night, then woken up with his hands around Jack's neck. He could see the fingerprint bruises on Jack's neck, and it sickened him to know he was responsible. Hurting the man in any way was unacceptable, yet Rex wasn't sure what to do about that.

So, after a shower and breakfast, Rex headed down to his workshop. Jack arrived a short time later, glancing around as though looking for something.

"What's up?"

His eyes scanned the space. "Please tell me there's something I can do here."

Rex wiped a hand on a rag. "You build furniture yet?"

Jack frowned. "Uh. No."

"Well, then I guess painting is the only thing on the menu."

His eyes lit up. "I seem to have that down."

Yes, he did. Rex had scrutinized the pieces Jack had worked on, and he'd found no issues. Not that he expected there to be. Jack was quite competent from what Rex could tell. It was more the fact that Rex was hypercritical when it came to his work, always reaching for perfection whether it was attainable or not.

Rex pointed at the two nightstands that had been drying for the past couple of days. "Could you start by moving those out of the way? If we can make a path through here, it'll be easier."

"Absolutely."

Jack got to work, relocating the pieces that were finished, pulling forward those that needed to be stained.

Rex found himself staring at the city boy, a smile on his face. Honestly, he had expected Jack to freak out today. Last night had been … unexpected to say the least. Of course, phenomenal also came to mind. And Rex wasn't merely talking about the sex. Sleeping with Jack—the actual act of sleeping—had been a comfort Rex hadn't known in far too long. Jack seemed to fit perfectly against him, and Rex hadn't wanted to let him go this morning. Not even so Jack could explore his cock with his mouth.

However, it brought to mind what had happened, and Rex knew they needed to discuss it.

"Hey, Jack?" Rex moved toward him.

"Hmm?"

"About last night…"

Jack turned to face him, and Rex's gaze instantly slapped right to the mark on Jack's neck.

"I am so fucking sorry," he whispered.

Jack stepped forward. "It's not your fault, Rex."

When Rex didn't look away from the bruised skin, Jack's hand moved under his chin, turning his head away.

"It is my fault," he admitted. "I told you—"

"Yes, you did." Jack stepped closer, their eyes locked. "You told me you couldn't sleep in the same bed and I asked you to." Jack's head tilted slightly. "I don't regret that, Rex. I wanted to sleep with you last night. Hell, I want to sleep with you tonight. And every fucking night I'm here. So this is something we'll have to deal with."

Rex wasn't sure how they could do that. He'd been having the nightmares since that horrible night. Sure, they would go away for a while and he could get some rest on occasion, but whenever he felt vulnerable in any situation, he was once again terrorized by them.

"Look at me," Jack whispered.

Rex hadn't realized he'd looked away, but he met Jack's gaze anyway.

"We'll get through this. And like I told you, when you're ready to talk, I'm here."

Nodding his head, Rex turned, needing to get back to work. He wasn't ready to talk about what had happened, to share the details. It was a horrific event that Rex wished like hell he could forget. He didn't want to drag Jack down that path, to subject him to the hell of what that bitch had done. What his father had allowed to happen.

In fact, he wished he could forget about it himself.

It was just after two when Rex went up to the apartment to find something to eat. The first thing he noticed was that the kitchen was spotless. As in everything shined as though it had been thoroughly cleaned.

Had to be Jack.

The guy was obviously getting bored.

Rex figured he'd go find him to see if he wanted lunch before he made himself something. He heard Jack's voice coming from the guest room, so he made his way down the hall, noticing that the dining table and living room had both been cleaned as well. The wood furniture gleamed with polish and the hardwood floors shined. Even the windows seemed cleaner.

Hmm. Rex kind of liked having him around.

For more than cleaning, of course.

"Yep, I agree, Shawn," Jack said, his voice drifting out from his room. "She does look better like this."

Rex stopped in the doorway and leaned against the jamb, watching as Jack paced at the end of the bed. He had a sketchbook open on the comforter and he kept glancing down at it. Rex skimmed the paper, admiring the drawing. The female character seemed to come off the page, so lifelike he had to do a double take. The man had some serious talent.

"Well, if you're good with that, then I'll get to work on her part. And while I'm at it, I'll start drawing up some sketches for the hero and the two villains."

Jack pivoted, his eyes lifting when he saw Rex in the doorway. He smiled but continued his conversation. "Yeah. Let me jot down your thoughts."

When Jack took a seat on the mattress, Rex stepped into the room. Jack's eyes widened, but he managed to continue his conversation.

"Yeah. I got that," Jack said. "Tell me about his bone structure. How do you see his face?"

Rex stopped at the end of the bed and went to his knees, shouldering Jack's legs apart. He obviously knew what Rex's intention was because he quickly tried to close his legs. Rex pushed his knees apart, then placed his hand on Jack's chest and urged him to lie back.

When Jack was flat on the mattress, Rex pulled Jack's sweatpants down to his ankles, then wasted no time taking Jack's cock in his mouth.

"I ... uh... Yeah, Shawn. I ... heard you."

Rex worked him relentlessly, focusing on the sensitive crest. He wanted the man to come while he was on the phone with whoever this Shawn person was.

"Yep. Strong chin ... fuck. No. Sorry. I ... broke... I broke my pencil. Just a sec."

Jack pulled the phone from his ear and tapped the screen to mute it.

"What are you doing?" he whispered roughly.

Rex chuckled but didn't release Jack's cock from his mouth. He knew damn well what Rex was doing.

"Rex…"

He paused and nodded toward the phone. "Keep talkin'. Don't pay any attention to me."

Jack huffed a laugh. "Yeah. Like that's possible."

Rex sucked him deep into his throat.

"Fucking hell."

While Rex bobbed up and down on Jack's shaft, he glanced at the phone again. Jack turned it toward him, tapped the screen, then put it back to his ear.

"Hey, Shawn. Yeah. I'm here. Sorry about that. You were saying about the eyes…?"

Another couple of minutes passed before Jack finally gave up. He said his goodbyes and disconnected the call before tossing the phone onto the bed.

"Rex! You're gonna… Oh, shit!" Jack's hips shot off the mattress as his cock pulsed in Rex's mouth. He came on a long, strangled groan.

After licking him clean, Rex stood and leaned over him, pressing his lips to Jack's, then pulling back and smiling. "I was gonna ask if you wanted lunch."

Jack was breathing hard as he stared back at him, a full-fledged smile on his face. "Is that why you interrupted my business call?"

Rex laughed, standing tall. "Best damn business call you ever had, no doubt."

"Well, yeah."

Jack's smile made Rex grin even more. He loved seeing this side of him. The carefree part, the side that wasn't so tense. Rex chuckled and turned to head back to the kitchen. "I'll throw some sandwiches together. So … whenever you're ready."

As Rex left the room, he heard Jack laughing behind him. "Okay. Sure. Let me just catch my breath first."

"Take your time," he called out from down the hall.

Rex had to admit, he happened to enjoy the hell out of having that man at his mercy.

Saturday, February 2, 2019

JANUARY FADED OUT AND FEBRUARY CAME IN with a roar, yet Jack didn't seem to notice. Not much, anyway.

He spent most of his time focused on his own work for a change, attempting to get some drawing done while he had the mind to do so. Probably helped that during that time, he and Rex fucked around at every opportunity.

Of course, they didn't limit their encounters to the bedroom. No, they were far too spontaneous for that. There were random blow jobs in the kitchen and the stairway leading down to the second floor, fucking in the living room—Jack bent over the arm of the sofa—even once in the workshop when Rex cornered Jack while he was applying a coat of lacquer to one of the dressers.

To be fair, Jack had never given much thought to what it would be like to have a partner with so much stamina. Keeping up with Rex wasn't easy, but it was definitely fun.

Needless to say, Jack didn't have any complaints.

At least he hadn't. Right up until he got the phone call from Tina. For some dumb-ass reason, Jack answered the call on the first ring.

"Jack?"

"Hmm?"

"Do you know what today is?"

"No, I don't," he admitted.

"It's the second."

"Of?"

"February."

"Okay." Where was she going with this?

"You were supposed to be back yesterday."

"No," he clarified. "You were supposed to be *gone* yesterday."

Funny how he hadn't even realized it, hadn't actually thought about Tina once.

Tina sighed. "I think we owe it to ourselves to have a conversation face-to-face before either of us makes a rash decision here, Jack."

"Rash decision?" Jack barked a laugh, but there was zero amusement in it. "You fucked another guy in my bed, I left, and you somehow think that was rash?"

"We need to talk."

"We have nothing to talk about."

"That's not true. We've been together for a year and a half, Jack. We have *plenty* to talk about. Even if this is not going to work out, we have to sit down and hash it out like adults."

"I really don't think so." The last thing Jack wanted was to sit down and talk to Tina. Hell, he didn't even want to do it on the phone.

"I'm not moving out until you do," she snapped.

"You were supposed to be out by now."

"Yeah, well. Obviously, it doesn't matter too much to you since you haven't been back to the apartment."

No, it didn't matter to him, although it should. Jack knew he had to go home eventually, but he was enjoying his time with Rex.

"Let's talk, Jack. Then I'll be out of your life for good."

Fucking hell. Although he doubted she would keep that promise, Jack knew he had to make the effort. "Fine. When?"

"Today."

"Can't be today, Tina. I've got shit to do."

"It has to be today, Jack."

He heard the insistence in her tone, knew she wasn't joking. For whatever reason, Tina had it in her head that they had to meet today. And when she got her teeth into something, it was damn hard to get her to give an inch.

"Fine. What time?"

"Meet me at the apartment at noon."

Jack sighed, hating himself for giving in. "I'll be there. But you've only got an hour, Tina. And if you pull any bullshit stunts, I'm not staying."

"Thanks, Jack."

As soon as she disconnected the call, Jack replayed the conversation in his head. Tina was up to something, he could feel it. As for what that might be, he had no idea.

Tossing his pencil onto the bed, Jack pushed to his feet and stretched. It was already ten, which meant he needed to shower and hit the road. It would take roughly forty-five minutes to make it to the apartment. Maybe while he was there, he could get more clothes. He would need to take his suitcase to do that, though.

Or he could just wait Tina out. If all went well, she could be out by tomorrow night. Then, Monday he could be back to sleeping in his own bed. While he headed for the shower, Jack tried to ignore the pain that came with thinking about leaving Rex. What happened when he did go home? Would Rex still want to see him? Or would this thing be over?

"Get out of your head," he insisted, his tone forceful. Jack refused to go there.

A short time later, after he showered and dressed, Jack was walking into the kitchen. He found Rex glancing at his laptop, a half-eaten protein bar in his hand.

"Want me to make you something?" Rex asked when Jack headed for the refrigerator.

"No, thanks. I need to head back to my apartment."

Rex's head snapped over, his eyes narrowing. He placed the protein bar down and turned to face him. "That's it? You're headin' out without givin' me any sort of warnin'?"

"What?" Jack frowned. "No. I'm just—" Jack noticed the insecurity in Rex's eyes. The man thought Jack was abandoning him. "I'm not leaving for good. Not yet. I won't be gone long. I just need to talk to Tina. She asked me to come over to the apartment. Said she wouldn't move out until we sat down face-to-face."

Rex nodded, but he didn't appear pleased by the news. "I get it."

He didn't get it, Jack knew.

When Rex turned away from him, Jack moved closer, coming to stand directly behind him. He kneaded the tense muscles in Rex's shoulders, then leaned down and pressed his lips to Rex's neck. "I'm coming back."

Rex shrugged.

Jack wrapped his arms around him. For whatever reason, he felt comfortable touching Rex. He liked it, even. He'd never been the touchy-feely sort, but Jack enjoyed every moment he got to put his hands on Rex. Even innocent moments like this.

"I swear, it won't be long. Tina and I have to hash this out so we can move on with our lives."

Another nod from Rex was all he got.

Releasing Rex's shoulders, Jack moved around him, taking a seat. "Talk to me, Rex."

"Nothin' to talk about. You've got a life. I never expected you to stay."

Jack frowned, hating that Rex wouldn't look him in the eye when he spoke. They'd had an amazing few days. They'd worked, talked, made love, even slept in the same bed together. Yes, Rex was still having nightmares, but he wasn't hurting Jack the way he had that first night. Jack considered that progress and no way was he planning to give all that up yet. Certainly not for Tina.

Knowing he could talk until he was blue in the face but it wouldn't do any good, Jack decided he would simply prove it.

"I have to meet Tina at noon. I'll let her say her piece, then I'll be on my way back. I'll text you."

Rex nodded but, again, didn't look at Jack.

Figuring the least he deserved was Rex's attention, Jack pushed to his feet, stepped right up to where Rex was sitting. He cupped Rex's face, tiling his head back until their eyes met.

"I promised you I wouldn't run," he said softly. "I'm not running, Rex. I'm coming back. The least I deserve is a little trust."

Rex's eyes bounced over his face as though he was searching for something.

Knowing actions spoke louder than words, Jack leaned down, pressed his lips to Rex's. The kiss was gentle, sweet. It punched Jack somewhere in the center of his chest, but it wasn't painful. It was … promising.

An hour later, Jack was stepping into his apartment. He scanned the space, noticed the Christmas tree was gone. Unfortunately, Tina—as well as all her shit—wasn't.

"Jack." Her smile was radiant when she turned toward him, picking up two glasses of wine from the bar. She started toward him, held one of the glasses out to him.

Jack's gaze darted from her face to the wine, then back. "Can't. I've got things to do later today."

Tina had gotten all dolled up. The dress she wore highlighted her curves, her long hair shiny and smooth, her makeup flawless. Jack wasn't sure the last time she'd put that much effort into looking good for him. Not that he'd done the same for her, either.

"Let's get this over with, Tina."

Her eyes dropped momentarily, her smile faltering.

"Can we at least sit?" She motioned toward the sofa.

Jack dropped into the chair, ensuring they would not be close together. He stared at her, waiting for whatever she'd concocted to convince him to stay.

Tina moved to the couch, setting the wineglasses on the table before sitting down, gracefully smoothing her dress. When her eyes met his again, there was light.

"So, how have you been, Jack?"

"Fine."

"You look good."

Leaning forward, Jack rested his elbows on his knees. "Tina."

She frowned. "I'm sorry. It's just… I haven't seen you in a while and now that you're here…"

"I only came because I need to know when you're leaving." He watched her face and he suddenly knew. With a sigh, he pushed to his feet. "You're not leaving, are you, Tina?"

Light blue eyes peered up at him. "I don't want to go, Jack. I want you to come home. Give this … *us* … another chance."

Shaking his head, Jack started for the stairs. He figured he could grab a couple of things while he was there. "It's over, Tina. You ensured that by inviting Max into my bed."

She shot to her feet before he could pass her. "I haven't seen Max since that night, Jack. I swear it. I told him it wouldn't work out."

He laughed, a strangled sound that held absolutely no humor. "Wow. I'm so happy to hear that, Tina. And what? You think that'll make me come running back into your arms, telling you it's all right that you've been screwing some guy on the side?" He shook his head again. "Not gonna happen."

Tina reached out, her fingers wrapping around his arm. "I love you, Jack. I'm so sorry." The tears came, just as he'd expected, but these weren't ugly tears. They were too controlled.

Too fake.

"Funny way of showing it."

"I said I was sorry," she declared, the pitch of her voice rising. "What more do you want from me, Jack? What do I have to do to get you to come home? To love me again?"

He pulled his arm out of her grasp. "You should've thought about that before you started fucking other men."

"It's not entirely my fault," she snapped.

Jack rolled his eyes, sighed. "Oh, I know. If I'd only taken care of your needs, you wouldn't've had to get it elsewhere."

The crease in her forehead smoothed out. "So you do understand."

Jack let out a hysterical laugh. This time he *was* amused. "Oh, yeah. I understand. If I don't give you everything you need, you simply get it elsewhere." He glared down at her. "I'm done, Tina."

"You can't say that," she demanded. "You asked me to marry you, Jack. I know you love me."

"I thought I did," he admitted, staring into her eyes. "I truly thought I did, but that was before…"

His thoughts drifted to Rex. To the time they'd spent together. The past month—even with all the ups and downs—had been amazing. The times they'd simply hung out, worked beside one another, watched television, shared a meal. And yes, especially when they'd been fucking like rabbits. The past month with Rex had been the best of Jack's entire life.

"Before what?" Tina reached for him, but Jack backed away.

"Before you decided to throw it all away." Now was not the time to tell his ex-fiancée that he was in love with a man.

His heartbeat skipped.

Love?

Wow.

Talk about revelations.

"Sorry, Tina. But I've got to go." Jack spun around and headed for the door. "Since you don't want to go, I will. I'll take myself off the lease and I'll be back for the rest of my shit later."

"You can't take your name off unless I agree to it," she stated firmly. "I've already checked."

Of course she had. "And you won't agree to it?"

"No. Not until you move back in here and give us another chance."

Jack planted his fists on his hips and stared at her. "I can't do that, Tina."

Her eyes were wide, a single tear leaving a mascara streak on her cheek. "Why?"

"Because I can't."

"That's not good enough," she exclaimed. "I need a reason."

Jack felt his temper rise, knew he was going to regret this later, but he couldn't seem to get through to her. "Because I'm in love with someone else, Tina."

Her jaw fell open, her eyes widened even more. Jack had never seen Tina speechless. "You're ... *what?*"

"I'm in love with someone else," he repeated. It felt good to say it, too.

"Who is she, Jack? I deserve that much."

"Actually, you don't," he countered. "But I did give you a reason, and I'm willing to remove myself from the lease. If you can't live with that, then you need to be out of here by tomorrow night."

They stood there staring at one another for the longest time before Tina managed to compose herself somewhat.

She took a deep breath. "Fine. When can you remove your name from the lease and get the rest of your stuff?"

Jack shrugged. "I need to figure out a couple of things first."

"What? What do you have to figure out?"

How to say the right thing.

To the right man.

But Jack didn't tell Tina that.

Instead, he walked out the door and headed back to the only place he'd ever felt as though he belonged.

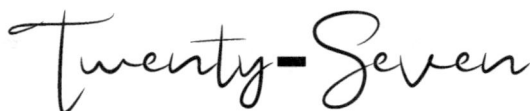

Twenty-Seven

REX WASN'T THE SORT TO BROOD.

Usually.

Which was the very reason he'd gone down to the main floor the instant Jack left. He immersed himself in work, putting up Sheetrock alongside the crew he'd hired to do it. Although he was still on the fence as to how much he wanted to contract out, Rex knew he had to be reasonable. The first couple of months of a new construction project were always hectic and this house was no different. They'd already tackled the new roof, new windows and doors, electrical upgrade, plumbing changes and fixes. The inspector had come out at every step, giving his seal of approval and allowing for the next stage to begin. Now they were focused on Sheetrock, then paint. Floors would come next and then onto the actual design. It was well underway.

Rex was overseeing every project, ensuring they were right where they needed to be. While they had months of work ahead of them, he wanted to get as far as possible before he started focusing on the individual tasks, such as installing the tile in those bathrooms or putting up the backsplash in the kitchen. Those were the jobs he wanted to do himself, which meant the further they made it before he went solo, the better off he'd be. Rex was still hoping he could beat Travis's expectations, get the place open a couple of months earlier than planned.

"Knock, knock," a voice rang out.

Rex pulled his earbuds out of his ears, turning to see Bristol marching across the living room, a beaming grin on her face. She looked like she always did when she was working. Jeans, sweatshirt, Converse on her feet. Her long hair was pulled back in a tail, her face clean of makeup except for mascara and lip gloss. Staples, she called them.

"Well, this is a nice surprise," he told her, hugging her back when she wrapped her arms around him.

"This place looks amazing, Rex," she announced, dramatically peering around. "I can't believe all that's been done already."

The woman was always so optimistic. It made Rex grin. "Yeah? I was thinkin' it looked a little empty."

"Well, sure. A little. But it won't. Before you know it, you'll be ready to hang curtains." She grinned wide and proud. "And Kylie showed me the design. It's gonna be incredible when you're finished." She scanned the room. "Where's Jack?"

The abrupt subject change had him sobering somewhat. "Had to go back to Austin."

Her smile instantly fell, that groove in her forehead appearing. "He's *gone?*"

Rex gave her a one-shoulder shrug.

"Like *gone* gone?" She did not appear happy about that.

He could only offer another shrug.

Bristol squared off with him momentarily, her blue eyes staring into his face. He'd seen this look a million times over the years. She was trying to read something that wasn't there. That or trying to decide if he was at fault for running off the city boy.

With her hands on her hips, she stared him down. "When's he comin' back, Rex?"

He shrugged again, dropped his gaze to the floor.

To be honest, Rex wasn't sure. He knew Jack had promised to come back today, but he wasn't holding his breath. The one thing he'd learned about Jack in the time they'd spent together was that the city boy was a very indecisive man. Plus, he liked to run from his issues. Considering what was transpiring between them, it wouldn't surprise him if Jack never came back. There was no denying that things had heated up a few degrees. They'd somehow managed to overcome their obstacles and had settled right into an actual relationship whether they acknowledged it or not. Rex figured that had freaked Jack out a bit, hence the reason he'd run back to Austin so abruptly.

"Oh, Rex."

Locking his gaze on Bristol's face, he shook his head, forced a grin. "Don't you dare feel sorry for me, woman. Jack was just passin' through town."

She swallowed hard, frowned. "Yes, I can see by the look in your eyes that you aren't bothered by that, too."

"I'm not." *Much.*

Bristol huffed. "Did he say he'd be back?"

Not wanting to lie to her, he told her the details of their conversation that morning.

She exhaled deeply, lightly smacked his arm. "You scared me for a minute, Rex. I thought you meant he was *never* comin' back."

Yeah, well. That was still to be determined.

Wanting desperately to stop talking about Jack, Rex shifted the direction of the conversation. "What brings you by, Bristol?"

She watched his face closely. "Just checkin' in. Haven't heard from you in a while. Decided I'd grab some lunch and stop by before I finished runnin' my errands."

"All's good here," he said, inserting some cheer into his tone. "Just workin' away. You know me."

And while he was hoping that would be the end of her interrogation, Rex got the feeling she was just getting started.

OH, BRISTOL KNEW REX, ALL RIGHT. SHE probably knew him better than he knew himself.

The man was many things. Smart, handsome, intelligent. Kind, giving, compassionate. But a liar, he was not. He was horrible at it. The worst, in fact.

Rex had never been good at hiding things from her. Oh, he thought he was, and he'd been doing it since they were kids.

He'd started off trying to hide the fact that his father was abusive. It hadn't taken Bristol long to realize there was something significantly different about her father and Rex's. But she'd never called Rex on it because they were too young to do anything about it. Then, when his mother and grandfather had died, Rex had pretended he wasn't shattered by that. Bristol had known better.

Through all of that, Bristol had remained by his side, pretending to believe him because she loved him that much. As a friend.

Bristol loved the man with all her heart, always had, always would. With her father gone, Rex was the closest she had to family, more of a brother than a friend. Which was why she couldn't sit back and watch him get his heart broken. As she stared at him now, Bristol was seeing something she'd never seen in Rex's eyes. Every time Jack's name came up, there was a spark there, a shimmer of... It looked a hell of a lot like hope. If it weren't for the fact that Rex would get defensive, she would accuse him of being in love with the man.

As it was, she could see the blatant insecurity etched on his handsome features. It was rare for Rex to show quite so much, even to her. However, she'd also been expecting it. While they hadn't been hanging out the way they usually did, Bristol knew there was only one reason for that.

Jack.

Well, mostly Jack. She had to admit, she had been a little sidetracked lately, too. Granted, she wasn't exactly ready to share the details of what was transpiring between her and Kaden and Keegan just yet. Once she figured out what it was, perhaps she'd share some of the details.

Maybe.

What she was worried most about now was why Jack had gone back to Austin. And when was he coming back?

Bristol stared at her best friend, desperately wished she could eradicate the clouds in his eyes. It was clear that Rex was hoping Jack would reappear at any moment. The way his gaze frequently darted to the door told her he'd been waiting long enough.

"What's been up with you?" Rex asked, reaching for a bottle of water. "You give in to those twins yet?"

Her mouth fell open. "To the … what?" She frowned, trying to play it off. "What are you talkin' about?"

He grinned, and for the first time since she'd walked in, it was actually genuine. "Kaden and Keegan."

"Who?"

Rex laughed, an abrupt sound that had her smiling. "Last I heard, they were still tryin' to get your attention."

Bristol waved him off. "Yeah, well. You know." She could feel herself blush. "So, it's comin' along, then? The house?" She tore her gaze from his face, peering around the wide-open space. The house looked nothing like it once had, back when Rex's mother had been alive. While it hadn't been the fanciest house in the area, Adele had done her best to make it nice for her boys. Now, down to the studs, the main floor seemed cold, lifeless. There was Sheetrock in a few places, but it didn't help to warm the space at all. Granted, when it was all said and done, she knew it would be phenomenal, a place Rex could be proud of.

"Nice subject change," he said with a chuckle. "But yes. It's comin' along faster than I'd planned."

"Yeah?" Bristol plastered on a genuine smile. "So does that mean we can grab a bite soon?"

"Definitely soon."

Knowing he wouldn't commit until he checked his schedule, Bristol nodded. "Let me know."

"I will."

"Talk to you later!" Bristol gave him a quick hug, a peck on the cheek before she danced back out the front door and into the cold February day.

Before she made it down the porch steps, a familiar sports car was pulling into the driveway. Bristol grinned and waved at Jack, grateful that he'd come back so quickly.

"Hey," he greeted when he climbed out of his car.

"Hey, back." She motioned toward the house. "Rex said you went back to Austin."

He nodded. "Just a quick visit. Needed to have a conversation."

"Did you?"

Jack studied her momentarily and it was obvious he wasn't sure how to answer that question.

"Yes, to clarify," she stated with a grin, "I'm nosy. Rex is my best friend, and I tend to ask questions when I'm worried about him."

Jack's concerned gaze shot to the house. "Is he all right?"

"Well, I figured you could answer that question better than I could."

Those soft gray eyes darted to her face and remained there. Bristol could see the wheels turning, but she waited, hoping he would open up to her.

When Jack leaned against his car, her stomach fluttered. He seemed sad.

"I went back to talk to Tina," he explained. "She said we needed to hash things out so we could move on."

Bristol joined him by the car, leaned her hip against it, and crossed her arms over her chest. "And?"

"She refused to move out of the apartment. Said we owe it to ourselves to work things out."

Oh, crap. Bristol did not like the sound of that.

Jack shook his head. "I told her I'd be back to remove myself from the lease and to get my shit. If she's not leaving, I am."

Relief swamped her, but Bristol knew she was the only one feeling it. "Are you okay with that?"

Jack's gaze dropped to the ground. "I don't know. I told her I was in love with someone else."

Bristol's heart squeezed in her chest. "With Rex? You love him?"

His eyes lifted to her face and he nodded.

"That's wonderful, Jack."

"I don't know about that." Jack peered up at the house. "I'm not sure where I'll go from here. But I don't have any more excuses to stay."

"Excuses? Why do you need excuses?"

"Because I'm intruding on Rex's space."

As though they had a mind of their own, Bristol's eyes shot across the street, locked on the bookstore, then inched up to the second floor. She happened to know that there was a vacant space up there. It wasn't anything fancy, but it had once been used as an apartment. Perhaps Jack could stay there.

"You know what?" she said quickly as she stood tall. "I need to talk to someone. But don't you go lookin' for anything until you talk to me. Okay?"

Jack frowned. "Uh…okay?"

"Great! I'll talk to you later." Bristol clapped her hands, then strolled over to her car.

As she backed out of the parking space, she glanced up, noticing Jack was still watching her.

And something told her Jack wouldn't be needing another place to stay, but she would check it out anyway.

Just in case.

"REX?" JACK CALLED OUT WHEN HE STEPPED into the farmhouse.

He'd taken his time after Bristol left, choosing to stand in the yard and contemplate his next steps. Did he admit to Rex that he'd fallen in love with him? Did he hold out hope that they could make this work? Would Rex even want something more? There were so many questions. But, after twenty minutes and no easy answers, Jack realized he had to go inside.

"In here!"

Jack followed the sound of Rex's voice into the back of the house, where he'd seen the layout for the new kitchen. "I just wanted to let you know I'm back."

Rex spun around, his surprise apparent. It was quickly masked, followed by a simple nod of acknowledgement.

"Did you think I wasn't coming back?" he asked when Rex didn't say anything.

A shrug was all he got, and for some reason, that pissed him off. They'd spent far too much time doing this exact thing, skirting the issues, ignoring their feelings, pretending nothing was happening. While he would shoulder some of the blame, Jack was still tired of it.

"That's getting old, Rex."

"What is?"

"Your lack of verbal response."

Rex turned away. "What did you expect me to say?"

"Something. *Any*thing."

Rex pivoted back around, crossed his arms over his chest. "Fine. How'd your visit with Tina go?"

"As I expected," he admitted. "She tried to convince me to work things out, then said she wasn't moving out."

"So, you're gonna patch things up? Get married in a couple of weeks?"

Jack sighed his exasperation. "Not a chance. But I did tell her I was leaving. That I'd be back to get my shit and take my name off the lease."

He was hoping Rex would get the hint, understand that Jack was finished with Tina. What he wanted was standing right in front of him, even if the man was frustrating as hell.

"Well, good for you." Rex took a step back.

"Good for me?" Jack couldn't hold in the anger. "That's all you've got to say? Good for me?"

"If it's what you want," Rex stated, that devil-may-care attitude securely in place. "Glad it's all gonna work out for you."

There were a million things Jack wanted to say right then, but he realized he had no place. If Rex didn't care, then why should he? They'd had a phenomenal few days, but that didn't mean Rex owed him anything. And it certainly didn't mean that Rex felt the same way he did. Rex had proven how easily he could write Jack off in just a few short words.

"You know what?" Jack turned, started toward the stairs. "I've got some shit to tend to. I need to find a place to stay and I'll be out of your hair as soon as I can secure something. I just need a day or so."

Jack didn't look back. His blood roared in his ears as he stomped up the stairs to the third-floor apartment. He went in, slammed the door, and headed for his bedroom. There were hundreds—probably thousands—of apartments in the area, from Georgetown to San Antonio, and any one of them would work for him. With his credit and rental history, Jack could probably move into one tomorrow.

It wasn't like he needed much. One bedroom, one bath. Hell, he could even live in a studio if necessary. As long as he had a small space to work, he was golden. Back to the grindstone for him. He could find something in the city, even. Close to shopping, restaurants, all the things he'd cared about before he found himself trapped in this small town.

Jack fought back the pain that clawed at his chest. He was stupid for allowing himself to get in too deep. But that was the way he worked. He didn't look before he leaped, and this was what happened. One more heartbreak in the grand scheme of things.

But he'd survived all the others. Surely he could survive this one.

Twenty-Eight

REX KNEW HE'D BEEN AN ASS TO Jack. He knew it and he hated himself for it.

Which was why he'd marched up the stairs shortly after Jack had. He tossed Duke a chew bone, then headed right for Jack's room, intending to apologize for his irrational behavior. It wasn't warranted and Jack deserved a hell of a lot better than that.

All his good intentions disappeared the moment he stepped into the room to find Jack packing his things.

"What're you doin'?" His heart thumped painfully in his chest as he watched Jack toss a shirt into his suitcase.

With hardly a glance in his direction, Jack said, "Packing. It's what you wanted, right?"

"No, it's not," he insisted.

Jack continued to toss clothes in the direction of his suitcase. "Could've fooled me."

Suddenly panicked that Jack would walk out and Rex would never see him again, he walked over and inserted himself between Jack and the suitcase.

"You're in the way, Rex."

"Don't leave," he whispered, his throat suddenly scratchy with emotion. "Not like this."

Jack spun around to face him. "Like what? Angry and hurt? Because that's what I am, Rex. You don't have a lick of faith in me."

Although he wanted to argue that point, Rex couldn't seem to find the words. It was true. He hadn't thought Jack was going to stay. From the moment he mentioned going back to see his ex, Rex had expected the worst.

"I think I've overstayed my welcome," Jack said, moving around Rex.

Rather than get out of the way, Rex took a step over, got up in Jack's face. "You haven't."

"I have and we both know it."

"Damn it, Jack." Realizing he couldn't express himself using words, Rex grabbed Jack and pulled him close. He melded his mouth to Jack's, then slid his arms around him.

And to his surprise, Jack didn't fight him. The kiss went from zero to sixty in less than a second. The next thing Rex knew, he was on the bed, hovering over Jack while he tried to inhale him. Their bodies moved as one, the inability to get close enough evident. The suitcase thudded onto the floor as they fought to remove clothes, clawing at one another as painful lust tore through Rex. He'd never wanted another man the way he wanted Jack. Didn't matter how many times he had him, he still wanted more. He doubted he would ever get enough.

"Rex…"

Pulling back, he stared down into the man's beautiful face. God, he loved his face. Hell, Rex loved every damn thing about Jack.

"You have to trust me," Jack whispered.

Holding his stare, Rex nodded. "I know."

"But you don't."

Rex swallowed hard. "Doesn't mean I don't want to." It was just too damn hard for him.

"Do you trust me with your body?" Jack asked.

Rex knew what Jack was referring to and he didn't even have to think about it. "Yes."

"Prove it."

That he could do.

"Strip," Rex insisted as he launched up off the bed, grabbing a condom and lube from the nightstand drawer.

Within no time at all, they were both naked, once more rolling around on the big bed, hands fumbling, hearts pounding, mouths searching, seeking.

"I don't want to hurt you," Jack muttered as he slid over him.

"You won't." And even if he did, Rex wasn't sure he cared. It had been a long time since Rex had bottomed, but he was eager, desperate even. He needed to feel Jack inside him. Needed it with an intensity that defied logic. It wasn't simply pleasure he was seeking here. Rex wanted to prove to Jack that he did trust him on some level. If not with his heart, certainly with his body. Which meant there was hope for him. For them.

Jack kissed him again, his lips soft and gentle.

"How do you want me?" Rex asked when they broke apart for air.

Jack didn't seem to have an answer to that.

"Then I'll tell you what I want," Rex said, cupping the back of Jack's head and staring into his beautiful eyes.

"Tell me," Jack rasped.

"I want to feel you inside me. I want you to fuck me. Hard, fast, dirty. To claim me the way I've claimed you."

"Fuck." Jack slammed his mouth to Rex's, shocking him for a moment.

Rex kissed him back with fervor, showing Jack just how much he needed this, how much he wanted him in every way possible. When they broke for air again, Rex flipped onto his stomach, relishing the warmth of Jack at his back. The man certainly didn't have a problem working him into a frenzy. While Jack appeared hesitant, the man knew how to touch him, kiss him, drive him higher and higher.

"Fuck me," Rex insisted, fisting his hands in the comforter as Jack drove two fingers into his ass. "Fuck me, now."

There was a rustle as Jack opened the condom, but then he was instantly pressed against Rex's back, his lubed cock sliding between Rex's ass cheeks. He held his breath as the initial intrusion burned. When Jack went too slow for his liking, Rex shifted, pushing back until Jack's cock was lodged balls deep inside him.

"Oh, fuck, Rex." Jack's breath fanned his neck, his voice so soft he barely heard him. "This is … fucking heaven."

Jack slowly retreated, then thrust back in. Rex relaxed as best he could, ignoring the pain, allowing the sensations to consume him. The way Jack's lips trailed over his neck, his teeth nipping every so often, had goose bumps breaking out over his skin.

And when Jack began fucking him in earnest, Rex groaned his pleasure.

"Don't stop," he warned as Jack's hips began to slow. "Fuck me harder."

Jack's fingers curled over Rex's shoulders, holding him in place as he impaled him again and again. "Don't … want … to hurt … you."

"Fuck me, Jack. Damn you. Fuck me."

That did it.

Jack slammed into him over and over, changing his position so his hands gripped Rex's hips almost painfully. It was intense and so fucking good. Rex held on for as long as he could, but when Jack cried out his release, Rex chased his own, giving in to the painful pleasure that racked his entire body.

And when they fell onto the bed in a heap, Rex couldn't stop the smile.

He had needed that. Perhaps they both had.

Tuesday, February 5, 2019

THE NEXT THREE DAYS PASSED IN A blur.

Jack was able to get more work done in that short time frame than he had in the past two months. The creative juices were steadily flowing, and he couldn't help but think Rex was the reason for that.

When they weren't fooling around—which, admittedly, they did quite often—Jack was sketching or talking to Shawn. Hell, he'd hardly slept a wink, but for whatever reason, Jack was filled with energy. Mental and physical. He felt damn near invincible. For the first time in a very long time, Jack wasn't overwhelmed by his thoughts.

And he'd accomplished so much with the project, Shawn had been impressed. Although Shawn still had to finish up a couple of scenes before Jack could move forward, if they kept up this pace, they would likely be done a few weeks ahead of schedule.

That had never happened to him before.

While Jack spent most of the day alone in the apartment, he spent every night with Rex in his bed, and for the past two nights, at least, Rex hadn't had a nightmare. Not that Jack knew of, anyway.

And they'd fallen into a fairly nice routine. Rex would wake up, make breakfast before heading downstairs or over to his workshop. Jack would pause in the middle of the day to make lunch, seeking Rex out to ensure he ate. By the time evening rolled around, they both ended up in the hot tub. Rex would toss something on the grill—burgers or chicken—before they spent a half hour or so relaxing in the water. Once they'd pruned, they would race out to avoid frostbite on their dicks.

Evidently, the stress-relieving powers of the hot tub were worth the risk because that was where they were now.

Jack watched as Rex sank down into the water, his eyes closed as he relaxed. While he wanted to enjoy the downtime, he knew there was a conversation they still needed to have. One they'd been avoiding since Rex confronted him the day Jack had attempted to pack. Avoidance had become their crutch. Rather than talk about what was happening, they simply filled their time with sex. While it was a great alternative, it wasn't solving anything.

Which meant they needed to discuss which direction they were headed. Jack couldn't deny he was still concerned that he was moving too fast. It was easy to do considering how he felt about Rex. Didn't mean it was right. That was the way he did things, after all. Head first without looking to see how deep the water was. Proceeding with caution wasn't his strong suit.

"What's on your mind?" Rex asked, drawing Jack from his thoughts.

Jack glanced over to see him reaching for his beer, then settling back down. "Nothing."

Rex studied Jack's face for a moment, and it was obvious he knew Jack was lying, but as had been the case lately, Rex didn't have anything to say.

"Okay, fine. I actually need to talk to you about something."

Rex's back straightened and his expression hardened. He'd definitely been waiting for the other shoe to drop. Which meant this conversation wasn't going to go well no matter how Jack approached it.

"I've found an apartment," he blurted.

Jack had never seen a man go eerily still before. The only muscle in Rex's body that moved was near his eyes as he stared back at him.

Jack wanted him to say something, but he didn't.

"It's actually really close to here," he explained. "I've already submitted the application and they've approved me for move-in whenever I want. I can finally get out of your hair."

Rex didn't appear to find the humor the way Jack intended. With a sigh, Jack set his beer on the edge of the hot tub and quickly moved over to Rex, wanting to reassure him that this wasn't him running away. Without an ounce of modesty, he put his arms around Rex's neck and stared into his eyes.

"I did my research, found a place that I thought would work well for the situation," Jack assured him.

Rex still didn't move, his eyes locked somewhere over Jack's shoulder. "What situation would that be?"

"You. Me. Whatever this is that's going on between us."

Rex wasn't looking at him and it was starting to piss him off, so Jack turned his chin, forcing Rex to meet his eyes.

"Go check it out with me?"

Rex instantly shook his head. "Sorry. No can do."

Yeah. That was a fucking lie if Jack had ever heard one.

"Why not?"

His eyes shifted away again. "Too much shit to do here."

Jack laughed, but it was tinged with anger and frustration. Why Rex felt the need to close himself off was beyond him, but it seemed to be the man's default setting.

"Bullshit. You can't take a couple of—"

Rex's eyes narrowed as they landed on his face. "I have shit to do."

"We all do," Jack snarled. "But I would drop everything if you asked me to go somewhere with you."

When Rex tried to push him away, Jack didn't fight. He released him, even though it choked him up to have Rex turning his back.

"I did what you told me to do," Jack said, his voice lower as he sat watching Rex move toward the side. "I made a decision. I came to you, remember? This doesn't change that. I'm simply getting out of your hair, back to my own space. It'll give us a chance to slow things down. Perhaps have a traditional relationship."

"There is no relationship, Jack," Rex muttered as he stepped out of the water.

Ouch. He was pretty sure that sound … it was his heart snapping in two. But whatever.

"If that's the way you want it," Jack told him, unable to muster the energy to fight.

Rex didn't look at him. Instead, he marched toward the house.

Jack was really getting tired of this shit. For someone who was constantly on Jack's ass for running away, Rex had a penchant for walking away in the middle of a conversation. Whenever Rex didn't like the outcome, he simply didn't stick around. The bad news was that Jack had no fucking clue what he was supposed to do. Did he go after him? Or did he simply pack his shit and leave? A rational conversation seemed the smart way to go, but it wasn't like he could have this chat with himself. Clearly, Jack wasn't the one who needed convincing. Rex was.

Jack hadn't been planning to disappear for good. He still wanted to see Rex. Hell, he was hoping they could continue this … whatever this was. And that was the reason he'd jumped on the opportunity Bristol had presented him with. Evidently, the bookstore owner across the street had been looking for someone to rent her second-floor apartment to. Initially, Jack had been hesitant, but then he'd figured he might as well give in. It was what he wanted. To stay close to Rex, to see where this *non-relationship* relationship went.

Seriously? He didn't understand why Rex was so pissed. Jack couldn't simply shack up with him indefinitely. They didn't have that sort of relationship. Not yet, anyway.

Maybe not ever.

Not to mention, that was a bad habit Jack had to break. He couldn't continue this cycle of jumping from one relationship to the next without thought. Sure, he enjoyed the hell out of being with Rex. In fact, he'd go so far as to say he'd never felt more content in his entire life.

Didn't mean this was going to be a lasting thing and Jack had to take care of himself. He was a grown man. He had obligations and responsibilities of his own.

With a sigh, Jack moved back to the contoured seat, grabbed his beer, and relaxed into the water. He rested his arms on his knees and stared up at the giant sky.

At least there was one positive in this whole thing…

For the first time, Jack wasn't the one running.

Twenty-Nine

JACK WAS MOVING OUT.

The thought made Rex want to put his fist through the tiled wall, but he wasn't exactly sure why that was.

Not true. He knew exactly why.

However, he also knew he didn't have the right to confront him on it. Jack didn't live there with him. He was a guest. It made sense that he had to get on with his life. But it still pissed Rex off.

No. That wasn't the right emotion.

It hurt.

It fucking *hurt* to think that Jack was going to leave. After all they'd shared together, Rex... Well, to be fair, Rex had wanted it to keep going the way it was going. Simple, easy, no strings, but a hell of a lot of convenience. Yeah. He wanted Jack to stay. There was no denying that Rex had gotten caught up in having him around. He liked having Jack there. In his house. In his bed. In his arms.

That was it.

Rex didn't want to let him go. He finally had someone he wanted to spend his life with, and the man was only temporary. The pain lanced his insides, made his heart physically hurt.

Okay, so maybe it was a little more than mere convenience.

Rex stood in the shower while the hot water beat down on his tired muscles and he fought for breath. What the hell was he going to do now? Did he let Jack walk out? Worse, did he push Jack away? Because that was certainly the direction they were headed. Rex was handling this the wrong way, even he could admit that. Instead of compromising, he was practically sending Jack on down the road.

"I don't want him to go," he muttered, his chest tight with emotion.

Rex's eyes had been wide open going into this. He knew what it was, knew what it wasn't. And to be fair, he'd never told Jack he wanted anything more than sex. Of course, that had changed, but had he bothered to voice his true feelings to Jack? Hell no. Why? Because he was fucking terrified it would all blow up in his face the way it was now. Because he couldn't admit the truth, couldn't tell Jack how he felt because it made him vulnerable.

Rex sighed, pressing his palms to the wall and hanging his head down. The water beat against his scalp, pouring down his face. His shoulders were tight, his anger barely restrained. He was pissed at the way things were turning out, more so about how he was handling them, plus a myriad of other reasons. Not only because he'd allowed himself to fall for Jack in the month he'd been there but also because Rex had somehow lost sight of what he was after. At some point in the past few weeks, he had lost his focus. He'd been playing house with Jack and gotten caught up in it.

This wasn't what was supposed to happen.

"Son of a bitch," he growled, frustration dripping from the words.

If he allowed Jack to leave with so much left unsaid between them, Rex knew they wouldn't find their way back to one another. Which meant Rex had to make a stand. He had to—

His body went still when he felt the air shift in the bathroom. Rex knew Jack had joined him. He had been expecting him to. After all, Jack was leaving. Of course he would want to say goodbye. And what better way than to fuck. That seemed to be what Rex was good for. Getting Jack off.

Rex felt Jack's hands glide over his back first, then his lips followed the same path. His skin tightened over his entire body as it always did when Jack touched him. Those slick, warm palms slipped around to Rex's chest and he stood when Jack pulled him back against him. Unable to resist, Rex closed his hands over Jack's, holding him there, enjoying the strength he felt in the man's hold.

He let his eyes drift shut when Jack's chin met his shoulder. This was where he wanted to be. Right here.

Rex's breath halted in his lungs. His heart pounded, but not from lust. The emotion swamped him. He didn't want Jack to go. That was all there was to it. He fought to regulate his breathing so he could tell Jack that. Before he could get the words past the lump in his throat, Jack spoke.

"I don't want to leave you," Jack whispered, his arms tightening around him.

Rex didn't want him to leave, either. So who said he had to?

"But it's time, Rex."

Yeah. Not at all what he wanted to hear following that initial confession. His blood pounded in his head, making it hard to focus.

Jack sighed, kissed Rex's shoulder. "I have to get back to my life, figure out what I'm going to do from here. I have a job I've been neglecting, and responsibilities."

Yep. Rex knew that.

Because Rex was only a temporary stop on his path. It wasn't like Rex had spent the past month falling in love with him or anything. Only he had. Head over fucking heels.

Rex turned to face Jack because he had to do this. He had to tell Jack how he felt. Otherwise, the man would leave, and he would never know.

When they were face-to-face, Jack's eyes met Rex's and a sad smile formed. "Rex, I don't plan—"

Rex cut Jack off with a look. "My turn."

He cupped Jack's face, tilting his chin back so Jack was looking directly into his eyes. They stood like that for several long seconds. He was terrified to say the words, to open himself up that way, but Rex knew if he didn't, he would regret it for the rest of his life. And to be honest, he had too many regrets. He'd wasted too damn much time as it was.

"Rex?" Jack whispered. "Are you all right?"

Rex nodded, and when the words finally came, his heart lodged in his throat as he said, "I love you, Jack. I don't want you to leave."

Jack's eyes widened, his Adam's apple bobbed as though that was the very last thing he would ever expect Rex to say.

"But I get it. I know you have to take care of things. You were stayin' here so you could figure things out. I didn't mean to complicate your life."

"You didn't," Jack argued.

"I did." Rex held his gaze. "I fell in love with you, Jack. I know you didn't plan for that to happen, nor did I. But that's the way it is. I love you. I honestly never thought I'd find love. I don't expect you to reciprocate, but I need you to know."

Jack still didn't speak, and Rex felt his chest tighten, a vise squeezing until it was hard to breathe. It would've been easy to take it all back, but no matter the outcome, there was no way for Rex to do that.

He'd laid it all on the line.

Now it was Jack's turn.

REX LOVED HIM.

That was what he'd said.

He loved him.

Love. As in, something far more potent than mere like or lust or…

How could that be possible?

Not that Jack had the notion to argue. Hell, he felt it, too. Still, he knew he had to rationalize this, had to figure out where along the way they'd stumbled onto something more.

"You love me," he whispered.

"I do," Rex confirmed, his dark eyes glittering with what looked like fear and insecurity.

Jack cleared his throat and continued to stare into Rex's face, not wanting to break the moment. "This didn't start out normal, Rex. I mean, I met you in a bar a month ago. Then, I stumbled onto your doorstep because I was looking for a hotel. You weren't even open for business."

Rex smiled, just a slight lift at the corners of his sexy mouth. "I know. I was there, remember? And your point?"

Jack's heart beat rapidly, his mouth suddenly dry. "Have you ever seen that movie *Speed*? The one where the guy and the girl meet under extreme circumstances? On the bus, I think that's where they met. Not that it matters. But they did. And they were suddenly thrown together in this whirlwind of activity."

Rex smirked. "I don't see how this is the same as that, no."

"So you have seen it?"

Rex nodded. "I don't consider meeting in a bar the same as having a madman threaten to blow up a bus full of people."

"Fine. Maybe that wasn't the best example. But that doesn't mean this was normal. I've practically been living with you since the day we met."

"Practically?" Rex's tone was teasing and some of the strain eased out of his face.

"Okay, literally. I have *literally* been living with you since the day we met."

"The day after," Rex corrected. "You were hugging a bar the night we met."

"Whatever. My point is, I don't want this thing to end between us, but I thought maybe we could take things slower."

"Slower?" Rex took a step back, dislodging Jack's arms from around his neck. "We're standing naked in my shower, Jack. I just told you that I love you and you want to take things slower?"

Jack knew now wasn't necessarily the best time to address a couple of things, but they had to be brought up, so he swallowed down his nerves. "Love is supposed to come with trust, Rex."

"Agree."

"But you don't trust me," Jack told him, remembering the first night he'd begged Rex to sleep in the same bed.

"Not true. I do trust you."

"With your body, yes. You've proven that time and again, but you don't trust me with your secrets, your pain."

Rex stared at him, and Jack knew he'd hit the mark.

"Tell me something, Rex. Why do we only fuck in my bed and not yours?"

Rex's eyes widened and flashed with what Jack could only assume was anger. When the man marched out of the shower without turning off the water, Jack knew he'd hit pay dirt. The answer to that question, whatever it might be, was the root of a lot of issues. Issues that would only get more difficult as time went on. Especially if they didn't talk about them.

Not willing to let Rex off the hook for this, Jack turned off the water, snagged a towel, and followed Rex out of the bathroom. After scrubbing the towel over his hair, he ran the cotton over his body as best he could, then wrapped it around his hips.

"You say you love me, Rex," he said, following Rex into his bedroom. "Then why can't you answer the question?"

Rex spun around quickly. "Because I don't have an answer you're gonna like."

"Why am I supposed to like it? The truth is what I want, Rex. I want to be there for you. To help you through the hard times, to protect you when you need me to. I can't do that if you don't share things with me."

"You've never asked," Rex argued.

"I told you I'm here to listen anytime you need me to. I was hoping you'd open up on your own. But now I'm asking."

They both stood there, clad only in towels while they squared off with one another in Rex's bedroom.

"It's not something I can talk about," Rex finally admitted.

"There's the problem." Jack sighed. "And if you don't trust me…"

He waited to see if Rex would say something. When he didn't, Jack turned, fully intending to go to his room and finish packing his things. He didn't even make it to Rex's bedroom door when the torment in the man's voice had him turning back around.

"I didn't grow up the way you did, Jack. My life wasn't … simple."

He didn't bother to mention that his wasn't simple, either. He knew Rex was merely trying to figure out how to talk about this. In a way, Jack even understood, so he held his tongue and waited.

Finally, Rex sighed, his voice deeper when he spoke. "I've never had a man in my bed before. Not to fuck, not to sleep. It's too difficult for me to deal with."

Jack turned to face Rex. "What is?"

Rex took a deep breath, his gaze somewhere on the wall. "The night my brother shot and killed my father…"

Jack's heart leapt into his throat as he waited for Rex to continue, knowing whatever Rex had to say was going to rip Jack to shreds.

"After my mother died, my father got a girlfriend. She was only a few years older than me. Far too young for him, and crazy to boot. But Billy Don—my father—he only gave a shit about himself. She was always coming around, damn near every day. We stayed out of the house as much as we could, but it never seemed to matter. When we were in the house, she paid way too much attention to me and Rafe. Not in a motherly way, either. Like I said, she was crazy and more than a little sick in the head.

"Anyway, I made dinner for the old bastard that night, fed Rafe, then sent him upstairs so he didn't have to deal with Jolene. She showed up before I was done cleaning the kitchen. Like usual, she was acting strange, flirting with me, asking about Rafe. I shrugged it off, figured she was high, like usual. I managed to avoid her by going upstairs. Whenever she was at the house, I let Rafe stay in my room. I didn't trust her. Rafe didn't complain. He slept in my closet, said he felt safer there. That night, I hadn't planned to fall asleep until she left. I must've passed out at some point because I woke up chained to the bed."

"Rex," Jack whispered.

"Let me finish."

Jack nodded, hating that he'd pushed Rex to this, but needing to know.

"I woke up with handcuffs on my wrists and my father was zip-tying my ankles to the footboard. They were both talkin' nonsense. At first, I figured they were on drugs. I tried to get away, tried to break the zip ties, but I couldn't. I was trapped, completely at their mercy. I remember panicking, my heart pounding so hard I thought I would have a heart attack. When I tried to break the restraints, my father threatened to get my brother, to make him watch. The only thing I could think about was protecting Rafe. I knew if they got to him, I would be helpless to defend him, so I complied."

Rex took a deep breath, his eyes distant as he relived the pain from that night right before Jack's eyes.

"Jolene said she was there to prove to my father that I wasn't gay. Said she knew exactly how to do it. Said she would make my dick hard, then make me come." Rex shuddered. "I can still smell her; the stench makes me ill. I can feel her hands on me … her disgusting mouth … and I want to vomit. In my nightmares, she's right there, laughing at me, insisting that I just need a woman to fix me."

Jack leaned back against the wall, his legs suddenly weak. He could see the pain on Rex's face, knew that bitch had scarred him for life.

"I don't know how long it went on," Rex continued. "A few minutes, maybe. Jolene got her hands into my pants, touched me. She was tryin' to get me hard, but it wasn't working. I tried to block it out, to focus on other things just to get through it. I wanted her to be done, to leave me alone. When she put her mouth on me, I broke. The fear overwhelmed me. The thought of her raping me had me screaming, pleading for her to stop. Evidently, I was loud, and I must've woken Rafe.

"I remember the closet doors opening, my kid brother standing there with my grandfather's shotgun. The sound of it being racked is something I'll never forget for as long as I live. My dad's girlfriend kept yelling, insisting my father get Rafe out of there, said she wasn't finished with me. Rafe didn't budge, told my old man not to come closer." Rex stood there, staring at the wall, his chest expanding rapidly. "When my father went to get Rafe, my brother shot him. Once. In the chest. Killed him instantly."

Fucking hell. Jack inhaled sharply, realized he was on the verge of tears. His imagination conjured up something hideous, and he knew that was only a fraction of the hell Rex had gone through that night.

Rex swallowed hard, inhaled slowly, exhaled deeply. "Rafe saved me that night. Hell, he saved both of us. And I've never allowed myself to be vulnerable like that again."

Jack wasn't going to clarify that he'd seen Rex vulnerable many times. They didn't have to be in his bed for him to put himself out there. Every time they'd been together, making love, Rex had been vulnerable. And Jack had been right there with him.

"What happened to Jolene?"

Rex continued to stare at the floor. "She was arrested but got out while they awaited trial. She overdosed." His eyes lifted. "I've never felt so much elation. The day I learned she had died, I had prayed that it had been a horrible death. That she had suffered immensely."

Jack could understand that. Hell, he was hoping that bitch was burning in hell right now.

"It's not that I don't trust you, Jack," Rex said softly.

"Do you?" Jack couldn't help but ask. He pushed off the wall, closed the distance between them. "*Do* you trust me, Rex?"

Their eyes met, held. "I fell in love with you, Jack. That's more than I can say for anyone in my life. I've never felt this way before. The thought of you leaving…"

Jack reached for Rex, curled his hand around the back of his head. "The apartment is just across the street."

"That's too far."

"Across the street," Jack repeated.

Rex took a step closer. "I don't care if it's next fucking door, Jack. It's too far. I want you here. With me. I can't explain it."

Jack understood because he felt the same way. "I don't want to go."

"Then don't."

"Okay," Jack conceded. "I won't go."

Rex frowned, clearly confused by Jack's quick turnaround. It hadn't actually been all that quick. Jack had been thinking about it for hours, days. He had tried to figure out what to do to make this work between them because it was the only thing he wanted. Even if he knew he would probably get hurt in the process.

"But we have to do this the right way," Jack told him.

"And that would be?"

"That's what I don't know. I don't have a clue how this is supposed to work. I've never felt this way about anyone, either. Sure, I've been scared. Terrified, actually. My past relationships haven't worked out, and I'm okay with that. But this"—Jack motioned between them—"this feels different."

"It's because I'm a man, isn't it?" Rex asked with a chuckle.

"No." Jack couldn't help it, he laughed. "Okay, maybe a little." He sobered, needing to explain this. "But that's physical, Rex. You feel different to my body, but not to my heart. That particular part of me doesn't seem to discern gender, it merely knows what it wants. And my heart wants you."

Wow. Jack hadn't meant to say that, but now that the words were out, he saw everything clearly. One thing above all else. "If this doesn't work out, Rex, I'll be shattered."

"No one can guarantee an outcome, Jack."

He knew that. He did. Didn't make it easier to swallow. "I love you, Rex. That's what it boils down to. I love you and I'm terrified about how I feel."

"I'm terrified, too, so that makes us even."

Jack took a step back. "Even, maybe. But does that also make us broken?"

He instantly thought about what Rex had shared, about the horrific incident that had altered the course of his life. Rex had obviously survived, persevered.

"If we're broken, then we pick up the pieces," Rex stated firmly.

"Do we?" Jack wasn't sure Rex believed what he was saying. "Does that mean I sleep in your bed? Or you in mine? Because, Rex, no matter how you look at it, you're vulnerable no matter where you are."

"I know," Rex admitted softly, stepping closer. "But I've never slept with anyone until you."

"And I'm okay with that," Jack admitted. "I like being your first."

Rex smirked. "Ditto."

Swallowing past the lump in his throat, Jack stared at the man he loved. "So what do we do now?"

"We move forward."

"And which direction is forward?" That was what Jack wanted to know. Half the time, he wasn't even sure which way was up. And since he'd met Rex, his life had been a whirlwind, a mixture of chaos and uncertainty.

Rex lifted his hand, cupped Jack's cheek. "It's whatever direction we want it to be."

Yeah. Okay. When Rex said it, for some reason, Jack believed it.

Now only time would tell.

Epilogue

Seven months later…
Friday, September 13, 2019

"HEY, THERE YOU ARE!"

Rex turned at the sound of Jack's voice, peered up at the second floor. "What's wrong?"

Jack practically ran down the stairs. "Nothing."

"Nothing?" He grinned. "Then why're you breathin' hard?"

Aside from the fact that Jack's eyes were wide and he was out of breath, Rex knew something was up because the man was fidgeting. The way he rubbed his fingers together rapidly was always his tell, the sign that told Rex something big was coming. The first time he'd noticed it had been the night they'd declared their love for one another. Then, when Jack had asked if they could move into the same room only a week after that, more fidgeting. Followed by the time Jack asked if they could adopt Snowball, the bright white Pomeranian he'd seen at the pound. And the last time had been when Jack told him that his latest release had gotten some kind of award and was being considered for a television series.

Rather than urge him to speak, Rex stood there and waited. He knew Jack would come around sooner or later.

"Okay, so…" Jack shook out his hands, took one step back, followed by a deep breath. "Can we go in there?"

Rex turned toward the living area, glanced back at Jack briefly, then walked over to one of the two sofas that filled the space.

"Sit," Jack urged.

Rex sat, waited until Jack eased down beside him. Then waited a little longer while Jack apparently caught his breath.

"Okay, so you know how this place is opening for business tomorrow?"

Technically, they'd opened the Double R Retreat today and had their first guests coming in tonight, but Rex didn't bother to correct Jack. Tomorrow was the official grand opening for the town, which would include a huge shindig that Travis had put together. Rex figured that likely wasn't the point Jack was trying to make, so he merely nodded.

"And remember how you mentioned that you'd like to build a house on the property? A place to live once this place was open?"

Rex nodded. "I also remember sayin' I'd do that once I turned a profit."

"Whatever." Jack waved him off. "That'll be in no time. We're already booked almost solid through December."

They were, that much was true. With the help of the Walkers, word had spread far and wide.

Rex waited for Jack to continue, but it was clear the man was nervous about something, so he gave him a little nudge. "And your point...?"

Before Jack could spit out whatever he was trying to say, there was a knock on the front door. Figuring it was one of his cousins stopping by to check out the finished project, Rex held up his hand to Jack.

"Hold that thought?"

"Yeah, sure," Jack blurted, but he didn't appear pleased. "I'll get the door."

Rex shoved his hand into his pocket, fingered the ring he'd slipped in there. He smiled to himself. The interruption was just what he needed. It was a distraction until Rex could corner Jack, not vice versa.

Rex didn't even get to his feet before he heard the door open and Jack greet whoever was out there. He was already heading toward the kitchen to grab a couple of beers when Jack's voice pulled him up short.

"Uh, Rex."

He turned, noticed Jack's face was pale. He instantly went on alert, ready to defend the man he loved, to put himself between him and whoever was at the door. "What's wrong?"

Jack took a deep breath. "There's a man on the porch."

"Okay."

"He … uh … he said he wanted to talk to you."

"Is it a potential guest?"

Jack shook his head.

Rex smiled, relaxed somewhat. "Why didn't you invite him in? I'm sure it's one of my cousins."

"It's not."

Rex walked toward Jack, unsure what was going on or why he was acting so strange. "Did he say who he was?"

Jack nodded.

Rex glanced at the closed front door.

"It's your brother, Rex."

His gaze shot back to Jack's face and he knew he couldn't hide his shock. "My brother?"

Jack nodded. "Rafe. Yes. He's at the door."

The next thing Rex knew, he was marching to the front door with Jack in tow. Without looking, he pulled it open and his heart instantly lodged somewhere in his throat. He half expected to jolt awake from the dream, and he actually waited for that moment, because there was no way he was seeing who he thought he was seeing.

"Rafe," he whispered roughly, clearing his throat as emotion threatened to choke him.

"Hey, Rex." His brother—much older than Rex remembered—smiled as though years hadn't passed since the last time they'd seen one another.

"Should I pinch myself?" Rex asked, his voice shredded by the gravel he could feel in his throat. "Or are you really here?"

Rafe's expression didn't change, but he did glance across the street, scanned the businesses lining Main Street. When he turned back, his eyes were narrowed. "I'm really here."

The warm hand on his shoulder settled him somewhat and Rex was grateful for the man he loved.

Rafe's gaze moved past him and Rex found his manners. "This is Jack," Rex told Rafe. "My boyfriend." He glanced over at Jack. "Jack, this is Rafe."

"Very nice to meet you," Jack said, not moving toward Rafe, as though he knew the man might bolt if he did.

"Same," Rafe said, his eyes darting back and forth between them.

Rex could only stare at Rafe. His kid brother looked good. Healthy and strong, but still lacking the smile Rex had remembered him having before that fateful day so long ago. Rex had been waiting for this moment, but he'd honestly thought it would never come. And now that it had, he wasn't sure what he was supposed to say.

Rex swallowed past the lump that had formed in his throat, then remembered where he was, what he was doing. He shoved open the screen door and urged Rafe to come inside. "You wanna come in?" Rex offered. "How long are you here for?"

Rafe didn't budge, his eyes darting into the house behind Rex only briefly. "No. Can't stay. Just thought I'd stop by."

Rex frowned and a spark of anger lit inside him. "You just got here."

Rafe took a step back, his defenses clearly falling into place. "Just wanted to stop by. Let you know I'm back in town."

"You're stayin' here? In Coyote Ridge? For good?"

Rafe offered a casual shrug. "Not sure yet."

Okay. No need to push the kid. Rex took a deep breath. *Start with the basics.*

"Okay, where're you stayin' for the night?"

"Don't know that, either."

Rex stepped to the side once more. "Come inside, Rafe. You're more than welcome to stay here."

Rafe shook his head, his eyes hardening. "I'm not goin' in that house, Rex."

The conviction in Rafe's tone took Rex by surprise although it shouldn't have. Rafe hadn't stepped foot in the house since the night the sheriff dragged them both out in handcuffs.

"I promise, you won't recognize it," he assured Rafe.

His brother shook his head again, took another step back.

"All right, then." Rex stepped out on the front porch, held the door so Jack could join him. He couldn't voice how much he needed Jack right then, but he didn't have to. The man knew him well.

When the screen door shut behind them, Rafe took yet another small step back.

Duke came out right behind them, nudging the door open with his nose. Rafe's eyes shot down to the four-legged animal, and what could possibly pass as a smile ghosted across his face.

"You got a dog."

"Two, actually. His name's Duke. He's an awful guard dog but the best damn friend I've got."

"Hey," Jack harrumphed, sounding offended.

Rex chuckled. "Fine. Second-best friend I've got."

Rafe leaned down, held out his hand for Duke to sniff. When he received the dog's approval, he gave his head a scratch, earning a tail thump.

"So, what's your plan? You gonna get a hotel?"

"Figured that's the safest thing for now," Rafe said, his tone soft.

"If you plan to stay for a bit," Jack interjected, motioning across the street, "there's an apartment available on the second floor above the bookstore."

Rex turned to look at Jack at the same time Rafe did. "And you know this how?"

Jack chuckled as he held up his hands. "I inquired not too long ago to see if it was still available. Considered renting it out for a workspace for me."

"Oh, really. You didn't mention it."

Jack waved him off. "Changed my mind. Doesn't matter. But it's still vacant. Violet's had it renovated a little. One bedroom, one bath. Perfect place for you to crash."

Rafe's gaze swung over to the other side of the street, past the sign that was standing proudly in the yard.

"The Double R Retreat?" Rafe asked, turning back to Rex. "Interesting name."

"He came up with it," Rex said, motioning toward Jack.

"What's it stand for?"

Rex smiled. "Rest and relaxation."

Rafe nodded, then frowned when Jack smacked Rex's arm.

"It does not," Jack stated. "It stands for Rex and Rafe."

Rafe chuckled. "He's right. It does. But I like givin' him shit about it."

Rafe's gaze darted to Jack briefly, then back to Rex. A real smile formed, and his tone was sincere when he said, "I'm glad you're happy, Rex."

Rex had no idea how the man knew he was happy, but he nodded in agreement as he reached for Jack's hand. "I am. Very."

"So, y'all livin' here?" Rafe asked, motioning toward the house.

"Third-floor apartment." He glanced over at Jack. "But we're lookin' to build a house. Still on the property, but maybe a little distance from here. When I do, we'll hire someone to run this place."

"Is that so?" Rafe glanced at the farmhouse but didn't say anything more.

For whatever reason, Rex had expected his kid brother to look older than his twenty-six years, perhaps a little more worn. He didn't. In fact, he looked good. As though whatever he'd been doing for the past eight years agreed with him.

When the silence became awkward between them, Rex decided it was time to put an end to it once and for all. His kid brother had been running for too damn long, and though Rex had no idea what had brought him back to Coyote Ridge, he damn sure wasn't willing to let his brother disappear on him again.

He turned to face his brother fully. "If you're back for good or even for a little while, I'll take you to talk to Violet."

Rafe's shoulders seemed to relax somewhat, but his tone was still rough. "Yeah?"

"Yes." Rex released Jack's hand and stepped toward Rafe. "I think it's great that you're back, but I won't lie, I don't want you to bolt in a week. If you're gonna stay, then stay. For a while. That's all I ask." He put his hand on Rafe's shoulder. "I've missed you so fucking much."

Rafe didn't say a word, but he leaned in, hugged Rex. The emotion threatened to choke him, but he didn't fight it.

"I promise, if I decide to head out, you'll be the first to know. How's that?"

"Better than nothin'."

Rafe stepped back, dropped his head, stared at his boots.

"I'm just glad you're home, man. Now, what the hell. Let's go talk to Violet. You know … just in case."

Rafe peered up, offered a semblance of a smile. "Yes. Let's."

JACK PACED THE BEDROOM.

He knew Rex would be back any moment. The man had spent the last hour or so with Rafe over at the bookstore. Although Rex had invited him to tag along, Jack had come up with an excuse. No way was he going to intrude on Rex's time with his brother. Not after the man had been gone for eight years. No way.

Of course, Jack did have something he really wanted to ask Rex and it was killing him to wait. Patience was a virtue, sure, but at the moment, Jack was running on empty in that department.

It was a big question. "Giant. Enormous," he told Duke. "Don't you think?"

One that, for perhaps the first time in his life, Jack hadn't taken lightly.

"I'm gonna do it, Snowball," he said, looking between the two dogs. Duke was sprawled out on the floor, uninspired by the conversation, while Snowball's tongue was lolling out of her mouth, a smile on her face.

Yeah. He was going to ask Rex to marry him.

"Big step," he told the fluff ball wagging her tail excitedly. "Huge."

But totally worth it.

Then again, maybe now wasn't the right time. After all, it wasn't every day that someone's estranged brother returned to town after being gone for so long. Perhaps Jack should take that into consideration. Rex would likely need some time to sort that out and Jack wanted to be there for him.

Which he would be. Married or not.

When the apartment door opened and closed, Jack stopped pacing, held his breath.

What the hell did he do now? Should he wait? Or pop the question and hope for the best? What if Rex's brother's return threw a wrench into everything? What if they both needed time to deal with this new development? Jack could wait. Not forever. Just a couple of weeks. Yeah. He could hold off, that way he could see how everything unfolded.

"Shit," he muttered, hating himself for doubting everything.

"Hey, Jack!" Rex hollered.

"Yeah?"

"Could you come in here for a minute?"

"Sure." Squaring his shoulders, Jack forced his feet to move.

He would hold off for now. There was plenty of time for them to get married. Things were really just getting started for them, anyway. After months of hard work, the B and B was opening, Rex was already mapping out plans for the outdoor entertainment on the property, plus Jack's solo novel had hit pay dirt and now they were considering it for a television series.

Jack turned the corner into the living room only to stop suddenly when he noticed Rex.

"What are you doing?" Jack whispered, hoping like hell his eyes weren't playing tricks on him.

"Come here," Rex motioned with two fingers.

Jack moved closer, one small step at a time, his eyes never leaving Rex's face. When Rex reached for Jack's hand, he knew the man could feel it tremble.

"Jack Cunningham," Rex began, staring up at him from where he was kneeling on the floor. "I'm gonna keep this simple."

Jack couldn't help but smile.

"Marry me," Rex said, his voice firm, his eyes intent.

"That was supposed to be my line," Jack said softly.

"I'm sorry to tell ya, but there's no more proposin' in your future, city boy," Rex said, a teasing grin on his face.

"No more?"

"Nope." Rex tugged him closer. "Marry. Me."

It wasn't a question, Jack noticed. Then again, it really *wasn't* a question. Jack wanted to spend the rest of his life with this man.

"Jack?"

"Hmm?"

"Say somethin'."

Jack grinned. "Okay, fine. Sure. I'll marry you."

Rex smirked, that wicked gleam backlighting his eyes as he got to his feet. "A little nonchalant, don't ya think?"

"Eh." Jack grinned. "I mean, it's not like I've got anything better to do."

"Nothing?"

Jack laughed. "Not that I can think of."

"Are you sure about that?"

Jack pretended to consider it. "Positive."

Rex steered him backward until Jack was up against the wall. "*Absolutely* positive?"

All thought fled when Rex's mouth crushed down on his.

Now this was what he'd been hoping for. It didn't matter how many times Rex kissed him, touched him, made love to him, Jack couldn't get enough of him.

"Now I know I kept the proposal simple," Rex whispered, sliding his mouth down Jack's jawline, his neck, "but I'll leave the weddin' up to you."

"Yeah?" Jack liked the idea of a wedding.

Rex slid his hands underneath Jack's shirt, pushed it high on his chest, then over his head.

"Can I have a big wedding?" Jack asked as he removed Rex's shirt, shifting their positions until Rex was against the wall.

"Anything you want."

Music to his ears. "Anything?"

"Yes."

"I can ask Bristol to help me, then?"

For a moment, there was what looked a lot like panic on Rex's face, but it disappeared quickly. "Sure."

Jack put his hand on Rex's chest, held him in place against the wall before dropping to his knees before him.

"Jack ... baby..."

"I love when you say that," Jack whispered, staring up at Rex as he quickly unhooked his jeans, then tugged them down.

Rex's palms flattened against the wall, his body going taut as Jack took him in his mouth.

"Fuck."

Knowing Rex wouldn't allow him to get him off this way—not if he had other things in mind—Jack worked him slowly, wanting to get him as hot and bothered as possible. It didn't take long.

The next thing Jack knew, they were on the couch, Rex's cock lubed as he slid deep inside him. The man always seemed to be prepared, didn't matter where they were or what time of day it was. Another one of Rex's many fascinating traits that Jack admired.

Jack stared up at the man he loved, saw the emotion dancing in Rex's dark gaze, and he fell a little more in love with him right then.

"I only have one request for the wedding," Rex said softly, rocking his hips, driving Jack slowly insane.

"What's that?"

"That you don't wait too long."

"It'll take some time to plan a wedding," he replied, pulling Rex's hips into him.

"Fuck, that feels good." Rex moaned, shifted, drove into him again. "Just don't take too much time."

"Any reason why not?"

Rex smirked, leaned down, and buried his head in Jack's neck. "Because I'm ready to make you my husband."

"God, I love you." Jack moaned the words as Rex bit his shoulder.

"And I love you right back. So ... fucking ... much."

Yeah.

What he said.

ACKNOWLEDGMENTS

As always, I have to thank my husband because he puts up with me each and every day, regardless of my mood. Steven has always been my rock, encouraging me to follow my dreams. If it weren't for him, I wouldn't be writing today. He is the very reason I believe in myself. I love you, babe!

My amazing daughter/assistant/office manager, Taylor. You don't know what it means to me to have you at my side in all things. Not only are you my daughter, you're my friend and for a mother, that means everything. I am grateful that you are along on this journey with me.

Chancy Powley – You continue to come through for me in every way. You even tolerate my inability to answer my text messages in a timely manner. I will apologize for that now and for all future instances because we all know, I'm horrible at it. Just keep in mind, you are the absolute best friend I am forever grateful for your friendship.

I also have to thank my street team – Naughty (and nice) Girls – Your unwavering support is something I will never take for granted.

I can't forget my copyeditor, Amy at Blue Otter Editing. Thank goodness I've got you to catch all my punctuation, grammar, and tense errors.

Nicole Nation 2.0 for the constant support and love. You've been there for me from almost the beginning. This group of ladies has kept me going for so long, I'm not sure I'd know what to do without them.

And, of course, YOU, the reader. Your emails, messages, posts, comments, tweets… they mean more to me than you can imagine. I thrive on hearing from you, knowing that my characters and my stories have touched you in some way keeps me going. I've been known to shed a tear or two when reading an email because you simply bring so much joy to my life with your support. I thank you for that.

ABOUT NICOLE EDWARDS

New York Times and *USA Today* bestselling author Nicole Edwards lives in the suburbs of Austin, Texas with her husband and their youngest of three children. The two older ones have flown the coup, while the youngest is in high school. When Nicole is not writing about sexy alpha males and sassy, independent women, she can often be found with a book in hand or attempting to keep the dogs happy. You can find her hanging out on social media and interacting with her readers - even when she's supposed to be writing.

Want to know what's coming next? Or how about see some fun stuff related to Nicole's books? You can find these, as well as tons of other stuff on Nicole's website. You can also find A Day in the Life blog posts, which are short stories about your favorite characters, as well as exclusive contests by joining Nicole Nation on Nicole's website. To join, simply click **Log In | Register** in the menu.

If you're interested in keeping up to date on any new releases and preorders, you can sign up for Nicole's notification newsletter. This only goes out when she's got important information to share.

Want a simple, fast way to get updates on new releases? Sign up for text messaging. If you are in the U.S. simply text NICOLE to 64600 or sign up on her website. She promises not to spam your phone. This is just her way of letting you know what's happening because Nicole knows you're busy, but if you're anything like her, you always have your phone on you.

CONNECT WITH NICOLE

Website: NicoleEdwardsAuthor.com

Facebook: /Author.Nicole.Edwards

Instagram: NicoleEdwardsAuthor

Twitter: @NicoleEAuthor

DEAD HEAT RANCH
Boots Optional
Betting on Grace
Overnight Love

DEVIL'S BEND
Chasing Dreams
Vanishing Dreams

MISPLACED HALOS
Protected in Darkness
Salvation in Darkness
Bound in Darkness

OFFICE INTRIGUE
Office Intrigue
Intrigued Out of the Office
Their Rebellious Submissive
Their Famous Dominant
Their Ruthless Sadist
Their Naughty Student
Their Fairy Princess

PIER 70
Reckless
Fearless
Speechless
Harmless
Clueless

SNIPER 1 SECURITY
Wait for Morning
Never Say Never
Tomorrow's Too Late

SOUTHERN BOY MAFIA/DEVIL'S PLAYGROUND
Beautifully Brutal
Without Regret
Beautifully Loyal
Without Restraint

STANDALONE NOVELS
Unhinged Trilogy
A Million Tiny Pieces
Inked on Paper
Bad Reputation
Bad Business

NAUGHTY HOLIDAY EDITIONS
2015
2016